A DIVE ON THE
DARK SIDE

*A tale of murder, revenge, buried treasure, and a
desperate dive boat captain in Costa Rica*

PJ Probert

For Lola Jane and the Bear

Contents

Central America

Isla Del Coco – Cocos Island

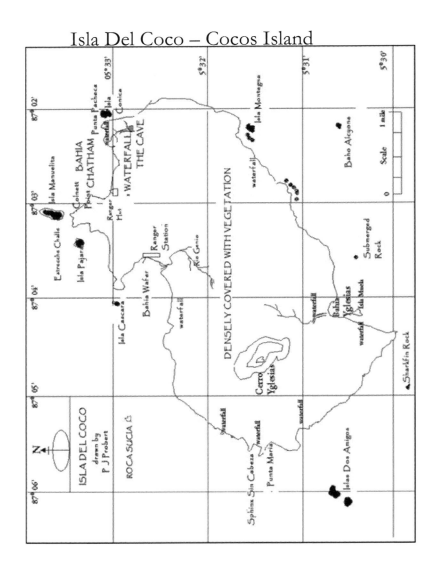

Preface

"If you will just start with the idea that this is a hard world, it will all be much simpler."
Louis D. Brandeis

I N THE DARKNESS, it's the things we can't see that often frighten us the most.

Here in the dead of night, swimming on the surface of the vast Pacific Ocean, pushing Molly my terrified brindle cat on top of a bundle of lifejackets, I'm wondering how many sharks are watching us from the darkness below.

Scuba diving on a nice protected coral reef at night with a flashlight is one thing; swimming with no light on the surface of one of the most notorious shark hunting grounds in the world, is another.

I can't see them now but I know there are packs of hungry sharks gliding around silently beneath us. In this very spot, I've seen an enormous school of jacks turn into a swirling tornado of panicking fish, prior to being repeatedly attacked by masses of ravenous Silky Sharks – yes, right here! The gyrating jacks were decimated from all sides in that onslaught and in no time at all there was nothing left of the once massive school but a few silvery sinking scales. But that was during the day. And I could see them. The sharks had their dinner on a plate. Who knows what they do at night? Who has studied them in the wild ocean after midnight?

The feel of the Glock in the waterproof bag pressing against my chest inside my wetsuit, doesn't reassure me at all. A hand holding a gun is not much use without a body attached to it.

I try not to splash, which isn't really difficult considering how tired my legs are. Stretching my legs out straight and pulling my fin-tips toward me, eases the cramp in my calf muscles, but the thought of drifting away with the current in the darkness with no hope of rescue, spurs me on.

I switch positions, and just as I did countless times in another life, swim on my back in the seated position; only this time, instead of dragging a waterproof pack containing explosives or weapons, I'm dragging a soggy, mortified cat who hates water, on top of an improvised raft of life-vests. At any second, she is going to slip out of her restraint, leap onto my face, and then claw my eyes out in a panic before jumping into oblivion. I don't know who is more afraid; her or me. I hope nothing touches my legs. That will really freak me out. There is nothing like panic to get the adrenaline pumping. My legs move faster.

Peering all around, I see no sign of the *Sea Searcher*.

What the bloody hell have I done?

I must be totally bloody nuts.

"Everyone is a moon, and has a dark side which he never shows to anybody."
Mark Twain

Chapter 1
Punta La Pesca

"Life is what happens to you while you're busy making other plans."
John Lennon

I N THE SILENT PREDAWN DARKNESS, sixty miles south of the Nicaraguan border, the Sea Searcher cruises slowly towards the dilapidated pier.

We are early.

After another 600-mile round-trip to Cocos Island with yet another group of gung-ho scuba divers, the crew and I are eager to berth alongside our dock, over on the northern edge of the narrow sandy peninsula we call home, despite spending most of our lives away from it.

As much as we enjoy being out at the island, we always relish coming back home - but isn't that just a sailor's lot?

Pointing west like a tinker's thumb, the two-mile-long, low lying peninsula jutting from the inner rim of Costa Rica's Gulf of Nicoya, embraces the fishing town of Punta la Pesca. The small town is a base for long-liners, prawn trawlers, and part-time, sport fishing tourists with oversized egos, and oversized Guy Harvey tee shirts featuring blue striped marlin of enormous proportions. The town is a haven for Jimmy Buffet wannabes. If you own a shiny trophy and can brag loudly and outrageously about impossibly large billfish, you are welcome in the local gringo bar.

The air is thick with bullshit and the smell of fish.

The fishy smell wafts from the canning factory cooking pots; emanates from the holds of countless small fishing boats tied to the docks, and oozes silently from the thick slimy mud banks at low tide.

Just off the western tip of the peninsula, hidden beneath the murky waters of the narrow channel between the headland and a massive mud bank stretching all the way to the other side of the bay, a sand bar blocks our entrance into the northern passage until high water at midday.

I could have planned our arrival here at high tide by reducing speed on the passage back from the island, but as a general rule I like arriving early. After we anchor, there will be plenty of time to brew a nice pot of Earl Grey tea, watch sunrise over the gulf, and then have a last Gallo Pinto breakfast with our guests before collecting any unpaid bills prior to their departure.

Closing on the anchorage just off the crusty old pier, I ease both engine control levers into neutral, waiting for the red flickering digits on the depth display to count down to 15 feet before gently pulling both shiny brass levers aft.

On the foredeck Raul waits for my signal to let go the anchor as the *Searcher* starts moving slowly astern. Raising my right arm, I give him the thumbs-down signal. Swiftly unwinding the brake handle on the winch, he gives the chain a quick kick; sending fifty feet of free-running, stainless steel, lugged anchor chain slamming through the metal hawse-pipe - shattering the early morning silence and destroying the dolphin dreams of any still sleeping divers.

We have officially arrived back home.

In the breaking twilight, waiting for the anchor to set in the thick mud beneath us, I walk out onto the foredeck and study the shoreline: no signs of life along the beach or along the Paseo De Los Turistas, but at dawn on a weekday this isn't really surprising.

A sleek looking tuna boat sits at anchor further out in the gulf, looking too sophisticated to be a fishing vessel. The little red helicopter sitting on her wheelhouse roof looks like a giant dragonfly.

The gulf is dotted with tiny fishing boats that the locals call pangas. I have to keep a keen eye out for them on my way in. The little wooden craft are smaller than the two fiberglass pangas we carry onboard to transport our divers to the dive sites. The little wooden boats out in the bay rarely show up on our radar screen. At night, the fishermen onboard these tiny boats usually carry a small flashlight which they sometimes turn on at the last minute, just as we are approaching. Luckily, I haven't hit one yet but I have run over a long line and that proved quite costly, not to mention the bad vibes I got from the fishermen. I've been buying beers for them ever since.

Raul, my oldest crewmember joins me by the guardrail. With his startlingly green eyes and thick, curly brown beard Raul looks like a mini Viking. Most of my crew members are short in stature with typically European features. Out of a population of three million, less than two per cent of Costa Ricans are Negro or Indian. Over the year's interlopers have pretty much decimated the indigenous inhabitants.

"Hey, Cappy, it's good to be home eh?" he smiles.

"Yeah, this is great,'" I reply, looking around the bay. "You'll be back with the family tonight. That's good."

"Si, too good Cap."

"Are Arcelio and Ronaldo up yet?" I ask.

"I'll go and check," says Raul "Ronaldo is maybe still sleeping." Ronaldo the steward is the youngest crewmember and he sleeps a lot.

"Hey Raul, don't forget the black ball."

"You know I never forget Cappy," he laughs.

The boat has to display a big black ball when at anchor during the day. Raul has it ready on the foredeck.

"Yeah, good man," I laugh back.

After waiting on deck for both main-engines to cool down enough to be shut off, I walk down the port side ladder to the main deck and then through a hatch down into the machinery room, where the compressor and air conditioning units are housed. A large, watertight door in the aft bulkhead opens into the engine room. A pair of ear defenders hangs on one of the door dogs. I put them on, un-dog the metal levers on the door, and swing it open. The combination of heat and noise slap me in the face. Luckily for the guests, the engine room is insulated because although you can hardly hear them outside the engine room, the two massive Detroit Diesels sound like hell-in-a-hurricane down here - even when idling. I walk past the port engine, open a couple of valves and start pumping fuel from our keel tanks into the engine room day tanks.

Walking from one engine to the next, I hit each engine kill switch in turn.

3

Suddenly, with both engines off and only the smaller of our two generators running, it is almost bearable without ear protectors.

Even the engine room sighs with relief.

Ten minutes later, sitting in the helmsman's chair up in the wheelhouse with Molly the cat purring away in my lap, I inhale deeply; relishing the semi silence. Through the wheelhouse windows I savor the panoramic view of prismatic sunbeams radiating skyward from behind a ridge of dark-green mountains to the east. I feel as relaxed and mellow as a manatee. If only I had more time off between trips. In the fifteen years I've been doing this job in various parts of the world, I've lived with hundreds of divers for days and nights on end. Although it's not easy living day and night with a group of total strangers for ten days every two weeks, I consider it the price to pay for having such a great job. With three nights in port before the next charter, I'm looking forward to getting ashore. Punta La Pesca is sure to be throbbing tonight in more ways than one. Ironically, the fishermen become pretty good bait themselves once they cash their hard-earned paychecks and start chucking their money about.

My reverie is broken by the sound of footsteps on the ladder leading up from the guest's area: it's Tom the barrel-chested American dive group leader.

"Mac, we need to talk." Oh, Oh! I knew this was coming. I've been avoiding him since leaving the island.

"What's up Tom?"

"You know the group isn't happy, right?"

"Yeah, I know, but it's hardly my fault there were no Hammerheads around the island during this trip. It's this bloody El Nino that's keeping them deep. I did warn you."

During El Nino, this part of the Pacific Ocean is like a warm bath, and the visibility is fantastic; but we see very few, if any, Hammerheads. Most pelagics live and hunt in the deeper, colder, thermoclines, where all the nutrients, and consequently every fish and its uncle live these days. There are still scores of white-tip reef sharks swimming around the island, and occasionally a teeming bait ball rises to the surface, but the huge Hammerhead schools are what everyone really comes to see.

"You warned us when we were heading out to Cocos that we might not see the usual schools of Hammerheads but you didn't tell us we wouldn't see any at all. Besides, what were we supposed to do: turn back and go home? Why weren't we told before the trip?"

That's a good question. I had previously suggested to the boat's owner that our guests should be alerted beforehand. "But that's bullshit," is what the boss had to say, looking at me as if I was crazy before dismissing the idea completely.

Recently a lot of guests have been pissed off about not seeing what they "paid good money to see." The trips have become more and more difficult for me. I'm just an ordinary bloke taking shots on the front line with no ammo to defend myself with.

"I'm sorry Tom, but you know I did what I could to make this trip special. What about the bait-ball? That was unique wasn't it? Not many divers can say they dived on one of those." Alerted by a flock of dive-bombing boobies on the way back to the boat from Dirty Rock, we dived on a school of green jacks being attacked by dozens of dolphins, scores of sharks and hundreds of tunas.

"Yeah, but not everyone got to dive on it. Most of us were out of air. And those who did see it were terrified. That was dangerous."

"We survived it didn't we?" I say defensively.

"I think it was foolhardy Mac. I told you that and I wouldn't be doing it again if I were you."

"Well... I'm not you, am I? You twat," I don't say.

"Well I'm sorry you feel that way," is what I really say.

"I do feel that way. And the group thinks you should refund us some money. I know you have a shit load of cash onboard. I personally gave you $10,000 at the start of the trip for the late bookings. Not to mention the money you made on all the Nitrox courses and overpriced T-shirts."

"That's not my decision to make Tom. You made the trip and I did my part. You had some good diving and I brought you back safely. You need to speak with the boss.'

I could take him in a fight but I'm no longer a fighting man.

"Oh, I'm going to talk to the boss alright Mac... And I'll be writing a piece about this trip in a dive magazine - and it won't be complementary, I can assure you." With that off his big hairy chest, he stomps out onto the side deck.

Bollocks. I hate this. I hate it when the guests are not happy. I hate it even more when they complain about things beyond my control.

Seconds later Arcelio the chef walks up the ladder, looking concerned.

"Did you hear that Arcelio?"

"It's OK Cappy, we have time off now. Why don't you stop by my house tonight and have dinner with my familia?"

"I'd love to, but I have to go to the city."

"Maybe when you get back?"

"Yeah I'll try. Thanks buddy."

"You want Gallo Pinto for breakfast?" He asks. "I'll make you a special plate." Scrambled eggs, black beans and rice, with Salsa Lizano and a touch of Arcelio's magic.

"That will be great. I'm starving."

"Con mucho gusto," he says, his blue eyes twinkling before disappearing below.

Despite the kind invitation to his home, I think about getting off the boat and away from town as soon as I can.

✳ ✳ ✳

This little port town has changed dramatically over the years; going from sleepy little fishing town, to wealthy bustling hub, back to being the poor neighbor in what seems like a fortnight flat.

During the 1800's, a series of rickety oxcarts rolled out of the lush green interior, bringing bananas to town for export aboard small steamships bound for the Northern Temperate Zones. A century later, when Costa Rica became the first Central American country to cultivate coffee, the town adjusted accordingly. The completion of a winding railroad, connecting Punta La Pesca to the Central Plateau changed things drastically. The Gulf of Nicoya was always the golden gateway to Costa Rica's rich bountiful heartland, but now Punta la Pesca held its key.

Like ants following a sugar trail, fleets of weather-beaten merchant vessels exporting fruit and coffee, docked in continuous lines alongside the brand-new municipal pier, together with a growing number of luxurious modern cruise liners traveling the west coast of the Americas.

Up and down the newly named Paseo de los Turistas, the town's mile-long beachfront drive, crowds of smiling locals mingled with the tourist hoards strolling past colorful colonial buildings, housing customs and immigration officers, shipping company officials and tourist agents. All along the freshly paved seaside sidewalk, throngs of local artisans sold brightly colored arts and polished hardwood crafts from portable wooden tables set up outside the rustic restaurants dishing up delicious meals of freshly caught seafood.

In the narrow Calles adjacent to the Paseo, a host of bustling bars and brothels appeared attracting an increasing number of randy sailors and lonely cruise-ship passengers, which in turn attracted a stream of working girls from afar.

For a good while the town prospered and a profitable living was made by all. But just as sometimes happened to me when things were going great, a kick in the balls was just around the corner.

In the name of progress and profit, shipbuilders started building bigger ships with greater cargo capacities calling for more efficient loading and unloading techniques. As the town's pier and docking facilities aged, they couldn't keep up with the rigorous new demands. When a modern, deep-water port was built across the bay, Punta la Pesca was promptly abandoned by all the shipping companies. Even the steam trains stopped chugging to town after a particularly bad earthquake destroyed the railroad. From that point on, the town's glory faded faster than the peeling orange paintwork on the flaky municipal pier. As the empty pier and docking facilities fell silently and sadly into disrepair, their approaches silted up along with the town's economy.

Although some picturesque beaches and high-class tourist resorts line the gulf, Punta la Pesca is not quite in their league. The black sandy beach along the southern edge of town is a graveyard, dotted with dog droppings and strewn with flotsam. Umpteen piles of dried out tree trunks, leafless tree branches, and old wooden pallets are interspersed with variously sized, oily plastic containers; tarred rope ends, and various other turtle and bird killing plastics, like cheap toys; plastic bags; plastic bottles, fishing lines, and dozens of multi-colored plastic cigarette lighters.

Soccer playing kids, dog walkers, and amateur fishermen use the beach during the day, giving it up to rats and drunken adulterers in the dead of night.

Backpackers sometimes stay in town for one night on their way to catch the local ferry over to Naranjo, or the National Park at Cabo Blanco, but the occasional tourist doesn't usually stay here too long. If you don't know the town as I do you might think it a sad little place - but there are still plenty of happy bits to it. The Mariscos and Korean restaurants are fine, and the small dingy bars are cheap, friendly and enjoyable - until a bloody knife fight breaks out.

A few years ago, the Chinese appeared on the scene to teach the local fishermen the art of long line fishing. Apparently, that was the thin end of a wedge. The fishing industry is gradually being taken over by Chinese and Taiwanese businessmen who now have their own boatyards, where they build fishing vessels shaped like junks, with high bows and poop decks, and names like 'Dragon' and 'Emperor'. But despite that, the majority of fishermen are still locals; as tough as old boots, but as friendly as you can imagine until someone upsets them. I try not to piss anyone off in town, especially fishermen who've been drinking. Franco, a crewmember from a fishing boat berthed in front of us was recently involved in a drunken brawl over a local bar girl. In the ensuing fracas Franco killed a guy.

"I don't suppose we'll be seeing Franco again will we?" I ask Mano, our agent and Mr. Fix-it.

He doesn't even stop to think about the reply. "Hey, Mac, this is Costa Rica. He'll be out in a couple of years if he can prove self-defense; it shouldn't be too much of a problem." Mano may have been exaggerating slightly, but apparently Franco doesn't need a big-shot Hollywood lawyer to defend him.

Even though the modern port across the bay took away the shipping trade, there is no actual town there. There really is no need for one because as soon as the cruise ships dock, streams of luxury, air-conditioned coaches whisk the majority of passengers away on sightseeing tours, and for any crewmember with time to spare, Punta La Pesca is still the nearest place to pump their personal bilges. The gaggle of 'good-time-girls' adds to the flavor of it all.

✳ ✳ ✳

Pulling up the anchor at noon, I can't wait to get to the dock and offload our guests. Even though it will be nice and quiet once they are gone, I'm not staying onboard. I'm getting off the boat as soon as I can. The city of San Jose is calling my name.

Steering the *Searcher* close to the beach on the way to the western point, I spot a brand-new neon sign outside the little red painted Beach Club Hotel and Casino, and it occurs to me that I probably paid for that bloody sign single handedly on my last visit.

I've lost mucho-dinero in that blood-sucking, money-pit of a casino.

Cruising past the large, white roofed, open sided ferry terminal at the tip of the peninsula, I turn into the narrow, muddy brown estuary to the north, just missing a small wooden fishing boat scuttling in front of me at full speed.

Bloody hell!

Some skippers think that having a hard time at sea, and a hard-on for their wives and girlfriends or both, gives them exclusive rights to the channel. We all know that the consequences of a collision are dire for every one of us, so it pisses me off that *I* have to avoid *them* because I drive the larger vessel. Normally when the buggers sneak in front of me at full speed, I grin through gritted teeth and suffer their rude disregard for the rules of the road, but this time, even though I know it does no good, I blow the horn and shake my fist. The fishermen don't take a blind bit of notice. Sometimes I feel like increasing speed instead of slowing down, just for the hell of it - but what good would it do? I am, and always will be a foreigner here. I don't need jail time or a war with the fishermen any more than I need an extra dick; besides, our relationship is pretty good right now so why screw it up?

Vowing to disregard the future antics of any randy fishermen, I concentrate on the job at hand: steering warily up the channel on full alert for fishing boats fleeing both ways; avoiding the gamut of floating moorings and dodging the odd assortment of small craft haphazardly anchored in the center of the tapering tideway.

Up ahead, I spot a small grey cloud hovering over the channel. Rain is well overdue but this isn't a rain cloud - this is something special. There hasn't been any rain for months because El Nino is squarely upon us and we are in the middle of 'Veranillo' or 'The Little Summer'. I know what this cloud is though: a farmer up north has burned the remnants of his sugar cane field, and the resultant mass of black and gray cane-cinders is now wafting ominously towards us.

Six guests standing on the *Searcher's* foredeck taking in the sights, have no idea what the floating ebony nebula is, until we plow through it. In an instant, our nice white paintwork and their previously spotless t-shirts are spattered with sooty Rorschach blotches. Brushing themselves off, the divers look down, startled to see the logos on their t-shirts change from testimonials to exotic dive locations, into psychiatrist's ink dot tests.

I bet if I study those blotches in detail, I will see a mass of naked women writhing suggestively across a giant poker table - but that's just me.

The attacking black ash sends three divers scurrying away back aft, which is good because the *Searcher's* raised bow is level with the wheelhouse, and although the high bow is helpful in big seas, anyone standing there now restricts my view of the channel ahead. Despite my pleading beforehand to keep to the sides, someone usually takes up post there when we enter port as if to deliberately piss me off.

My tolerance levels are getting lower.

Opening the starboard wheelhouse door to ask the remaining divers on the foredeck to move, I'm instantly saturated by a sticky wave of midday heat and humidity, as if someone just emptied a bucket of tepid olive oil over me.

Stepping back inside the air-conditioned wheelhouse, I close the door and grab the wheel; turning it slightly to starboard; hugging the right side of the channel; passing closer to the town's hodge-podge of faded wooden houses, cracked concrete docks and flimsy floating pontoons. Over on our port side, a hundred yards away, another unmarked mud bank lay hidden beneath the high tide. For obvious reasons I don't like getting too close to it.

Rooted in the shallow, murky waters beyond the mud bank, miles of tightly packed, twisted mangrove trees and low-lying shrubs stretch far away to the north like a bonsai forest on steroids. Hosts of sea creatures hatch in the protective waters beneath the mangrove jungle; growing up in a safe fantasy world before anxiously migrating into the open-ocean. The local fishermen cultivate this giant nursery by regularly dumping huge bags of rotten fish guts here. Consequently, at low tide when fully exposed, the black shiny mud-bank oozes oil and burps the unique nasty odor of putrid fish.

The massive mangrove swamp meanders inland for miles, running parallel with the estuary as far as the eye can see. The network of interlacing tributaries feeding the estuary is colonized by huge, sinuous snakes and colossal armored crocodiles. When I first arrived here five years ago, I was astonished to find snakes slithering across the *Searcher's* decks in the early mornings.

No one told me to expect those buggers.

The heavy pelting rains regularly dislodge snakes of all sizes from their jungle habitats, and as the fast-flowing swollen tributaries disgorge into the estuary, the snakes are swept along for the ride. The lucky ones somehow manage to wrap themselves around our horizontal wooden fenders at the dock, and from there, wriggle up onto the decks - claiming sanctuary from currents that might otherwise send them sailing off all the way to Hawaii.

I once found a huge, brown-mottled python onboard big enough to eat a child – *no shit!* After discovering that big scaly bastard laying in ambush, I always make certain to check the decks thoroughly before letting Molly out in the mornings. *Stone the bloody crows!* Molly could have been eaten alive and I would never have known what happened to her. Funnily enough, even though the large pythons scare the shadows off the locals, some keep pythons as pets and I have a standing order for more – but only for the smally ones.

I had the bright idea of keeping the big python around to cure the rat problem at the dock, but common sense and pressure from the local fishermen forced me to round the big bugger up, and dump it back into the estuary.

Rounding the big beefy bastard up in a cargo net was not easy. Raul refused to help. "No Cappy, es muy peligrosa. I don't like to do it!"

Ronaldo relishes the idea, even getting close enough to poke it with a small stick to see if it is alive. "La calebra is moi benita Cappy," he says with his lopsided grin, minus two front teeth.

"No Ronnie! Es muy, muy peligrosa!" shouts Raul from the safety of the top deck.

"We need your shotgun, Cappy!" says Pedro, one of our panga drivers, as we lift the big beast up in the net. Having the shotgun around might be a bad idea, especially in Raul's panicky hands. Anyway, it's a little late. The python's sheer weight startles us, making us even more nervous in case we drop it, it escapes, and then eats one of us – and that bugger might still be digesting me today. We are doubly surprised when the python slithers out of the net into the creek and swims straight to the nearest row of houses before slithering ashore there.

"Isn't that your house over there?" I ask Ronaldo jokingly.

"No Cappy, it's my coosins house," he laughs back.

Now as far as I know this snake has never been found and no small children have yet gone missing - but I hear talk of missing dogs…

Anyway, despite the pile of pythons, dog eating or otherwise that the rains bring swimming to town, everyone now prays on their knees for precipitation and the end of El Nino.

Steering slowly up the channel, I watch two divers standing on the side-deck wave to a long liner's crew casting off from the crowded co-operative dock. The disinterested fishermen don't bother waving back. They barely notice us, despite our size and solid, pristine white appearance contrasting starkly with the rest of the town's colorfully painted fleet. The townies see us coming and going regularly - the only ones remotely interested now are my crew's family and friends; the casino owner; and a few local whores.

Approaching the coastguard station, I slow down so as to not piss off the sailors onboard the small patrol boat berthed there. Speeding past will create a wake big enough to spill their midday mugs of high-octane Costa Rican coffee.

A hundred yards ahead, on the right side, just beyond the bright-orange, wooden building, housing the fish and veggie market, the channel splits into two forks. Turning the wheel sharply to starboard at the dogleg, I gently ease both engine control levers into neutral, giving a quick burst astern with both props to stop all forward movement. The remnants of the incoming tide do the rest. With the current carrying the *Searcher* slowly sideways towards the dock, I look down to where Mano stands waiting; sweltering beneath his oversized baseball cap.

Mano is such a comical character that I can't help but grin. I gave him that pair of gold-framed Elvis-sunglasses as a joke; I didn't expect him to wear them constantly. Those glasses, combined with the oversized baseball cap and his long black, mutton-chop sideburns, above his dark wobbly jowls make him look like a poker playing bulldog in a velvet painting; waiting for a chance to cover everyone in sweat and mucous with just the slightest shake of his corrugated head.

"Hey Cappy, welcome home," he shouts.

"Pura Vida, it's great to be back, Mano," I reply.

A thin ribbon of swirling blue smoke curls up slowly from a seemingly perpetual cigar, clamped firmly between his yellow teeth. The curly cigar smoke darkens the orangey-yellow nicotine-stain beneath his broad nose. Big beads of sweat drip steadily off his nose just missing the cigar. I wonder if the eternal flame is about to be extinguished. Will the cigar's tar-filled stump unravel damply and disintegrate between his lips?

I have no time to find out.

As the *Searcher* draws closer to the dock Mano suddenly comes alive. With wild rotational arm flourishes he gestures the usual docking instructions to me up in the wheelhouse, revealing dark wet patches in the armpits of his light blue safari jacket. Despite his well-intentioned efforts, I ignore him and his signals completely. After docking the boat here every two weeks for the past five years I'm too proud to seek his help; besides, I still have no bloody idea what some of his signals mean.

The very first time I docked here I needed his help badly, but to my consternation I ignored him then too. As I drew close to the dock that first time, things were already going horribly wrong. I used the wrong angle of approach and to my horror, the current in the tight little corner was much stronger than I expected. Barely having enough space to squeeze between a prawn trawler and a funny old catamaran at the dock, I could not see a bloody thing astern of my position at the wheel because my newly constructed cabin blocked the aft view. I made the mistake of relying on Raul, the one crewmember I thought I could trust, to stand on the aft deck with a handheld radio and relay distances from our stern to the dock, and to the catamaran alongside it. Like an idiot I waited expectantly for distances to be broadcast over the radio in the wheelhouse. But as the current carried us rapidly towards the dock Raul panicked. All I heard over the airwaves was silence, interrupted by loud bursts of static. I had no idea that in a panic Raul's mouth and throat would seize tightly shut.

Darting outside to the starboard bridge wing, I took a quick look aft and swallowed hard.

Fuck a duck! I was in big trouble.

At 120 feet, the *Searcher* is twenty feet longer than the previous boat I skippered and I underestimated her length. As my stomach tied itself in knots, I walked back into the wheelhouse nonchalantly - so it didn't look as if I were the one panicking. Turning the wheel swiftly to starboard, I gave the port throttle a quick thrust ahead to kick my stern out, but I knew whatever I did next wouldn't stop me hitting something.

I was completely bollixed.

Holding my breath and squeezing my arse cheeks tight, I waited for the crunch. At worst, our solid steel, starboard quarter would crush the dilapidated catamaran. At best I might win the lottery.

Stone the bloody crows.

I heard the shouts before I heard the crunch and it all sounded horrible, until it went mercifully silent inside my head. Standing outside my body, outside the wheelhouse door, I gazed down at the small crowd staring up at me. Everyone looked at me as though I had just fallen into a sea of shite, which I had, figuratively speaking. Fortunately for everyone concerned, the crunch sounded worse than it really was. The startlingly loud crack was nowhere near in proportion to the damage. Miraculously, the catamaran still remained afloat. Maybe the quick burst of throttle helped, but the feeling inside me wasn't good. My bowels dropped.

I picked a fine time to discover that Raul is prone to panic. This wasn't the time to find out that every time he panics, he freezes up like a bloody snowman - *The Wanker!*

But to be absolutely fair to him - it wasn't his fault at all. The fault was mine and mine alone. I was the wanker. I had miscalculated my angle of approach; I misjudged the strength of the current close to the dock, and I didn't really know how to handle the extra twenty feet of length on the Searcher's stern compared to the last boat I drove. And it's hardly Mano's fault that I ignored him. I can't blame him just because he looked like a bookmaker at a racetrack, giving odds on how hard I was going to hit the catamaran.

I learned a valuable lesson from that incident though. By paying proper attention to the current, and letting it work for me, I don't need help from a panicky wanker standing on the aft deck with a radio. Nor do I need the assistance of a twit with funny sunglasses giving me hoodoo-voodoo signs from the dock.

"Hey Cappy, don't feel bad; it was your first time. That piece of shit boat shouldn't be here anyway; it should be making a nice fire somewhere," says Mano afterwards.

Now, because he doesn't want a repeat performance of that faux pas any more than I do, Mano still gestures to me anyway. Tick-tack-toe - there you go. If it makes him feel like a kingpin, parked in his puddle of perspiration on the dock then let him signal.

Mano helped me negotiate with Macho Gordo, the damaged catamaran's owner, for the cost of repairs. But Macho Gordo, the big, crooked, no necked slimy bastard, demanded more money for the cost of repairs than the catamaran was actually worth. In my estimation we overpaid him, but he still thinks I owe him money. He needles me about it every time we meet. So now I try avoiding him.

To be honest, I couldn't stand the sight of Macho Gordo even before that incident. And just for the record let me say this: I loathed the big bad bastard even before I discovered the true extent of his evil - even before I knew of the drug dealing or heard the dark murmurings around town about his sickening involvement with youngsters.

Yes, I really hate the bastard.

Although his catamaran remained alongside the dock unused for months after the 'incident', it wasn't because she couldn't be used. The fact is, nobody wanted to book her at Macho's price. The boat was a mess even before I hit her. Previous attempts at covering parts of her hull with glass fiber were evident, because osmosis caused the fiber matting to delaminate, giving it the warped syrupy look of a typically bad fiberglass job. She looked like she was built by a shortsighted mountain-dweller who never even saw the sea, let alone sailed upon it. In a country thick with exotic hardwood trees it's also a mystery to me why she was constructed from softwood. Softwood is harder to get in Costa Rica than hardwood.

The catamaran was totally top heavy, with her misplaced dancing deck balanced on stilts across the width of two rotten pontoons. You didn't even need to close your eyes partially and look at her a bit skewed, to see she resembled two double-decker buses welded together with scaffolding poles.

The boat's name was a joke too. 'Momma de Super Hombre' - Mother *of Superman…?* What the hell was that all about? Obviously, somebody with a sense of humor was smart enough to sell the boat to Macho on a dark and rainy night; probably when he was drunk or stoned or both.

Although I know nothing about the first chapter of her life, the final chapter came as no surprise to me at all. When a group eventually chartered her for a day trip, the illustrious *Mother of Superman* encountered the kryptonite factor.

According to some reports, she left the dock completely overloaded with an unspecified number of passengers, and by the time she rounded the western point, on the way to a small island in the gulf, she was already sinking. A crewmember serving beer and chicharones started screaming to Guapo the skipper that there was 'mucha aqua', gushing up through a deck hatch on the port side pontoon. Not surprisingly, mass panic ensued with everybody on the high dancing deck running over to see what was what. With all the weight on her port side she immediately tipped over sideways, throwing everyone and everything, including a crewmember still clutching beer and chicharones into the sea. Most passengers swam for their lives through the current. But the current was fierce that day and not everyone could swim. The fact that nobody wore a lifejacket further compounded the disaster, and even if they were able to find the stashed life vests, there were reportedly an insufficient number of lifejackets onboard anyway.

Some poor souls never made it through the current alive.

I thought Macho Gordo might face trial but he mysteriously managed to avoid legal action, unlike his skipper Guapo, who now awaits trial for manslaughter because he overloaded the boat. Guapo should have known better but all he has to say is "I didn't think the boat would sink that easily," which is a bit like saying, "it came apart in my hands chief."

The disaster did have some positive repercussions though: the government tightened up the inspection and licensing requirements for all local boats, and the *Searcher* became the first vessel in port to have all the required bells, whistles, and maritime safety equipment necessary to undertake international voyages comfortably and safely.

And that is a blessing in itself.

Since the catamaran is no longer with us, the *Pirate,* a new 60' aluminum pleasure craft is now in her old berth. As we approach the *Pirate* each of her crewmembers stops painting to grab a large white inflatable fender. Holding the fenders over the bow rails, the crewmembers laughingly swap rapid greetings and friendly profanities with my crew, in a local dialect I can't follow.

Carefully wedging the *Searcher* into the gap between the prawn trawler ahead of us and the *Pirate* astern, I inch our big bow slowly forward until it hangs over the trawler's transom by a few feet. With our high bow looming menacingly above them on the aft deck, the three fishermen standing there peer up nervously; their tight-mouthed looks of concern betraying the memory of me hitting the catamaran five years ago. I smile at them and wave. By now, they should all know it's a piece of cake.

Once in position at the dock, I give orders for the crew to secure the lines and set up the gangway; orders that are totally redundant because they do this so many times it's now automatico.

No problemo.

Ashore, a blue two-story wooden building stretches the whole length of the dock. On the ground floor of the building at the extreme eastern end, just in front of, and to the side of the Searcher's bow, Mano disappears into his small office adjoining our bodega. Next to the bodega, directly opposite the searcher's wheelhouse, my blond German mate Claus, the owner of the dock, stands outside his office with a nice-looking young woman dressed in very tight clothes. Claus is not so much talking to her as inhaling her. From my vantage point up on the bridge wing, I have a sneaky bird's eye view of her enormous wobbly brown breasts straining to break free from a tank top and bra that are at least three sizes too small. Claus somehow manages to wrench his eyes away from her tits long enough to give me a nod and wink before virtually dragging her into his office.

I glance along the dock hoping to catch sight of Maria, but she obviously hasn't turned up yet.

At the western end of the dock, adjacent to the street, three locals emerge from the doorway of a small shop, stopping next to a gaudily painted wooden sign propped up with a broom handle on the tarmac. The sign, featuring a fan belt, an oil filter, and something else rubbery, looks like it was painted by a drunken child. Happily-oblivious to the amateurish nature of the sign the three smiling men raise their beer cans in salute, shouting "Buenos Dios" to all and sundry.

The atmosphere on the dock is distinctly carnival-like. The rich smoky smell of barbecued seafood wafts around the dock, and the sound of a Mariachi band playing the "Macarena" echoes from the purple painted bar across the street. My crew sings along, substituting the word "Puntarenas" for "Macarena". Puntarenas is the Costa Rican province the town is part of. This is great - the weekend has started already.

Guapo the frog, the ex-skipper of the doomed catamaran, stands in the shadows holding what is probably his second bottle of guaro of the day already. Guaro is the national drink made from sugar cane. Most downtown bars sell it in recycled Jonnie Walker bottles. I'm not really sure if it's rum or not, but I can personally testify that some brands are fierce - requiring a slice of lemon, a little soda, and a strong constitution. If I drink too much of the questionable brand my eyes twinge, my hair stands on end, dastardly demons dance in my mind, and I usually do unspeakable things I am sorry for later. In the morning, when the host of demented demons awake, they bash my brain repeatedly with big chipping hammers and I want to die. I can't see the brand of guaro that Guapo clutches, but it is almost certainly the cheaper, nastier version. Struggling with the nightmare of the sinking catamaran, Guapo is usually drunk before midday.

"You have work for me Cappy?" he shouts to me loudly.

"Sorry Buddy, not this time." I answer.

"Esokay Cappy. Tomorrow?" He slurs back.

"Maybe," I reply

He always asks if we have any work for him when we come back to port. Ideally, he wants a job keeping watchman's duty on the dock, thinking that it will be a good opportunity to get paid whilst catching up on his sleep. There is fat chance of that happening; we already have night watchmen who sleep, but at least the barking dogs wake them if there are intruders on the dock – and after drinking all that Guaro, Guapo won't wake up if you launch him into space.

Soon there will be nobody onboard the *Searcher* except the watchmen. As soon as the crew finishes cleaning the boat, they are going straight home, and once I've sorted things out onboard, I'm going to leave the boat in Manuel's capable hands, and zoom off to the big city to raise a rumpus myself.

Chapter 2
The Island

"There is a pleasure in the pathless woods,
There is a rapture on the lonely shore,
There is society, where none intrudes
By the deep sea, and music in its roar."
Lord Byron.

SITUATED 300 MILES FROM COSTA RICA, its territorial guardian, Isla Del Coco, or Cocos Island as it's known in English, is just a tiny speck of dust on a map of the vast Pacific Ocean.

Bombarded by twenty-five feet of rain a year, this towering, partially impenetrable rainforest island is one of the wettest places on the planet.

Measuring only four miles in length and two miles in width, the island's meager square footage belies its actual land mass. Shrouded beneath a tropical cloud forest, the volcanic peak of Cerro Iglesias soars almost 3000 feet above sea level.

Throughout the island, tightly woven masses of green jungle undergrowth snake up and down countless slopes; hiding the deadly pitfalls of an ultra-jagged terrain.

Oh, and the surrounding sea harbors a traffic jam of sharks.

But despite all this, or more likely because of it, Cocos Island was once the perfect pirate hidey hole, where several buried treasures estimated to be worth over five hundred million dollars reportedly still lay buried.

Considering the potential wealth buried on Cocos Island, it may seem surprising to hear that it is inhabited by only a handful of rain-soaked Costa Rican Park Rangers bravely protecting its soggy jungle heights and fish filled corridors.

Two bays with sandy beaches provide sheltered anchorages on the northern shore, whilst to the south a boulder ridden shoreline next to Teacup Island provides another.

Over the years, passing sailors regularly stopped off for respites from the weather, to replenish their water supplies and supplement their larders. At one time there were all the coconuts you could eat on the island, but a series of destructive whaler's crews soon put paid to that. Stopping off on short breaks from decimating the Pacific whale population, intrepid whalers chopped down whole trees just to harvest the nuts; so, it is hardly surprising that by the time the whaling industry collapsed in the late eighteen hundreds, there were very few coconut palms left standing.

The harsh topography and remoteness of Cocos Island has inhibited all attempts at prolonged mass settlement there; in fact, the only people who lived on the island for any substantial length of time until it was declared a National Park in 1982 were prisoners, pirates and treasure hunters. Since then, only the trusty Costa Rican Park Rangers take turns in staying there.

Reports regarding the origin of the island's name conflict. Some said it was originally named Isle de Coques: The Nutshell Island, but some also said the world was flat. Although the island may look like a giant nutshell from a distance, once you arrive there and take in the jungle vista and smell the wet earth, you'll be thinking of coconuts, and to me the word Cocos is close enough to the word coconut to make sense.

Details of the island's discovery are also sketchy, but Cocos can be seen on old charts and maps in various inaccurate positions and with dissimilar names. On at least one old chart I've seen, it was considered part of the Galapagos Islands. But this is not surprising when you consider that until the advent of accurate navigational instruments, relatively recently, pinpointing Cocos was such an exacting task that only highly skilled navigators could find it; and only then with the greatest of difficulty. With over three hundred inches of torrential rains pouring down annually, almost continuous cloud-cover envelopes the island's heights. And as all that moisture evaporates and condenses amongst the island's craggy folds, a veil of mist arises, shielding its vista from all but the sharpest eyes. Cerro Iglesias is seldom seen through her cloud-forest canopy.

Lying 300 miles southwest of Costa Rica at Latitude 5 degrees 32 minutes north, and Longitude 87 degrees 4 minutes West, Cocos Island sits almost slap bang in the center of the Cocos Ridge, an undersea mountain range 376 miles northeast of Isla Darwin, the northernmost Galapagos Island.

The Cocos Ridge was originally part of the Carnegie Ridge from where the Galapagos Islands began forming 22 million years ago; but since its formation, tectonic plate movement has shifted the Cocos Ridge northward at the speed of the average fingernail growth. The 10,000 feet high ridge stretching up from the sea floor runs in a northeasterly direction for 620 miles until disappearing into the Middle American Trench off Costa Rica's Pacific coast.

Considered young in geological terms, Cocos Island itself was formed three to four million years ago by a hotspot, a concentrated area of intense heat below the Earth's mantle. When the Cocos Plate paused long enough for the hotspot to melt a hole in the Earth's crust, plumes of molten larval material spewed out, piling up toward the sea's surface. A series of eruptions during the next thousand years or so produced a volcanic mountain of magma 2788 feet above sea level – thus becoming the only volcano in the Cocos Ridge to have breached the sea's surface.

When the Cocos Tectonic Plate resumed its northeasterly journey towards the Caribbean, the volcanic vent beneath Cocos Island closed, extinguishing its firestorms forever.

As the years slowly passed, the extinct volcano island gathered dust and more dust, and bird crap, and seeds - until a period of continuous heavy rainfall encouraged its emergence as the only major island in the eastern Pacific supporting a wet, vibrant, tropical rainforest; a rainforest now alive with an inherent population of over 200 plant species, 97 different bird types, and more than 350 diverse kinds of creepy-crawlies - not to mention the hoard of feral cats, pigs, deer, and goats running around willy-nilly since being introduced by passing sailors over the years.

Cocos Island has long attracted adventurers to its steep, mysterious shores.

Michael Crichton surely had Cocos Island in mind when he wrote 'Jurassic Park' – and if you go there, you'll understand why.

Among the many adventurers captivated by the beauty and intrigue of this amazingly exotic island was Jacques Cousteau who thought it "The most beautiful island in the world," when he stopped there aboard his research vessel *Alcyone*. He commissioned an artistic crewmember to carve the ship's logo into a block of pink granite on a small beach, bearing rock carvings from as far back as the sixteenth century.

Scuba divers worldwide now know Cocos Island as 'Shark Island' - the penultimate A-Z of pelagic creatures; one of nature's outstanding marine playgrounds where massive armies of sharks constantly prowl through its underwater corridors.

Whether you are flying like a flag in a storm in the strong current, or clinging to a sea mound 120 feet below the sea surface, or zooming along at 80 feet, letting the sea sweep you with it, there is little to beat the sight of a few hundred hammerheads swimming right at you. If you bear in mind the majority of these stalk-eyed creatures is between 8 to 12 feet long, and as ripped as heavyweight boxers, you might wonder why anyone would want to do that – unless you are a diver yourself.

Strangely enough, most divers feel no fear when they encounter a tightly packed army of hammerheads; there is just a tremendous rush of excitement. If you race towards the school, or breathe out fast, the hammerheads scatter like skittles. And, unless you sit quietly and hold your breath, or are wearing a rebreather in the middle of a hammerhead cleaning station, you won't get close enough to stare into their big stalk-like eyes; stealth is an absolute must for getting that close; close enough to study their strange rituals in detail. The hammerheads appear out of the blue, swimming into areas where Barber fish and Queen Angels dwell waiting to pick parasites from the scars on the hammerheads backs; scars caused by infighting amongst elders in efforts to get alfa positions for feeding and mating in the school.

Weird-looking hammerheads aren't the only sharks swimming around the island. Great congregations of other fierce looking sharks also lurk there. And if you're lucky, you might see them feeding ferociously from a passing school of prey - a truly astonishing sight.

When one of the great waves of green jacks running the Pacific migration-gauntlet pass by Cocos Island, they stand little chance against the island's hungry hunting pelagics. On very special occasions I took divers out to witness these mad feeding frenzies. Jumping into the center of the action we watched spellbound as dozens upon dozens of dolphins, scores of big, sleek, silky sharks and hundreds of huge, shiny yellow fin tunas ganged up for bacchanalian feasts.

With their high intelligence and unique communication skills, dolphins use a series of grunts, clicks and whistles to herd green jacks into whirling polarized hornet's nests. Attempting to escape the inevitable onslaught, the jacks race to the surface in teeming tornados, but the constantly smiling dolphins have all the time in the world as they gracefully swim through the maelstrom picking off the panicking fish one by one. The dolphin's swimming-buddies, the scowling sharks, aren't anywhere near as delicate in their approach. With the course skins of their robust bodies glistening; swinging their fearsome pointy heads from side to side in rapid zigzag movements, sharks streak menacingly scabrous through the whirling nest of green jacks capturing all the fish their steely mouths can hold in one go. And as if this isn't enough for the fish to panic about: once the swirling mass of jacks hits the surface, the air force moves in.

Flocks of flying boobies with baneful beaks break off from flying formations; descending swiftly to dive-bomb the desperately dense storm of fish.

There is no escape then. As death comes from all angles, the desperate fish swirl in smaller and smaller circles until there is nothing left in the sea-column they once occupied but blood, feathers, and shiny sinking scales.

Despite it being the most exciting thing I ever witnessed underwater, some guests thought it the scariest; and I can't say I blame them; it was pretty scary being surrounded by shit loads of sharks sniffing at your socks. But what a rush! A lot of guests preferred seeing a huge school of slow-moving hammerheads from the safety of a seamount, but I am a bit blasé after seeing so many.

In the shallower areas, closer to shore, white-tip reef sharks are more prolific than anywhere else in the world; thanks to the park rangers' efforts in protecting them from fishermen. Being lazy by nature, white tip sharks are very easy to catch. They relax in large scattered groups in shallow sandy patches; stirring only occasionally to mate or form hunting parties in collaboration with schools of voracious Crevalle Jacks. During the hunt for reef fish, jacks are normally the first fish to strike, often only injuring the fish they chase. When this happens, the injured fish take refuge in the nearest rock crevice and it is not uncommon to see 15-20 white-tips wriggling furiously trying to squeeze themselves into that crevice - no matter how small the crevice or the trapped fish.

Apart from the numerous shark species, including massive but harmless whale sharks, just about every pelagic you could wish to see swims around Cocos Island: killer whales, humpback whales, manta rays, giant tuna, dolphins, sailfish, blue striped marlin, mobila rays, eagle rays, marble rays, sea snakes, turtles, octopus, lobsters by the hundred, and at one time there was even a lonely stray Galapagos seal living on the beach.

With such a major diversity of pelagic action on its doorstep, Cocos Island is one of the finest dive sites in the world.

But Cocos Island is not renowned only for its traffic-jam of sharks.

For treasure hunters, the enormous amount of treasure reputedly buried there makes it highly desirable real estate — it tops a long list of locations said to be the inspiration for Robert Louis Stephenson's *Treasure Island*. And whether Stephenson knew of Cocos or not, countless treasure hunters have long believed it to be the depository of a series of highly sought-after pirate treasures with an estimated combined value on today's market, of over half a billion dollars U.S. Yet despite over three hundred documented treasure hunting expeditions to Cocos, no group has ever been publicly successful in recovering anything more valuable than a few doubloons.

In 1869, long after the pirate's heyday, the government of Costa Rica took possession of Cocos Island, and from 1872 to 1884, used it as a perfectly placed penal colony for high security prisoners.

After that, for almost twenty years beginning in 1889, an august German gentleman settled on the island with his wife and for a very short time with others, in an effort to colonize Cocos while he searched tirelessly for its buried treasures. During this period the government sent their own team of researchers to explore Cocos Island. But shortly after arriving and discovering the fascinating abundance of flora and fauna, all thoughts of treasure went on the back burner, and the expedition turned into one of a more scientific nature.

There is no doubt the island attracted pirates. Reports from as the early as the 1600's suggest it was an ideal rest and recreation center for buccaneers who took full advantage of the natural safety deposit facilities. After engaging in audacious inland raids and clashes with Spanish galleons bearing gold shipments along the coast of the Spanish Americas, Cocos Island was the perfect pirate hideout.

The treasure hunters I took to the island told some outrageous stories. About ten percent of those stories were pure poppycock, whilst eighty-eight percent were sheer horse cock. One bloke I took out to lead a treasure hunt told a different story every night. And each night, as the magical effects of alcohol stimulated his brain cells, the stories became more elaborate and less believable. He told me once that he'd found a box full of silver ingots on the seabed during a dive in the Gulf of Mexico, and, in his exact words, "by the time the box was hoisted to the surface, the silver bars had turned into lead. But hey, that sort of thing often happens in life."

And I'll be blowed if it doesn't; the twit.

Anyway, shortly after he made that statement, he dropped his drink and fell off his chair, as pissed as a parrot.

After hearing stories like that I tried digesting only the facts. For example: I knew it was a fact that numerous treasure expeditions had taken place because I'd taken some out myself. And there were also numerous expeditions documented before my time; some led by renowned personages such as Sir Malcolm Campbell, who, during the 1920's and 30's held the world land and sea speed records. Sir Malcolm travelled to Cocos onboard the yacht belonging to his friend Lee Guinness – of the brewing family. In fact, Sir Malcolm published an account of his expedition in 1926 that may have helped alleviate the financial burden of his fruitless search.

In 1904, the Earl Fitzwilliam, a wealthy English coal magnate bought the steamship *Harlech Castle*, which previously ferried British troops back from South Africa after the failed Mafeking Conflict, (when Britain attempted to bring the Transvaal into South Africa). The Earl renamed the steamship *Veronique* and refitted her as a private yacht, ensuring that his Cocos expedition was as comfortable as it could possibly be.

But even the Earl hadn't the resources at his disposal that his onboard partner had on *his* last visit to Cocos.

Before he retired and accompanied the Earl on his expedition onboard the *Veronique*, Admiral Henry St Leger Bury Palliser, of Her Britannic Majesties Royal Navy, tapped the might of the British Empire, employing some of the 555 crew of his battleship *Imperieuse* - the British flagship of the Pacific - to blow up and dig up great portions of the island in search of treasure. Before the *Veronique* was evicted from Cocos by the Costa Rican army, the Earl and some of his crew almost blew themselves to kingdom come in a last ditch, botched attempt at obliterating the island from the planet. The incident caused a major international scandal and led to the cooling of relations between Costa Rica and Great Britain, and the subsequent banning from Cocos of all vessels belonging to Her Britannic Majesty the Empress Queen Victoria. This was a diplomatic feat of major proportions by Costa Rica, considering the British Empire encompassed two thirds of the world at that time.

Even Theodore Roosevelt, the onetime President of The United States of America, sent his crew off treasure hunting during deep-sea fishing expeditions there.

From all the treasure tales I heard over the years only two seemed to have a consistent basis for mounting an expedition. Mariners such as: John Cook; Bennett Grahame; William Dampier; Edward Davies; and the dreaded 'Bloody Sword Benito Bonito' soon became familiar to me. Edward Davies and Benito Bonito were major players in the art of pirating, being responsible for hijacking butt-loads of booty from boats bearing treasure all along the Spanish Main.

The very sight of Benito and his vessel *Relampago* was enough to strike terror into the hearts of lesser men. Well known for his ruthlessness at sea and for daringly cunning raids on the mainland, Benito had a huge spy network on his payroll. After paying off his spies ashore, he and his men hid in rocky outcrops adjacent to dusty roads before ambushing guarded specie-filled wagon-trains on their way from the mint in Mexico, to Pacific seaports such as Acapulco. And whenever Benito's ship filled with treasure he headed straight to Cocos.

Cocos Island was Benito's and Davies' favorite home away from home, partly because it housed their favorite banking facilities – hidden caves and discreet holes in hillsides, that could only be accessed with a great deal of difficulty. In one notorious incident, Benito reputedly slaughtered several members of his own crew after they helped him bury a particularly sizeable treasure. After that, unsurprisingly, there were scant few volunteers when it came time to bury the boss's share of booty.

Unfortunately for him though, Benito the Pretty One of the Bloody Sword was eventually trapped and surrounded during one raid too many in Southern Mexico. Rather than be captured and tortured by those wishing to know where he had stashed his tremendous fortune, Pretty Boy Benito took his own life. And many still believe that Benito's fortune lays buried in a series of unmarked graves on Cocos Island.

Many also believe that somewhere else on Coco Island, another, even greater treasure waits to see the light of day. But I'll tell you about that later.

It's all about timing.

Chapter 3
El Nino

"In all things of nature there is something of the marvelous.
Nature does nothing uselessly."
Aristotle

IN THE DAMP, DEBILITATING HEAT, the crew busy themselves securing the mooring lines. Mano's two waiting maintenance workers walk the shore-power-cable and telephone-lines onboard, dodging small groups of guests milling around on the side deck. Once all the mooring lines are secure and the gangway is in place, we begin unloading the stack of garbage bags that have accumulated during the ten-day trip. After gingerly removing the bin bags from several small lockers situated on the wheelhouse roof, the guys carry them ashore. Grabbing a bag, I saunter across the gangway to chat with Claus and Mano.

As soon as I set foot on the hot dock, Claus' dog Kaiser lopes over wagging his tail wildly. Kaiser is a beast: a mixture of German Shepherd, Rottweiler and Great Dane, whose brain is lost somewhere inside a huge head. When Kaiser was a monstrous puppy, I cunningly fed him food scraps, hoping he wouldn't rip my head off later in life. Now fully grown, he slobbers all over me every time he sees me, hoping I carry food somewhere on my person. But it could be worse; he could try humping me every time he sees me, just as he does all the women he encounters – he's a lot like Claus in that respect. As it is, Kaiser manages to break open one of the many garbage bags Carlos the engineer is carrying, scattering assorted trash all over the gangway.

"Hijueputa perro," mutters Carlos, backing away from Kaiser who is now sniffing the spilled garbage, with one threatening eye daring Carlos to go near.

The garbage stinks to high heaven, despite us giving our leftover food scraps to the Park Rangers to feed to their captured pigs at the island. After helping clean up the mess and calming Kaiser down I saunter back along the dock, inspecting the boat's black speckled paintwork - the sugarcane ash has certainly left its mark.

Molly the cat jumps ashore and follows me, ignoring Kaiser in the hope he will go away. I have no idea how old Molly is but she was a pathetic looking creature when I first encountered her in the corner of our bodega, four years ago. She was so skinny and moth-eaten I felt sorry for her. After curing her acute flea problem, I made her a small nest on the aft deck. My crewmembers thought I'd gone nuts - but once she fattened up a bit, she looked as good as new. Now, she looks ten years younger and is my first mate and chief rat deterrent. There were problems with rats sneaking onboard before I found her, but now, even though she seems to do nothing but eat, sleep and poop, she has cured our rodent problem and never misses a single trip.

I knock loudly on Claus' office door but there is no answer. He is most likely up in his bedroom with the girl. I don't expect to see him again for an hour or so.

After greeting the guys from the hydraulic shop and declining a beer I say 'Ola' to the crewmembers of the *Pirate* before walking back to Manuel's' air-conditioned office. I know what the office smells like before I open the door. Manuel has a penchant for munching raw cloves of garlic. His truck reeks of garlic even with the windows open, making it a nightmare riding anywhere with him. I guarantee there are no vampires within twenty miles of the dock.

Taking a deep breath, I open the office door. Mano sits at his desk with sweat dripping down his face, despite a portable fan blowing full blast two inches from his head

"Hey Mano, you old bastard, how's it going?"

"Hey Mac, good to see you back, God Save the Queen. Pura Vida." Pura Vida, meaning pure life, is a national greeting in Costa Rica that always brings a smile to my face. "How was the trip?"

"It sucked Mano. The weather was great but the diving was shit. The guests are not happy."

"Did you lose any divers?" Mano asks with a grin.

"Not this time."

"Well, it was a successful trip then," he smiles.

"I wish it were that easy Mano. What I need now is a good stiff drink and a good loose woman to relax me. Have you seen Maria today?"

"Didn't see her this-morning boss, maybe your milk brother did."

He is referring to Claus. They call you milk brothers if you've slept with the same woman – not at the same time mind you; I'm not into that.

"Claus is busy. Did you see the girl he was talking to?" I ask.

"Yeah; one more to add to the list," he replies.

"Speaking of lists, I have two for you. There are a few things I want you to get for me, and there are a few jobs for the maintenance boys to get on with. I need the usual, but I don't need diesel this trip; I have enough for two more trips. I do need oil though, and of course gasoline. No oxygen: the next trip is with treasure hunters so there won't be any diving."

I watch him study the first list before handing him another. "These are the supplies needed for the galley. We'd better start putting fresh water onboard now too, the Americans nearly cleared us out on this trip, the water maker couldn't keep up."

"Don't you fill up from the waterfall, at the island, no more boss?"

"Not since it was analyzed by the Park Rangers and found to have traces of pig shit in it."

"Really?"

"Yeah, really. I thought I told you that. Anyway, we'd better start filling up." Claus has a huge concrete holding tank under the dock from which we pump fresh water onboard.

"No problemo boss. Don't you worry I'll fix everything for you. Are you going to the big city this time in?"

"Yeah, I'll go later." He loves me leaving the boat. Claus tells me Mano sometimes 'auditions' women for non-existent jobs in the bunk bed in the room behind his office. I know he takes over as "Lord of the Manor" when I'm gone, but I never worry about him using the boat for his 'auditions' because he rarely steps onboard: walking up the gangway is too much of an effort for him, especially at high tide when the water level is ten feet higher and there is a sharp incline to negotiate.

"Has my passport come back from immigration yet Mano?" Mano sent it off two weeks ago to get my work permit renewed.

"Not yet boss. You know how these things work; they take forever."

"It's just as well that I'm not planning to leave the country anytime soon."

"Heh, they wouldn't let you out boss, so now you are stuck with me," he laughs.

His garlic breath threatens to envelope me in its haze.

"What time is the bus due to pick up the guests; did they call yet?"

"They called and said they will be here at any minute boss; perfect timing."

"Great, everyone's packed up and ready to go. I'll come back over when they're gone."

"No problemo boss. Oh, I have some fan mail for you." He hands me the usual pile of credit card bills.

"You've lost weight," I say walking to the door.

"Have I?" he asks, with a smile.

"No," I reply, with a big grin.

"You Limey bastard! This trip didn't change you at all, did it?"

"Nothing will, Mano," I reply, laughing to myself. "Nothing will."

Walking out of Mano's office back into the oppressive heat makes me feel like a soggy sock. I think about how nice it will be in San Jose, the capital city. Punta la Pesca may be the hottest place in Costa Rica right now, but San Jose is a perfect 78 degrees year-round - not that I spend much time outside during my stay there. If I do stay here in town there won't be much to do except hang out with Maria, and she hasn't even shown up. As much as I like spending time with her, going to the city is a far more exciting prospect. As for the little casino here in town – forget it. Besides, if I stay on the boat I will be badgered constantly by Mano and the maintenance workers.

I am anxious to say goodbye to our somber guests. They will soon be on their way home, or maybe taking one of Costa Rica's famed ecological tours. The government does a great job of protecting and maintaining her numerous National Parks. A well-organized network of buses, taxis, and light aircraft is available to whisk tourists off to the remote National Parks and to all seven active volcanoes. I've been there and done that, and now I'm over it. I've even stayed in a couple of nice resorts, but I'm not a laying on the beach type of person and anyway, after spending almost every working day out at a beautiful, isolated island, surrounded by nature's finest, I prefer spending my time off enjoying the hustle and bustle of a big city; wasting what little money I don't have. I enjoy the excitement of the city. I have a penchant for the larger casinos and the endless supply of beautiful women hanging out in the bars and clubs.

Outside the dock gates, the heat shimmers off the road. Four hundred yards away, on the right side of the road, past the remains of an old abandoned building allegedly burned down by crack heads one night, the indoor fish and veggie market is bustling. Despite El Nino, fish is still available in the market, but the selection is nowhere near as abundant as in a normal year, and what little is on offer, sells for at least double the usual price. The bright orange façade of the market forms a colorful backdrop to the lines of glistening locals standing on the steamy pavement outside. Picking through cheap trinkets laid out on trestle tables in the shop-front doorways, they wait patiently for the small beat-up buses to transport their tired, damp bodies back home after shopping in the miserably exhausting heat.

Just to the right of our dock gates, behind an old red-brick colonial style building, the bare-chested crew of a long-liner are busy unloading their catch; tossing fish carcasses to three darkly tanned locals dressed in muscle shirts, cut-off blue jeans, Wellington boots, and surfer-dude sunglasses. Next to their dock, a bright red pickup truck with a blue fiberglass cooler box on its flatbed is parked on the ramp. Before heaving the fish into the cooler box, they weigh them on a scale fixed to the side of the truck. A pair of 'Bad Boy' eyes, painted in black on the truck's red door, stares in disgust at the long liner's meager haul. Most of the town's long liners, although only 30-60 feet long, carry up to ten crewmembers, even though there are no cabins and only one deck above a small engine room and fish-hold. On the stern, four large steel reels hold approximately ten miles of spooled, nylon fishing-line each; with a series of hooked, six-foot lengths attached at intervals along their entire lengths. A number of poles topped with brightly colored plastic flags and strobe lights are lashed all around the aft deck; others lay strapped across a wooden canopy above the wheelhouse. The poles mark the long lines at sea, and in port serve as perfectly placed perch pads for passing Pelicans.

Before departure, the fish holds are filled with huge, crystal clear blocks of ice from one of the town's ice factories.

As soon as they are positioned at sea, the fishermen bait the lines with small pieces of calamari or dried clam; attaching the marker poles every quarter of a mile or so. Left floating in the open ocean overnight, the flags and flashing strobe lights warn other seagoing craft of their position, while the baited hooks do their dirty business. A small location finder attached to one of the poles indicates its position if they leave the area to lay more lines.

The long lines are a pain in the arse on crossings to and from Cocos. Sharp eyes are needed to spot them all. Although they may be in my path, I haven't the slightest intention of going ten miles out of my way to avoid them, so I put both engines into neutral and cruise over them. Sometimes, if they are very close to the surface they hook up on the props. And if the props aren't turning, we can usually pull the line clear. But if a line gets tangled around the propellers it's a right old mess; especially with all the hooked sharks and whatnot zooming about in a state of panic. I could keep motoring and cut the line with the props, but I would then have a mass of melted nylon around the shafts and some very irate fishermen wanting to kill me. Usually I volunteer one of my brave crewmembers to jump in and nervously cut the line for me.

Well I'm not going to do it am I?

Some small long-liners have a range of up to twelve hundred miles in open-ocean if they take enough spare fuel drums onboard – six hundred miles out, and six hundred miles back; that's a hell of long way for these small vessels to go to catch fish. Usually, if they are close enough to Cocos Island they might anchor and stay overnight, returning to sea to retrieve their lines the following day; often after a furious game of football on the beach.

Retrieving the lines is a bit dodgy if you ask me.

A lot of fishermen lose fingers or worse. I frequently give first aid to fishermen who've suffered nasty fishing line cuts, or are the victims of an angry shark's last ironic bite. Some even know me as 'Medico Mac'; and in the town's bars, I often have grateful, drunken, three fingered fishermen offering to buy me drinks.

The long-liners haul in a variety of fish. The sharks are mostly unidentifiable to me because the heads are cut off and ditched at sea - fish rot from the head first. The highly profitable shark fins are also removed; for sale to Chinese markets. The carcasses are sold in the local fish market or directly to restaurant owners. Some boats just deal in shark fins. After cutting off the shark fins they dump the still live shark back overboard where it sinks, suffers and dies. Macho Gordo is one of the biggest culprits.

A while ago, when Claus' dock was closed for maintenance work on the pilings, I berthed at the co-operative dock closer to the western point. In front of us, a big converted oilrig tender about 200 feet in length had so many shark carcasses onboard that it took two days to unload them all. The crew unloaded forty tons of sharks into a series of huge freezer container trucks destined for Mexico - that is 80,000 pounds of weight *after* they had been gutted and the fins and heads lopped off. I was told they were paid $67,000 for the fins and about $60,000 for the carcasses. Incredibly, this boat went back out after unloading and was back within two weeks with another thirty-seven tons. The fishing lines this boat used were sixty miles long. *No shit.* The captain told me the Pacific Ocean can never be fished out like the other oceans of the world have been - no sir! He said he heard that straight from another fisherman who heard it straight from the Japanese who did a study on it - so it must be true. Yeah right... We ought to seriously wonder about the number of wankers walking around in our world.

Here in town a shark-processing plant buys all the shark cartilage they can get; grinding and processing it into pills or liquefied solutions that they sell to suffering cancer victims desperately seeking 'the cure'. I've heard from a sound source that these painfully expensive injections don't work, but obviously the word hasn't gotten around to everyone yet.

I am obviously totally biased about the overfishing of sharks because I make my living taking divers to see them in their natural habitat and no matter what you hear about them, sharks are the guardians of the seas - they have a purpose in life: keeping fish stocks strong and healthy by eating the sick, dying, weak and dead, thereby preventing wide scale pollution.

Along with sharks, the long liners catch many other pelagics, including: Yellow Fin Tuna; Sailfish; Marlin; Wahoo, and Dorado, or Mahi-Mahi - the Hawaiian name for Dolphin. Although Dorado have a big bulbous head that may indicate a large brain, they are not really dolphins. They are beautiful multicolored fish when first hauled out of the sea, but unfortunately for them, they happen to taste delicious. Over the years I've seen many horrified looks on guest's faces when told they were having Dolphin for dinner.

Long lines don't discriminate about what they catch. Sometimes hapless turtles end their days on these lines; hooked up just a few feet below the surface desperately struggling for air until they die. Even birds get hooked up. They die too.

I think most fishermen don't really care about what they catch as long as they can pay their bills. They have no choice. They have lives to lead and families to feed and are paid according to their catch. If it's a good catch there is a good payday followed by the inevitable fiesta. And if it's a bad catch, with the resultant bad pay, they still have a fiesta – "Screw it, let's party!" - but with lots of unpaid bills to add to their hangovers. Regrettably that just happens to be the case now.

Times are particularly hard right now.

When the dreaded 'El Nino' rears its ugly head we all suffer. The fishermen of South and Central America are not the only ones who suffer, but they are the first to realize its effects. They've known about the El Nino phenomenon for eons. Now known as ENSO (El Nino Southern Oscillation) the effect was first noticed around the time of the Christian celebration of the birth of Jesus Christ the boy child. Consequently, the name "El Nino" (meaning boy child in Spanish) has become synonymous with the phenomenon.

Every three to seven years the temperatures of the surface water in the Eastern Pacific Ocean undergo a drastic change. For reasons that are still not fully understood, during the El Nino cycle the Trade Winds die. Instead of blowing the warm surface waters of the Pacific Ocean from East to West and creating a warm water basin around Indonesia and Australia, as is the norm; during an El Nino cycle, the Trade Winds stop and sometimes even reverse. Subsequently the top layer of warm water normally resident in the western Pacific travels in an easterly direction, toward Central and South America. This influx of extra warm surface water causes the temperature of the water around Central and South America to heat up to as high as 86 degrees Fahrenheit - ten degrees higher than normal. Although this temperature is great for swimming, it's really crap for fishing.

The extraordinarily warm layer of surface water acts as a blanket, preventing deeper, colder waters from upwelling. And there lies the fishermen's problem: the deeper, colder waters are rich in phytoplankton on which fish feed. Fish in coastal regions die off in their thousands - around Peru and Ecuador schools of sardines and anchovies virtually disappear altogether. During El Nino the fishermen of central and South America have to travel much further afield in search of a decent catch; and frequently the catch is meager or non-existent. The local fishermen here, sometimes have to travel 200-300 miles beyond Cocos to get a decent catch.

El Nino can last from weeks to months; not only disrupting the lives of fishermen and those who depend upon them, but also upsetting the delicate balance between atmospheric pressure and temperature. This has a catastrophic worldwide effect, causing severe droughts, floods forest fires, and other destructive weather patterns.

It is also said that El Nino drives people nuts.

A Dive On The Dark Side

* * *

On the *Searcher's* aft deck, I walk under the big extending crane that I use to unload our pangas from the sun deck, and maneuver my way between a pile of dive bags and the two rows of bench seats, with their built-in dive-gear lockers and tank racks. Dive bags are stacked all around the deck. Very few divers travel light – in fact, some bring more gear than the treasure hunters.

A single set of dive gear takes up quite a lot of space but it seems, as a matter of status, the more baggage some divers bring the better diver they think they are; or think other people might think they are. In addition to large dive bags, some bring big ice coolers packed to the brim with underwater photographic equipment.

Pulling open the aft deck door I walk into the main salon. The sweat on the back of my neck freezes in the icy air. The A/C system is going full blast. With Americans onboard I swear it is like living in the Arctic Circle. Despite me asking everybody politely not to touch the thermostat in the main salon without consulting me first, someone usually clandestinely turns it up to maximum, causing us to either freeze our bollocks off in the resulting frost, or sweat like saboteurs because the system doesn't work when it is completely ice bound. I like it when it's cool inside, but there is a limit. Most European guests suffer when the air conditioning is full on, but Americans seem to thrive in it. There is a constant battle between different nationalities over the internal temperature of the boat - this time the warm bloods have obviously won.

A few guests sit around on the built-in sofas chatting, as others make last minute adjustments to their hand luggage.

"Ok ladies and gentlemen, my man tells me the bus will be here any minute. You should be out of here pretty soon. Please don't forget to sign the visitors' book. If you leave your name and address, we'll send you a newsletter. And don't go writing anything nasty about me because I'll just tear the page out." *I mean that.*

"EL NINO SUCKS!" is the chorus I hear.

'You'll have to come back after El Nino. It's going to be great then -in fact, it'll be unbelievable!" I reply.

"Yeah."

"Right."

"Sure."

I know my optimistic comment was not what they wanted to hear, but hallelujah! The bus just arrived on the dock.

Tom, the group leader strides past me without a glance.

Fuck him and the horse he rode in on.

On the aft deck, my crew-members strain to lift the dive bags and carry them out to the bus as the guests start moving onto the dock. When all the bags are loaded, my red-faced crew-members stand around waiting for the bus to drive off. As it disappears slowly through the gate-way, we wave a sad farewell. But as soon as it is out of sight, we all dance in the air. Ten days can be a very long time indeed for the crew of a diving charter boat.

Chapter 4
The Crew and the Tip

"Silent gratitude isn't much use to anyone."
Gertrude Stein

ONE ANNOYING THING about this job is meeting people who think I should do it for nothing because I have so much fun – and that includes the boat's owner. Believe it or not some people resent paying for me to have fun; completely disregarding the fact that my job actually involves work. Although I do enjoy it, and do have lots of fun, there is a certain amount of stress involved, and when a guest asks if I've thought about getting a proper job, I feel like giving them a good slap.

My philosophy is this: if you make your work look easy you are doing a good job. Obviously not everyone sees it that way. Relative to the cost of each trip per guest, the crew's pay is really pretty meager. We all rely on tips to boost our earnings to an acceptable level but few guests realize this. I have the impression they all think we are paid great wages for being their slaves and it never occurs to them, and nor do I tell them otherwise. Each crew member always goes out of their way to do that little bit extra as part of the job, but I know the thought of the tip is always in the back of their mind. The boat is chartered to individuals who book through various dive-travel agents and each trip is arranged well ahead of schedule. Even though the trips are expensive and we are a little floating hotel - a mini cruiser with very personal service - we aren't quite in the league of luxury yachts.

Dive boat owners assume a big financial risk. The maintenance and upkeep of any boat is expensive, so in order to make a profit on their investment they have to fill each charter trip and if the boat runs at full capacity every day it can become highly profitable. On the other hand, if a dive charter boat doesn't fill every trip, or if the boat breaks down and can't make a charter, or if there is a diving accident, the compensatory payment together with the loss of revenue and subsequent bad reputation can prove disastrous.

I was once given a piece of advice: *If it flies, fucks or floats –RENT it.*

Although I've found wages in the dive industry to be relatively low, there is no shortage of dive boat skippers looking for work because it is a dream job. The food, a cabin, tips, and diving are all included in our wage package, and while I do the job more for the fun and excitement than the relatively meager wage I earn, the Searcher is different from many other dive charter boats I've worked on, particularly in the Caribbean. Many boats use crewmembers that work temporarily. Maybe they are fresh out of college, or working their way around as many tropical destinations as they can while young enough to do so. But all my crewmembers here are professionals, dedicated to their jobs, working a minimum of sixteen hours a day, seven days a week, year- round, with regular paid vacations and all the benefits. While we are in Costa Rica the crew are given two days off after each ten-day trip, but during the three months we spend in the Caribbean each year, we all work none-stop. To be fair, the wages are not too bad by Costa Rican standards, but the tip, which I always divide equally, makes it worthwhile. If the crew makes a good tip, they are happy to work hard and away from their families for days, weeks, and sometimes months on end.

Every year, starting in December, the Atlantic Humpback whales migrate down from the cold, North Atlantic Ocean, to the warm, sheltered Caribbean reef areas to give birth. In January I take the Searcher from Costa Rica down to Panama; transiting the Panama Canal and then cruising across to Puerto Plata on the north east coast of the Dominican Republic. After picking up our guests in Puerto Plata, we travel eighty miles north to the site of the largest Humpback Whale mating orgy in the Caribbean - anchoring for six days at a time inside the Humpback's major mating ground: the huge reef complex at Banco Del Plata or Silverbank as it's more commonly known. From there, our guests ride out twice daily in our two, 24 feet tenders to snorkel with the giant Humpbacks. The guests have an incredible time but it is tough for the crew and stressful for me when the wind rattles the boat at night. We sit on a mooring, surrounded by umpteen, unseen coral heads and if that mooring breaks we are in deep shit. We stay in Puerto Plata every Friday night, so the guests can leave early on Saturday morning. The next group arrives Saturday afternoon for an evening departure. This means the crew has only a few hours ashore each week to go nuts. And go nuts they do. But who can blame them?

In order for the *Searcher* to get an international license we had to take an examination on safety procedures and first aid onboard before we left. A government instructor from the ministry of maritime transportation lived onboard with us for two weeks, giving us a refresher course before a series of examinations. The government course included a section on childbirth, and I had a good laugh watching the guys assist each other giving birth to a child's doll on the carpet of the main salon. I can't imagine a woman in the late stages of pregnancy coming on a diving or treasure-hunting trip to Cocos with us, but my crewmembers are always having new additions to their families, so it is worthwhile for them to know the procedure. Another part of the course that tickled me pink was when the instructor made us all don lifejackets and jump off the foredeck into the sea together. We had to swim like the clappers to get back to the boat before we all disappeared over the horizon in the strong current leaving the instructor onboard by himself.

Training with the crew is always good practice. Being competent in any emergency is imperative.

It's an exciting life alright. In fact, the excitement of it is the main incentive for my pandering to the whims of countless guests - some of whom are spoiled, others who are not, and some who leave a nice tip, and others who are as tight as a duck's arse. As much as I love the job, I don't know how much longer I can keep doing it. I am starting to feel burned out - but not from living and diving in Paradise; it's living so close to so many people every day that drives me nuts.

For the last fifteen years, every seven to ten days, I've lived with all kinds of people from all corners of the globe: hard core divers, hopeless divers, fanatical treasure hunters, touchy feely, hippy whale watchers, demanding, fussy filmmakers, magazine editors, journalists, doctors, and some high powered, hard-arsed lawyers; amongst whom are some really nice people. Most come to have a good time but there are some really miserable bastards in this world; people who actually enjoy being shit-heads and making all those around them miserable. I try not to let them leave the longest impression but it grates on my nerves being around such twats. And there are more twats than you can possibly imagine in this world. I've met more than my share of those. *Why do so many people enjoy making life difficult for others?*

The majority of our guests are relatively wealthy, by which I mean that as expensive as it is, they don't have to save up for a long period of time to afford the trip. We have a variety of punters onboard, but regardless of who they are, there is one thing I detest as much as running across an instant expert. I hate being asked a question by someone who isn't remotely interested in the answer. Do you know what I mean? I mean those who are already asking the next question before the answer to the last question is only half way out of your mouth. I mean those twits who usually ask what they think are the right questions to make everyone else think they're smart. Believe me it happens a lot. And they all ask the same bloody questions.

Some guests think I am the luckiest guy alive for being paid to do what they are all paying to do, but they have no idea of the responsibility I carry in ensuring their trip is safe and successful.

Can I blame anyone for being jealous of me being paid for what many would give up anything to do?

I know I am a really lucky bastard. I have everything I need. I have a great job on a floating home in a tropical paradise, there is no shortage of lovely female companions and there is the opportunity to visit a casino whenever the boat is in port. I spend two to three hours underwater almost every day in one of the most fantastic diving areas in the world and on top of that there are the frequent treasure-hunting trips to add to the excitement. Even better, I am in charge of the whole operation because my boss lives in the city and hardly ever comes onboard for a trip.

After being in the military, this kind of freedom really appeals to me. As soon as we leave the dock every decision is mine alone. I am responsible for the welfare of everyone stepping foot on the boat. A few lucky divers come to one of the wildest dive sites on earth and I make damn sure I bring the same number back safely. My job is to make everyone feel at home, in my home, on the boat. The crew and I keep everybody happy no matter how miserable they are and I keep them safe no matter how dangerous they are to themselves or to their buddies. I eat with them and amuse them for days and nights on end no matter how demanding they are, and I smile at them every day and pretend to love them all equally. Yet when they leave, I never see ninety percent of them ever again.

No matter what their character, or however much a pain up the arse they are, and regardless of whether I like them or not, they are there to have the best diving of their lives and expect to be entertained accordingly. They need to be convinced they are enjoying themselves even if they aren't, and they have to believe they are somehow superior to all us peons as we run around acting like genies in the lamp, making their every wish come true.

Despite having a laidback attitude, I'm kept busy. Apart from organizing all the diving, there is a boat to run and a crew to take charge of. I have to be sure the small, exclusive floating hotel and all its systems work properly. Sometimes I assist the engineer with repairs and sometimes the engineer assists me, because often when something breaks down it is swiftly followed by other problems.

The engineer and I sometimes find ourselves up to our elbows in crap, because somebody shit a brick, or threw something into the toilet bowl they shouldn't - despite my emphasizing it in the briefing when they first come onboard. And often when I find myself with my gloved hand immersed in a bowl-full of smelly brown human waste, trying to arrest an offending object that is blocking the system, I hate boats and boat's toilets with a bloody vengeance.

And then there is the air conditioning problem I spoke of earlier: *Temperature up full, temperature down full.* Although everyone whines about it, the onboard system isn't meant for that kind of treatment and even though I explain it with special emphasis during my initial boat briefing, it is evident that I either speak in an alien tongue or a lot of people have cloth ears.

Every day at the island, in addition to organizing the diving, I dive two or three times with the guests. I drive the *Searcher* around the island, anchoring in different spots every day. I organize shore excursions and panga trips and give Rebreather Courses and Nitrox courses. I check that the crew has cleaned all the cabins and bathrooms and made all the beds properly, and I make sure the food is always on time and at its best. Divers love to dive but they also love their food. The fresh Cocos sea breeze and exciting diving makes everyone ravenously hungry.

After doing this in various parts of the world for fifteen years, I don't own a house or have a pension fund and my only possessions are a set of diving gear and a few clothes. I don't have medical insurance or a savings scheme. A deckhand on a private yacht earns more money than me. What I do have is a bad gambling habit and a lot of rather large credit card bills (which doubled on my last couple of trips to the casinos). There is also a very high risk of me catching some tropical disease - but more of a sexual nature than from the tropics. The longer I do this job the greater chance there is of me losing my patience and seriously smacking someone in the gob, hard.

And I used to be such a nice guy too.

But every choice is mine. And I never really take time to think about what I don't have, because I still have a hell of a lot going for me, and I work for it every day onboard the boat.

All in all, I consider myself a really lucky bloke, but I desperately need a break. I haven't been off the boat for longer than two days in the past year, during which time I've worked virtually none stop. Sometimes I feel I live in a kind of shadow world, with only me in it. I have no family and no one I really care about deeply except Molly, the cat and maybe Maria, but I'm not prepared to commit to one woman. Occasionally I wonder about the future, seeing myself as a hermit living in a cave later in life. On these occasions I usually change my thoughts to sex.

Sitting at my desk in the wheelhouse counting the tip, I glance up to see "Raul the Mini Viking" peering in as he cleans the windows. He is trying hard not to make it obvious he is waiting for me to finish dividing the tip equally for each crew member.

I beckon him inside. Raul once told me that when he was younger, he was a merchant seaman with an unhealthy appetite for drinking that cost him the loss of his family. He is now a sober born-again Christian remarried to a nice forty something divorcee with a bunch of children.

"I'm sorry Raul the tip isn't much this week."

"Si Cappy, we know the guests were not happy with the diving," he says disappointedly. "But we do a good job, no?"

"You always do a great job, but these guys were just miserable. It's been tough the last couple of months."

"Si, pero when El Nino is gone it will be better."

"Yeah, let's hope so."

My crew speaks pretty good English; it's a requirement for them. They need to be able to communicate with the guests. Costa Rica has an extremely efficient and productive education system, with the government spending a considerable amount of money per capita ensuring the literacy rate is high – over ninety percent in fact. I get by with my Spanish but when I encounter the local dialect spoken rapidly like machine gun fire, I feel like a total idiot. I have no idea what is being said. The crew uses the local dialect if they don't want anyone to know what they are saying - often using it when talking about guests. They give everyone nicknames. I don't know what mine is but I'm willing to bet it's one I don't want to know anyway.

"As soon as you finish washing down you can go home. Do you need more help?"

"No gracias Cappy. Nico is helping me." Nico is Nicaraguan; one of the three shore-based maintenance crew. The Nicaraguans I meet are all nice people. Nico is great, but Mano the agent gives him a hard time just because he is Nicaraguan. Mano is not a benevolent soul when it comes to Nicaraguans. He blames them for virtually all the problems in Costa Rica. One particular instance immediately springs to mind. For one of our scheduled trips, our guests requested an extra-large stock of cola. Seeing as how there is a factory just up the road that bottles cola in copious quantities, you would think it would be no problem getting as much cola as we need. Because Mano has a tendency to forget things, I had to remind him about the cola right up until the day of the boat's departure. Just before we were ready to leave there was still not enough cola onboard.

"Mano, what about the cola?" I ask.

"The supply truck from Nicaragua tipped over on the road boss - you know these Nicaraguan drivers. Now there's no cola in town."

He must think I just rowed in on the last banana boat. The excuse is obviously the first that comes into his head. He thinks he can save face by making up a good story and making the Nicaraguans take the blame at the same time. I end up getting the cola from the local supermarket; they have piles of it in stock. I have a good chuckle when I think of that story.

Another time, when there was an outbreak of dengue fever - a mosquito borne virus transmitted by the bite of a mosquito - it didn't stop Manuel telling me, "We didn't have the focking dengue before the Nicaraguans came here. We didn't have all this crime either."

Although every window in almost every building in Costa Rica is barred or grilled, paradoxically Costa Ricans are generally honest, straight, and nonviolent. There are the usual petty crimes in the poorer, depressed areas, but some locals use an age-old excuse and blame the bad crimes on immigrants from other Central American countries - particularly Nicaragua. Many genuinely honest immigrants come to work in the coffee and sugar plantations but there are inevitably 'the undesirables' - bad eggs who cross the border seeking to enrich their lives through crime. Costa Rica has no military and there has been no armed conflict in the country since the 1948 civil war. In Nicaragua it is a different story. The population was all too familiar with the concept of violence during the 'Contra War', when weapons were carried openly and many died. But now the war is over and people are trying to get their lives back.

As Raul leaves the wheelhouse, Carlos walks up the stairs from the dining area. He has the furthest distance to go home and has to catch a ferry to get there. He usually wants to leave early. At twenty-eight years of age he is married with five children, and like the other crewmembers is always smart and cheerful, despite working in the engine room in the intense heat. When he was eighteen, he had a scholarship to study in the USA. Unfortunately, while there he fell in with the wrong crowd and dabbled with drugs, which got him kicked out of college and sent back to Costa Rica. I admire him because he managed to straighten himself out, and is now a sober and upstanding family man. He once spent time working at a government radar station here, from where the DEA track drug shipments around Central America. Even though the Pan American Highway - the pathway from South American drug producing countries, to the United States, runs through Costa Rica, the incidence of hard drug abuse was relatively low until just recently. Lately, the crime levels - particularly those of violence – have begun to increase. Before joining the boat, Carlos worked with his father repairing cars and trucks in the city.

"Did you finish the check list?" I ask him. I already checked the engine room with him earlier, going over our inventory of spare parts. Luckily the systems on the boat rarely cause major problems but there are always hiccups – it *is* a boat after all.

"Si, claro. Todo listo, Cappy. I checked the fuel level; oil, engine hours log and spare-parts list; todo bien; all done."

"Ok Carlos. Good job. I'm sorry but the tip was lousy this week." I give him an envelope.

"Well, we do our best Cappy."

"Yes, you do Carlos, gracias. Have a good time at home. Be back here by nine on Monday morning."

"Okay. Gracias Cappy. See you then. Hasta luego." And he is off.

Moments later Arcelio trudges up the stairs. He is a good chef; always laughing and joking, with that constant twinkle in his blue eyes. Now into his third marriage with six children and two ex-wives chasing him for alimony, he is a bit of a rake.

"Are you sure you can't come to my home tonight Cap? You know you are welcome anytime," he says.

52

"I'd love to Arcelio. But I really do have to go to the city tonight. I have to see the boss. Thanks anyway."

"Okay. Tell the boss I say Hi, and ask him for more money for us," he smiles, half-jokingly.

"Okay Arcelio, you did a good job again. Gracias. See you Monday."

Once he's gone, I sit back down at my desk in the corner and pull out the account sheets. I really don't cherish this part. It is my last task before leaving the boat to start partying. Sorting out the accounts is a complicated procedure that makes my brain hurt. There is a long list of payments made by guests, with various commissions to be calculated for the crew and myself. The guests are told to bring only cash to pay their bills. There are U.S. dollars, German marks, British pounds and Colones, the local currency. The exchange rate changes daily so I have to call the head office in San Jose on the single sideband radio the day before I arrive, to get the correct exchange rate in order to cover my arse. The radio reception was so bad during this trip we couldn't communicate, so I'm hoping I get everything just right.

Distractedly, looking through the wheelhouse window I watch Juanita the cleaning girl, arrive. She's a beauty, but unfortunately for me she is happily married.

Engrossed with the accounts I don't hear Pedro until he is standing right behind me looking over my shoulder. Pedro recently separated from his wife after going out, getting roaring drunk and then threatening her with a gun because he heard a story in a bar about her being out on the town while he was away. Since his wife kicked him out, he usually heads off to a small beach town in the south to spend his time off. I feel sorry for his three children. Spending all this time away from home is hard on all six crewmembers.

"All is finished Cappy. Can I go now?"

"Si, muy bien, Pedro." I give him his envelope. "Are you going to the beach?"

"Si Cap, es moi tranquillo, you should go."

No chance

"Yeah, maybe I will. Have a great time."

"Gracias Cappy. Lo haz hasta luego el lunes nueve." These guys are so polite. Obviously, word has spread about everybody having to be back on Monday at nine.

After he's gone, I watch Ronaldo help Juanita take the last of the laundry ashore and load it into Mano's truck. Juanita washes and irons everything by hand. With three sets of sheets and towels for fourteen guests and seven crewmembers she has her work cut out.

I am so busy trying to look up Juanita's skirt as she bends over the truck-bed that I don't hear Roberto the dive-master coming up the stairs. He is different from the other crewmembers. He regards himself as a higher-classed citizen, which jars with them because Costa Ricans in general consider themselves a classless society, frowning upon any form of boasting or arrogance - except in relating exploits with the opposite sex, which Roberto is really good at. Being a handsome, twenty-five-year-old, Roberto is a big hit with our guests. He's the only unmarried crewmember. He always spreads it on thick with the women guests, regardless of whether they are married or not. Roberto uses his Latin charm to try and talk their knickers off at every opportunity. The first question he asked when he joined the boat as a crewmember was: "Am I allowed to sleep with the guests?" I told him that he can only sleep with the men because I am saving the women for myself. He didn't quite know how to take that. Roberto will shag a sheepskin rug if he can find a hole in it.

"OK Mac, all the dive gear is stowed away and all the dive tanks are full." He's the only one who doesn't call me Cappy. He hands me an inventory of dive equipment.

Mostly, the divers bring their own equipment but on odd occasions someone forgets a vital piece of gear and we rent it to them. We also have a set of rebreather equipment onboard for rent. Rebreathers are very expensive. They are also heavy items to carry around. Only a few wealthy die-hard divers bring one with them. If any guest is qualified to use a rebreather, they can always rent one from us, and if anyone wants a course qualifying them to dive in one: I am only too willing to oblige.

"What time do I need to be here on Monday?" He always wants to turn up later than the other guys.

"You're in luck. We don't need a dive-master for the next trip - the treasure hunters are coming."

"You mean I get a vacation?"

"Correcto.'

"With pay?"

"Negativo. You can work if you want. I'm sure I'll find something for you to do; like cleaning and painting." I know that will discourage him.

He screws up his face. "No, that's OK. I will take the time off. When do I need to be back?"

"The next trip is only six days. So that would make the start of the trip after that…" I look at the calendar behind my desk, "…So, we have three nights in now, then six days out, so that makes it a week on Tuesday. But if things change, I'll give you a call when I get back from this next trip. I've got your cell phone number." I am surprised his cell phone doesn't go off while I am talking to him; it usually rings constantly while we are at the dock and it annoys the shit out of me – probably because I don't have a cell phone of my own. I make a mental note to look into buying one. This new technology is passing me by.

I give him his tip. "Have a good vacation Roberto."

"Okay, Gracious. See you in nine days."

Ronaldo ambles up next. When he first came onboard his English was nowhere near as good as my Spanish so we communicated in Spangleasy; with me trying to teach him a few words of English. Occasionally I taught him the odd phrase like: "Have a good shag," which in England means, "have a good fuck", but I told him it was English slang for "have a good time," and I loved it when he said it to the Brits. They thought they'd misheard him. The crew went along with the gag until one of the Brits told him what it really meant. He no longer trusts me when I try teaching him new words.

"Cappy, I finish to helping to Juanita. I checking all cabins, no problemas. Por favor, I can go home?" Ronaldo gives me a toothless grin. He had a nice set of false shiny white front teeth when he first came onboard, but during his first sea crossing to Cocos the sea was a rough and he puked the gleaming plastic pearly whites over the side, where they sank in several thousand feet of water. The crew members had a good laugh about that and still tease him constantly. He is trying to save up for his next set of false teeth but the poor bloke always has some kind of disaster befalling him. I don't know how many times his home has been flooded or his roof has blown off. He tells me his house is also burgled repeatedly – although I'm not quite sure what he can possibly have left that is of any value. I feel particularly sorry for him. He is deeply in debt, and although he's the youngest crewmember, he still has an army of children.

I give him the tip envelope and he looks at it before rubbing it between his fingers. "Cap, is possible I borrow mooney for until next trip, I have some small problemo in my hoose."

"Sorry Ronaldo, we don't have divers next trip – it's with the German treasure hunters. Maybe if they find the treasure, we will all get a big tip and you can buy a new house, no? He grins once more, knowing full well the Germans won't leave a tip, nor will they find the treasure after so many futile attempts at searching for it. He looks despondent. Being the steward, his pay is bottom of the scale so he always asks for a loan to be paid off from his next tip. I feel like lending him money myself, but I need all the money I can get to try and recuperate some of my casino losses. I don't tell him that though.

Once he's gone, I relax in the silence.

After a quick stroll around the boat, checking on things in general I settle back down at my desk to get on with the accounts. When I'm finished, I bundle up the money and lock it in a drawer in my cabin.

Thank heaven for that.

Chapter 5
Claus

"It's choice, not chance, that determines our destiny."
Jean Nidetch

REALIZING THE THREE maintenance workers are still onboard, I go looking for them to tell them to go home.

Descending the stairs from the wheelhouse I walk into the dining area, past the Galley on the port side. Outside the galley a buffet counter runs the length of the bulkhead. Part of the galley is visible through a serving hatch in the bulkhead on my right. In the galley, beneath the hatch, a table with two benches serves as the crew's dining area.

In the center of the carpeted dining room, secured to the deck, thirteen teak chairs surround a large elliptical polished mahogany table. On the teak paneled bulkheads around the dining room, a series of large framed photographs of coral reef scenes add a touch of color.

I usually eat at the table with the guests during the week, changing seats daily so I can chat with each individually. Sitting around that table I tell the same jokes and answer the same questions and hear total strangers swapping personal details that I wouldn't even tell a shrink, but as long as they are all happy, I am too.

Passing the watertight door that opens on to the port side deck I walk into the aft salon. Around the perimeter of the salon, large built-in sofas surround a custom-made teak entertainment center. On each side of the room two oblong windows look out to the world. To the right of the door leading to the aft deck, a permanently open watertight hatch sits above a stairway leading down to the four aft cabins. After descending the stairs, I check each cabin and bathroom; satisfied they are clean, I make my way back up to the dining area. After ten days at sea it's nice and quiet here without the engines or generator running.

Inside the galley, the walk-in cold-room usually full of provisions at the start of a ten-day trip is now empty. Standing there in the cool silence makes me think of what it once held.

During a dive charter at the island three years previously, a park ranger was out hunting pigs with another ranger when he fell into a ravine and broke his neck. His body had to be brought back to the mainland for an autopsy and a proper burial, but the only way to get him back to the mainland was by boat. There isn't a landing strip for fixed-wing aircraft on Cocos or even a clearing big enough to land a helicopter. A seaplane can land on the waters of Chatham Bay if it is absolutely flat calm, but that only happens with any regularity during an El Nino or in the summer-months. Only one aircraft has ever landed on the island, and that was a tragic mistake. During a routine flight many years ago, a United States B24 Bomber crashed into Cerro Iglesias the island's peak, killing all onboard.

The coast guards have two patrol vessels in Punta La Pesca but I have never seen them at Cocos, and since none of the fishing boats would do it, I volunteered to bring the deceased ranger back onboard the *Searcher*.

There was no alternative but to bring the unfortunate park ranger back with us: we were his only ticket out. So, while the guests were out diving on the last day of the trip, the galley crew emptied out the cold room and in a clandestine operation laid the ranger to rest for his final voyage back to the mainland. Leaving Cocos that day was a sad affair, but as if by magic, the most enormous school of dolphins I have ever seen there, escorted us for several miles, as if bidding the poor guy a final farewell.

Standing in the silent galley I hear my name being called in an eerily deep voice, and it puts the shits up me. With shivers running down my spine I turn and bump into Marco, the son of Guapo. Marco is one of the maintenance guys.

"Cappy" he says in a husky voice.

"Hey Marco. Todo bien?"

"Si Mac. Todo is good all." Is what I think he says with his lopsided smile.

'Marco the Pump' was a crewmember who now has a bullet in his brain. I never really learned the real story but I heard it had to do with a .22 rifle and an argument with his wife. The doctors decided it was too dangerous to remove the bullet from his brain so it remains somewhere inside his head. The left side of his face is paralyzed and he occasionally dribbles from the corner of his mouth. There is a big round scar beneath his Adams apple, which I assume is from being resuscitated. I have a hell of a job trying to understand what he says. He also keeps losing his balance and falling over. Every time he does something strange, which he often did before the accident, it is explained away as 'the bullet moving.' Now, despite a lopsided face, a glassy eye and a hoarse voice that is still difficult to decipher, he is as fit as he can be and taking a college course in engineering. Marco is as happy as a poor boy can be under the circumstances. I have a soft spot for him.

Marco always wants to chat for as long as he can, but I don't understand half what he says so I always try and dodge him when I can.

My main maintenance worker, Ricardo, is an all-round handyman with the ability to do most small repair jobs; outside tradesmen do the jobs these guys don't have the necessary skills for. Ricardo, constantly tears his hair out over Marco's' insistence on taking things apart just to see how they work. This in itself would not be half bad if only Marco were able to put things back together correctly. He inevitably puts parts back together wrong, causing minor disasters in his wake, so I have to make sure he doesn't have any technical jobs on his list, and I try keeping the two of them working at opposite ends of the boat, out of each other's way.

There is an excellent little boatyard in town owned and operated by a hyperactive seventy-two-year-old Costa Rican character whose English father came to Costa Rica to help build the railroad and ended up staying and marrying a local girl. There is nothing this guy doesn't know about, or cannot manufacture for a small boat. He has equipment from all over the world in his yard. Along with giant lathes of various shapes and sizes, and machines for welding any kind of metal, there are wood working machines, metal working machines, and machines for making machines. You name it; he has it.

Although the *Searcher* is too big to go up on his slipway for dry-docking, it is still great for me because I don't have to worry about missing trips due to breakdowns or a missing spare part. He can replicate as new, any vital, previously irreplaceable part that may be broken, worn out, or lost by Marco.

Being a fishing port, there is always someone available to fix boat stuff. We don't have much electronic equipment onboard; just a basic Satellite Navigation unit which gives me five chances in a twenty-four-hour period of getting an accurate position at sea – if I'm lucky. There are two radar sets; a depth sounder; a VHF radio for local calling and a Single Sideband radio that enables me to talk to the office in San Jose while we are at the island. There is also an autopilot, which saves us from the tedious and tiring job of hand steering the boat for thirty-two hours to reach Cocos. Luckily none of the units give me major problems.

The maintenance guys don't bother me too much about the jobs they have to do onboard, they just get on with it, which is great because it means that I can leave the boat to Manuel and these guys, and shoot off to the city.

I tell Ricardo he can leave whenever he's finished up and to tell Nico he can leave also.

Walking outside for a cigarette, I catch sight of Claus, beer in hand standing outside the fan belt shop.

"Hey, you old bugger, what's happening?' I shout.

"Mac, my brother, come on over. Have a beer." Claus speaks English and Spanish with hardly an accent.

Claus arrived here ten years ago.

While cruising the Pacific coast of Costa Rica in a small yacht he bought with the proceeds from a restaurant sale in Germany (which he bought after working as a chef on several cruise liners) the potential he saw in the tourist industry here prompted him to start a small charter boat business - at least that's what he says; I think it had more to do with the attractive women and sexual freedom than any business potential. Anyway, he was successful in chartering his yacht, and with his blonde hair and Germanic good looks is a novelty to the local coffee-skinned ladies. Beginning with daily trips to a small island in the Gulf of Nicoya just around the corner, he eventually branched out; making frequent trips to Cocos Island during the dry season - December to May. During the rainy season the prevailing winds and stormy weather make passages to Cocos too long and arduous for a relatively small sailing yacht.

Claus once made a weeklong trip to Cocos during the rainy season and spent most of that time battling against the weather trying to reach the island. He had to turn back before he got there because he ran out of time. Needless to say: his guests were not amused or impressed by that little adventure.

Anyway, four years ago, his charter boat career came to an abrupt end when his yacht sank. And that incident forged a unique bond between us.

Anchored at Cocos Island in the middle of a treasure hunting charter, I heard Claus' mayday call over the radio. He was in big trouble about five miles from the island so I took off immediately with the *Searcher*. When we arrived at the scene his yacht was wallowing up to the gunnels. Nearby, Claus and Leona, his sometime girlfriend, sat forlornly on top of a hodgepodge of belongings in a small inflatable dinghy surrounded by floating debris. After rescuing what we could, I let Claus and Leona stay onboard the *Searcher* for the remainder of our charter before taking them back to port. They both pledged eternal gratitude for saving them, and we have been good run-ashore buddies ever since. Oddly enough Claus was on a rescue mission himself that day, intending to deliver a vital spare part to a fishing boat stuck at the island with engine trouble. The fishing boat had to wait until I got back there on the next trip with another part before they could leave.

Although Claus lost his yacht, he shrewdly bought this dock with the insurance money, and now earns rent from any boat docking here. Before we started using his dock, another dive boat had exclusive use of it, and that vessel was strong competition for us, but luckily, she sailed off to the South Pacific to do a film project so now the *Sea Searcher* has Cocos Island all to herself.

I wander over and shake hands with Claus, gladly accepting the proffered icy cold Imperial beer; my first for ten days.

"Hey buddy. How the devil are you? Who was that young lady you were with earlier?"

"She just came for a job in my office."

"I'll bet she did, you prick. You don't need anyone to work for you; except maybe with their lips and hips. Did you?"

"Hey buddy, would I do something like that?"

"I'd be surprised if you didn't."

"So, what's happening in town now; anything new?"

"Oh yeah! I've something huge to tell you my friend." Claus is a great source of local knowledge. The locals love to gossip and Claus seems to know it all. I never know if half of it is true but like everyone else, I don't really care; it's interesting hearing the stories – the wilder the better.

"Tell me now." I urge.

"Well, it's about Maria," he says smiling. "She wants to see you. I think she is in trouble."

"She said she would be waiting for me when I came in but she didn't show up. Don't tell me she's pregnant."

"It's worse than that," he says, becoming serious.

"Holy shit, what could be worse: some kind of communicable disease?"

Claus laughs. "It's pretty bad my friend. Let's go for a few drinks and I'll tell you all about it."

"I'm going to San Jose as soon as I've finished here mate," I tell him.

"Go to San Jose tomorrow; we haven't had a good night out for too long man. Hey, there's some nice new talent in town." He means ladies.

I think about it. "I don't know mate. I've got to get away from the boat for a couple of days. The punters are driving me nuts now that we don't see Hammerheads."

"Fuck the punters Mac, they have gone home," he laughs.

"Yeah, fuck'em. But I need to get off the boat. Anyway, what's so important I have to stay in town and put up with you for the night?"

Before he can answer Manuel shouts for me to take a phone call in his office; it's the boss in San Jose.

Claus makes a big 'O' with his mouth. "Mac, meet me over in my second office as soon as you are done here." His second office is the bar across the street.

"Tell me, quickly about Maria."

"No. Go take your phone call."

"OK pal, I'll see you over there. But this better be something good; I could go to San Jose."

"Stay here. You're not gonna believe it Mac. See you later."

"Alright, see you over there."

The boss is pissed. He wants to know when I will be delivering the large sum of cash I collected. I should have given Mano the balance for the group's late bookings before I left port on the last trip but I had to catch the tide. I left as soon as the guests arrived onboard. I tell the boss I'll bring the cash to San Jose tomorrow but he is still not happy. *Well...screw him.*

Claus is gone by the time I come out of Mano's office.

Back onboard I shower; put some smelly stuff under my arms and around my balls; drink another beer and then go over and chat with Mano again - he is just about to go home. One of the night watchmen has arrived. Claus has one for the dock and I have one for the boat. Felix is my watchman. A big stocky guy, he doesn't take any shit from anyone, but he sleeps during the night. Luckily Claus' dog Kaiser barks like a killer if anyone appears at the gate.

After making sure Molly the cat is in her spot on the aft deck, I leave for the meeting with Claus. I'm anxious to hear the news.

Chapter 6
A night on the Town

"The hardest thing to understand is why we can understand anything at all."
Albert Einstein.

C LAUS' 'SECOND OFFICE', is directly opposite the dock, on the corner of one of three main avenidas running east to west. None of the streets in town have names: Claus' address is: De Mercado 300 E. Muelle Claus - which translates as: Claus' dock, 300 meters east of the market.

Crossing the street to the bar, I glance at the cinema to my left: this is the dark side of town. Crack City is just fifty yards from the dock gates. The filthy foyer of a dilapidated cinema and its pavement outside are home to some of the crack addicts attracted to town. The area stinks. Regular folk don't walk on that side of the street. The cinema front is a freak show. Crack addicts sprawl there on the dirty cracked mosaic tiles in various stages of undress day and night. The posh ones lay on pieces of cardboard. The poorer ones lay in puddles of piss. I once saw an unconscious crack-head lying on the paved sidewalk in the afternoon sun with a river of steaming urine flowing from the leg of his shorts. The stream of piss evaporated on the hot pavement before it even reached the curb. The stench outside the cinema is at its worst during the dry season, without the cleansing rains washing it away – another good reason to pray for rain.

A few weeks ago, out of the blue, two policemen arrived in Claus' upstairs apartment to ask if they could video the street from his kitchen window. Claus' kitchen has a bird's eye view of the cinema and the small tin shack on the derelict building site opposite from where drugs are sold. Claus was only too happy to let them use his place as a stakeout for a few days – the area badly needs cleaning up.

Surprisingly there are no signs of crack-heads outside now.

"Hey Mac," Claus shouts from inside the bar. He is sitting at a table behind a slatted wooden fence-gate that is propped against the side door entrance. Smiling, I walk around to the front entrance.

Just inside the main door, in the right-hand corner, I notice a new addition to the room: a small triangular cubicle with a waist high door.

"Have a look inside," Claus shouts from across the bar room.

Nailed to the wall inside the cubicle is the smallest urinal I've ever seen. Beneath it, attached to the outlet pipe, a small hose snakes across the floor and out through the main door. I follow it outside. Partly buried in the paving stone cracks, the hose continues along the sidewalk and disappears into a storm drain. What a nice little setup.

The bar is abuzz.

Several Ticos dressed in shorts, flip flops and T-shirts, sit nursing beer bottles around a circular blue-tiled bar at the back of the room. Costa Rican men are known as Ticos, and the women Ticas: maybe because they used to address each other respectfully in the past as Hermaniticos – little brothers. By the bar, I recognize a couple of fishermen I saw earlier unloading their boat.

"Ola. Como estas?" they both smile.

"Moi bien. Pura Vida," I reply.

Two ceiling fans whizzing overhead challenge flies to land on the bar. Despite the funky facilities, Pablo serves tasty bocas: dishes of fried chicken or fish handed out gratis with each round of drinks. A favorite of mine is ceviche - raw fish marinated in garlic, lemon-juice, onion and cilantro; I am told it puts lead in your pencil. Thursday is chicharones day - pork skins cooked slowly in their own fat until light and crunchy – the aroma is mouthwatering. Of the two brands of beer on offer, most men choose Imperial because the big black, imperial eagle on the label looks a lot more macho than the pink label on the stronger Pilsner beer, which many consider to be a lady's drink. You are only given a glass if you drink spirits.

"Hey Pablo, Como esta?" I ask the bartending owner.

"Moi bien Mac. Usted? Que pasa?" he asks, smiling broadly.

"Moi fantastico. I'll have a guaro and soda, con limon per favor."

"Sure thing Mac," he replies pouring a good measure of guaro into a wet tumbler and adding a lemon wedge. With drink in hand, I move over to the table where Claus sits with two workers from the hydraulic shop and a couple of other locals I know vaguely. The table is completely covered with empty beer bottles. Being careful not to knock the pile of bottles over, I shake hands with everyone around the table. Pablo's unique way of calculating the final tab is to count the bottles on the table and on the floor next to it, if the table is full. Every customer drinking beer is surrounded by a mass of bottles testifying to their fortitude. Pablo calculates the bill mentally; trying to rip us off by counting some bottles twice. When we find him out, which we usually do, he claims it is a joke. But by that time, we are usually too intoxicated to take it personally.

One old guy sitting at the table usually performs party tricks for us when he's had too much to drink. His favorite stunt is stubbing a lighted cigarette out on his tongue. After watching him a few times I noticed he clandestinely put ice cubes under his tongue beforehand. I make a mental note to check his tongue the following day, wondering if it was swollen to the size of a salami sausage, but he is usually nowhere to be found the next day.

Pulling up a chair, I sit next to Claus. "What's up with the new toilet? Can anyone actually fit into it?" I ask.

"Yeah, if they don't get a hard on," Claus laughs. "Pura Vida buddy. Now that women come here in regularly, Pablo has made the old men's toilet the ladies room."

I laugh, "Has he cleaned it up?"

"Probably not."

The "ladies room" is situated inside a dark, door-less hole, close to the bar — *a little too close if you ask me.* Inside, at knee level, a smelly orange-stained steel trough runs the length of the wall next to a partly painted brown stained wooden door. When it was the 'men's room' that forbidding looking door was usually kept locked, but when it was once unlocked, I opened it out of curiosity. *Fuck me!* After taking in the nightmare of the toilet bowl I peered upwards to where the orange-stained walls meet the cobweb-laced ceiling. I discovered a lost world of giant hairy spiders. I almost screamed like a girl. I get goose bumps on my ball bag just thinking about it.

"I'm glad the bar is being upgraded; it'll be full of yuppies before we know it. So, what's happening buddy? What's so important that I have to stay here and put up with you for the night?"

A big grin creases his face.

"You look tired Mac. You need a good night out."

"I could have one in San Jose."

"Yeah, but the girls are so expensive there," he laughs.

"I don't buy girls, Claus."

"No, not fucking much. Why are you always broke then? You need to have some proper fun for a change."

"Okay Claus, you win. But before we have fun, tell me what's so importante?"

Claus looks around the table. All eyes are on us. "Is Julia still at the island?" he asks.

"Not right now. She's back home in the States."

"Is that why you have lumps under your neck?" he laughs.

Julia and I have a thing going - thanks to James Colnett.

In 1793, James Colnett, captain of the good ship *Rattler,* was on a voyage studying the whale fisheries and anchorages of the Pacific when he stopped off at Cocos Island to fill his water barrels and stock up on coconuts. In exchange for the sustenance he took onboard, the well-intentioned captain deposited two lucky little pigs on the island, hoping to benefit future mariners by adding to the island's live food larder. Good old Captain Colnett had no clue that Mr. and Mrs. Porky and their multitudinous offspring would cause devastating damage to the island's ecology over the coming years. He had no idea that the island would be overrun with porkers constantly foraging for worms, their only good source of protein. The pigs leave trenches all over the island that fill with rainwater, overflow, and wash valuable, nutrient rich soil into the sea. Now, as the little bastards go about destroying the island, Julia tracks them down and studies them.

She's been studying the porky family on a government grant for a couple of years, on and off. I took her out on her first trip and when she saw the conditions on the island that she had to live in for the next two years, she seduced me into letting her stay overnight on the boat whenever possible. Although she's a tough cookie, Julia loves warm showers, good food, and most importantly the run of the laundry. With a bit of persuasion on her part it didn't take long for her to move into my air-conditioned cabin. And I must admit: when she is out at the island I look forward to her company at night. Fortunately, she spends a lot of time on the mainland so I don't feel in any way committed to her, nor she to me.

"Is this about Julia? I thought it was about Maria." I ask.

"Not really," he says looking around the table, "it's about Maria."

"So, tell me."

He spends the next five minutes or so regaling me with the latest chapter of his own love story. Apart from the young girl that afternoon and a couple of other girls he recently met, there are no new serious novias in the picture. Serious for Claus means going on two dates. Curiously, he has a long-standing relationship with Leona, the girl I rescued with him from his sunken yacht. Leona is a bar girl in the Royale, the town's biggest brothel, where Maria works as bartender.

Prostitution is legal in Costa Rica and some girls make a good living from it. In the Royale, girls try to seduce customers into going upstairs to one of the poky little rooms for anything from five minutes to chucking out time. Punters usually pay by the hour and the bar takes a chunk of the money.

When I first arrived here, I didn't speak or understand a word of Spanish, so Mano suggested getting myself a walking dictionary. I got one in the form of Maria, who, unlike Leona isn't part of the merchandise on offer.

I am genuinely fond of Maria and we get on famously. After sleeping my way around town, I started spending a lot of time with her. We developed a regular relationship. When first arriving here to take over the Searcher, I spent a lot of time in port. At that time, we only journeyed to Cocos occasionally with treasure hunting groups. The dive boat here before us: the one that left for Fiji, did most of the dive business at that time. At first Maria didn't ask much of me. She has a small apartment in town but we slept onboard the boat most of the time. As far as I know I am the only guy sleeping with her and I like it that way, but when she mentioned marriage, I had a bad attack of the heebie-jeebies. She is a great girl but I know she uses cocaine and I don't like it. I don't want to break off with her entirely because she is very convenient and I like her a lot. Occasionally we took other girls to bed with us and I liked that a lot too. But funnily enough, she became jealous of every girl I looked at, and I wasn't sure if it was because she fancied the girl herself. But whatever the reason, I started feeling uncomfortable about our relationship. Things changed. After spending a weekend alone in San Jose, I discovered a whole new life. The big city offers an obscene number of beautiful women and a great choice of casinos, and the freedom to do it all. As the *Searcher* became busier and busier, I started spending less and less time with Maria. I still spend the occasional first or last night in port with her, but it isn't the same anymore.

The last time in port I didn't see Maria until just before leaving on the trip to Cocos. She came to the dock to see me and I promised to spend time with her when I got back. I am still surprised she didn't show up this afternoon.

With everyone now preoccupied with their own conversation around the table Claus turns to me, and in a low voice says, "Hold on to your hat my friend - Maria has a boyfriend."

"Yeah right!" I don't believe him. Claus likes to joke around.

"I'm serious," he laughs.

"Fuck off."

He stops laughing. "No really. She has a new boyfriend."

"Yeah, right. Who is it?"

"Macho Gordo," Claus replies, laughing again.

"Now I know you're joking." I don't expect to hear that, and funnily enough, it pisses me right off. At the mention of Macho's name, I notice everyone around the table stops talking.

"Would I joke about something like that?"

"With your sick sense of humor? Yes, you would, you twisted prick." I still think he is lying, just to get a reaction from me.

"Honest buddy, it's true. What do you expect? You only see her occasionally now.

"She still thinks I'm in love with her. You're lying – you dickhead."

"I'm sorry buddy. I'm serious."

"Are you?"

"Yep."

"Okay, but tell me she's not really going with that fat ugly bastard Macho. Who is it really?"

"Mac, I swear it's true, she's been with Macho all week and now he's in love." Claus looks deadly serious.

"Fuck off. What's he doing? Giving her free coke? I don't believe it. Isn't Macho married?"

"His wife left him months ago, but if she were still with him, would that stop him? Does it stop anybody here?"

"I don't suppose it does; but Maria with Macho?"

"Mac, it's serious."

I can't believe it. And I feel astonishingly jealous. I could probably accept her going with anyone except Macho.

"You have to be careful amigo. You don't want to fuck with him."

"I wouldn't dream of it, but if this is true, Maria must be in trouble. I should talk to her."

"Leona said Maria wants to see you at the bar, buddy."

This is a bad turn up for the books. Macho is the owner of the Mama De Super Hombre, the disastrous catamaran, but the thing I hate most, apart from him being a dope peddler and shark finning boat owner, is the undercurrent of evil surrounding him. I've heard dark rumors concerning his taste for youngsters, and as far as I am concerned there is no smoke without fire. And it seems that everyone except the police knows about it.

Since the catamaran incident, I've seen Macho often at the town's Casino. I avoid sitting anywhere near him. He takes up two spaces, wasting perfectly good air that other people can breathe. He is a totally obnoxious bastard. Usually he has a big stack of chips in front of him, and an entourage of cronies huddling around placing large bets for him on the roulette table whenever it takes his fancy. Shouting out the numbers he wants playing, he hands over a pile of chips, usually dropping a few on the floor for his cronies to pick up. I hate it even more when he wins.

It isn't only Macho I dislike; I hate drug peddlers in general. I see too many people fucked up by drugs. I don't want Maria going down that road. I know she uses coke, despite my pleading for her not to. I once smoked a joint with her: Holy smoke! It messed me up so bad I have no intention of trying drugs ever again.

As far as I am concerned Macho is a sleazy crook who will cut your heart out as soon as look at you. I hear that anyone who upsets him disappears from the streets; and as far as I know, nobody even bothers to check on that. I never feel easy around him, especially when he sleazes around Maria trying to act cool. I never imagined in a million years they would get together. I am furiously jealous, even though I have no right to be. I am also worried about it. She's a nice girl.

"So, you're still seeing Leona?" I ask.

"Yeah, a couple of times a week. She was the first to tell me about Macho and Maria."

"She was the first? How many other people told you?"

"Come on buddy, this is Punta La Pesca, there are no secrets here; you know that."

"I wish you'd told me earlier; I could have prepared myself better for tonight. I would have gone straight to San Jose."

"If you didn't go to San Jose every time you came in, she wouldn't be with Macho."

"You know what Claus? You're right. You want to go to the Royale for a quickie? A quick drink I mean. I'm curious to learn more. Something's not right."

"I know that brother. You're crazy to go, but why not? If Macho is there be very careful. Don't upset him - he has a lot of friends."

"Hey, I have no intention of upsetting the fat bastard - I value my balls dearly."

I don't intend confronting him. I'll probably end up lying in a pile of garbage on a dark night with my balls wedged down my throat - and despite them smelling nice, that's a taste I would never get out of my mouth. Having witnessed our conversation, the other guys around the table nod gravely in agreement.

After a few drinks, a couple of bocas, and the usual argument with Pablo about the size of the check, Claus and I are ready to move off to the Royale.

Chapter 7
Flora

"He who has a thousand friends has not a friend to spare, while he who has one enemy shall meet him everywhere."
Ralph Waldo Emerson

WALKING DOWN THE DIMLY lit street opposite the cinema, we pass the garbage-strewn rubble site with the shaky-shed-drug-shop in its corner. I expect to see the usual crack-heads loitering around, but the cinema and site are both abandoned.

"What happened to all the crackies?" I ask Claus.

"Since the police were watching from my place, they cleaned them out. I heard the site was sold to a developer. I guess whoever bought it has some influence."

"Wow." I am impressed. "This must be a blow for Macho. Wasn't it one of his best vending sites?"

"I guess you could say that."

Further along the street, the residential houses are barred and shuttered. The Cabaña Bar, the popular gringo watering hole for American and Canadian ex-patriots on the corner of the main street, looks pretty quiet. The bar can be either extremely boring with tales of boats and long accounts of fighting fish with long poles, or throbbing with giggling girls and drunks who don't know a Sprat from a Springer. Not wanting to be bored shitless, we walk past.

The main street is busy. The Tico Fried Chicken Shop has the usual walk-through line at its window – there are no drive-through places in this town. The smell of crispy barbecued chicken wafting into the air makes me hungry again. The bocas in the bar were good but the portions are small. Walking along Main Street, listening to salsa music echoing from the interiors of numerous bars gives us the 'Saturday Night Fever' feeling. I almost want to dance but quickly suppress the feeling. Passing the bars and a few stores closing up for the night, we check out the girls in their tit hugging outfits.

Girls here seem to mature very early; many already have children by the time they are teenagers. And it seems to me that the older ladies, who grow progressively rounder each year, still manage to squeeze into the same size clothes they wore when they were teenagers – some may even be wearing those actual same clothes. Not that the guys are any different. There are some gruesome pot bellies around town.

Many girls make the trip into town from the poorer housing areas on the outskirts. They come for the fun and to hopefully meet someone who will take care of them financially, even if only temporarily. But the end result is often the creation of another hungry baby: and so goes the vicious cycle of survival.

The fishing industry, with its canning and exporting facilities, provides a reasonable amount of employment, but there are a lot of single parent families struggling to survive. In town, the inhabitants seem to be more prosperous and live more comfortably - *if you don't count the crack heads, whose days may be finally numbere*d.

Walking one block further, we turn left into a street lined with insalubrious bars and brothels - the red-light area. The Royale is 100 yards south.

Grasshoppers jump in my stomach as we walk into the dimly lit bar. It is quiet. The lighting is almost too subdued, but I've seen this place in the light and believe me it is better in the dark. Soft, fuck-me-slowly music oozes through the stereo speakers above the bar. I glance around. At first, I can't see if Macho is there or not. But as my eyes adjust to the gloomy interior, I see no sign of him or his buddies.

Two Latino guys, sitting at the end of the semi-circular bar, have their arms wrapped around two bar girls' shoulders, as if they are long lost friends. Three other young Latinos sit around a table in the far corner, taking everything in. Just inside the front door, a couple of oriental looking gentlemen are deep in animated conversation with two black girls.

From behind the bar Maria looks at me sheepishly.

In the rear lounge I can just about make out Leona, sitting and giggling with three other painted ladies around a small wooden table. As soon as she sees us, she comes bounding over with a big smile.

She gives me a hug and a kiss on the cheek, before jumping on Claus and giving his balls a squeeze. He doesn't wince so I assume it is just a loving cup. Since I last saw her, Leona has dyed her normally dark hair blonde, and now looks astonishingly Germanic. I suddenly realize what Claus sees in her.

Taking a stool at the bar, I turn to Maria. "Ola, mi amor. Que pasa?"

Half smiling, she reveals her gleaming white teeth and although her dark eyes look tired, she still looks stunning. With her coffee colored skin and lithe little body, she makes me horny – *not a good sign.*

"Muy bien Mac, e usted?"

"Fantastica."

"How was the Isla?"

"Great. But I missed you. Give us a couple of vodkas on the rocks would you baby?" Maria glances towards the back of the room nervously. "It's okay, I heard about you and Macho? Is it true?"

I smell her familiar scent as she leans close to me across the bar and whispers, "Mac. I'm sorry, but you are always away, how can I not go with someone else?"

"But how could you go with HIM?"

"It's not what you think Mac. I'm not going to talk about it. But you don't even stay here in town anymore, except for maybe the first night your damn boat comes in. You never spend time here like before. Sometimes you spend one night here then go off to San Jose and play and don't even think about me. And last time you didn't even come to see me. I had to come to your dock to see you. I need someone to take care of me and lately you only think of yourself." She is right. I am a selfish bastard, but it hurts hearing her say it. I actually feel sorry for her.

"Don't be angry Mac. It had to happen sooner or later. You know, I couldn't pay the rent I owe on my apartment and you never help me. You know I owe a lot of money, Si?"

I want to answer but don't know what to say. She is so incredibly beautiful.

She could have a thousand men better than Macho.

"Why Macho?" I pull a face.

"It's not what you think Mac."

"I think it's crazy that's what I think."

"You don't know Mac. You just don't know."

"Well talk to me."

"I can't, not now."

"Okay later then."

"I can't Mac."

"So, I guess one more night is out of the question? For old times' sake?"

"Don't be crazy Mac. If Macho finds out, there will be big trouble."

"Is he coming in tonight?"

"He could be. I never know when he will show up. Please be careful Mac."

"Just dump him. I'll take care of you."

"I can't Mac. Not now. It's too late"

"Why? Just ditch the son of a bitch."

"Mac, please. I can't talk about it."

"Okay. Don't worry about it then, mi amor. Be cool."

"How can I be cool? You know Macho is very jealous."

Claus told me you wanted to talk, so here I am."

Maria looks around nervously and then waves towards the table at the back of the room. "It's very difficult Mac. I have big problems. I just wanted you to know it is not what you think. But Mac, I am sorry. Be very, very careful."

Maria is one good-looking girl. But I am not going to slink around town hiding from Macho. I'm not afraid of him. I can take care of myself. But then, he can pay someone peanuts to do some serious damage to me when I'm not looking or when I least expect it. I'm not going to bed Maria tonight that's for sure; but there's no use crying over un-spilled milk.

I turn to Claus and Leona.

"Well, suck me sideways. What do you say? Should we yalla out of here, or just get pissed and start a fight?" *I am joking about the fight.*

"Wait Mac." Maria steps away from behind the bar and wanders off into the back.

I glance at Claus. He is smiling.

"Watch," says Claus, gesturing towards the rear.

I turn around and watch Maria walk back with another olive-skinned little beauty.

"Mac, this is Flora. Flora this is Mac."

The clever girl!

"Flora, mucho gusto, want a drink?" I ask.

Things have just changed. Claus, Leona, Flora, and me are now a foursome and Maria is free to tend bar, and if Macho comes in what the fuck does it matter? It doesn't. I am with a new girl.

During the next two hours, with one eye on the door and the other oscillating between Flora's breasts and Maria's bum, I get to know Flora quite well. Her dark beauty increases in direct proportion to the number of drinks I consume. She tells me she is not for sale; she just has to get the punters to buy her sticky green drinks at vastly inflated prices. I believe her. In her late teens, she says that just this week she moved into town from the country. She never worked in a bar before and sees it as a great adventure. It may be a great adventure for her but I can't understand how the other girls around can sell themselves; there are some really gnarly men with some very nasty diseases visiting these bars.

I often spoke with Maria about prostitution, trying to get an insight into the girls' psyches. Curiously fascinated by them, I try understanding how they can carry on the age-old business of whoring. Until coming to Costa Rica I haven't even been remotely connected to this kind of thing. Well, that's not true. As a young seventeen-year old in the Far East I did visit a couple of brothels. But I was just tagging along with my older, wiser shipmates – yes, really. I never actually went to bed with a girl in a brothel, preferring instead to sit and watch the strange goings on around me while getting shit-faced drunk; even though I was hornier than the devil in those days. The truth is: I was shit scared of catching some horrible disease. I am one of the few who paid attention to the grossly disturbing graphic lectures they gave us during training, about vital body parts being eaten slowly and painfully away after going with an infected woman; even after using a condom. I tried my best to stay away from dirty women; unlike some of my 'wiser worldlier' shipmates who ended up with nasty diseases of the dick and had to be shipped back to Blighty to undergo painfully mysterious treatments, which we were told involved umbrella like instruments being inserted down the pee-hole and opened up rapidly. I was told later it wasn't true about the umbrella needles, but the thought of it certainly did the trick: it scared me off prostitutes for the whole of my naval career. Mind you, as I later discovered: you always end up paying for it somehow anyway; and you don't have to go with a prostitute to get a nasty disease.

Maria tells me some girls are just lazy and see whoring as an easy way to make money; others are excited by it. Some feel there is no other option. And then there are those who are abused as children. I can't even think about that subject because it makes me furious. Who am I to sit in judgment on anyone? I'm just morbidly fascinated. Spending years in the military gives you a strange outlook on life. Many girls use drugs to obliterate thoughts of what they are doing, but in turn that causes them to become obligated to fund their drug abuse. And drugs are readily available thanks to fuckers like Macho and his cronies. But Flora is not at that stage, yet. So, in my partially intoxicated state I think I should sleep with her while she is still relatively fresh - I am a bit of a stupid bastard really. When I ask if she uses protection, she tells me she only gives hand jobs. And I believe her.

I am so bloody naïve.

Claus is still busy groping Leona at the bar when Flora and I move off to a table in the back. When the place starts filling up, Flora tells me she has work to do and seeing as how I am not paying for her company in the bar, she kisses me on the cheek and promises to meet me later at the disco, warning me mockingly about not being with another girl when she arrives. She skips over to a group of young studs just coming in. Isn't love grand?

I am ready to leave anyway. I should go before I am tempted to grope Maria one last time.

Back at the bar Claus is also ready to leave; Leona has a regular customer.

The next stop is the Disco.

Now forget any preconceived ideas you have about discos because this is something different again. Claus and I call it The Zoo.

The street outside the Royale is getting lively. With the salsa music turned up a notch, the other bars are hopping and young studs are cruising. I notice a couple of crackies wandering around begging from anyone who appears to be drunk or foreign, or preferably both.

The Zoo is another block south, over on the Paseo del los Turistas. We hear the music thumping before we even turn the corner. The disco is enclosed by vertical metal bars embedded in a half wall topped with razor wire; probably to stop anyone from escaping from inside without paying their bar bill. Outside, a group of penniless locals gawk jealously through the bars at the mob enjoying themselves inside. Others watch enviously as street vendors cook kebabs on crude barbecue grills on the sidewalk. The kebabs smell great; maybe tonight's meat isn't quite as dubious as normal.

The place is crowded. Pushing our way through the front door, past the big bouncer who never charges us admission as long as we buy him a couple of drinks, we walk past the energetic salsa dancers crowding the circular concrete dance floor. The bar along the rear wall is crowded. A large group of locals, some of whom I know to be fishermen stand huddled at the very end of the bar in the far corner. The crowd is bigger than normal. The crews of every boat in the bay must be ashore. Working our way through the crowd towards the bar, our built-in radars are on full scan; even though I hope to see Flora later, I still scan for new talent. Before reaching the bar, Claus walks over to a table and into the presence of six girls of various ages and sizes. He obviously knows them – but who doesn't he know? Introducing me to the girls, he grabs a chair from the next table and sits down. Standing there smiling, I wonder if I should grab a chair for myself when suddenly I feel a grip on my arm. Each of the faces around the table fills with alarm.

"Hey Mac. Amigo."

It is the big bad ugly bastard himself.

I turn slowly. Standing inches from his fat gut, I look into his broad smiling face some distance away. I don't think I ever stood this close to him before. He is a big guy.

"Hey Macho. Como esta?"

His puffy dark eyes look like elephant's arse-holes and he really has no neck. He looks as though someone once hit him on the head with a massive mallet. A pair of rubbery lips is just visible above a succession of wobbly chins, above a tent-like shirt that can't disguise the extra arse protruding from the front of his trousers. What an ugly bastard! What the hell is Maria thinking?

"Hey Mac my old friend. Que Pasa?" He looks me up and down as if it's the first time he's seen me, and he's measuring me for a coffin.

"Pura crap mate. E usted?" The ugly twat doesn't seem to notice my attempt at humor.

"¡Venga hay un trago y Maine!" He gestures to the corner of the bar, to the vicinity of the large group I noticed as we came in.

"I just got one. I'll come over later."

"Where you drink? Com now, tenemos que hablar." He is insistent; wants to talk, and obviously doesn't like being refused.

I look around the table. Everyone's eyes seem to be imploring me to go – Claus' especially.

"Bueno, Buddy, ve." There is no sense in upsetting Macho here in the bar.

Walking over to the bar together he puts his pudgy arm around my shoulder, giving me a whiff of his obnoxious armpit: Eau de colon. I want to puke.

I didn't notice him when we came in because he was sitting in the corner surrounded by his cronies. After a bit of handshaking and banter with his buddies, someone pulls up a stool for me. When Macho sits down on his stool the cheeks of his arse hang over all the edges. It looks about as comfortable as I feel right now. After buying me a whiskey – he didn't ask what I wanted - he looks at me through half closed eyes; cocking his head to one side and smiling at me with brown jagged teeth. How the hell could Maria spend one minute with him?

"So my friend, how long you in town?"

"Just the three days, para usual."

"How was you trip?"

"Great." I just want him to say whatever it is he really wants to say, so I can leave.

"So… Claus he tell you 'bout me and Maria?" He smiles but his slitty black eyes are as unsmiling and as dark as coal.

"Yeah, he told me. No problemo my old friend. Good luck to you." I am a dive boat skipper and I know how to appease people.

"So you don't be going to the Royale Bar no more eh?" This sounds like a command.

There are lots of things I can say, like: "Fuck you, you fat ugly bastard, it's a free country." Or "Bollocks to you Macho, I'll go where I fucking well please."

But instead, as much as I hate to, I demur like a pussy.

"I guess not. That's historia, ahora, my friend. 'Malesh." I love that Arabic word. It means: forget it; it's over; it's done; we can't change it; it doesn't matter – all in one word.

"Good. You understand me huh?" The 'you' sounded like 'Hugh'.

"Sure Macho. Don't worry. I guess I will spend more time in San Jose now. It's mejor."

"I don't worry my friend. You are sensible guy eh? Maybe you don't need to be worry. Okay. You need something you call me." I am dismissed.

I wander back to the table with a bad taste in my mouth, as if I've just chewed on a rotting skunk.

Claus is all smiles when he realizes there will be no trouble. He loves stuff like this. He really thinks it's funny. His sense of humor is warped at the best of times.

I sit down and swallow my drink in one go, smiling at the ladies - a smile that feels as crooked and false as it is.

Although I felt quite inebriated when we walked in, I suddenly feel dead sober and am ready to leave. Somehow the fun has stopped and the girls don't seem anywhere near as attractive as they were when we first walked in. I don't even feel like going to the casino; my karma feels that low. Why the hell did I stay in town?

"Have another drink Mac, the night is young." Claus senses my mood swing.

I pause for a moment to consider.

"C'mon, you only live once my friend. Hey, you have that beautiful new chica Flora coming to see you. Stay here my friend, let's have fun." He is standing, ready to go to the bar. "Get over it buddy, it's your own fault."

"Okay. Fuck it. Get me a big one."

He smiles at me, glances toward the door and nods his head in that direction. Flora walks in and makes a beeline for me, drawing jealous looks from girls around the table. After a few more guaros my bad mood passes and everyone is attractive again, and I don't give a flying fuck about anything except sticking my end in something juicy – and the sooner the better. I even get up and dance with Flora, doing my best not to look like a complete gringo prick with two left feet and arthritic hips. The locals know how to dance alright, with that natural flowing rhythm and swinging hips. We gringos are shit dancers and anyone who says we aren't is taking the piss. Flora oozes sexuality in every enticing step.

I love it...

Sitting close to her I feel Macho's raven eyes boring icily into the back of my head. But I no longer care. Flora is like a breath of fresh air.

At around two in the morning it seems to me as though Flora wants my body as badly as I want hers. She says Maria has told her all about me - whatever that means. I am flattered anyway and signal to Claus, whose eyes are glued to the breasts of the not so young, not so attractive lady sitting next to him. I indicate that I am leaving with Flora. He looks back at me completely shit faced. He is in an even worse state than me. I tell him I will see him in the morning before I leave for San Jose. I still need to talk to him.

A Dive On The Dark Side

Flora says she is staying with a friend outside town so, at her suggestion and not wanting to waste any valuable time, I decide to take her straight to the boat for the night. Although the dock is only a couple of blocks away, I grab a taxi outside the door.

When we pull up at the gates, true to form, both watchmen are sound asleep. I think about climbing the gates and screaming into their ears to frighten the crap out of them, but can't be bothered. I rattle the gates instead. Kaiser goes bonkers as soon as he sees Flora. Garcia, the *Searcher's* watchman, wakes up abruptly and comes bounding over to unlock the padlock securing the gates. With a disapproving look he struggles to hold Kaiser back while letting us both in. The old bastard is dead jealous. And *I am disapproving of you sleeping whist on watch, so don't come the old acid with me.* I've caught him sleeping loads of times and he doesn't seem to realize he can be fired for it. I will definitely have to have a word with him later. Right now, I have a job on my hands keeping Kaiser's nose out of Flora's snatch while guiding her across the gangway. Molly the cat is sleeping by the window on top of a carpeted shelving area, where the punters usually keep cameras and accessories during the trips. I walk over and stroke her under the chin, waking her up. As soon as she sees Flora, she arches her back and hisses. *Fuck me. I've never seen her do that before.* Flora jumps back, telling me she doesn't like cats. I understand. We have lots of guests, mainly women, who don't like cats. And on more than one charter I've had to keep Molly in my cabin because someone is allergic to her. I am surprised she hissed at Flora though. I usher her into the salon.

Flora asks for a drink so I grab two cans of cola from the fridge. Declining a glass, she asks where my cabin is. *Great, let's get straight down to business.* Walking up the steps to the wheelhouse ahead of me she gives me an amazing view of her beautiful thong slit buttocks beneath a very short skirt. The sight of her smooth olive cheeks causes a stir in my boxers. Opening the door to the small passageway leading to my cabin in the rear of the wheelhouse, I guide her inside. Sitting on the bed, she opens a can of cola and offers it to me. I take a quick gulp before disappearing into the bathroom.

I am slightly drunk but I've been a lot worse. Despite the large quantity of booze I've consumed, I still feel pretty good. Staggering slightly, I stand trying to point my prodder at the porcelain. I think about having a shower and trying to sober up a bit more but I can't wait to get stuck in. When I emerge from the bathroom Flora is lying on the bed in only her underwear, sipping her cola. Her big dark eyes look at me over the rim of the can. She is like an innocent young deer; delicious. Taking off my shirt and shorts I crawl onto the bed in my boxers, which are now tent like in the front. Stretching my hand out to feel the silky-smooth skin of her legs, she stops me.

"Drink, Mac." She leans over my face, brushing her breasts across my nose. I aim my tongue towards her nipple under her bra, but she sits up and hands me the cola can from beside the bed.

The cola tastes good.

"You have hard muscles. Do you exercise a lot Mac?"

"Only in bed. Usted es muy Hermosa Flora."

"Do you think so?"

"No, I was just saying that to get you into bed!"

She hands me her can. "Usted me hay ahora aquí bien." I place her can by the bed and empty mine in one go; all that guaro made me thirsty. I throw my can into the waste basket and lay there looking at her. She wants to talk a while, about the boat and the trips we do but I am impatient and lightheaded, afraid I will fall asleep if we don't soon get down to business. Kissing gently, we caress each other slowly. The kisses become more passionate as I clumsily unclip her bra and swiftly roll her thong down to her ankles. Kicking the thong off, she straddles me, pulling my boxers down to my knees, whilst I stroke the backs of her thighs and cup her buttocks in my hands. She is silky soft to the touch. As I lay there ecstatically, eyes closed, wrapped in a thick pink haze, her lips make a wet trail down my body. And suddenly, a two-headed monster straddles my chest and the light inside my head changes to red. Very slowly, I disappear down a long psychedelic tunnel, into total darkness.

Chapter 8
Hung Over and Done Over

"As our circle of knowledge expands, so does the circumference of darkness surrounding it."
Albert Einstein

I AWAKE WITH AN uneasy feeling in my bowels. My tongue feels like a Bedouins starboard flip-flop.

The clock shows eleven thirty, but surely it can't be: it is light outside. Is it morning? *Holy shit!* I never sleep this late. I normally never sleep past six thirty.

Trying not to move my head too much, I ease myself out of bed. Standing up, head pounding, I gingerly walk into the bathroom and look in the mirror. *Fuck me! My eyes look like two cigarette holes in a flannelette blanket.*

After spending an uncomfortable time on the toilet, I wash my hands and try cleaning my teeth without gagging. Not possible, I am as sick as a dog.

Bending over the toilet bowl, I heave until it hurts. I am in a bad state. I feel like I've just stepped out of a spin dryer. Standing under the shower trying to compose myself I will the nausea to go away; but it doesn't. After drying off, I drag on a pair of shorts, take two aspirin from the medical cabinet outside my cabin door and trudge slowly down to the galley. With a glass of orange juice and ice, I sit down at the crew's table.

What the hell happened last night? I'm like a bloody zombie this morning.

I vaguely remember leaving the bar.

Sitting there in a daze I watch Molly the cat walking towards me. The maintenance workers must have let her in. She rubs herself against my legs. Shit, she needs feeding. After dumping some meow mix into her bowl, I wander back up to my cabin, still in a foggy haze.

Details of last night slowly come back. The Maria chapter is over, that's for sure; but what about the new girl? I don't remember much after leaving the bar. I think about wandering over to see how Claus made out.

I put on a clean T-shirt and look around for my watch: I can't find it anywhere. Checking through my trouser pockets I find nada, zero, nothing; not even that mysterious bit of fluff I normally find there. Did I empty my pockets before leaping into bed last night?

Oh, Oh!

I look through the top drawer of my bedside cabinet: it is cashless. I thought I left a couple of hundred colones in there before I went out last night. Slowly, through the pain, a light starts flickering inside my woolly head. I rifle through my underwear drawer looking for the lucky ace of spades key ring I bought in Vegas. The key is still there but so is the uneasy feeling in my stomach.

With my hand shaking, trying to put the key in the lock of my bottom drawer I dread what I will find - or not.

Bollocks! The drawer is empty. I am dumbstruck and suddenly twice as nauseous. I dry-heave on my way to the bathroom.

Stone the fucking crows; so much for my lucky Vegas key ring. I've been fucking robbed.

I sink down on the bed.

Despite the pain, I want to bash my head against the wooden bulkhead. I am an idiot! And now, I am really, really pissed off. Boy, am I pissed. I can't believe it. A flaming red rage comes over me. In a spin, I fly outside, over to Mano's office. Stopping outside the door, I try composing myself, trying not to puke or show the fury blazing inside.

Mano sits at his desk attacking a huge plate of pasta.

"Mano. Buenos dias."

"Hey, boss. Buenos tarde ¿Cómo está? Man, you look real bad. What happened? I heard you had a good time last night, eh?" A wicked grin parts his pasta-flecked lips.

"Yeah. Not bad. Who told you?"

"Garcia said you brought a young Senorina to your bed last night."

84

"Yeah, Garcia was jealous. Did he say what time she left?" I don't really want to hear the reply.

"He said she left about four o'clock this morning, I guess," he smiles. *Bollocks!*

"Did he say if anyone else came to the boat last night; any of the crew; any other visitors?"

He looks at me suspiciously, "No. Why? What's up boss?"

"Nothing. I'm just curious."

"I guess you don wanna ride your bike to the city like this. What time you wanna go to the bus station? I'll give you a lift." Mano is eager to see me go to the city.

"I don't know yet. I'll let you know. I have a couple of things to do first."

"Okay, let me know. You sure you're okay? You don't look too good."

"Just a heavy night that's all. See you later."

"You should go back to bed," he laughs.

"I might just do that."

On the way back to my cabin, the wheels in my brain turn slowly. Flora - the name just popped into my head. How long did we make love? I can't remember. I don't remember anything. Is it possible I fell asleep before anything happened? I look around for an empty condom wrapper. Did I have unprotected sex? Not likely. Did I have sex at all? Maybe; but I wouldn't have unprotected sex with a girl I just met. Whatever happened, it looks like she screwed me good and proper; but not in a good way. One thing is for sure though - I have no intention of being front-page news. A large amount of dosh has been stolen and I will look like a complete and utter idiot if it emerges that I, a former sea borne warrior has been duped and robbed by a young girl.

Something niggles at my brain. Although my brain hurts, I am thinking hard, and the germ of a notion is growing in my mind.

Lately, a great deal of press coverage has focused on the increased usage of a particularly insalubrious drug - a drug that produces a rapid high when mixed with marijuana, cocaine, or alcohol. A drug also used to perpetrate acts of rape, robbery, kidnap and murder. 'Flunitrazepam' is manufactured under the trade names Rohypnol or Revitrol. Also known as the forget pill, the date rape drug, the mind eraser, roofies, ruffies, roche, R-2, rib, and rope; the drug comes in tablet form; is ten to twenty times more powerful than valium (diazepam); and can easily be slipped into an unsuspecting persons drink, where it dissolves readily. Tasteless, odorless and colorless, it is a particularly nasty drug; rendering the victim unconscious shortly after being taken; leaving no memory of any dirty deed that might subsequently take place. The effects of alcohol are intensified and a state of amnesia begins as soon as ten minutes after its administration. Even low doses cause loss of inhibition, lack of judgment, drowsiness and uncoordinated motor functions. Stomach upsets are common afterwards, but larger doses mixed with alcohol and or other drugs cause unconsciousness and, in some cases, death.

Articles about roofies are a regular feature of the gringo weekly newspaper. I've researched it, because in the city I'm vulnerable, but I never imagined it would happen to me here in this small town. I am quite sure I was not drunk enough to fall asleep with a beautiful woman in my bed, leaving unfinished business outstanding - many moons have passed since I was in that state.

I have been date robbed.

She could have fucking killed me!

This explains why I feel so shitty and woke up so late with my stomach tied in knots; and why I didn't hear or see her go. And it explains why I remember so little about what happened once I left the bar. I am normally a very light sleeper; I have to be. I am usually aware of every strange noise onboard. I notice changes in pitch from the generators, the air-conditioning systems, and the water pumps. Birds walking across the wheelhouse roof sound like clog dancers to me. I hear the sound of the wind and the sea and I hear the mooring rope squeaking. I would notice someone leaving my bed and opening the door; and for sure Kaiser barked when she left.

I sit on my bed looking over the account sheets from the previous day. It is the largest amount of cash I ever had on the boat. *Bollocks!*

I lift the plywood cover from the boards under my mattress. At least everything is still here, including the two thousand dollars I keep for emergencies. Why the hell didn't I put all the money under the bed last night? *I'm a bloody idiot that's why.*

I go over to Claus' office - the real one on the dock – but it is locked. Trudging up the steps to his first-floor apartment I feel like a piece of shit on a shovel.

Claus is in his kitchen.

"Hey Mac, what the fuck happened to you? You look like shit."

"I feel like shit; I had a hell of a time last night."

"Yeah looks like it. Nice one there man, I would have taken her myself if I had seen her before. Nice Nicaraguan pussy."

"What? Nicaraguan? Why do you say that?"

"Leona told me about her after you left the zoo; said she was a hot young thing from across the border."

"She's a Tica isn't she?"

"Na. She came down from Nicaragua last week with her boyfriend."

"Her boyfriend?" *I can't believe it. That isn't what Flora told me.*

"Are you sure?"

"You think a girl like that will be by herself?"

"No. I mean about coming from Nicaragua last week. I really thought she was a Tica."

"You ought to know the difference by now man."

"There's a difference?"

"If you don't know - I can't tell you."

"So, what do you know about her?"

"Leona said she arrived here with a guy last week."

Bollocks. Bugger. Shit. More lies.

"Any idea where she's staying?" I ask hopefully.

"No. What's up? You look sick, man."

I feel worse than sick.

"Listen Claus: last night someone cleared out my fucking safe and stole all my fucking money." I can't tell him I kept the money in a drawer; he would laugh his cock off. I wish I had a safe but I thought a locked drawer in my cabin was safe enough. I trust my crew implicitly. "I've got to find Flora."

"What? Someone stole your money? You think she did it?" he laughs.

"It's not fucking funny, buddy. All the money I had is gone, even my watch is missing. Garcia and the crew didn't do it; they wouldn't even think about it. I don't think anyone snuck onboard from the estuary either - It must have been her."

"How much money was there?"

"Claus, you don't want to know how much money there was; it was a lot, believe me." In fact, it is almost fifteen grand but I'm not going to tell him that; I don't want word spreading around town.

"Hell! That's bad Mac." The amused look on his face fades. "Call the police right now. You really think she broke into the safe?"

"I think she spiked my drink and when I passed out, she helped herself to the keys."

"Aw, come on man. You really think she did that. How would she know?" Claus laughs again. *The bastard.*

87

"She probably went through the drawers and found the key. It would have been easy. I was unconscious. Do me a favor will you Claus? Phone Leona and ask if she knows where Flora is staying. I know it's difficult for you, but don't say anything to anyone about the money - please." It is the first time I've asked Claus for anything.

Nothing like this has happened to me before. Not only have I been made to look a complete idiot, I've lost a vast amount of cash that I will have to replace. I don't think for one minute that Flora is still around but I have to check. Claus gets on the phone, chats for a while, and then turns to me.

"She's staying in the Chino pensione around the corner."

I feel a chill in my bowels. She lied about where she was staying too. "I'm going around there now." And I am out the door at a fast trot with my red eyes blazing and my head pounding to the beat of my footsteps. The bitch lied to me from the start.

The flophouse is just a couple of hundred yards around the corner. I've never been inside but I've seen some of the residents lurking outside while walking by on occasion - they aren't the type of people one invites for tea. I recognize the Chinese lady from one of the town's take-away restaurants. She tells me Flora left very early that morning.

"With her boyfriend? Con el novia?"

"No, no."

"No novia?" I ask.

"NO novia." She looks at me as though I am as dull as a brush.

So Flora left without him. *Fuck me running*. She definitely did it. I am such an idiot. I ask if Flora's boyfriend is still there.

"No novia here..."

So, where is he? I try, but can't get much sense out of the old Chino lady with her mixture of a little English, a bit more Spanish, and lots of Chinese. I have to go and get Claus to talk to her. A few minutes later we all stand in the flophouse doorway with Claus rattling away to her in Spanish. Their conversation is earnest. I hear the name Macho mentioned several times before Claus thanks her with a broad smile. His smile isn't returned. He motions for me to walk back to the dock with him.

"Well amigo, Flora's boyfriend did not stay there with her."

"I thought you said she came here with her boyfriend?"

"Yeah, that's what Leona told me."

"So where is he, and what was all that stuff about Macho?"

"I asked if Flora had any men coming around and she told me the only man who called was Macho; on the phone."

"How does she know Macho?" I ask, intrigued.

"Maybe because he sold her the place," Claus replies, eyebrows arched.

"You're joking!"

"Not this time buddy. He sold the pensione to the chinos a couple of months ago."

"Jump me. What else did she say?"

"Flora moved in there the day before yesterday. Then early this morning she gave the chino's husband, the night watchman, some cash, and left in a taxi with a small bag. The Chino said she is never surprised by anything her guests do. After all buddy, it's not the Hilton."

"Did she know which taxi it was?"

"The usual: one of the locals."

"Well, how do we find out who picked her up? You must have contacts in the taxi business." There is only one Taxi Company in town, and Claus knows all the drivers; he is one of their best customers.

"I'll ask around."

"Okay pal. But do it quickly, please. She's got a big start on me but I'm going to find her and get my damn money back, even if she's bathing in ass's milk somewhere in Nicaragua. Nobody does this to me and gets away with it. And buddy, please don't say anything to anyone about this."

I want to drive up to the Nicaraguan border, capture the sweet little woman and then scare the bejasus out of her, before reclaiming my cash. But she could be in Panama, or Limon on the Caribbean coast, or who knows where. Having a large sum of money gives her a lot of options. I have no doubt whatsoever now that Flora, or whatever her real name is, has ripped me off. And she ripped me off big time. I can't even remember exactly what she looks like.

What an idiot I am.

I don't want anyone but Claus to know about it. I certainly don't want to call the boss in the city and explain how I lost fifteen thousand dollars belonging to him. Why did it have to be this bloody week? Why couldn't it be a normal week when I only have a fraction of that amount onboard? And why hadn't I gone to San Jose the night before? Fuck it. I am in a mess. It will take me years to pay that off, and it will severely restrict my gambling activities - providing the boss doesn't fire me over it. He could easily get someone else to skipper the boat. I am by no means irreplaceable. But if he does that, he will never get his money back. Of course: I can do a runner but I have no passport because it is with the ministry. I protested about giving my passport up, but there was no way around it – I need that work-visa.

Claus makes a couple of local phone calls. Surprisingly, the information I need doesn't take long to get.

Bless the small towns of the world.

A taxi-driver just finishing his shift, picked Flora up from the flophouse at four forty-five in the morning. He drove her to Fortuna just outside town and dropped her off outside the front door of a restaurant. He doesn't know where she was heading but he is sure it wasn't the restaurant, because it was closed and shuttered, and no-one lives there. He says he drove off leaving her standing outside the door.

Fortuna is an area of pricey summer homes close to the beach. I add two and two together and get five. Why the hell would she leave the flophouse at five this morning with her bag and fifteen grand in her purse to go to some restaurant outside town that is closed? Obviously she is meeting someone. I want to go out to the restaurant to take a look but I need more information. Claus vaguely knows the restaurant; he ate there a while ago. He says there are definitely no living quarters on the premises.

I have another nagging feeling in my gut: So far, there is at least one common denominator.

"What happened last night when I left the zoo? Did you come home alone?' I ask Claus.

"Yeah, I stayed until about three o'clock. I was too drunk to screw."

"Did you see Macho leave?"

"Yep, he left just after you."

"Did he leave alone?"

"No, he had a couple of his buddies with him."

"Last night in the Royale, did you know that Maria was going to bring a girl over to me?"

"What do you mean?"

"Well, just before Flora came over with Maria you seemed to know." I remember Claus' reaction just before Maria brought Flora over to me.

"Leona told me that Maria said if you went into the bar to see her, she would get another girl to sit with you, so there wouldn't be trouble if Macho came in."

"Did Leona know it would be Flora?"

"She didn't tell me that. Why? What are you thinking?"

"I'm thinking I was set up."

"You think Leona and Maria set you up?"

"I don't know Claus, maybe not Leona, but there are too many coincidences. Maria brought Flora to me, and obviously Macho knows her, because he called her at the flophouse."

"You think he's involved?"

"You know Maria as well as I do; do you think she would do this to me on her own."

"Well, you did piss her off Mac."

"That's true but she couldn't do something like this to me on her own. At least I don't think she could. I need to talk to Leona. Can you call her again? But for fuck's sake don't tell her what happened."

"She's coming by here anyway, later this afternoon."

"Okay, great. Give me a shout when she arrives. I'll be on the boat. Oh, by the way; do you know where Macho lives?"

Claus' face drops. "Yeah, out near Fortuna!"

Well, well. Surprise, surprise!

This whole thing stinks. Am I just being paranoid in assuming it is a conspiracy to rob me? If Maria is involved, then by default, so is Macho. This virtually proves it; but why? My brain might be a bit foggy but I haven't just flown in on a shag carpet. *This is too much.*

Maria knows I keep money on the boat but she has no idea how much. I joked about having everything I own on the boat, but surely she doesn't think I have a lot of my own money onboard. She doesn't know I'm broke but she slept in my cabin numerous times, so she knows about the drawer. She also knows that on the day I arrive in port I take the money I collected during the trip to San Jose. I use that as an excuse for actually going to San Jose. Would Flora do this of her own volition? Maybe she would, but what does it have to do with Macho?

If Macho sold the pensione he must need money. I've never heard of a drug dealer being broke, but what do I know? I only know what I hear second or third hand. I consider him a small-time crook. He definitely isn't in the big league - those guys are much flashier. Maybe he does have serious financial problems. With the police cleaning up the town, it must be affecting him in some way. And with El Nino seriously hurting his shark finning business, his boat won't be paying much either. He paid for an apartment for Maria but that is probably a rental. What if, like me, he hasn't been doing well at the casino, and what if he needs ready cash for a drug deal?

If 'ifs' and 'buts' were crisps and nuts we'd all be munching and crunching until Christmas.

I know Macho is involved; I feel it in my aching gut. But then again, what do I really know? Only that nobody fucks with me and gets away with it.

I can be a really nasty bastard when I get upset.

I have to arrange a meeting with Maria without Macho knowing. From now on I have to act as normal as possible. It doesn't take a mathematician to figure out that Flora won't be showing her face around town anymore. For all she knows I *could* have called the police. Maybe I should. But I am a gambler. Even though my luck has been lousy lately I know it is going to change. Of course, like all gamblers, I never imagine it will change for the worst.

Chapter 9
Fighting Fire with a Flamethrower.

"Be careful when you fight the monsters, lest you become one."
Friedrich Nietzsche

I DECIDE TO CALL Maria's sister, Rosa.

She is happy to hear from me. I haven't seen her for a while. We arrange to meet at the dental office in town where she works. It only takes ten minutes to walk there, past the market and coastguard station, but by the time I reach the small office, just off the main road, my head throbs and I am drenched in sweat. Rosa is alone and eager to talk.

"Ola Mac. What happened to you? You look ill."

"I'm just upset about Maria." I lie – well, partially lie.

"What happened between you and Maria? Why do you have to spend so much time in San Jose every time you come in, instead of being with her? I thought you two were getting along great."

"We were Rosa, but I have to go to the city to see the boss. He's too busy to come here."

"Well it's not good Mac. I'm not happy about Maria. She is in trouble. She asked me to lend her money, but I don't have the kind of money she wants. I think she is using drugs. Our parents are worried about her too." They are a respectable couple, and although disapproving of her working at the Royale, they still dote on her.

"Do you know about Macho Gordo?" I ask.

"Of course I know. It is terrible - he is scum," she spits. "I don't understand it; he must have some kind of hold on her. You know her. She wouldn't be with him if she had a choice. She told me he pays the rent for her new apartment at Las Brieses, but he has a lot of problems now since the police are cleaning up the town and making drug busts all over. He must be paying someone off because everyone knows he sells the drogas. Don't you think it's strange he has never been caught? They say his wife left him and took everything, and he had to sell his pensione close to your dock a few months ago. El Nino has been very bad for all the fishermen, and everyone has lost mucho dinero because they don't catch fish."

Add that to gambling heavily, I think to myself.

"Do you have a telephone number for Maria?" I ask.

"Si."

"Can you do me a favor and call her: tell her I want to help her but Macho mustn't find out. I'm sure she's in a big mess. I need to speak with her alone as soon as possible. I don't want to phone her myself in case Macho is there."

"What is going on Mac?"

"I can't tell you right now Rosa, but Maria is in deep trouble. Trust me."

"Yes, I *know* she is in a big mess but please be careful Mac, Macho is a terrible person. He could hurt you and Maria. I hear bad stories about him all the time but he never gets in trouble with the police."

"Don't worry Rosa, I can handle it."

"I hope so Mac. I hope so."

"Can you call Maria now and tell her I need to talk to her as soon as possible. Maybe I can meet her at your place?"

She rings Maria's number, but there is no answer. *Shit!*

"Keep trying Rosa. If you get hold of her, get back to me. I'll use Claus' mobile phone so she can call me at any time. Make sure she is alone when you talk to her. If there is someone there, get her to call you back when she is alone."

"I'll try, but it could be a problem."

"There are no problems Rosa, only solutions."

I'm gambling. If Maria did plot with Macho, I hope to hell she won't tell him I want to see her. *If I am wrong, I am in even deeper trouble.* On the other hand: if she isn't involved, she will just think I want to see her because I can't live without her. I give Rosa, Claus' mobile number and make my way back to the dock.

Leona is already in Claus' office when I get there.

"Hi Leona, mi amor. Que pasa?"

"Ola Mac. You look like mierda." *I will knock out the next person who tells me I look like shit.* "Cool Mac, Claus was telling me that you are coming to the bar tonight to see Flora again. She is cute, no?" This is good. Claus hasn't told her the bad news about me being robbed.

"Yeah, she's cute alright. How long has she been working in the bar?"

"Just a few days, she must like you because she doesn't do business in the bar."

I wonder about that.

"Well that's good for me no? Do you talk to her much?"

"No. She don't talk a lot, not like the other girls - guidy, guidy all the time." She laughs.

"Does she get on okay with Maria?"

"I think Maria don't like her too much."

"Do you know if Flora knows Macho?"

"Si. Everyone know Macho."

"No. I mean does she talk to Macho when he goes in the bar?"

"Oh, si, she talk with him when he come in, but I don't take notice."

"Do you know where Macho lives?"

"Si, in Fortuna, in una casa grande cerca de le playa. Por que? You want to go to his house?"

"No, I'm just curious. Do you know which house?"

"It is from the road to the beach, with a small statue of La Virgen Maria at the cancilla."

"Is he still selling the drogas?"

"Why? You want something now? That's why you want to go to his house? I can give you."

"You have some?"

"You know a lot of caga happen in town now. Mucha actividad de policia, but maybe I can get you something."

"Well, what about roofies?"

"Ah! You want some good high eh?"

"Yeah. Can you get me some?'

"I have some. I can give you. How much you want?"

Unbelievable. Do all these girls have them? I haven't a clue how many I want.

"Give me ten."

"Whoo, you plan a big party, huh?"

"Yeah, I am at sea too long."

"You must be very careful with these mi amore, too much and all is caput." Leona laughs again. Claus has been giving her German lessons. She digs into her shoulder bag and pulls out two bubble wrapped packages. "Give me cinquenta dolares."

She had them with her! Amazing!

"Great. What else do you have?"

"Just some amphetaminas and some small coke. You want some?"

"No, this is good."

"You should try some with coke, is very good."

"No, this is fine for now. Where do you get all this stuff, if it is so hard to get in town now," I ask.

"There is always a way honey, but I don't tell you," she teases, giggling.

"No problemo. I'll give you the money later okay?"

"Si, por usted Mac: is ninguna problema."

"Why is Maria with Macho?" I ask.

"She not happy now. Why you leave her?"

"Well it's a long story, but what is she doing with Macho?"

"I think Maria get in trouble with Rudolpho."

Rudolpho manages the bar but usually leaves everything to Maria until it is time to close and collect the money.

"You think Maria had trouble in the bar?"

"I don't know too much, but there was big fight with him couple of times, Maria say she is leaving, but she still there, no? I think Macho help her."

I knew there had to be a reason. After chatting some more, she leaves to go home and change for her night's work.

"What do you think Claus, any ideas?"

"I think you should be very careful my friend. What are you planning to do?"

"I'm just going to relax and enjoy myself for a couple of days."

"What about Macho and Maria and Flora and the money?"

"They can wait. I'll go out tonight and have some fun."

"Mac, you are a very strange bugger, as you would say."

"Yeah, well, stranger things happen at sea."

Before I leave, Claus lends me his mobile phone.

Back on the boat the shore phone is ringing. It's connected to Mano's office so I wait for him to pick it up. He usually picks up all the calls, even the ones I pick up, so he can listen in on my conversations. I don't bother answering. It might be the boss and I definitely don't want to talk to him just yet.

Right now, I have a few things to do.

Lifting the boards under my bed, I go through my inventory. There is a small arsenal under there. I wondered when all this stuff was going to come in handy. I bought it all on a stopover in Miami when we went to the Caribbean. It's unbelievable what you can buy there, at gun shows.

I pull out the Mossberg stainless steel pump action shotgun with its snug pistol grip but I don't think I will need anything this drastic. From a canvas sack I take two 113gram canisters of foam pepper spray and put them into a small black backpack. Effective up to ten feet away, foam helps the spray to stay on the face, so if the recipient tries wiping it off, it makes matters worse. I throw in two large canisters of fifteen per cent pepper spray, each with two million Scoville heat units. Effective close up, they might prove handy if there is no wind. Although pepper spray won't stop everybody, it will certainly cause a distraction – it's difficult to see with hot pepper burning into your eye sockets.

My Glock 17 is next. A 9mm handgun manufactured all in plastic - except for the steel slide. In 1980 Gaston Glock switched from producing plastic curtain rods and kitchen boxes to developing a gun. In 1982, the Austrian army was the first of many militaries to adopt it. The Glock handgun has an overall length of seven inches and weighs just over two pounds loaded. I added a luminescent tritium site - a green dot on the front with two very dim red dots on the rear - and another cheap and effective improvement in the form of a molded rubber finger slip over the grip. I like the feel of it. After a lot of practice, I can field-strip it in about thirty seconds.

I take time cleaning and lubricating all the stripped-down parts before loading a seventeen-round magazine with jacketed hollow points. Weighing 115 grams each, they are +p+, high-power high-performance rounds, with a velocity of thirteen hundred and forty feet per second. The hollow cavity in the nose expands, stopping in the body and transferring all kinetic energy into shock waves, for maximum stopping power. They are ideal self-defense rounds, particularly in a confined space like a boat, where you don't want the round coming out of the assailant's body and carrying on its trajectory into something or someone else, as ball ammo does. Instead of making two holes in a person, these just make one. I chamber a non-lethal rubber round. I don't really intend croaking anybody, but I am fully capable of it if the first round doesn't do its job. I put the Glock in the holster. I can wear it inside my trousers or shorts with a loose shirt covering it.

The next item is a lovely little Berretta 21A - a great little .22 caliber weapon with an alloy frame, blued steel slide, and nice walnut grip. The barrel length is only two- and three-quarter inches, so it fits snugly in a wallet holster and slips nicely into my pocket. The tip-up barrel feature allows me to check the bore; load a round directly into the chamber quickly and easily, and makes it safe, quick and easy to clear a live round. The open slide design shared by all Berretta small frames virtually eliminates jamming and stove piping problems. I keep the seven-round magazine in tiptop condition by meticulously cleaning and lubricating it regularly. I choose 33-gram yellow jacket hollow points for the load. I am a good enough shot to be able to rely on this weapon alone in close quarters – it's worth its weight in gold. I place everything in the backpack and put it back under the bed.

"Mac!" it's Mano calling from the dock.

"Hey Mac, Jimmy has been calling, he wants to know where you are. I told him you didn't look so good.

"What did he say?"

"He said you should be in San Jose."

"If he calls again tell him I had to go to the dentist. Toothache."

"OK. But he sounded really pissed off."

"Yeah, well you know Jimmy."

"Yeah, I know him alright," he scoffs.

"Thanks Mano."

He wanders back into his office.

Fuck. That's not good.

I need an ally.

A few years ago, I made a good friend here. 'Big Al' is a diamond: an ex-platoon sergeant still recovering psychologically from his tours of duty in Vietnam. He isn't a raving psycho or anything like that – but he is slightly whacko. Al was a patriotic volunteer, but despite that lapse in judgment, he is an extremely intelligent bloke. He'll talk about every subject under the sun except the Vietnam War. His tongue never gets tired. One of the many ex US servicemen to call Costa Rica home, he lives out in the sticks about thirty miles from town in a house he built entirely by himself. The house is only accessible by a long driveway he personally cleared through thick jungle undergrowth.

I first met him when he volunteered to teach the Park rangers how to use their M1 Garand rifles to shoot the wild pigs at Cocos. The chief ranger asked me to take Al out to the island and I willingly obliged. Al wanted to shoot the wild pigs and sell the meat. The number of pigs involved is enormous. Unfortunately for him and the island, a couple of minor details scuppered that idea. Firstly, the pigs don't taste very good because of their diet of roots, grubs and dirt. And secondly, there is the logistical problem of transporting the pigs from their deathbeds to the shore through a virtually impenetrable jungle. Pigs are smart creatures. After a while, the survivors will hide and become extremely difficult to track. Al has friends in Columbia, with hunting dogs, who were willing to go out to Cocos just for the hell of it. He was going to buy freezers with generators to run them, and then ship the meat back to Punta La Pesca in large ice boxes onboard the Searcher. After all his planning the National Park directors decided to carry out research on the pigs before he tried annihilating them. Al taught the rangers how to handle their weapons so they can go out on patrol alone and shoot any pigs they can find, leaving them to decompose where they fall and be eaten by vermin.

So, the pig study was given to my friend Julia.

Al and I formed a bond that ex-servicemen often share. I used to visit him and his wife regularly on my way to or from San Jose. Al is a bit of a loner but still likes having someone other than his wife to talk to. He is a keen gun enthusiast with an amazing armory of weapons at his home. 'Big Al' is not a man to be trifled with. We've practiced with our weapons for hours: popping a variety of homemade targets from up to thirty feet away; blasting away to our hearts content. I would not want to be a burglar attempting to rob his place. He carries a handgun in his fanny pack everywhere he goes. I am convinced he has no qualms about shooting someone, even if he doesn't have to.

Al's wife is bored being so isolated, so, when I visit, the noise we make gives her an excuse to go shopping.

I give him a call and we trade the usual banter.

"Hey Al, can I stay at your place tonight?"

"Hey Mac, of course you can, anytime you like. The wife is in the States for a couple of weeks, visiting her parents. I'm getting bored out here on my own. I was thinking of looking you up anyway. Maybe we can go out to one of the local bars." Al doesn't drink but he still likes to look at the girls."

Perfect. At least something is going right. I arrange to see him at his house later.

I study a map of the area around Fortuna. I know it vaguely: the houses are large with huge gardens close to the beach. The details on the map give me a vague idea of the area. Claus' mobile phone rings. It's Rosa. She hasn't been able to contact Maria. *Bollocks!*

It is now five o'clock and the bar opens at six. Although I awoke late this morning, it seems like it's been a long day already - and this is only the beginning.

Maria usually arrives at the bar at about five thirty. I have to catch up with her then. I'm sure she is a key piece in this jigsaw puzzle. Manuel shouts from the dock to tell me he is going home. Garcia, the watchmen has just shown up. I tell him I am going to San Jose on my motorcycle soon, but will be back in two days. He is happy to hear that.

I'm hungry. I have to eat before I go. I make a cheese and tomato omelet in the galley. Before I finish eating, Rosa calls again. Maria is now at the bar in an agitated state and wants to see me but she can't leave. I tell her I'll be on my way to the rear entrance of the bar in minutes. I wolf the rest of the food down, and then grab a can of cola from the fridge. I stare at it for a second, remembering last night. Before opening the can I check the roofies in my pocket. On my way out I grab a baseball cap. Telling Garcia I am going to buy a newspaper I stride out onto the street. Once there, I walk quickly up the street to the Royale, ducking into the alley at the side and trying the gate – it is unlocked. At the back door I wait a few seconds before knocking loudly. After what seems like an age the bolts shift inside. Maria opens the door and falls into my arms crying.

"Oh Mac. What has happened?" she sobs in my ear.

"I was hoping you would tell me, Maria." I answer softly.

"I don't have much time but I am in terrible trouble Mac. I have been borrowing money from the bar to pay my rent and Rudolpho found out. He was going to the police but Macho paid him back, and then one-night Macho drugged me and did terrible things to me and took photos while I was asleep and threatened to send them to my parents. Now he threatens to kill me if I leave him. Oh Mac, I'm so sorry. What can I do?" The words gush out as big tears roll down her beautiful face.

"What about Flora - and last night?"

"I'm sorry Mac but Macho told me to get you to the bar and introduce you to Flora. He said it would take your mind off me."

"Do you know what happened last night?"

"I'm not sure, but I know something happened, Macho made me stay at his house last night. Flora arrived there early this morning and he was shouting at her about money and her stealing from him. But after that he was happy."

"Well let me tell you something, mi amor: Flora drugged me last night and cleaned out the money from the boat. How did she know about that?"

She trembles as she looks at me. The tears running down her face are huge. "Macho asked me about you and the boat, and money and things, but I didn't think he would do anything like that. He said he was curious about the boat and everything."

"Doesn't he have money?"

"No. He is very broke. He lost a lot of money with the boat that sank, and because of El Nino the fishing is bad and the police broke up his drug operation and he is paying someone in the police to stop them arresting him. His wife took everything she could from him and he wants to kill her, but because of the problems with the police he can't do it now. He said you owe him money too. Everything is so bad. What can I do? Macho told me to come to work and act normal, but you know how I feel about you even if you don't feel the same for me."

"What's Macho doing now?"

"He is at his house. He says he is going to the casino tonight. He told me to wait at my apartment for him."

"Before or after going to the casino?"

"Before. He wants me to go with him 'for luck'."

"Why aren't you living with him?"

"Gracias Adios, he doesn't want me to live there."

"Where is his house exactly?"

"In Fortuna. It is at the end of the long beach road, three blocks from the main road."

"Does Macho usually have people visiting his house at night?"

"Sometimes his friends go there to party."

"How many usually?"

"Depends; from two to six sometimes."

"Do they stay the night?"

"No usually Macho likes to be alone with 'his girls'."

"Does he have an alarm?"

"No. Nobody would be stupid enough to rob his place."

"Is Flora still there?"

"No. She left this morning."

"Do you know where she went?"

"No. Macho took her somewhere."

"When Macho picks you up, is he usually alone?"

"Si."

"In his car?"

"Si."

"Great. Okay, listen carefully. I want you to act as normal as possible tonight when he comes to your place. Tell him you are not ready. Get him to have a drink before you leave." Reaching into my pocket I take out a package of roofies.

"You know what these are?"

"Yes, the girls use them sometimes."

"Do you use them?"

"I have before, but not now. It was the drugs that got me into trouble."

"Does macho use drugs?"

"Si, mucho."

"What does he drink?"

"Rum and coke. And lots of coke"

"Right, I want you to put some of these into a coke bottle before he arrives - then make sure he finishes his drink. When he's finished get him out to the car as quickly as possible. Try and stall him once you are in the car - tell him you have forgotten something - then go back to your apartment but don't let him drive off. Make sure you give him enough of these to knock him out. I want him totally comatose." I give her Claus' mobile number.

"Call me at this number when you think he is unconscious. If there is anybody with him, make sure they have a drink too. I'll be close by - watching and waiting. Be very careful mi amor. Now go and open up. I'll wait here for two minutes before I leave. I'll see you later. Be careful. Don't ask any more questions. I'm going to get you out of this."

"I don't know if I can do it Mac."

"Listen. He won't know what's happened and I have a plan for later, so don't worry. Trust me." *I am lying; I don't have a plan for later – not yet. I am playing this by ear.*

"Okay Mac, but please, you must be careful also." She gives me a hug before walking back into the bar. She isn't that tough. I just hope she can keep it together.

I slowly saunter down the alley to the street. Good, it's getting dark. Peering out, I pull the cap down over my ears, hunch my shoulders and walk out at a fast pace; trying to act as inconspicuous as possible, which is a bit of a joke seeing as how I am the tallest guy around.

On the way back to the boat I make a quick detour to the only ATM machine in town, hoping there is something left in my account. After waiting nervously for cash to pop out, the machine tells me to go fuck myself because I am broke.

I pay Claus another quick visit and beg him to lend me his mobile for a while longer, telling him I am off to San Jose for a couple of days, which he still can't believe. The next part of my plan excludes him. The less he knows the better.

Back on the boat I sit and ponder what Maria said. She played the keyboards on the cash register and got caught. Rudolpho the manager is a big buddy of Macho's and they probably worked it out together. She must have taken a fair amount of money. I hope she can pull this thing off tonight but I figure that *if she can sleep with Macho, she can do anything.*

After making one last phone call to San Jose, I pack a few more things into the backpack from under the bed, pull on a pair of black jeans and a black polo shirt and walk out to the bodega where I keep my motorbike. Luckily there is enough gas in one of the spare jerry cans we keep there, to fill the gas tank. Satisfied I haven't forgotten anything I wheel the bike out onto the dock, put on my helmet, and start her up. With a quick wave to Garcia I take off into the night.

The ride to Al's place takes 45 minutes. The roads are atrocious. There are no street lights and no moonlight. I have to avoid several large craters in the road whilst dodging all the mad truck drivers along the busy Pan American highway. Turning off into a winding country road, I reach Al's driveway and stop to call him on the mobile - I don't want the mad fucker shooting me before I arrive at his front door.

Although tall and rangy, Al is a regular looking guy with glasses - but as strong as an ox. He gives me a bear hug and then punches me playfully in the chest, almost knocking the wind out of me.

"Mac, great to see ya."

"Great to see you too Al."

"Come inside." he leads me through the front door to a huge wood-paneled lounge area. "Want a drink?"

No thanks Al I've got some business to do tonight."

"Oh yeah what's that?"

I sit down and tell my story, watching his eyes go wild. He is ready to do battle. "You know Mac I've been kind of bored lately. I've heard of that fucker Macho. Let's go and stage the Fortuna Chain Saw Massacre."

My plan however, is slightly subtler.

Chapter 10
Even the Best Laid Plans…

"Before embarking on a mission of revenge, dig two graves."
Confucius.

THE ROYALE CLOSES around midnight.

At eleven fifty-five Al and I sit in his parked trooper in front of a construction site on a quiet, tree-lined-street, close to the beach. We have a clear view of Maria's one-story apartment block fifty yards away, on the opposite side of the road. Maria's apartment is the closest to us, the front entrance sitting slightly back from the sidewalk behind a low wall with several cars parked in front. The three apartments in her block are barred and shuttered showing no light from inside, as with all the other buildings in the street. To our advantage, only one of the half dozen streetlights is lit, shining dimly at the end of the block, next to the intersection at the Playa de las Turistas.

Al has parked his old Trooper beneath the spreading branches of a tree, facing the direction from which Macho will arrive if he drives via the beach road. Directly opposite Maria's apartment, just past the construction site's driveway ahead of us, a vacant car is parked in front of a large brick wall topped with razor wire. We can't see the house behind the wall.

"I hope she turns up soon," says Al, staring straight ahead.

"She should be here by twelve thirty at the latest." I reply.

"Let's hope it's soon. She must have finished work by now."

We wait anxiously for twenty minutes, tensing when two cars turn the corner from the beach road. One car drives by, but the other pulls up in front of the walled house, opposite Maria's apartment: it looks like there are two occupants.

"What kind of car does macho drive?" asks Al nervously.

"I don't know, but this doesn't look good. If Macho has a buddy with him, it makes things more complicated. We don't want anyone else involved."

Al stares through the window. "Is that her?"

Maria emerges from the parked car and walks towards the apartment, followed closely by Macho. He must have picked her up at the bar. She looks up and down the street nervously.

"That's her. There's no one else in the car," I say, relieved.

Sitting hunched up in the trooper with our baseball caps pulled down over our ears, the next thirty minutes drag like an eternity. Two couples walking by glance at us curiously.

"I hope they are the last passers-by we see tonight," mumbles Al.

"If any more come by we'll have to have a cuddle," I joke.

"Good luck with that," growls Al.

This is normally a very quiet neighborhood.

Suddenly Macho appears from the apartment block, with Maria following. My hand is on the door latch and I am ready to move. Macho approaches the car. Maria glances nervously up and down the street. When he reaches the driver's side door, Macho leans with one arm on the window, searching through his pockets. Maria stands by the passenger door, watching.

"Not yet, don't let him fall down in the street," I murmur.

"Keep him standing girl," breathes Al.

Macho shakes his head. Fumbling with the keys, he opens the driver's door and squeezes himself inside. Maria stands hesitantly by the passenger door. The next part is critical.

She opens the door and leans over to get in.

"Don't get in!" hisses Al quietly.

Stopping half way, she suddenly withdraws from the car and walks back to the apartment.

"Good girl," I whisper.

She is following the plan.

"Thank the Lord," says Al.

You can cut the tension in the Trooper with a teaspoon as we wait for the next move. Maria re-emerges from her apartment several minutes later and I hold my breath. Glancing up and down the street again, she walks the short distance to the car. By the time she sits down in the passenger seat my heart is ready to tango. Now according to the plan, the car should not move, but suddenly the lights come on and the car pulls out slowly into the street.

We both tense up. "Bollocks! This is not supposed to happen."

"For fuck's sake."

The plan is going awry.

The car takes off slowly, traveling toward us on the opposite side of the road. With the trooper's engine already running, Al quickly pulls out onto Macho's side of the road with his headlights on full beam. I see Macho's face lit up in the headlights as he veers across the road to his left and mounts the sidewalk. His car crashes into the wooden fence of the construction site and stalls. This is not good.

"Let's go!" says Al.

As quick as a flash Al jumps out of the Trooper and races towards the car with me following right behind. Al pulls open the driver's door. Macho just sits there, looking at us through glazed eyes.

"Allow me," I say, pushing past Al.

I hit Macho square on the temple with the heel of my right hand. He falls sideways onto Maria who looks at me, horrified.

"Get out." I whisper harshly. "Go back into your apartment. Quickly! If anyone asks, say Macho is completely drunk or doped up. I'll call you later."

She shoots out of the car and hurries away. We don't have much time. The noise surely alerted the neighbors. Al goes around to the passenger's side and together we unlatch the two front seat backrests, lowering them backwards and pushing Macho down with them until he is lying completely flat. Pulling Macho's fat legs out of the driver's foot well and sliding them over to the passenger side, we roll his upper body onto the back seat. Hopping into the driver's seat with the backrest still down, I re-start the car.

"Meet me in the next street," Al says urgently.

He is already in the Trooper and driving off down the street by the time I reverse. Through the rear-view mirror, I see lights come on in nearby houses. Curious neighbors appear in the street close to the construction site as I drive off swiftly to the next block and park behind Al's trooper. Macho is out cold in the back seat. From my pocket I take two thick cable ties and bind his hands together. Ripping two strips of duct tape from a roll, I cover his mouth and eyes. After a brief struggle, Al helps me pull the driver's seatback into the upright position from underneath Macho's fat carcass., After collecting my backpack from the trooper, I jump into Macho's car and gun the engine, driving away with a screech of tires.

Thank fuck for that!

With Al following, I drive Macho's car carefully along the back streets until reaching the main road out of town. The drive to Fortuna takes over thirty minutes and it takes another twenty nervous minutes to find the house with the statue of the virgin in the driveway. Al goes off to park his trooper a couple of blocks away as I drive into Macho's driveway.

The large, single story house is centered inside a grassy expanse obscured from the roadway by a thick growth of tall bushes. Two security lights come on as I park the car outside the carport adjoining the house. I take the keys from the steering column and try the garage door lock. None of the keys fit. I feel very vulnerable standing under the bright lights, trying to get the door to open. Back at the car I search through Macho's pockets. Whilst groping around I recoil, feeling my stomach turn as I realize they are wet with warm urine. I find a key ring with two sizeable bronze keys and four smaller ones that look like house keys. I am not surprised to find a wallet holster along with a billfold in one of his pockets. Thankfully one of the smaller keys opens the garage doors. Once the car is inside, I swing the doors closed behind me.

Standing in the darkness of the garage with my heart racing I wonder if I've been seen. The house is isolated from the road but the security lights are intense. From my backpack I pull out a pair of thin neoprene diving gloves and a flashlight with a red transparent lens cover that I normally use for night vision in the wheelhouse.

The kitchen door is unlocked and inside the house it is surprisingly cool. Standing in the gloom sweating, alert for the slightest sound, I pause before drawing the blinds and turning the kitchen light on. The room is a mess. Garbage overflows from a black greasy bin in the corner and there is cigarette ash all over the tiled floor. The table is full of dirty glasses and an empty rum bottle sits in its center next to two ashtrays piled high with cigarette butts. Plates of half eaten dried beans and rice are piled high in the sink and a half full bottle of whisky sits on the dirty worktop next to it.

I hear tapping on the front door and my skin crawls. Hoping feverishly, it is Al I walk through the living room and peer through the spy hole in the door. To my great relief it is Al. I open the door.

"Fucking amazing! After that dodgy fucking start everything is going according to plan and not a single shot fired," he whispers through a grin that runs from ear to ear.

"I know. This is too good to be true. Here, take these." I give him another pair of gloves from my backpack. "Let's get Macho into the house. I don't want the fat fucker to wake up just yet."

We struggle to get him out of the car. I have to cut the cable ties from his wrists so we can drag him out by his arms. We both drag the big heavy bastard unceremoniously by his arms into the kitchen. Once inside, I tape his wrists behind his back, tape his ankles together and join the two with duct tape. If he wakes up, he won't be going anywhere trussed up like that. An apple in the mouth would be a nice finishing touch, but the duct tape will keep him quiet if he wakes up.

Leaving him in a big heap on the floor we walk into the sparsely furnished living room. Macho's wife must have taken everything when she left. The only things in the living room are a reclining chair and rattan sofa sitting in front of a television set. There are no ornaments, nor any items of furniture to put an ornament on. On the facing wall, a framed oversize photo of Macho with a large marlin hangs askew. I cross the room and peer through the bars of the rear door. Outside, a small swimming pool surrounded by a paved patio, has a large expanse of lawn beyond, which stretches to the bushes along the rear boundary.

Drawing the blinds in the living room, I turn to Al. "Can you look for the fuse panel? We need to disable the security lights."

"I saw one in the garage. I'll try that."

Al finds the panel and flicks off every switch. All the lights go out.

I adjust to the darkness and switch on the flashlight as Al returns.

"Do me a favor Al. Can you go out into the garden at the rear and make a hole in the bushes facing the beach, then wait for me there, out of sight? I'll be as swift as possible."

Back in the living room I stand in front of the large hanging picture of Macho. Pulling the picture of the bad bastard aside I expect to find a safe behind it but instead I'm staring at a blank wall - nothing. There isn't much else to search through in the room. I know exactly what I am looking for: I have evidence of it on Macho's key ring.

I walk down the corridor leading off to my left. The first door is locked. Fumbling with the key ring I find a key that unlocks the door. This is creepy. A desk in one corner has what looks like a photo enlarger sitting on it. Papers are scattered all over the floor and a freestanding closet against the far wall holds a stack of photo paper and some plastic chemical bottles. The adjoining bathroom has been used as a darkroom. The sink is deeply stained and more chemical containers stand on the washstand with a number of flat trays stacked in the corner. A clothesline with pegs attached, hangs across the shower stall. The toilet bowl is filthy.

In the bedroom opposite, a mattress covered with crumpled sheets lays on the floor. The built-in closet yields only a cheap duffel bag. Rifling through the bag I find a few small tank tops and some make-up items. There is also a woman's purse that is empty except for a photo of a girl and a baby - it is difficult to see the faces in the light but the girl looks a lot like Flora.

I walk down the corridor and enter the master bedroom at the end on the right. In the center of the room is an enormous unmade bed. I stop in my tracks. There's a body lying under the sheets. I freeze, before creeping over and gently prodding the mound in the bed, preparing for movement. The hairs on the back of my neck dance on end. I pull the top cover back. The mound is just a pile of pillows. Relieved, I go straight to the built-in closet and stare at the row of extra-large clothing hanging there. I take all the clothes out, throwing them onto the bed until I reach the far end of the closet. Underneath a pile of shirts, I find what I am looking for.

Bingo - a safe! This has to be poetic justice.

The two large bronze keys on Macho's key ring fit both locks. I kneel down and swing the door open. Staring me in the face are four bulging brown envelopes and a pile of cash.

I take everything out of the safe and sit on the bed. A few 8mm videotapes and a note book are amongst the pile. Flipping through the book I know immediately it is something to do with drugs. There are lots of figures, names and dates. *I'll bet the police would love to see this.*

The cash is in mixed currency, so I know straight away it is from the boat — *the thieving bastard.*

I open one of the envelopes, hoping to find more cash but the blood slowly drains from my face as a variety of photos assault my eyes. The envelope contains debased images of seemingly unconscious naked young girls in unimaginably cruel and sordid poses. They look like very young girls. Incensed, I sort through them looking for pictures of Maria. There are also photos of young boys that could have been taken in this very room. I grit my teeth, wishing I had never seen these images, ashamed of seeing something so shameful and sinister. I scan through rapidly, not wanting to look, but needing to make sure I remove all the ones of Maria.

I also take the videos, which I suspect contain much of the same, and put the remainder of the photos back in the envelopes, placing them under one of the pillows at the head of the bed.

This whole thing has just reached another dimension. It takes all my will power to regain my composure. I can't show them to Al; nobody should have to see stuff like this - except the police; as evidence.

I have a major 'red out' and feel physically sick. I want to take a baseball bat and beat Macho's head to a pulp.

I close and lock the safe and replace the clothes in the closet. Suddenly the house shakes from a loud pounding on the front door. My heart leaps. My already taut nerves are about to break. My first instinct, thinking it is Al, is to run and open the door, but a loud voice calls Macho's name, stunning me; stopping me in my tracks. I breathe deeply, trying to regain my composure before shuffling silently to the end of the corridor. The door is thumping on its hinges. I reach into my pocket for the Beretta in its wallet holster. *Bollocks!* I gaze across the dark interior of the living room trying to make out my backpack. The backpack is lying on the easy chair where I left it earlier. The Berretta and the Glock are in there - what am I thinking? I would dearly like to have the Glock in my hand right now. If that door opens, I will have very little time to grab the Glock from the backpack, remove it from its holster, and fire - but I surely will in my present state of mind. I don't care who, what, or how many people there are, they will all die. I am burning with rage.

With someone trying to knock the door down and Macho still lying still on the kitchen floor, I face what I think might turn out to be my death and rebirth as a dung beetle. I don't want to crawl across the living room floor in case they can see through the small spy hole in the front door. But that's crazy; it is as black as fuck without the lights on in here. No one can possibly see inside. Waiting with baited breath, straining to make out the gist of the discussion outside, I hope they don't decide to wait around. I can't see what is happening but I sure as shit am not going to risk parting the blinds to have a peek; even though I would like to know how many there are out there.

Voices are laughing and joking in Spanish, about Macho being in his bed and not wanting company. The banging continues. Someone conjectures that maybe he isn't even home. The voices gradually subside until it becomes silent once more.

Once I'm sure they are gone, I retrieve my backpack, take out the Glock, and rush back into the bedroom where I stash the liberated items and remove the tape from the handy-cam. Finding a still camera in the cabinet beside the bed, I remove the film.

Having completely checked the contents of each cabinet, I leave the bedroom to check the last room. I am relieved to find it completely empty. I now have what I came for and don't relish the thought of finding more surprises. It is time to leave but I can't risk going outside just yet. I hope Al is still hidden away somewhere out back.

There is one more thing to do before leaving.

Creeping back into the kitchen I kneel over Macho's evil fat body. I can hardly tell if he is breathing or not. But I don't care. I have a last plan for him but as I'm rifling through his wallet and removing a large wad of banknotes, I jump at the sound of another knock on the front door; this one quieter.

Please, let it be Al.

"Mac, Mac, it's me, Al."

I rush to the door and open it. Al quickly steps inside looking seriously alarmed.

"Let's get the fuck out of here now Mac; that was the cops."

"Jasus."

"Let's go, quick." He is understandably agitated. "Did you find what you wanted?"

"Yeah; and more. You go. I have one more thing to do."

"What could be so important? If the cops come back now, we're screwed."

"I just have to take care of something."

"What?"

"I can't tell you."

"Fuck, don't do anything foolish Mac." Al obviously senses my mood.

"I'm going to say goodbye to our friend here."

"Are you serious?"

"Never been more so."

"Are you fucking crazy? Do you realize what that means?"

"Yeah, I am and I do, but you don't want to know what this sick fucker has been up to. Anyway, he'll know that Maria had a hand in this and he'll link it to me and then we are both dead walking."

Al looks at me in disbelief. "I can't be a part of this."

"Listen buddy you don't need to have anything to do with this next bit. I'll manage it on my own. Can you go and wait in the car for me? I won't be two minutes."

What happened to the bloody chain saw massacre he promised earlier?

"What are you going to do Mac?"

"The pool out back: he's just going for a midnight dip."

"I don't fucking believe you. That's madness."

"Yep; I know."

"What the fuck happened to you?

"You don't want to know."

He looks at me exasperatedly. "I'll get the car."

"Don't bring the car here. Wait around the corner. I'll come to you."

"Okay, but don't be long."

"Right."

So, I guess Al isn't crazy after all. *I'm the crazy one.*

Walking back into the kitchen, I stand for a few seconds looking down at the bad ugly bastard in the red glow of my flashlight. He's a drug dealer, a thief, a pedophile and possibly a murderer. I want to kick the shit out of the bad, bad bastard but I have the wrong kind of shoes on. I am going to do the world a favor. After untying the ropes and checking his wrists, I massage the marks left there by the cable ties. Pulling the duct tape from his mouth is easy, but when I rip the strip of tape from his eyes, most of his eyebrows come off with it and I resist the urge to laugh and punch him in the face. I remove his shirt and grab the bottle of rum from the table. His breathing is shallow as I lift his head and pour the whisky down his throat. He chokes and gags but I persevere, almost emptying the bottle. In an effort to remove any tape glue residue, I use his shirt and the remainder of the whiskey to wipe the spillage around his mouth and eyes.

Dashing into the bedroom, I take the cover from the bed and spread it on the floor next to him. After clinically divesting him of his remaining clothes I roll the ugly bastard onto the cover and drag him out of the kitchen, across the tiled living room floor and through the patio doors to the pool outside. Lifting the cover high I pull it from beneath him. He rolls into the pool with a nice big splash.

Sink like your catamaran, you bad ugly bastard.

I search through his trouser pockets once more, taking all his remaining cash except for about two dollars in colones, which is more than the fat fucker is worth.

After switching the electrical breaker back on in the garage I wipe the car's steering wheel and doors clean. As quickly as I can, I return the bed cover to the bed and sweep away the tracks on the floors. In the kitchen I grab the two full ashtrays, and throw them one by one into the air from the doorway. They both shatter, scattering ash and cigarette butts all over the floor. Grabbing my backpack, I have a final look round before running out through the patio doors, leaving them wide open behind me. I make the hundred-yard dash across the lawn in two seconds flat and dive into the hole Al made in the bushes earlier, pausing for a minute to look back at the pool, now bathed in the bright security lights that came on as I rushed out. After being sure there is no sign of movement anywhere, I bolt out to the deserted beach and race up the road to where hopefully, Al is still waiting with his car.

I am lucky; he is waiting but the mood is somber on the drive back to his place.

"I don't understand you Al. You were willing to do battle tonight and I thought you would gladly shoot someone in the eye at a moment's notice, yet you don't like what I did to that no-good fat bastard."

Maybe I should tell him what I found in the safe. Maybe I should have shown him back at the house, but I feel a heavy burden after seeing such degradation. I feel violated. I feel I will never get those images from my head.

I left the filthy envelopes under the pillow, optimistically hoping that when Macho is discovered, the police will find them during their examination of the scene. I don't really know whether leaving them is the right thing to do or not, but I definitely don't want them in my possession. Those kids are deeply scarred and will need serious counseling. I thought of burning the place down with Macho and everything inside. But as it is, after seeing the photos, if the police find any foul play, maybe they won't be in too much of a hurry to find his killer.

Al is silent.

When he does eventually speak, it gives me a chill. "This is different Mac. It is in pure cold blood. I couldn't do that. But now you've made me an accomplice, and I don't like that either. I'm really pissed."

Well, well. I guess that puts me in my place. But do you know what? I feel good about slotting Macho. I touch my backpack with my right foot, wondering how quickly I can get a weapon out if I need one.

Oh, oh. The rot is setting in.

Al doesn't say another word for the rest of the drive to his house. I don't feel the love anymore. When we arrive, he shows me straight to the guest room and mumbles "goodnight" as if it is a strain to even talk to me.

I feel uncomfortable about our relationship now. When Al and I discussed what we were going to do, we were prepared for a shootout if we had to follow Macho home and something went wrong. Maria did surprisingly well. I didn't really expect that part to go according to plan. This morning I thought the money was gone forever.

I've been lucky.

In the bedroom I take out the cash and count it on the bed. There is absolutely no doubt it is the boat's money, although it is about twelve hundred dollars short of the original amount. I look at the book too, with its names and numbers and decide to hold on to it. I will destroy the videotapes and negatives. I don't want to know what is on those; maybe Maria is.

Now I start thinking of the links connecting me to Macho. I don't think Al is a real problem, despite our good relationship being destroyed. Claus might be a problem, but I am counting on him not saying anything to anyone and maybe not even connecting me with the incident – but that is a bit optimistic. Leona is a danger though. If she thinks back to our conversation about Flora and Macho, she might suspect me, but if those photos come to light it might exonerate me in her eyes. Rosa might also be a threat, even though I have done her and Maria a big favor. I am curious about Flora though. Where the hell is she? If she has gone off somewhere, what was her bag (if it was her bag) doing at Macho's house? I've had a hectic day I am still very jacked up. Sleep doesn't bring its escape until much later, after all those random thoughts stop bouncing about inside my head.

Chapter 11
Got to get a Witness

"Do not take life too seriously. You will never get out of it alive."
Elbert Hubbard

THE BEDSIDE CLOCK READS 6 AM.

For a few seconds I wonder where I am.

Holy shit! What the hell was I thinking last night?

I use Al's phone to call Maria: it rings a half dozen times before she answers.

"Maria, it's me, Mac. Are you okay?"

"Si Mac, what happened last night? I was so worried, why didn't you call me?"

"Listen carefully mi amore. I got my money back and I also got the photos of you. What happened last night after we left? Do you think anyone saw us?"

"Gracious a Dios. After all the noise of the car hitting the fence a few people came out to see what happened. I told them that Macho was drunk and his friends were helping him. Some of the people were laughing and some were disgusted but nobody seemed to think it was anything other than a drunken driver. But what happens now? Macho might know I did something to his drink. I'm frightened Mac; he could kill me if he found out." Her voice quavered.

"Macho won't find out anything anymore, mi amor."

"What do you mean?"

"Macho was so drunk that he decided to go for a midnight swim in his pool."

"I don't understand."

"Well, I don't think he made it through the night."

"¡Caramba Dioscito!"

"Maria, you have to stay calm.

"Ay Dios. Oh Mac. Oh…" I cut her off. "Maria, listen to me. The police will probably ask you questions about last night. If they call on you, stay calm, except when they tell you what happened to him. Don't over react. Remember this: all that happened was that Macho picked you up from work and dropped you off. Tell them you think he was drunk or on drugs. Say some Ticos helped him after the accident, and they all drove off together. Do you understand? That's all you know. Make sure you get rid of that package I gave you. How many did you give him?"

"I put the whole packet into a big bottle of cola. I didn't know how many it would take. He drank two glasses." That alone would probably have killed him.

'Okay, make sure you dump the rest and rinse out the bottle. Then dump that as well. I have to stay in San Jose tonight but I'll be back tomorrow morning. Come to the boat tomorrow if you can. Stay strong baby."

She is crying.

"Hasta mañana Maria mi amor. Call me if you have to. But it's better you don't - unless it's an emergency." I give her Claus' number again and hang up.

After a cold shower and shave I walk into the kitchen. Al sits at a table nursing a cup of coffee.

"Look Al, I'm really sorry I dragged you into this."

"Yeah, well, I'm not happy about it Mac, but I did offer help, and I was prepared for trouble. My worry now is if anyone saw us during the incident with Macho's car, outside Maria's place. How do you think Maria will hold out?"

"Well Troopers are pretty common cars here, and I just called Maria and told her, to say that it was two Ticos involved, if anyone asks. The street was pretty dark and we left pretty swiftly. I'm betting no one got a bead on us."

"I hope not. Why did you have to kill the guy Mac? You did, didn't you?"

"Listen Al, I had my reasons, and right or wrong it's better this way. There was only one possible conclusion to last night as far as I was concerned. He was an evil, evil bastard. Believe me."

"Well, I suppose things could have been a lot worse: at least we didn't have to kill anyone else, and I assume you got all your money back?"

"Yeah. Most of it. Look, I can't thank you enough for helping me out Al, but I need one more favor, then I promise I won't bother you again."

"I'm not getting involved any further Mac."

"No, it's nothing like that. I need to leave some stuff here while I go to San Jose. I'll pick it up on my way back tomorrow."

"Okay, but you may need an alibi for last night, did you think of that?"

"Yeah I thought I'd use you."

He looks at me aghast.

"No, I'm joking Al, I've already thought about it. I called Jake."

"That's what I was thinking."

Jake owns a guesthouse in San Jose. Before I left the boat the last call I made was to Jake. I 'booked a room' for last night at his place. He didn't ask any questions.

"Okay Al, thanks again. I'm really sorry to have gotten you involved in this but I couldn't have done it on my own."

"I know - that's what bothers me."

"Look I'll give you a call tomorrow, before I come to pick up my things."

We part with a rueful handshake and I roar off on my bike toward San Jose.

In the daylight, without rain, the ride is refreshing. The wind blows some of the cobwebs out of my brain. I take the mountain road instead of the Pan American highway because I know where most of the big potholes are up there. Thankfully El Nino is holding off the rain. When it rains, potholes appear all over the roads, and that can be deadly for a sucker like me on a motorbike. I usually take the bus.

Closer to the city the weather is cooler; much cooler than on the coast. San Jose sits in the central valley four thousand feet above sea level. About a third of the country's total population of three million live here and just like any other big city, the traffic is atrocious.

After winding my way through the bustling metropolis with my finger on the horn most of the way, I arrive at Jake's Guesthouse, a big old colonial building not far from the city center. Jake rents about ten rooms out. Parking the bike outside, I stroll in through the main door. Dropping my helmet behind the small desk by the entrance, I walk on through the dining room into the kitchen. A local girl preparing food looks up at me questioningly.

"Ola. Donde es al senior Jake?" I ask.

"Momentito."

She picks up the phone and speaks rapidly into the receiver.

"Esta viniendo ahora."

"Okay gracias."

I walk back into the dining room and wait. Eventually Jake swaggers in with a big smile, gesturing for me to follow him. He takes me to a room in the rear of the house. Once the door is closed, we shake hands.

"Hey Mac, good to see you. What's up? You in some kinda trouble?"

"Something like that Jake. Hey, it's good to see you too. Thanks for doing this for me. You busy right now?"

"So-so. I've been taking the opportunity of doing a few improvements around the place so I don't have many rooms available right now. This is my boy's room. He's back in the Mexico right now. The maid never comes in here. She would know you weren't in one of the guest rooms last night, but this way she don't know shit: just what I tell her," he laughs.

"That's great. You going to play poker tonight?"

"Maybe. But I got me a fine woman now and I need to take care of her. She don't like me wastin' my time and money around no casinos." This is a turn up for the books.

"Are you sure you are okay vouching for me last night? It may involve the police."

"Holy shit what d'ya do, rob a bank?" he asks, breaking down in a phlegm-filled fit of laughter.

"No, nothing like that."

"Hey buddy it's none of my damn business. Why hell, I can't even remember what day it is most of the time." I am surprised he remembers my call last night. Jake's face is like a relief map of the Rocky Mountains, with the typical features of an alcoholic: broken nose veins, whisky breath, ruddy complexion and bloodshot eyes. He stays on the same level of inebriation until about three in the morning, when he starts to unravel a bit. He has a big Texas heart and is as funny as hell and I liked him from the moment I sat down next to him on a flight from Panama a few years ago. During the flight, sharing a few drinks together and swapping our life stories, he tells me he once made "a huge business deal" that set him up for life. After living in Mexico for a while he decides to settle in

Costa Rica. Coincidently he is also a great friend of Al's and the more I get to know him, the more convinced I am that the "big business deal" was related to some kind of illegal activity.

"Here Jake, I'll pay you for two nights and you can give me a receipt, just to keep things on the record. I checked in late last night and you haven't seen me till this morning. I'll probably stay in the Rio Hotel tonight though; I need a woman desperately." Jake doesn't allow non-guests to bring 'one-nighters' in any of his rooms, regardless of whether you are a friend or not. He's had plenty of trouble with that and I respect his policy.

After chatting a while longer Jake lets me park the bike in his garage at the rear of the house. I have to go to our office but I can't be bothered to drive around the city anymore, even though it will be a lot faster. Avoiding the potholes and pedestrians is too much hassle, and besides, I am beginning to feel pretty knackered. Before I take off in a taxi, to the boss's office on the other side of town, I try calling Claus on his mobile. The battery is dead. *Shit!* I should put it on charge but haven't brought the charger with me - I didn't think of it. *What a wanker I am!*

The taxi pulls up outside the office. I give the driver a reasonable tip because he doesn't try to rip me off. Since I started speaking Spanish, I found some things a lot cheaper - especially Taxis. If you are a foreigner, taxi drivers sometimes drive around without the meter on and charge what they like.

Lena, the office secretary, is sitting in the outer office talking on the phone when I walk in. She gives me a curious stare and holds her hand over the phone. "Hey Mac. Jimmy is waiting for you, he's not happy."

Jimmy the boss' son is waiting for me in his office. He's five foot nothing; a spoiled rich kid who got a gold Rolex and a Porsche for his eighteenth birthday and now looks down his nose at all us poor people. He handles the boat's business for his father but his dad makes the major decisions. Jimmy and I have clashed heads a few times about things I want done on the boat but he has a grudging respect for me because there are no problems I can't handle. Despite El Nino, the guests usually respect the way the boat is run.

"Where the hell have you been?" he asks straight off the bat. "You have the money?"

"Yeah, I have it all here." I hand him the envelope. The cash is all accounted for because I used money from the boat's emergency fund to make up what was missing. I now owe the emergency fund fifteen hundred dollars, which is a lot better than owing twelve thousand dollars.

"I've been trying to get hold of you since yesterday."

"Yeah, I had to go to the dentist. Toothache emergency."

"Well you should have called."

"I told Mano to let you know I'd be late."

"Yeah, he called."

So why the fuck are you asking where I was?

"How was the trip?"

"It sucked. The guests were pissed off about not seeing Hammerheads. We really should warn them before they leave home. Give them a chance to cancel," I tell him.

"You must be joking Mac. They won't get their money back even if they do cancel," he says with the self-assurance of the very wealthy.

"Well, I'm the one taking all the flack. I should get a pay raise just for that alone."

"Yeah, I can just see that happening," he laughs.

"I'm serious," I shoot back. "I haven't had a pay raise for two years."

"No, but now you get commission on all the courses you teach."

"Yeah and I earn it *you maggot.*" I don't actually say "maggot", I just think it.

"I'll talk to my father," he says more reasonably.

"What about the coming trip?" I ask.

"The treasure hunters are in town but Dietmar has run into all sorts of difficulties trying to obtain the permissions he needs. One document in particular has to be signed by the President himself. Don't worry: all will be well by tomorrow evening, ready for the scheduled departure the next day."

I sincerely hope he's right. I don't want to hang around Punta La Pesca any longer than I have to.

"Did you know that Dietmar thinks he knows the exact spot the treasure is buried?" he asks.

"No, I didn't."

"Yeah, this trip is major. They are really going to uncover it this time."

"After seventeen years of trying it's about time Dietmar found something," I reply, hoping they don't actually find the treasure. I would like to stumble across it myself.

"All kinds of officials from the government and National Park Service are coming for the ride. There will also be a small party of police onboard for the trip."

This makes me nervous. I don't normally mind surprises because they keep me on my toes. But right now, my life is currently too full of surprises.

"Okay I'll see you tomorrow, I'll be coming along for the ride," he says, dismissing me. I am not too thrilled about that. "I'll call the boat tomorrow and let you know what time we will arrive: it will probably be late," he says as I leave.

Outside his office I flirt with Lena until a taxi arrives to take me back to Jake's place. I think about the treasure to take my mind off my predicament.

Chapter 12
The Treasure of Lima

"There is nothing so desperately monotonous as the sea, and I no longer wonder at the cruelty of pirates."
James Russell Lowell

IN 1821, REVOLUTION FILLED the colonial air, as Spain's New World fell apart at the seams. The viceroyalty of Peru watched apprehensively as liberating armies marched from all sides. Simon Bolivar was mopping up in the north after the liberation of Panama, Columbia, Venezuela and Ecuador, and General Jose de San Martin bestowed independence on Argentina and Chile. Now both had their sights firmly set on Peru.

The Catholic Church and ruling nobles of Peru had good reason to fear: untold riches were in their possession and there was no telling what the ungodly would do to get their grubby little hands on a small portion of it, in the current state of rebellion. Earlier, when the Peruvian fortress of Pisco was taken in the South, its army and Nobles escaped to Lima with their personal fortunes. But now, as liberating armies marched closer, the Viceroy of Peru, together with other Spaniards of wealthy nobility, plotted to move their valuables out of harm's way - with the church hierarchy deciding to follow suit.

Adding to his crisis, the Viceroy had been unable to remit the country's annual endowment of jewels and precious metals to the King of Spain for several years, because of the increasing attacks on convoys by privateers running amok up and down the Pacific coast. The Peruvian Viceroy sent a special request to the King of Spain for reinforcements, but the ships were either destroyed in action or captured by the Argentinean or Chilean Navies en-route to Peru. During the previous two years, all Peruvian ports had been blockaded fiercely by the Chilean Navy, effectively making Lima, with its vaults already overflowing with riches - the last outpost.

Lima's port of Callao was founded in 1537, as the main waypoint for shipments of gold and silver stolen by the Spanish from the Inca Empire. Its fortress defended the city from incursions by pirates - although it didn't stop Sir Francis Drake from sacking it in 1578. But in 1746 as fate would have it, the city was destroyed by an earthquake and the resultant tidal wave. The Viceroy at that time, Jose Manso de Valasco, immediately started reconstructing and rebuilding the city - subsequently creating the largest and strongest fortress in the Spanish Americas. He named the fortress Real Felipe, in honor of the Spanish King.

In what seemed like a logical move, the present Viceroy ordered everything of value be taken to Callao's heavily guarded fortress. The pious preachers took advantage of this guarded move, and shifted their own mountain of fabulous wealth to the stronghold of Real Felipe, after stripping their own personal treasure troves and denuding the churches and Cathedrals. Reports suggest that buried beneath the mound of priceless pieces of jewelry and fine church artifacts stood a solid gold, jewel encrusted, life size statue of the Virgin and infant Jesus – and that alone was worth a bob or two.

When it became clear to the wealthy citizens and men of the cloth that the liberation of Lima might be unavoidable, the churchmen decided on a bold and as it turned out, foolish tactic for preserving the safety of their valuables. They decided to place everything on a ship guarded by trusted soldiers and priests and send them all on a sailing trip while things were sorted out ashore. They would then put their trust in God.

But there was one major problem: The devil waited outside the harbor.

In the British Navy, during the Napoleonic wars he was known as 'The Sea Wolf', but to the Spanish in the Americas he became known as 'El Diablo' – The Devil.

Lord Thomas Cochrane, who later became the 10th Earl of Dundonald, had been persuaded by San Martin's overseas agents to establish and oversee the running of the Chilean Navy - and he made a damn fine job of it. He was responsible for the sacking of Pisco. And he now waited outside the harbor with his fleet, forming the formidable blockade that kept all Spanish warships harmlessly in port. (In one of the many coincidences that crop up in this story, Cochran previously commanded the first British man o' war to bear the name *Imperieuse* - of Admiral Henry St Leger Bury Palliser infamy - in the Mediterranean years earlier.) But that's another story.

The theologians of Lima were faced with the problem of choosing a ship on which to load their treasures. They needed a ship whose captain could be trusted and one who could pass through Cochran's blockade unharmed. Luckily – or not, as it turned out - there just happened to be a merchant vessel sitting in port whose flag almost guaranteed neutrality.

The Mary Deare, or Mary Dyer, or Mary Dean – depending on whose account you listen to, was a British vessel well known for the integrity of its captain, William Thompson, who had traded along the Eastern Pacific coastal routes for years.

In a nighttime subterfuge under the strictest security, several merchant vessels in the port were loaded with boxes of heavy worthless junk whilst the *real* priceless cargo was loaded onboard Thompson's ship, accompanied by priests and soldiers. The following evening, just as the Cordilleras were disappearing in the dust and fading light, the merchant ships, all sitting low in the water, set off from the dock. Billy Thompsons' vessel managed to pass unmolested through Cochran's blockade off the tiny island of San Lorenza and with all sails set, headed out to sea and into history.

The instructions given to the officer in charge of the contingent aboard Thompson's vessel were to set a course northwest, out of reach of Cochran's ships, whilst avoiding the profusion of prowling Privateers whose numbers had increased dramatically since the liberation of Chile. Thompson was told to keep a good distance from land and await the outcome of the impending battle for Callao. Messenger ships would be sent out to find him when all was well.

In the mind of the priests and Viceroy, a Spanish victory was distinctly possible because large numbers of Spaniards resided in Peru, and its citizens were mostly indifferent to the idea of liberation. If they were successful in routing the marching liberation armies, the boat could return with the treasure and everyone would live happily ever after.

But this isn't a fairy story.

When Cochrane attacked Callao, the Viceroy ordered the evacuation of Lima. This action was swiftly followed by a case of premature declaration – San Martin announced himself Peru's protector, even though Peru wasn't completely subservient to independence.

Out at sea, meanwhile, although Billy Thompson and his men knew nothing of the events unfolding ashore, they weren't quite as dumb as they looked. They were plenty smart enough to realize they had something of extreme value and importance onboard and they were all itching to find out what.

Thompson steered his ship out into the Pacific away from the coastal shipping routes, and waited. His chance came one night during their first bout of bad weather, when the priests and soldiers were either asleep or seasick. The captain's mate took a peek into one of the trunks - and almost fainted.

There followed a heated discussion between the mate and the Captain, in which the mate prevailed with his idea of slotting all the guards and taking off with the precious cargo. Some crewmembers missed their supper because they were killed in the bloody action that followed that night, but the sharks didn't go hungry – they probably had bad cases of indigestion after gobbling up all those soldiers in their armor after they were unceremoniously tossed overboard.

The dead men bear the distinction of being at the very top of the list of victims of 'The Curse of the Treasure of Lima.'

Shortly after his act of outrageous treachery, Billy Thompson panicked. He and his crew would very soon be top of South Americas Most Wanted List and he needed a plan. His mate - whose convincing persuasion in the whole series of events suggests he may have had dark connections with the pirate trade in the past - knew just the place to go. Billy Thompson and the mate told the crew they were going to the Galapagos Islands to dump the bulk of treasure after sharing out a portion amongst themselves. The crew had no reason to doubt their destination; they weren't navigators and didn't know any different. Only the captain and mysterious mate knew the real destination, which was in fact further north.

When the ship eventually arrived at the island after a voyage of over twelve hundred miles, the crew realized just how much loot they had lifted - it took two days to stash the many boatloads of boodle. Then, when it was all finally hidden away, they faced another dilemma – where to go next? It was less than three weeks since leaving Callao, but during that time they had all become murdering criminals. The crew and once noble Captain had suddenly surfaced in the twilight zone of piracy, and judging by the theme of the greater part of goodies stashed on the island, the church was the most significant victim. Although the Viceroyalty had been virtually disbanded throughout Spain's New World, the church hadn't; it was still mighty powerful. And what you must realize is this: the church was the production company that spawned the dreaded Spanish Inquisition – and as the Monty Python Team perfectly put it: "Nobody expects the Spanish Inquisition."

After leaving Cocos, Billy Thompson decided to head north, thinking that neither the Spanish Nobles, nor the men of the church would have any idea of his treachery and would think he was still out at sea waiting for messenger ships to find him. But what he hadn't taken into account was the authoritative power of the church and the discontentment breaking out amongst his crew after leaving the bulk of their newfound treasure on an isolated island. Scared for his life, Thompson was forced to anchor in Costa Rica, where his crew immediately tried to sell their share of the swag to finance another boat to take them back out to the island. Wanting their full share of treasure, they then decided to slot Captain Thompson and take the Mary Deare for themselves.

Unfortunately for the crew, the church's lines of communication stretched from South America to Mexico and beyond. The churchmen of Lima had prepared for the worst-case scenario and word was already out. Although they weren't told why, a huge reward dangled in the faces of numerous seaman and church members up and down the length of the Pacific coast, with instructions to be on the lookout for an English Brig by the name of Mary Dear, Deere, Dyer, or Deary and to report its sighting to the nearest church authorities.

Consequently, sometime after Thompson and his men arrived in Costa Rica the boat was ambushed. Billy Thompson, the longtime honest captain and one-time pirate was killed in the ensuing fight. And only one man managed to escape. Before the fighting had even begun the mysterious mate jumped overboard and fled into the rainforest - and was next heard of in Nova Scotia many years later.

The remaining crewmembers were captured and expertly tortured until they gave the inquisition the exact meaning of life, the names and addresses of their next of kin, and the whereabouts of the treasure – which they thought to be on an island in the Galapagos. Once that little matter was cleared up, the crewmembers were painfully executed, and large parts of their dismembered bodies were reportedly nailed to various buildings around Latin America.

Costa Rica is situated on the Pacific Rim of Fire, inside a dangerous zone of frequent seismic activity. Ticos are used to the ground trembling from the effects of a succession of earthquakes. But they probably didn't even notice the one that occurred in 1821 out in the Pacific, two hundred and seventy miles from the coast.

The crew of the whaling vessel *Nora* felt it though. Having just stopped off at Cocos for a short break and some fresh air, a few of its crewmembers were investigating a recently cut trail through the dense jungle when the island shook like the clappers. Tons of earth and solid rock tumbled down the side of the island's high slopes; toppling trees, obliterating the trail and deleting all previous signs of the whaler's crewmembers. Moments later a huge tidal wave, caused by the seismic tremor deep beneath the ocean's floor, swept in and picked up the *Nora* like a balsa wood model, hurling it onto the shoreline, smashing it into tiny pieces and killing all but one of the remaining crew.

In the space of a month, the Curse of The Treasure of Lima had become the Curse of Cocos Island. There were only two survivors - the mysterious mate of the Mary Dear and the extremely fortunate crewmember of the whaling ship *Nora*.

From that point on, the story has more twists and turns than a snake pit in an Indian zoo. Characters appear, disappear, and then reappear like a conjurors' rabbit. Stories of Cocos treasure hunts always include a leading male or female whose life was somehow inexplicably linked to Benito 'of the bloody sword' or to William Thompson's mysterious mate, or to the *Nora's* one surviving crewmember.

The 'august German gentleman' who spent almost twenty years of his life living on Cocos Island was in fact a man named August Gissler: a man of great resilience, courage, and physical and moral strength. During that time, by his tenacious persuasion he was granted governorship of Cocos Island by the President of Costa Rica himself. August Gissler contracted the treasure-hunting bug after he met two people in two entirely different parts of the world, who both claimed to have maps detailing the exact spot the treasure was buried.

There is twenty-years-worth of stories regarding his efforts.

During his time of relentless digging and searching Cocos Island he saw the coming and going of umpteen different treasure expeditions - all with the same goal but different maps. Although Gissler tried fending off some of the expeditions, he was known to have collaborated with others in combined searches. But despite it all, he found nothing more valuable than a few coins. Unfortunately, August Gissler - the King of Cocos Island - died penniless in New York in 1935.

The common factor in every single expedition to Cocos is that they all left the island thoroughly disheartened and broke, after digging their holes and pouring their own personal fortunes into them.

But I'll tell you what: They were the lucky ones. There were others far less fortunate, who never even left the island.

Now I am about to take out yet another group who are positive they knew the exact location of the greatest known buried treasure in the world.

Cocos Island has been the scene of countless dreams. But it is also the harbor of horrific nightmares - a blood-soaked stage where Machiavellian dramas of treachery and death play to hostile crowds, and I am about to walk on that stage.

Chapter 13
Gringo Gulch

"Did you know we know we are all the object of another's imagination?"
Carlos Fuentes, The Old Gringo.

BACK IN JAKES GUESTHOUSE, I use the house phone to ring Claus; I am aching to know the local news.

There is no answer.

I now desperately need a siesta.

Stripping off my clothes, I lie on the bed and fall asleep before my head hits the pillow.

I awake from a dream in which I was standing next to the treasure hunters as they dug away at a wall of earth and rock. I don't usually remember my dreams but this one was vivid. Leaning against the rock wall I watched as they dug, and suddenly the rock wall I was leaning on rolled aside, revealing a small cave full of spider webs. Standing at the entrance I saw a skeleton wearing a suit of armor topped with a Conquistador helmet. Inside the cave, spilling from a pile of wooden chests, tons of gold and jewels reflected the light from the doorway and I laughed out loud, thinking what stupid bastards they were for digging in the wrong place. I tried to shout that I had found the treasure but I couldn't speak. I woke up instead.

Needing to use the bathroom, I hop off the bed, trying to remember the rest of the dream. Where was the cave situated? As I point Percy at the porcelain the dream fades into the distance; too bad; but I slept for four hours and that's good.

A hot soapy shower is followed by a cold rinse and brisk rub down before putting on a clean t-shirt, clean pair of boxers and a pair of shorts from my backpack. Taking a few hundred dollars from the envelope I am ready to take the city by storm. I give the money envelope to Jake to keep in his safe before I leave. At the intersection with the main road I hail a cab and jump in.

"Hotel Rio por favor. Vaya dirija."

I'm off to "Gringo Gulch," an area of the city popular with tourists because of the number of bars and casinos there. This is an area where anything is available: the perfect place to escape the beauty of nature.

The taxi deposits me outside Hotel Del Rio's main entrance. I am ready to rock. Walking through the crowded lobby, the subliminal coded tunes escaping from long rows of shiny slot machines are just audible above the taped music echoing from speakers mounted on the brightly painted walls. Sitting in semi-circles around several felt topped gaming tables, punters pensively ply their luck with the cards, with one eye on the raised bar area at the rear. Flirty cocktail waitresses dressed in skimpy dresses, show off shapely legs and smooth breasts as they whiz around from table to table serving drinks and smiles for tips placed in a glass on their tray. This is one of the busiest and liveliest casinos in the city. I love its spirited atmosphere. Making my way slowly past the tables I pause several times, watching the way the cards fall, trying to draw a feeling for a particular table - you have to have the feeling. But I need a beer and some food before committing to gambling.

Squeezing my way through the excited gringos and their attendant young women, I resist the overtures of a few unattached females before reaching the bar. This isn't the place to come if you want to be alone, that's for sure. This is a sports bar bordello style. I savor the beer while glancing around, taking in the menu of girls who are watching the menu of guys watching them. Giving a girl more than a passing glance will have her on you like a tiger cub - flirtatiously licking her lips whilst undressing you with kittenish eyes. If she doesn't give you a hard on within three minutes, she'll be telling everyone you are gay; then you will be approached by the guys. I am as horny as hell but if I succumb now, I will probably miss the best casino action. It's a toss-up between women or gambling first. On the one hand, if I wait too long all the best girls will be taken, but on the other hand many will reappear later and might even stay with me all night. It really is no contest - the gambling comes first. The bar is too crowded for eating in any comfort so I walk through the casino to the restaurant, where they have a fast food menu. I order a big steak and French fries.

Sitting there eating, I remember I have not called Claus back; but it is too late now, and I don't have the cell phone anyway. Maybe I'll call from the front desk later. I wonder what is happening in Punta La Pesca right now. I am pretty sure I am safe if I can make my alibi stick. I just hope Maria will hold out. As long as Claus doesn't blab about me having the money stolen the previous evening, maybe nobody will connect me to the fat dead bastard.

I also hope the police treat it as an accident. If not, I have no idea how this thing will play out. Now that I have time to reflect on it, I can't believe what I have done and how lucky I am that it went according to plan – more or less, give or take a death or two. I didn't really need much of an excuse for croaking Macho but the fact that I actually did the dirty deed bothers me slightly; but only with the thought that I could have gotten caught - and still can if I don't take care. It was an audacious plan but I bear a grudge like a wild boar. Macho felt my ultimate rage, although it's a pity he didn't know too much about it; if I'd had more time, I would have tortured him to death.

Maybe I should have set fire to him.

After the meal I feel great. Changing a bunch of dollars into colones at the cashier's cage, I am ready for action. I decide to play stud poker first. I win the first two hands, and because my luck is in, I start doubling up. This isn't such a good idea. I lose just about every hand from then on. After changing tables and more money, and after managing to stay in the game for a while without really winning or losing, I move to the blackjack table. Usually I do pretty well at blackjack, but not tonight. All I get from playing at that table is a few strong drinks and an equal number of smiles from the cocktail waitresses as my pile of chips diminishes into colored felt circles where my money used to be.

Bollocks! I couldn't win an argument right now. This is not good.

I am left with just under a hundred bucks, which is not the sort of situation I like to be in. I face the gamblers nightmare of trying to win back my losses or giving in to defeat. *Fuck it!* I try the roulette table and promptly lose another fifty bucks.

How stupid can I be? I wander out of the hotel and walk around the block to the Tropicana. Running the gauntlet of shady characters of indiscriminate sex standing around outside the walls of the colonial building, I duck inside the gate before one of the transvestites grabs my arse - these guys or girls or whatever they are, can relieve you of your wallet, watch, and underpants, in a flash.

The big building houses three large bar complexes on three floors. The noise level inside, is phenomenal. Music blasts through a multitude of speakers and everyone is to be heard shouting above it. There must be a hundred women of all colors, shapes and sizes hustling an even greater number of guys. I am approached by at least ten girls walking from the main door to the entrance of the ground floor bar. I pass painted ladies, unpainted ladies; black, brown, white and coffee colored girls, fat girls, skinny girls; girls with mighty breasts spilling from tight, low cut dresses. I see huge nipples through flimsy silk tops; small bra-less mounds with straight aiming erect nipples under tight fitting tank tops - lips, arses, teeth, and tits - the penultimate pussy parlor. Making my rounds of the bar, squeezing past numerous hot bodies I am groped surreptitiously and overtly by a number of females I recognize from previous visits. Smiling enticingly, they try making conversation, but the music is too loud to hear what they are saying. I circulate, taking in the sights, sounds, and smells. I want to be seen: not because I am a vain bastard but because I am so bloody guilty, I need two alibis. Finding a couple of quiet spots upstairs I chat with four different girls, telling them I saw them last night but it was too crowded to speak with them; they all say I should have anyway, which is good: it means I could have been there last night and nobody can confirm or deny seeing me amongst the crowd - part two of my alibi completed successfully. Unfortunately, I don't have enough money with me to book a room in the Rio and pay the girls 'expenses', so I have to head back to the guesthouse. I broke the golden gambling rules about continuing to gamble and doubling up the ante when losing so badly, but you never know when your luck will change; it could be the very next hand.

Arriving back at Jake's well after midnight, I let myself in, thinking about getting more money from my envelope in the safe but Jake is nowhere to be found. He must have gone to bed - it's amazing what a good woman can do for you. I haven't even been laid; and that sucks. In my room, thoroughly pissed off about being such a bloody idiot, I fall sound asleep.

I awake early in the morning: I need to stop at Al's before going back to La Pesca. After eating breakfast with Jake, I take my envelope, say a hearty farewell, and ride off to Al's to pick up my stuff, hoping he has mellowed out a bit. When I arrive, he is still in a dark mood. He's heard on the local radio that someone was found dead in a swimming pool. There were no other details but he is worried he might be implicated if the police decide it is murder. I assure him everything is going to be okay, but he is still hostile. I don't have much time; I have to burn the videotapes and photos of Maria. In the book I took from Macho's safe, there are a lot of numbers and words in Spanish I don't understand. They don't make much sense to me, but if Macho kept it in his safe it means it must be important. Maybe I should have left it with the other photos for the police to find, but it is too late now. Should I burn it? If I don't, I will be stuck with evidence against me; but if I destroy it, I will never know what it is; but then, do I really want to know?

I burn the tapes and photos of Maria, together with a pile of negatives in a big metal garbage bin in Al's yard. He doesn't even ask, but I feel better for it.

After collecting the rest of my things, I ride back to the dock – towards the mighty shit storm brewing on the horizon.

Chapter 14
There May be Troubles Ahead

"Not everything that counts can be counted,
and not everything that can be counted counts."
Albert Einstein

BACK ON THE BOAT my crew members are all busy cleaning and organizing their departments ready for the afternoon departure. Mano's truck is parked at the side of the bodega; so, I guess he is in his office.

Claus is nowhere in sight.

Walking onboard, I feel strange looks following me - but maybe it's the paranoia kicking in.

In my cabin I dump the backpack on the bed and return to the dock. Then, after stowing my bike in the bodega, I bowl into Mano's office.

"Hey Mano what's up?"

"Holy shit Mac you scared the crap out of me. Where have you been? I was trying to get hold of you. Why didn't you call me, I didn't know where you were?"

"I was in San Jose like I told you. Where do you think I was, Europe? What's up, an emergency?"

"Well, there's some real shit happening around here boss. Macho Gordo is dead. He was found in his swimming pool yesterday."

"Bloody hell, really? What's that got to do with me?"

"Well, the police came by asking for you yesterday."

135

"Why? What do they want from me?" I feel a cold sweat running down my back.

"They are looking for that girl you were with the other night!"

"What girl?"

"The girl you brought to the boat."

Fuck a rat.

I clench my arse cheeks tight. "What? Why are they looking for her?"

"I don't know. Claus told me the police were at the Royale last night asking questions about her."

"Well I don't know anything about that. What happened with Macho?"

"I don't know. They say he was drunk and drowned in his pool but I think it was some shit with the drogas."

"Wow."

"Maria came by looking for you too; And Claus was asking about you; and the boss called about an hour ago: he wants you to call him as soon as you can. He told me you were in San Jose yesterday, how was it?"

"So, you knew I was in San Jose?"

"Yeah, but you wasn't in the Hotel Del Rio, boss."

"No, I stayed at Jakes place."

"So, how was everything?"

"Great! But now I need some rest - you know what I mean?"

"Oh yeah I know how that is." A big cheesy grin split his face in two.

"Is everything ready to go on the boat?"

"Everything ready boss, but I don't think you are going today."

My bowels dropped another notch. "Why?"

"Jimmy told me the treasure hunters are still having problems with the permissions."

Shit, shit, shit.

I need to get away from here pretty damn quick. High tide is at ten-past-three in the afternoon, so we have until around 4.30 to make high water and cross the sand bar at the entrance. The next high tide is at 3.43 in the morning and if we miss that we won't be able to leave until four o'clock the following afternoon.

Bloody hell!

"I'll give Jimmy a call. I'll use the phone on the boat. Where's Claus - any idea?"

"No, I haven't seen him for an hour or so."

I need more information on the latest developments and Claus always knows more than most.

"What do you think about Macho Gordo," I ask Mano. I know from the time I hit the catamaran that Mano dislikes him.

"Everybody knows about that son of a bitch. It's no great loss boss." I need to hear that, just to feel a bit secure. I hope Mano will lie for me if he has to – he's a loyal old goat.

"Yeah, eso es la vida, Mano."

When I speak to Jimmy on the boat's phone, he tells me the treasure hunters are still having a problem with all the different permissions they need for the trip. The bad news is: the president has been in Nicaragua for two days, and no one has the authority to sign for him. Jimmy is hopeful they will have his signature by morning, but unfortunately it means they will not be in Punta la Pesca until then. I have one more night in town.

Bollocks!

I don't relish the idea of a visit from the police even though I can probably handle it okay. I still have no idea why they are looking for Flora but both she and Maria can link me to the fat bastard. And if the police got hold of Flora, she may blab about stealing the money for Macho. I will then appear to have a big fat motive for killing the big fat bastard. The old Chino woman might also tell the police I was looking for Flora if she is questioned, but I will just say Flora was so good in bed I wanted to see her again. I will of course deny knowing anything about any missing money. Maybe Maria will hold up strong. I've done her a mega favor by liberating the photos, and I've banished Macho from her life forever; whether she wants it that way or not.

Back in my cabin, I take the weapons from my backpack, put them in a plastic bag and lay them on the bed while I empty the rest of the pack. A knock on my cabin door startles me. It is Arcelio.

"Cappy the police are here." He calls from outside the door. "They ask for you."

"I'll be there in a minute."

Fuck me. They haven't wasted time getting here.

My skin goes cold. I rapidly take the bagged weapons into the bathroom. In a panic I put the weapons in the garbage bin and place another bag neatly back on top; I throw some toilet paper in for good measure and take a deep breath. Composing myself, I walk outside.

Jasus this isn't good - my cabin will pass a cursory inspection but I am a dead duck if they search it properly. It will be goodbye to the free world as I know it and hello to a sore arse and a miserable life in a Costa Rican jail. I can't really plead self-defense on this one, but I will die before going to jail.

Arcelio is still outside my door. "Is everything OK Cappy?"

"I don't know. Are they outside?

"No inside the salon."

I think of going back into my cabin to hide the bag under my bed, but decide against it. After locking the cabin door behind me I walk down to meet the two casually dressed policemen waiting in the main salon.

My smiling greeting is returned with two steely looks. The older, taller of the two has graying hair and a big droopy moustache that accentuates his glum look; I guess he is around forty years old. He flashes his ID at me. I scrutinize it. In the photo he looks like a funeral director; his dark eyes as unfriendly when it was taken, as they are now. Introducing his young partner to me, he studies my face. His partner smiles but I sense hostility radiating all around him like a steel shield. Frowning, I direct them both to follow me up to the wheelhouse where we will be alone - there are too many eyes and ears in the salon area.

"What can I do for you?" I ask, indicating for them to sit in the built-in seat beside the helmsman's chair. They both sit.

As I sit down in the helmsman's chair the older guy speaks. "Well senior we are looking for a young girl."

"Yeah who isn't?" I ask stupidly, turning the helmsman's chair on its swivel to face them. I am looking down at them and I can see it makes them feel uncomfortable.

"This is no light hearted matter Capitan. We are looking for the young Senorina who was here on the boat three nights ago."

Was it that long ago?

"You mean Flora, the girl who spent the night here? What has she done?"

"Well, we are concerned for her safety senior."

"Really?" I am trying to stay as calm as I can, but something niggles in my stomach. "How can I help you?"

"We are trying to trace her movements since she left here."

"Well it's strange, because she left in the early hours of the morning. I wanted to see her again so..." I give what I hope is an embarrassing smile. "...I went to the chino pensione where she was staying and the owner told me she moved out soon after she arrived back there. I was very surprised she had gone."

"What happened here on the boat to make her leave so early?" The moustache is doing the talking. The young one just stares through me.

"Well, I fell asleep and maybe she was upset because we didn't... err... You know?" I say, again feigning embarrassment.

"So... She left without waking you?" He gives me a penetrating look.

"Yes. I had a little too much guaro... I think." I smile, hoping he understands my meaning.

"Did she talk to you about where she came from or where she might be going?"

"I'm afraid I don't remember too much. As I said, I was a little drunk, but she didn't say anything about going anywhere. She did tell me she came from somewhere in the North. She said she usually stayed here with a friend but I can't remember who or where it was. I didn't really think about anything, other than... Well, I had other things on my mind."

"Where have you been these last two days?"

Oh-oh!

"I was in San Jose."

"And where did you stay?" *This is not good.*

"I stayed at a guest house."

"And what is the name of the guest house?" *Bloody hell, it is getting worse.*

"It's called 'Jakes Colonial House'."

"And when did you arrive there?" *Something is definitely wrong.*

"Oh... Friday night." Do they know something more than I give them credit for?

"At what time?"

"It was around seven thirty... I think."

"And you left... when?"

"This morning."

"I see. Okay. This is a very nice boat. Do you mind if we look around?"

"No, no problem." I try not to show my relief at being able to stand up and move around. I couldn't have felt any worse beneath a spotlight.

I walk them around the boat, showing them the cabins, the dining room and galley, and then take them out onto the deck where they walk me back to the wheelhouse.

"Where do you sleep?"

"Right behind the wheelhouse here."

"Do you mind if we have a look in your cabin senior." This shakes me to my toes. I don't want to ask why.

"No, not at all."

"It gives us a better impression as we piece together her movements," he volunteers, as if reading my mind.

"Why are you concerned about her? Do you think she is in some kind of trouble?" I ask, looking as concerned as I really am.

"I'm afraid I can't tell you right now senior but we have reason to believe she is in danger."

"From what?"

"I cannot tell you any more senior Capitan."

"Oh, that's too bad. Here, follow me." I walk them to the cabin and unlock the door.

"You always keep it locked Capitan?" he asks suspiciously.

"Not always, only when we are at the dock; sometimes there are many strangers around on the day we are leaving. It's my house, you know?"

"Si senior. You are leaving today?"

"Well, we were supposed to, but it won't be until tomorrow." I show them into the cabin, wondering why he is calling me Capitan one minute and senior the next.

"It's small no?"

"Yes, as you can see most of the space on the boat is for the guests."

They both stand in the doorway looking around. The young one walks in and looks into the bathroom.

"Ah, can I please use your bathroom?"

Fucking hell!

"Yeah, sure." I show him the button for flushing. "Con, mucho gusto."

"Gracias." He walks in, closes the door and I wait outside straining my ears, listening for any sound not associated with natural bodily functions. I am trying my best not to look nervous, feeling the eyes of the mustachioed one boring into to me.

"Senior, you know Macho Gordo?" *Jasus, he is full of bloody surprises.*

"What? Yes, I heard he's dead. What happened?"

"It seems that he went swimming the other night but was too drunk to swim and died in his swimming pool."

"Too bad."

"Could be." *What kind of statement is that?*

The Young One appears from my bathroom and actually smiles. "Gracias senior."

"Con mucho gusto." I reply trying desperately not to look in the direction of the garbage can. Why did I do a stupid thing like that? I obviously read too many spy novels in my youth.

"Well, thank you for your help Senior Capitan. We may need to ask you some more questions later." They actually look friendly now.

"Well, I'm sorry I can't be of more help. Are you sure you can't tell me why you are looking for her? It's a pity, because she seemed so nice," which is true, in a way.

"Hasta luego, senior. Maybe tomorrow we will come back."

I fucking hope not.

Once they have gone, I sit down in the helmsman's chair trying to relax. What the hell was that all about? I get up and go over to the side windows to peer out, to see if they are still on the dock. As soon as I see them getting into a car and driving off, I rush into my cabin and look at the garbage bin in the bathroom - it is in the same position by the sink, looking as it did before - undisturbed. *Jasus, this is nerve-wracking.* I have to hide all that stuff quickly, but first I have to tell the crew they can go home for the night.

I meet all the crew down in the galley. They are obviously discussing the police visit.

"OK, tripilantes, we aren't leaving until tomorrow afternoon."

"Is all good Cappy/" asks Pedro.

"Mas y minus." I answer.

They all look concerned. "Pero no problemo aquí." I add.

"All the supplies are onboard and everything is ready for the charter," says Arcelio. "Can we go home for the night?"

"If all the work is finished, Si, pero be back by nine o'clock in the morning. Anyone staying onboard tonight?"

"Si Cappy" says Carlos.

"Yo tambien." Pedro and Carlos live too far away to make the journey home worthwhile. I would prefer to be alone on the boat but they will probably go out on the town for the night.

"OK. Don't get too drunk tonight you two," I smile.

"No, no Cappy," They both laugh.

Arcelio comes up to the wheelhouse before going home to ask what the police wanted. I tell him they were just passing by and stopped in for a friendly chat. Of course, he doesn't swallow it, but it is none of his fucking business anyway. I am feeling far too polite to tell him that though.

After the crew is gone, I think about Maria; I need to see her badly. Thank goodness she didn't show up while the police were here, that really would have complicated matters. They must already know Maria was

Macho's his latest girlfriend. I start feeling even more uneasy about my current situation; I am at the very heart of all the nastiness.

I walk back over to Mano's office.

"Did you hear Mano? We're definitely not leaving today." He was probably listening in on my conversation with the boss over the phone.

"I thought so. Hey, what did the police want?"

"They asked me about that girl. They said she was in some kind of trouble. Have you heard anything new?"

"No. I don't know what's going on, but the rumor is that Macho was killed because of some kind of drog thing. Those bastards are always killing each other."

"Where did you hear that?"

"It's all over town boss. You know how news gets around here. Did they tell you anything?" A frown creases his forehead into a six pack.

"No, they wouldn't tell me anything; just that she was maybe in danger."

"Maybe she did it," says Mano, playing the great detective.

"Did what?"

"Fucked Macho to death," he laughs.

"Is everyone a fucking comedian now?" I laugh back.

"Lucky it was not you she killed," he laughs again.

"Yeah, I guess it is."

"Listen, most of the crew is going home for the night. You had better call Garcia and let him know we'll need him to do watch-man's duty tonight. And tell him not to let anybody in who doesn't belong here. Comprendo?"

"I called him already boss. "So, he was listening in on the phone call.

"Right, I'm off to see Claus."

"Okay boss."

Claus is actually in his dock office for a change.

"Hey Mac, you missed all the excitement..." he smiles with twinkling eyes. "Or did you?"

"What do you mean?"

"You know about Macho of course?"

"Of course. I've had a visit from the fucking police."

"They have 'fucking' police now?"

"Is everybody a fucking comedian now?"

"They have 'fucking' comedians too?"

"Claus, you are too fucking funny for your own good. What's going on? What have you heard?"

"I heard that Macho was found in his swimming pool and I heard that he was murdered." He is in his element.

"Who told you that?"

"Leona told me. The police were in the Royale last night asking everyone questions about Macho and Flora. You remember Flora - she stole your money. Do you remember that?"

The sarcastic bastard.

"And?"

"And now she is missing."

"Well of course she is; she has a lot of money in her pocket - my fucking money!"

"I heard she has a daughter and she left her somewhere. She didn't take her with her. Now that's strange, no?"

"Where did you hear that?"

"From the Royale; apparently she came here with her boyfriend and her young daughter. Her boyfriend disappeared. And then a day later so did her daughter. I also heard that Macho was a pervert with young kids."

"Was he? I'm not surprised about that. Nothing that fat bastard did would surprise me. So, what's the theory on the street?"

"The word is that Macho was killed by somebody. Maybe it was Flora, or maybe her boyfriend, maybe some drugs people got him or maybe somebody's father - or maybe even YOU."

"Fuck off Claus."

He is laughing again. "No not really you." He thinks that is hilarious. "But did you?"

"No, I fucking didn't, but even if I did, I wouldn't tell you, would I? By the way, have you seen Maria?"

"Oh yes... another suspect."

"Listen pal, everyone in town must be a fucking suspect."

"Well, I know I'm not." Again, he rocks with laughter. "How was San Jose? I tried calling you but you didn't have the phone on."

"The battery's dead, I'll bring it over. So, what about Maria, have you seen her?"

"The guys in the shop told me she came by looking for you but I missed her. She's not working at the bar anymore - she didn't turn up last night and Leona thinks she quit."

"Now why would she do that?"

"Do you think maybe she was upset about Macho? He was her boyfriend after all," he laughs.

"You think this is all so hilarious, don't you?"

"Well my friend, don't you?"

"It would be if the police hadn't been here questioning me. I mean, what do I know?"

"I think you know a lot more than anyone else that's what I think."

"Bullshit!"

"Hey, let's go out for a drink tonight."

"Okay, let's say around eight o'clock?"

"Yeah that's good."

"Okay, see you later."

I don't want to call Maria from the boat's phone, and Claus' phone is dead so I decide to take the bull by the horns and go to Maria's place. But first I take a shower. Standing under the warm water jet I take stock of the situation. I heard somewhere that the best place to think is on the toilet, but an old friend once told me he gained all his inspiration standing under the shower. He spends hours in the shower coming up with all kinds of brilliant ideas, or so I hear. I suppose the secret is all about being relaxed, but I am having a hard time relaxing with this shower of shit hanging over my head.

I wait until sunset before venturing out onto the street towards Maria's apartment. Stopping at a pay phone three blocks away, I call her number.

"Maria?"

"Mac," she breathes, "where are you?"

"I'm on my way to your place, can I come?" I am greatly relieved she is in.

"No. Better not. Meet me on the beach behind the cervesa kiosk. I'll be there in ten minutes." She sounds calm enough.

"Okay, bye."

The beach is a straight walk south across two intersections. The sky over the gulf oozes a dozen brilliant shades of red and purple as I walk along the black sand, passing the dog-walkers. How can they allow their dogs to shit willy-nilly all over the beach? Don't they know that hordes of harmful bacteria are sending kids blind? Of course, they don't. And why do I even care? I watch jealously as a courting couple stroll by hand in hand, carefully avoiding the dog shit. A group of young kids are playing beach soccer, using goal posts made with piles of driftwood. I hope they cleared all the dog shit away. During the rainy season huge logs are piled high on the shoreline; I've hit floating trees with the *Searcher* at night and it puts the shits up me to tell the truth. Two big Chinese long liners are still anchored off the beach behind the solitary tuna boat silhouetted in the sunset. I think about the rape of the sea and wonder about my morals and priorities. Do I really care about fish? I eat tuna, I love prawns, and I devour any fish served up on my plate; I love it. Oh, and by the way, I'm a murderer.

Before reaching the cervesa kiosk I pause to look around. Half a dozen patrons sit around small wooden tables drinking beer and munching bocas in front of the kiosk; others stand at the counter, laughing and chatting with the owner. A steady stream of locals walks slowly up and down the promenade next to the beach. Whole families are out strolling. Townies sit together on long benches lining a stretch of garden parallel to the beach, either watching the traffic or mesmerized by the sunset.

Closer to the point I wait in the half-light of dusk, anticipating Maria's arrival.

I am taken aback by her appearance. She is pale and drawn with deep black circles under her eyes. I try hugging her but to my astonishment she pushes me away.

"Maria, mi amor, how are you?"

"How am I? How do you think? I can't sleep and I'm terrified. The police took me to the station and questioned me for hours yesterday; about Macho and Flora and everything. Luckily my father knows one of the policemen and they let me go.

Why did you do it Mac?"

"Look I'm sorry, I didn't mean to kill him; I just wanted to frighten him a little. Anyway, this is really for the best."

"Don't lie to me Mac. Please, I deserve more respect than that. You killed him and killing someone is not for the best. You realize you will never go to heaven now?"

Damn. She is serious, but I never thought about that.

"Listen Maria, I found the photos of you in Macho's safe and I also found some very bad photos of children. Macho was abusing children for Christ's sake! He was evil to the bloody bone Maria. I was so mad I lost my temper. Can't you see I had no choice? If he remembered anything, he would know you had something to do with his abduction."

"You bastardo! You knew this would happen, didn't you?" she hissed.

"I didn't intend it to happen this way Maria. I promise you. I thought he would be unconscious before he had a chance to drive off from your apartment, and he wouldn't remember anything. But the way it was; he could have put two and two together. Anyway, now you are finally free of him. Get yourself a decent job and forget all about it."

"I can't just forget about it. You killed someone for God's sake. The police know he abused children. They found the photos. They even asked if I knew anything about it. I feel so ashamed."

I don't dare ask if she did know.

"What about Flora; what happened to her? Where did she go?" I ask instead.

"I think Macho killed her."

"What?"

"Flora came here with her daughter and a boyfriend. They came to deliver drugs to Macho but her boyfriend stole the drugs and the money and left town. Macho took Flora's daughter and gave her to his sister to look after. Flora was supposed to work and repay him the money for the drugs. Macho's sister went to the police about it yesterday as soon as she heard Macho was dead. Flora would never have left without her baby, so now the police think Macho killed her."

"He was totally evil, Maria. Don't you see?"

"Yes, he was evil, but so are you to do such a thing. You should have let the police handle it."

"Oh yeah. Great. What about the police Macho was paying off? How many crooked policemen are there? Do you think he would have got justice? And even if he got locked up, he would probably be out in a couple of years, and then what? Maria, I wanted to help you. I wanted to get you out of the terrible situation you were in. I love you." T

That last bit just slipped out.

"Why did you never say that before Mac? Why do you leave me longing for you, always waiting for you to show up at the bar? Why do you spend all the time in San Jose if you love me?" Those are damn tough questions and I don't even want to go there. But I try.

"I was frightened by it, mi amore. I have never been in love like this before. I didn't want to get hurt by you. I spend so much time on the boat away from you I can't stand it." *I am such a lying bastard.*

"Why didn't you tell me that?" Tears slowly begin streaming down her face as her breathing pattern falters.

"I love my job Maria. It's my life. I thought I might have to choose between my job and you - and I couldn't do that."

146

"Then you really don't love me."

"I do Maria, I do. Okay listen. What if I give up the boat for you?"
Fuck, why did I ask that?

Well of course, I want her to be on my side; why else would I ask?

"Do you mean that?"

"Of course I mean it." She looks so vulnerable she makes me feel very protective and in a strange way horny. I can't really help myself. She turns to me and falls into my arms sobbing her little heart out.

She feels so good in my arms.

"Let's go to your place mi amor." *I am such a bastard!*

"But what if the police come? I don't want them to find you there."

"Does your apartment have a back entrance?"

"Yes."

"Okay. If they come, I 'll go out the back door."

I feel like shagging her, right here and now on the beach in the moonlight, but there's too much dog shit around. "You don't think the police are really watching you, do you?" I ask, as we slowly make our way up the beach.

"No, I think they know I wasn't involved. My father's friend put in a good word for me and I know a couple of the police: they came to the bar a lot."

"What about Rudolpho?"

"Hijo un puta. He won't say anything, now his amigo Macho is dead. The police think Flora's boyfriend killed Macho."

"What? They don't think it was an accident?"

"Of course not... Macho couldn't swim."
Well, suck me around a fucking pipe bend.

"Are you serious? Why did he have a pool if he couldn't swim?"

"For his kids."

"Well, didn't he paddle?"

"He hated the water."

"I don't believe it. All fat people can swim and he lives in a fishing town... he owns boats." Well, he used to.

"He told me he nearly drowned when he was a boy."

I can't believe that fat bastard never went in his pool, shit... score one for him.

"Well, it's a pity he didn't drown when he was a boy: it would have saved a lot of people a lot of trouble. I hope the police don't point a finger at me. Did they ask questions about me?"

"No Mac... but don't underestimate the police here. They are not stupid. They are very clever and efficient."

The only thing that can incriminate me now, if Maria doesn't break under the strain, is if Flora is found alive and tells the police she robbed me. That will be bad. I have too many thoughts whizzing around my brain. I think about it as I wait and watch Maria walk along the beach toward her apartment: she is going ahead to open the back door for me. Standing on the beach in the growing darkness, studying movement in the street, I wait five minutes before slowly wandering over to the opposite side of the road, alert for anything out of place. I know I shouldn't do what I am about to, but the lure is too great. I am as hard as a bastard.

When I am absolutely sure it is all clear, I run down the street into the alley at the rear of Maria's apartment building and walk straight through the back door. She is in my arms in a flash.

Clawing at each other's clothes, we strip naked in seconds flat. In a muddle, our bodies entwine. My rod throbs as the skin stretches tighter than it has for months. Placing me between her thighs she squeezes both her silky legs together, surrounding me with smooth wet tingling flesh. In a fever, we kiss over and over blindly. Her hands move to my back and she rakes her nails down to my clenched buttocks. Holding her tightly my hands and mouth caress her cocoa-soft-skin. Pulling away, squeezing her perky plum shaped breasts gently, I suck her erect nipples, flicking each with my tongue, drawing loud gasps of excitement. I kneel with my hands on her small smooth hips, and make a trail with my wet tongue down her hairless belly to her thighs. At the soft bushy triangle of hope I stop and breathe deeply. My heart pounds in my chest, sending blood down to my loins, making me harder and more sensitive. Pulling my hair, she forces me to stand. Lifting her effortlessly onto the kitchen table I bury my head between her legs, using my fingers and tongue in harmony. She grabs my hair again, pulling my wet face away, gesturing and pushing towards the bed. I lift her from the table by her buttocks, and with her legs wrapped tightly around my waist, walk her into the bedroom area. Our mouths glue themselves together as I lift the silky cheeks of her perfect bum, take aim, and lower her gently on to my rock-hard shaft, carefully easing myself inside her. She cries out. Buried deep, supporting her weight, I walk slowly toward the bed, lifting her small body up and down gently, enveloped in the moist heat. I stop at the foot of the bed. A mirror hanging on the wall in front of me produces a vision of Maria's beautiful brown buttocks bobbing up and down on my stiff shaft. The sight of her biting my shoulder, looking at me from another mirror at the head of the bed almost sends me overboard. We watch ourselves front and back, the vision searing itself into my brain as Maria starts bucking wildly, uttering fierce cries and whimpering softly. Unable to wait any longer I fall over backwards onto the bed as she grounds herself violently onto the base of my penis. Blood pounds inside every vein in my body. Maria cries loudly screaming my name, but I am already in the throes of an orgasmic frenzy.

Fucking hell!

Our lips and eyes don't stop twitching for about ten minutes afterwards and I worry that her screams may bring someone to investigate. It sounded like a murder could have been committed, but when I mention it, she smiles tenderly and tells me she is the only one living in the apartment block. I want to stay and bathe deeper in the soft afterglow of our unbelievable togetherness but Maria is nervous and wants me gone. Wiping briefly and then dressing slowly I promise her my undying love and leave her with a kiss and an avowal to never leave her again – after my next trip. Moving out through the rear door I try to be invisible.

On the way back to the boat I can't help but smile as I replay what has just happened. I am one hell of a lucky bastard right now. Maybe Flora really is dead, but if she isn't, I face a nightmare. Having the police think her boyfriend is the chief suspect is a definite plus. Maybe things will work out okay after all, but how can this be so bloody easy?

I get back to the dock just in time to catch Claus before he goes out. After giving him back his phone we both go across to his second office.

Talk about déjà bloody vu.

Of course, all the talk in the bar is about the deceased fat bastard, and theories abound as to what has happened. Recalling the conversation Claus and I had about Macho, two nights previously brings a few verbal digs my way. I completely forgot about that; and it makes me nervous all over again. Apparently, most people in town agree that Macho has indeed been murdered, because it makes a far better story, seeing as how everyone knows about his drugs business, which is quite amazing considering he was never arrested. The topic of pedophilia is apparently also news all over town, and nobody seems to be the slightest bit sad about Macho's demise, which is a very good sign for me. Stories of his dirty deeds are plentiful. The general feeling appears to be that it was a justified end to a just dead bastard.

Changing the subject, I ask Claus what he knows about the treasure hunters coming the next day. I've never had an in-depth discussion with Claus about the treasure but I know he has good knowledge of it; stories of Cocos treasures are also well known around town because many boats were chartered from here over the years, for expeditions to the island. I ask Claus if he was ever involved in the preparation of any. Although his boat sank, Claus still holds a rare, valuable license issued by the ministry of tourism to operate a pleasure boat out at Cocos Island. We discuss trips he's made with treasure hunting groups. Apparently, some were unofficial, which he says he didn't know about that at the time. *He is such a wanker.* I ask about the exact areas his people searched and we compare notes over a few more beers. We should have done this long ago. I know that Claus, being German, knows Dietmar the leader of the expedition but I'm surprised when he says he spoke with him on the phone last week, and it is precisely because Dietmar thinks he knows exactly where the treasure is that he faces such problems getting permission. He wants to dig up the island, but Cocos Island is a National Park and proposed world heritage site, so the National Park's administrators will fight tooth and nail against anyone wanting to dig there. They are, and always have been fiercely opposed to giving permits for treasure hunting trips anyway. This new insight makes me even more nervous. This trip has to be on; I need to get away from here pronto.

After more interesting stories from the locals I am ready to go back to the boat and to my bed.

Back onboard I am sound asleep in a matter of minutes.

My deep state of slumber is shattered by the sound of a dog barking. I grope for my alarm clock; it is two-fifteen and there is some kind of commotion on the dock. I hear raised voices outside. As I lay there in the darkness the voices become louder, as does the barking dog. I raise myself from the bed, put my shorts on, and walk into the wheelhouse to peer out the side window. The security lights are on and I can see Garcia with Kaiser the dog at the gate. He and Diego, the other guard, are engaged in a shouting match with two guys outside the gate. At first, I think it is Carlos and Pedro returning from their night out, but they don't come in, so I wonder if it is the police. But if it is, Garcia would surely have let them in by now. Eventually the noise dies down and the two guards return to their chairs, with Diego on the dock and Garcia on the aft deck. Maybe it's a couple of drunks passing by. Anyway, I will check in the morning.

It will be so good to get out to the island - I am becoming more and more paranoid.

In the morning I awake early, and after eating a bowl of cereal and drinking a cup of fresh coffee I am ready to face another day. What will this one bring?

Garcia tells me the two guys making all the fuss at the gate were looking for me. They didn't say what they wanted but they threatened him and Diego, so he threatened to call the police on them in return. The two guys outside the gate said it was very important and they would come back this morning.

Great - now what? Do I keep my weapons ready?

Did he recognize them? Yes, he's seen them around town.

Were they Ticos? - Yes. Were they friendly? - No. Not at that hour.

That's all I need to hear.

Chapter 15
El Cabeza

"Life is a journey that must be travelled no matter how bad the roads and accommodations."
Oliver Goldsmith.

I AM ON THE EDGE; expecting a phone call from the boss; another visit from the police; or the reappearance of the mysterious midnight prowlers. At twelve fifteen I receive a phone call. *Thank feck it's from Jimmy.* The trip is on and the group is on its way to the boat and will arrive in an hour or so. This is great news. High tide is at three fifty; so, the earliest I can leave is two thirty - only a couple of hours to go.

Waiting for the bus is purgatory. I try contacting Maria several times by phone but there is no answer. I call her sister Rosa, but she doesn't know where Maria is either. I tell Rosa I am leaving and will see Maria when I get back from the trip. Then I wait; and wait; and make three or four 'final inspections' of the boat, and do more pre-departure checks of the engine room and wheelhouse, and chat with the crew; telling them all I know about the trip; and I worry myself sick about being arrested.

When the bus shows up I almost vomit with relief.

There are nine bodies in all: Jimmy and four treasure hunters, two National Park officials, and two policemen with heavy clanking bags. At the same time a couple of park rangers show up with their supplies, ready for their stint out at the island.

Supervising the placement of all the boxes on the aft deck, I feel a hand on my shoulder.

"Hi captain," a soft warm voice whispers in my ear.

"Julia! Welcome back. It's great to see you. How was it at home?"

"It was great Mac, but I'm glad to be back. I'll see you later," she smiles. The thought of having her as a cabin companion for the week excites me, making me extra keen to leave. A very interesting week lies ahead if I can just get out of port on time. This will be hugely different from any other trip I've made with divers, or treasure hunters.

The fact that there are only four treasure hunters surprises me a little. Even more surprisingly, I only recognize two of them. I thought Dietmar's usual group was coming but Dietmar isn't here. This puzzles me the most, because if he really does know where the treasure is, he wouldn't miss this for the world.

In his late sixties Dietmar has been coming to Costa Rica to search for the treasure for seventeen years straight. He makes at least two trips a year, and because he is getting on in years seems more desperate to find the treasure every trip. He spoke about the treasure a lot, but I'll never forget the look in his steely blue eyes, when he gripped my arm tightly during his first trip with me and whispered: "The Treasure is here Mac I know it!" If I had any doubts before, they left me right then. I absolutely believed him.

Because someone goes through the hassle of mounting a treasure expedition it doesn't necessarily mean there is any treasure where they say it is. People organize fraudulent expeditions all the time – some are out to make money from vulnerable investors and others are just out for the fun of an all-expenses paid trip in the tropics. Dietmar is absolutely for real though. He puts his money where his heart is.

He hasn't used only the Searcher for his expeditions; he hired other boats too. He once hired an old Panamanian tugboat for three-months with a group of characters onboard that could easily have been B movie extras; each was the difference between chalk and chewing gum.

Dietmar covered all his bases with that crew.

Two tough Soviet SPETZNAZ looking guys could be seen scaling steep cliffs around the island at all hours of the day. They both contrasted starkly with J.C., the elegant Californian restaurant owner and, his slim, silicon implanted girlfriend Ellie: J.C. was tall, blonde, and handsome in an effeminate way and Ellie was a musical actress constantly singing complaints about the state of her frizzy bleached blonde hair and fake silver fingernails. A little old lady Dietmar brought with him turned out to be a gold diviner who could supposedly find precious metals with a twig, a prayer, and a bent hairpin.

A little old man, who could have been anybody's grandfather, was in fact a clairvoyant, specializing in treasure recovery, who reputedly found treasure in the Urals.

Jack Crabshaw was a brave experienced cave diver who mostly snorkeled daily, deep into gnarly jagged caverns etched at sea level in the high rocky cliff faces around the shoreline. One day, armed with only a mask, a snorkel and a flashlight, Jack disappeared into the dark interior of a deadly looking cave on the crest of a bloody great wave and didn't reappear until everyone was completely convinced that he was dead. Eventually, when another huge wave spat him out with a load popping sound, he appeared covered in red raw scratches, deep jagged gouges, and bubbly, bloody froth. Dietmar brought him over to the Searcher to be fixed. I fed him whiskey and cleaned him up with large swabs of alcohol-soaked cotton wool, and then stuck him back together with the medical equivalent of duct tape and industrial-sized butterfly closures, I shortly thereafter took him back to the mainland with the group of divers I was just finishing my charter with. On the journey back to port a sorry looking Jack Crabshaw vowed to hang up his mask and snorkel and never-ever enter another cave again in his whole life.

Onboard the tugboat Dietmar also had a small sea-borne micro-lite aircraft, whose pilot was constantly coming over to the *Searcher* to buy the odd crate of beer or two. I watched him and his fascinating flying machine take off and land on the waters of Chatham Bay several times, each time thinking it might crash in a spectacular fashion; but despite its wobbly flight path, it never did.

Dietmar had void detecting apparatus onboard the tug for finding caves and caches of buried treasure underground, or undersea. He had the Russian industrial version of an accelerometer - I swear I didn't make that word up. This equipment utilized a series of extremely cumbersome heavy wires and probes that emitted strong electrical impulses. The returning waves were measured on a computer by two Eastern Europeans using newly developed software. This was all clever stuff - if they found the right location to place the wires and probes. Unfortunately for Dietmar and his gang, permission to use this piece of equipment wasn't granted by the National Park's administrators until the very end of the expedition - after Dietmar deposited a huge amount of cash with the government as collateral, in case he caused any damage to the island's eco-structure. To top that off, being constantly monitored by Rangers, the group wasn't allowed to physically dig anywhere on the island, and that, needless to say, made for a very frustrating time for everyone. Just before they were due to leave, the group did manage to use their void detector and collected a stack of data for later analysis.

Strange as that group seemed, the thing that banded them together was an unshakeable faith, and the absence of any doubt in their treasure bitten minds that more than one treasure cache was still there, on the island, and that they would surely find it – even though as the weeks wore on their search patterns became more and more erratic, and their efforts more frantic.

Being accompanied constantly by National Park rangers, they were ever mindful of security. Being paranoid about giving away clues that might lead the rangers to find the secret burial site themselves, a ceaseless game of cat and mouse developed between them, but Dietmar told me later that he won that game.

If I were a park ranger out on the island I would be up at the crack of sparrow-fart every day in search of that bloody treasure.

Jimmy comes over to me on the dock. "Hi Mac. The boat looks good."

"Yeah, we try to keep on top of things."

"You're going to have fun with this guy," he says nodding towards one of the group.

"Who is he?"

"He's the leader."

Watching the group on the dock, I am fascinated by the guy in charge. He is a big bloke, but the thing that strikes me the most about him is the size of his head. He has one of the biggest heads I have ever seen on a person. Marching around on the dock, giving orders to his group in a high pitched voice, his crisp commands instruct how to unload the luggage, how to handle it and where to put it, while at the same time directing the shooting of a video by another group member who is doing his best to make sure his leader is in the center of every shot looking busy and important. I leave Jimmy and walk over to him.

"Hi, I'm Mac, the captain; pleased to meet you."

"You are the captain?" he asks with a tinny voice. "My name is Herman and I am the leader." He stares at me through a very small pair of eyes, behind a very small pair of wire rimmed glasses. "I want a cabin with a double bed," he instructs without a smile. "I want the biggest cabin. I have a lot of equipment."

"Okay, no problem," I reply.

"Good. We must leave now. We lost too much time because of this bullshit government papers. We need to go immediately. Tell your crew."

"We can't leave until high tide," I explain.

"Shiese! When is that?' he asks. His two beady blue eyes stare at me as if I am apiece of dog shit he just stepped in with bare feet, and which has now squelched up between his toes.

"High tide is at…"

"Okay, okay. Just leave as soon as you can."

"We will…"

"Do you have Peach Snapple onboard?" This completely throws me.

"I don't think I've ever seen any here," I reply.

"This is bullshit and this is a bullshit country."

I look around hoping none of the crew hears our exchange. "Just a minute Herman, this is not a bullshit country and I'd appreciate it if you showed some respect in front of the crew. They are very proud of their country."

"What? I don't know why." He looks daggers at me and I think for a minute he is going to cancel the trip or have me replaced. I am suddenly very thankful we've already lost a day and the trip is only going to be six days in length.

"Look, we'll leave at two thirty," I tell him abruptly, before turning my back and leaving him on the dock.

What the fuck?

Why is it that events that seem to have all the ingredients of being really great in theory, sometimes turn out to be shit in practice because of one rotten egg.

Pedro walks over to me. "El Cabeza," he says smiling.

"What?"

"El Cabeza," he points to Herman. "Cabeza Grande, no?"

I laugh. The crew has already named him "The Head."

Once everyone is onboard, I allot the cabins and make sure everything is stowed away before walking down to the engine room. Carlos is pottering about with a cleaning rag. "El Cabeza is not a good man," he says frowning.

"Yeah, well at least we only have six days with him," I say laughing again at the nickname Cabeza has been given. "You can fire up the engines and generator as soon as you're ready."

While Arcelio, Pedro and Carlos disconnect the shore power cable, I give the group a boat briefing. I explain the use of the boat's facilities and safety equipment, and relay instructions on what to do if anyone sees someone falling overboard. I warn them not to smoke next the pangas or the gasoline tanks and ask them not to flick their cigarette butts into the wind. I explain what to do if there is a fire or flood and also tell them everything they need to know about using the boat's toilets without blocking them.

The briefing takes thirty minutes. At two thirty, after making sure Molly is onboard, I steer away from the dock in a highly relieved state of mind. In the wheelhouse I move Cabeza out of my way repeatedly as he fluffs around being filmed by his personal cameraman. At one point, while I am on the side deck checking the stern, he grabs the wheel and I almost have to wrench him off so I can turn the boat around.

On the dock, a group of the crew's wives and kids wave us off.

Claus gives me the finger - the prick.

I have the uneasy feeling that at any moment something will stop us leaving. Steering west into the estuary, negotiating the narrow channel, I pass the market and coast guard station with its patrol boat seemingly welded to the dock. Motoring slowly along the channel towards the western point I study every small craft leaving its own dock. Passing the terminal, I watch the ferry departing. It isn't until we round the point and head out toward the dozens of tiny fishing boats in the shallow waters of the gulf that I begin to relax. When we reach the calm blue water of the open ocean the knot in my stomach starts to fully unwind. With at least another week of freedom ahead I am so relieved I could gaily scream "Yippee-Ai-Ay".

The weather is expected to remain good for the whole trip.

Although I usually get Mano to bring me the weather report from the coastguard dock, it makes no difference what the forecast is because we have to leave no matter what. We never delay a trip because of bad weather. Not because I like bad weather. I hate it. The problem is that because everyone pays a small fortune for the trip, they don't want to miss one single minute of a dive, and they certainly don't want to hear excuses for not leaving on time. The majority of divers are mortally offended and unforgiving if they are given a low air-fill or are otherwise robbed of dive time.

Luckily, the *Searcher* is sturdy enough to steam through any really bad weather conditions. Apart from a couple of my crew and most of the guests being seasick, there are no serious repercussions if we do hit it rough. Battling through a tropical storm once, the *Searcher* handled every wave thrown at her, although we did lose a couple of deck lockers and a life-raft.

During the time it takes to clear the Gulf, Cabeza continues to make himself as much of a nuisance as possible. He wants to know all about charts and the essentials of navigation and about every piece of equipment that has a switch. The large professional video camera perched like a toucan on the cameraman's shoulder is permanently pointed at Cabeza. I didn't really listen when the cameraman introduced himself so I've conveniently forgotten his name already. I do that a lot lately - with so many guests coming and going on these trips I never remember all the names on the first day. Often, I forget someone's name as soon as I am introduced to the next person in line, but I usually figure it out by the end of the second day. The crew's method of making up names for everyone sometimes confuses me, but the cameraman will now be known as Cecil B. De Mille for the rest of the trip.

"Is everything okay," I ask Cabeza appeasingly. "Where is Dietmar? Why isn't he here?"

"All this bullshit from the National Park made him ill. He had a heart attack."

"Holy shit!" Is he going to be alright?" I ask.

"He is in hospital in San Jose recovering. He will be fine," he says offhandedly. He gives me a small box and microphone. "Put this on, I want to ask you some questions on camera," he orders.

With the microphone attached, he fires a series of questions and gives directions, whilst fiddling with every switch he sees.

"What are your plans for the trip," I ask. "I hear you know exactly where the treasure is."

He looks down his nose at me for what seems like a full minute before answering. "After Dietmar's last expedition on the tug boat, when all the collected data was analyzed, one area stood out as being the likely spot. The void detector found a promising echo that could be a cave buried under a few meters of earth. We also have other evidence to suggest there is a hidden cave."

I wait for him to say what the other evidence is.

"It ties in with my original calculations," he continues.

"So where is this cave," I ask.

"It is here," he says to my surprise, pointing to an area of the island on the chart. With Cecil filming he looks straight into my eyes and laughs. I don't know whether he is serious or not, but I have to take a step back to escape his smelly breath.

The area he points to is one I often thought of exploring myself, but it is far too overgrown for me to attempt a proper search, and besides, without a void detector up my kilt it will be like searching for a straight guy at a Cher concert. When I look for caves, I look in obvious places. I haven't the time or opportunity to go digging.

I picture the terrain at the spot Cabeza points out. A long narrow gully, completely overgrown with thick vegetation is flanked on both sides by steep sloping escarpments and trees, leading down to the shoreline.

"Why don't you come with us?" he asks to my utter dismay. "You can help us dig. You must clear it with the police first."

Although I want to steer clear of him as much as possible, I dearly want to be a witness to this potentially historic event.

Maybe I will actually get to like him after all.

Clearing the shallow gulf and moving a safe distance from the prawn trawlers and small fishing boats scattered around, I hand over the helm to Arcelio, the first of the crew on watch, with the usual instructions to call me if he is unsure of anything, or if any vessels are on a steady bearing. Happily escaping the major production in the wheelhouse, I leave him alone with Cecil and Cabeza, and wander down to the main salon, where the other guests are sitting around quietly relaxing.

The two National Park bigwigs, Orlando and Joachim, have both been out to Cocos with me before, but this is the first time I have taken any policemen. The two tough looking cops insisted on carrying their own heavy bags and boxes onboard when they arrived. I suspect they don't have sun tan lotion or beach towels in their luggage; more likely they are fully tooled up with a selection of weapons and ammo. If the treasure hunters do happen to find treasure on this trip, a whole new set of rules will apply - the *Searcher* might well be a floating bank vault on the way back.

My mind is suddenly filled with all kinds of dark imaginings, and I am reminded that the clock is still ticking for me.

Gunther and Willy, the two treasure hunters from previous trips with me are already trying their best to drink our beer supply dry. Willy consumes a crate of beer in one session without needing a piss, and strangely enough, never appears drunk. He is always pretty laid back but with a crate of beer under my belt so would I be.

"How's it hanging Willy?" I ask.

"Ya. Good Mac and you?"

"I'm okay. Who is Herman?" I ask.

"He is a Dietmar's partner. A computer wizard. He has a company in California. And lots of dollars," Willy replies. "He has invested a lot, a lot, a lot of money with us. He is paying for this trip."

"He's going to take some getting used to," I say.

"Ya. He's okay. He wants everything to be exactly his way, and no other way. Ya he's difficult sometimes, but you will get used to him."

"I don't know about that Willy. Too bad about Dietmar. Do you think he's going to be okay?"

"Ya, he'll be fine," he says smiling.

"I hope so. Is this the big one?" I ask.

"Ya. This is it Mac. All these years," he smiles again.

I look over at Gunther, who is connected to his laptop by a pair of seriously large headphones. Oblivious to his surroundings he taps away furiously at the keys; playing some kind of three-dimensional game that is incomprehensible to my tiny mind.

Leaving Willy, I go over and make polite conversation with Orlando and his buddy for a while before chatting with the cops. Being on an all-expenses paid cruise to a tropical island, with nothing to do but relax and enjoy themselves, they are tickled pink about such a choice assignment. I tell them if they need anything, they should not hesitate to ask and I will be only too happy to accommodate them. I have no idea whether these guys can be of assistance to me in my current predicament or not, but who knows? It's always good to have the cops on your side.

I keep out of Cabeza's way for the rest of the evening, hiding in my cabin or in the wheelhouse. Once everyone has retired for the night Julia joins me for the midnight watch in the wheelhouse.

Julia is a tough, independent woman, who knows exactly what she wants and how to get it. By no means ugly, she pretends to be, to ward off the horny Ticos. She deliberately tries to make herself look unattractive, but she has a way about her that makes me dig deep. Once I dig, I expose her inner beauty, and in return she exposes an amazing hidden body from beneath her drab baggy clothing. She might not look like the most feminine woman in the world, but when she is in my bed and going for glory - *Oi Caramba*.

If she wants to use the boat and my body while out at the island that's fine with me. She can eat all the good food she wants and use as much hot water in the shower and washing machine as she likes, because I'll tell you what: she certainly knows what her hands, tongue and lips are for – and they aren't just for counting pigs.

I'm not naïve enough to think I am the only one enjoying her favors. There must be at least one other horny bastard plumbing her depths, but out at the island, human nature exists on the most basic level. We suit each other's immediate needs with a symbiotic relationship - Just as a sailing ship needs a mast…

The wheelhouse is dark. The blackout curtain draped over the hatchway leading down to the dining room blocks all light from beneath the stairs. The fuzzy green glow of the radar screen and the dim glow of the instrument panel provide the only light inside the wheelhouse. Outside, the moonless night sky screams with blazing stars. There are no navigation lights visible and no contacts on the radar screen anywhere out to the horizon. As Julia and I chat I feel the old familiar warmth rising in my shorts. Her face glows in the darkness and I feel a tension building between us. Standing by the helmsman's chair, she leans in close now and again, rubbing her crotch intentionally on my right knee. Reaching out I pull her to me. I know she is ready.

"I missed you girl."

"I missed you too Capitan."

Our lips meet. We kiss gently at first, then more urgently. She stops me with a hand on my chest.

"Wait, I'll check there's no one around."

My throat is almost too dry to reply. "Okay. Good idea."

When she comes back, she assures me everyone has gone to bed.

We spend the rest of my watch having sex - straddling the helmsman's chair, leaning over the instrument panel, sitting on the window ledge and standing behind the chair watching the stars. The excitement of being caught at any moment by an insomniac intensifies our pleasure.

In the morning, another session follows in my cabin before breakfast, but this time we move slower and more sensually, taking time to watch each other and talk. I think again what a lucky bastard I am. I also think about what a damn fool I am. *But it's too late now buddy.*

161

Walking down to the dining area with a big smile on my face I'm glad to see everyone in a relaxed mood after finishing breakfast. "Where's Jimmy?" I ask Raul.

"He's still in his cabin." Jimmy usually sleeps because of his tendency towards seasickness during the rare crossings he makes with us - even when it is flat calm.

Oscar and Felipe, the two cops, remain quiet and unassuming, keeping to themselves as much as possible.

Although El Nino is having a serious effect on the world weather, the good news in this region is that the weather is beautiful. The deep blue sea is calm, the azure sky is intense, and there is no wind or swell. I don't see a single ripple in my coffee mug.

I feel good this morning. I managed to escape from town and the uncertain predicament I am in – even if is only for one week. I can't dwell on what might happen on my return though; speculation does about as much good as wheels on crutches. I have to keep that thought intact.

Cabeza bothers me all day long. I want to be with Julia in my cabin but Cabeza gives me a walky-talky radio to carry around, calling me constantly until I switch it off. I can't stand the sound of his voice. He won't let me rest in my cabin. He questions me repeatedly about the island and about boats in general. He is interested in boats and wants to buy one with his share of the treasure, to sail around the world. He wants to film the engine room and every piece of machinery in there.

He needs an electrical converter for his hairdryer and he wants extension cables and adaptors for charging his batteries. He wants me to move his boxes around on the aft deck so he can check his tools. He wants to fish from the aft deck. When he comes and tells me his toilet is blocked, my stomach turns and I want to knock him out cold. Carlos is off watch sleeping. As much as I hate doing it, I sometimes have to put my gloved hand inside the toilet bowl and grope around the pipe-bend to arrest the offending object. Luckily, I manage to clear this blockage with a plunger – but it still doesn't stop me heaving.

Cabeza stays in the wheelhouse during my watch to annoy me further with more stupid questions; some he's already asked. He uses my least favorite practice of not listening to my answers. He surpasses the "complete wanker" stage. When Willy, Gunther, and Cecil join us in the wheelhouse all speaking German at once, it sounds like a stream of nonsense.

Years ago, I had a German girlfriend who tried teaching me the language. Funnily enough, she told me I shouldn't learn because she was sure I didn't want to know some of the stupid things men talk about. I'm rusty not having spoken it for a while, so I understand little of what the guys are saying. Most of it makes no sense at all.

Despite the beautiful weather outside, Orlando, the older of the two park chiefs, sits in the salon with his buddy Joachim, reading and watching videos most of the day. We don't see a single cloud and the sea remains as anonymously calm as a pint of Guinness. We spot a couple of schools of dolphins but they don't approach. We chase after them for a while so Cabeza can film them, but the dolphins are too busy fishing, hunting, or on some other high-speed mission. We usually see at least one pod of pilot whales or dolphins during the calm crossings.

In the early hours of the morning I take over the helm from Pedro. We are five miles from Cocos. It's time for the dolphins to playfully escort us in. No matter what time of day or night, dolphins usually accompany us on our approach to and from the island, offering a magical brand of hospitality. Today is no exception. Our arrival at the island is usually in the early hours of the morning but dolphins don't sleep as we humans do: they put parts of their brain to sleep at different times. *How clever is that?*

With the auto pilot on, I leave the wheelhouse and walk across the foredeck to join Julia watching the dolphins swimming out of the darkness, leaving luminescent trails in their wakes. Dozens of sleek smooth bodies enclosed in phosphorescent cocoons, streak through the water towards us like silver torpedoes. Exhaling loudly through the watertight blowholes on the crowns of their shiny heads they surface to take a breath, sometimes leaping high into the air. The speedy dolphins dazzle us with their masterful display of maneuverability under the bow, each one jockeying for a prime position inside a group of fifteen or more. Squeaking and whistling with delight, several small juveniles try to keep up. A dolphin escort feels like an honor guard. Watching them racing through the sea, jumping into the air alongside us, gives everyone a great feeling; as if the boat is being blessed and nothing bad will happen on the trip. The dolphins escort us to where a fierce current line runs off the end of Manuelita Island, before departing one by one. I watch them swim off into the darkness before walking back into the wheelhouse.

I reduce speed.

Cruising slowly into Chatham Bay, we pass Isla Manuelita, Cocos Island's largest satellite, on our starboard side. The main island is clothed in darkness. There are no other boats in the bay and not a single light ashore. I see no sign of human habitation anywhere, which is another thing I love about Cocos.

Turning off the auto pilot I steer toward our mooring buoy, close to a small waterfall at the far end of the bay. The current has slowed us down. The passage usually takes thirty-two hours when the weather is this calm, but it is almost half past midnight now - thirty-four hours since we departed the dock.

Putting both engines into neutral I allow the *Searcher* to glide slowly towards the orange buoy tied to our floating mooring rope. Losing sight of the buoy under the bow I reverse, waiting for Pedro's directions. Throwing a grappling hook, he catches the small rope attached to the spliced eye of the larger, polypropylene rope. With a great effort he hauls it up to the guardrail, waiting for me to leave the wheelhouse to help pull it under the bow-rail, and across the deck, to the bollard in its center. The large waterlogged eye weighs heavily as we struggle to pull it under the guardrail and secure it to the bollard before the current catches hold of the boat and we lose the rope, making it necessary to go around again. Once secured to the mooring rope and hanging with all our weight, I thank Pedro and tell him he can go and turn in his bunk. The crewmembers usually stand watches here at night, but I have decided to give them all a break this week, seeing as how it is supposed to be a relaxing trip with no divers onboard. Once he leaves, I go back into the wheelhouse. On the radar screen I check the distances and bearings to both sides of the bay. I need to make sure the mooring rope is still secured to the big anchor on the seabed in the exact same spot it was when I left it a few days previously. I will dive first thing in the morning to assure it is still in good shape.

Completely satisfied everything is secure I set an alarm on the radar, set another on the depth sounder and one on the GPS system. This will warn me if the mooring rope breaks and we move. I don't want the boat to go on walk-about during the night. You can never be too careful when you have the responsibility of human lives on your shoulders - which may sound strange coming from a murderer.

Finally, content that everything is as it should be, I walk out onto the deck once again, breathing in deeply, filling my lungs and senses with the cool, rich smell of virgin earth. Although only five degrees from the equator, the temperature at Cocos is a good deal cooler than in Punta la Pesca.

I love arriving here in the dead of night – it's a magical time for me. I love the earthy smell of the island and the sight of her steeply vegetated slopes disappearing into the darkness. I listen in wonderment to the million alien insect choirs as it chirps away merrily into the night. The mooring is only 100 yards from the waterfall on the left side of the bay and 300 yards from the beach over on the right. I still don't see any lights from the ranger's hut hidden behind the palms in the center of the bay so I suspect they are asleep. They have an early start scheduled in the morning. Cecil and Cabeza appear on the top deck. I hope they aren't about to start filming with all their lights and shit, but thankfully their visit is brief.

After they have gone and both engines have cooled down, I descend into the sweltering heat of the engine room, grab some ear protectors and switch both main engines off. Changing generators, running the smaller, quieter one for the night, I start to relax. The feeling of arriving safely is like bathing in the afterglow of sex.

After checking around the boat making sure everyone is turned in their bunks, I set the A/C thermostats to the correct temperature for the island. Because it is much cooler here, I don't want Cabeza waking me to tell me he is freezing. I check the engine room once more for luck, and then walk back up to the top deck where Julia is waiting in the semi-darkness.

We stand side by side listening to the cacophony of sounds. The island's nocturnal inhabitants are busily going about their secret nightly business. The sky is also alive. Zillions of stars shimmer like tiny Harry Winston's diamonds. Standing hand in hand, staring up into the brilliant night sky, we marvel at the amazing phenomenon overhead, hoping to catch sight of a shooting star or two. I'm amazed at how the sight of major star clusters brings about such elation, such euphoria. The Southern Cross is up there somewhere, hidden behind the island's heights. Crosby, Stills, and Nash sang something like: "When you see the Southern Cross for the first time, you realize why you went away." They know how it feels alright.

Julia feels it too.

Letting go of my hand she pulls me close and our lips touch gently as we embrace. Holding her tightly I feel her wrap-around skirt brush past my lower legs as it drops to the deck and lands on my bare feet. Moving both hands down to her buttocks I cup them in my palms. I am only slightly surprised to find naked flesh in my grasp. She has no panties on. Pushing me back gently she unfastens my shorts, letting them fall to my ankles. Her hand is inside my boxers and holding me before I know it.

Turning around, she leans over the guardrail exposing her smooth naked buttocks to the night air. Stroking my erection, she guides me, groaning as I gently ease myself inside her. We both stand perfectly still; taking in the night sky; breathing deeply, inhaling the smells; listening to the sounds of the island; feeling each other's heat. With the warmth of her bum pressed against my crotch, I am deeply conscious of the hot moistness enfolding me. Julia takes off her top and gently plays with her nipples as I massage her clitoris. Moving my hips backwards and forwards slowly, I slide in and out until she begs me to go faster. Pumping her feverishly, I hold her hips as she tweaks her own nipples. Uttering several muffled groans, she climaxes just before I do. Shooting stars whiz around inside my head and I come with a blast that makes my knees weak and my vision fuzzy.

Later, in my cabin, lying in bed next to Julia, I think of Maria and suddenly feel a deep, inexplicable sense of sadness, wondering if she is sad and thinking of me.

What a bastard I am.

Chapter 16
Treasure Hunting

"Life is really simple, but we insist on making it complicated."
CONFUCIUS

THE MORNING COMES TOO SOON. I haven't even time to share my morning glory with Julia. Instead I have to get ready to unload all the rangers' crates, boxes, sacks of food, drums of diesel, and gasoline.

In the wheelhouse, bathed in the early morning light, Molly stares at the island through the window. Standing beside her, stroking her head, I study the island too. The normally lush green vegetation is dotted with brown patches and the waterfall is more of a gentle stream than the usual steady torrent. The island is suffering from an acute lack of rain – El Nino is in the treasure hunter's favor. Rain makes climbing on the island murderous.

The rangers have already berthed their blue-hulled motorboat alongside our aft deck and are all onboard, collecting their replacement buddies, as I walk onto the aft deck drinking my first cup of coffee.

Snuggled into the northeastern corner of the island, protected from the prevailing southeasterly winds and sea swells, Chatham Bay is the anchorage of choice. We are on the Eastern side of the half-mile wide bay, close to the small waterfall at Punta Pacheco. Onshore, stretching away to the north, a small sandy beach only emerges during low tide. The beach is strewn with large boulders bearing carvings from mariners gone past.

167

When she isn't on the boat or off exploring the island, Julia stays alone in a small hut nestled amongst a garden of spiraling orange and green bromeliads, and copie ferns. Sitting beside a small stream emptying into the bay, the hut is hidden behind patches of cupey palms and pond apple trees. The stream washes past an extensive bed of ancient, graffiti-covered rocks on the beach. Close by, two huge circular caissons dug in the sand by previous treasure hunters are supported internally by metal pilings and thick corrugated steel sheets. Per foot, they are probably the most expensive caissons in the world.

Jacques Cousteau has the ornate carving from of his research vessel 'Alcyone', chiseled into one of the larger rocks on the beach. A couple of years ago, a monstrous storm - the worst I've experienced at Cocos - forced me to take shelter close to the beach. I moved in closer than I normally would, putting two extra anchors out and staying awake all night. When the storm died in the morning, I heard on the BBC news, on our SSB radio that Jacques Cousteau had died that night.

His spirit surely passed us by on its way to Valhalla.

Most of the island's features and satellites have Spanish and English names. Many place names on English charts were given by persons working in the various Admiralty Hydrographic Offices. People who never traveled more than five miles from their homes in their entire lives, have their names linked forever to some of the most exotic places on the planet, but Colnett Point, the northernmost tip of Cocos Island, 600 yards northeast of the rocky portion of Chatham Bay beach, is named after the *Rattler's* captain who left his two little piglets here – it is also named Punta Quiros, after the Portuguese born navigator Pedro Fernández de Quirós who passed by in the 15th century.

Two hundred yards from Colnett Point, across a narrow channel named Estreche Challe, Isla Manuelita forms a natural extension to the bay. The tall-standing, quarter-mile-long-island is also known as Isla Nuez, because of its resemblance to a colossal walnut. Sparsely draped with foliage, it is home to a huge flock of rowdy, red-footed boobies.

Manuelita acts as a great natural barrier, keeping the swell heights down in the bay and making it easier for me to unload.

Down in the engine room Carlos and I start the main generator so we can put the big crane into action. Hauling on the big heavy metal lever, Carlos rams the clutch of the generator into the cogs of the large hydraulic pumping unit, which sends hydraulic oil rushing through various pipes and flexible hoses to the crane on the aft deck. The piping and hoses vibrate nosily through the aft cabins. The obnoxious, rattling, buzzing noise acts as a giant communal alarm clock, waking anyone having the audacity to sleep in.

Using the crane to unload the ranger's fuel drums into the large panga alongside is a piece of cake, but launching our pangas from the top deck is a wee bit trickier. Luckily there is hardly any swell, so everything goes according to plan. There's nothing worse than starting the day off with a ton of boat suspended in the air on a crane wire, waiting for a lull in a series of rolling swells. If I misjudge the timing, a lot of bodies will run for cover – and with good reason - once those big heavy pangas start swinging in the air they have to be grounded quickly, wherever possible. Thankfully the crewmembers do an excellent job. Mercifully I only have to unload and load the pangas once a trip.

Raul, Pedro, and Roberto have already swung out the large steel boat booms on each side of the Searcher's mid-ship section, and secured them in place with guide wires from above, forward, and aft. Once in the water, the crewmembers attach each panga to its own boom by a nylon line, interwoven with a bungee cord for extra flexibility. The boats stay secured to the booms every night at the island. As protection against damage that may be caused by swells ramming the pangas into the Searcher's sides, we tie big plastic-cushioned wooden fenders between them for the duration of our stay. My crewmembers scurry about on deck like worker-ants, needing no direction from me at all.

With both pangas sitting peacefully in the water alongside the aft deck, I use the crane again to lower the enormously heavy platform hinged to our transom.

Now, anyone who wants, can go for a swim. After finishing with the crane, I tell the treasure hunters it is safe to get their kit together on the aft deck.

They have a big selection of digging implements with them. They brought pickaxes and shovels of all shapes and sizes, and huge pry bars, presumably to move the rocks that supposedly cover the cave. There are also some seriously large sledgehammers for smashing any rocks they can't move with the pry bars, but I seriously doubt they will be able to use them. Maybe Cabeza has conveniently forgotten this is a national park, but Orlando and Joachim will remind him soon enough when they see this array of destructive weapons.

I watch both their reaction when they do come out on deck and see everything lined up ready to go. I wish I had a camera to record the looks on their faces. Despite the enormous prospective value of the treasure

169

that may or may not be uncovered, Orlando and Joaquin are not too impressed with Cabeza and what they see on deck. Frowning at each other, they seem to be cooperating under silent protest.

A large number of boxes previously stacked neatly on the aft deck are now scattered everywhere. Cabeza consults his clipboard and gives instructions to his minions in German - all the while being filmed by Cecil who strangely still excludes everyone except Cabeza from the shots. The group is highly excited until Cabeza starts shouting like a eunuch once again.

This prompts me to go inside and eat a quick breakfast before getting ready to go with them. Jimmy has actually surfaced from the depths of his cabin to ask me to go with the group and help with their equipment. I have already decided not to miss it - and because she knows the island better that most, Julia is also coming along with us.

During her study of the pigs' behavior she has probably traipsed through more hidden terrain than anyone else in decades.

After breakfast, Cecil, Cabeza, Günter, and Willy hop in Pedro's panga with all their equipment. I join the park guys and cops, with Arcelio as driver. The bags the cops bring with them clank noisily as they load them into our panga. I am absolutely certain they contain weapons. Casting off from the Searcher and heading towards the western corner on our way to Punta Pacheco, the excitement in the hunter's panga switches up a notch. Motoring a little way south past the tiny cone-shaped Isla Conico, we stop directly in front of a narrow-overgrown gully. There is no beach here, just a narrow, pebble-strewn ledge behind crops of large, submerged, and partially submerged boulders. This will make the landing difficult. A slight swell sends breakers up onto the shoreline and a series of completely submerged rocks further out makes it too dangerous to get any closer. If the pangas are lifted by the swell they could smash into, or overturn on these rocks, causing damage to them, the engines, and maybe bodily injury to any one of us.

When both pangas are close enough to the shore I lift my arm high in the air.

"Ok. We'll stop here while we unload. Just keep the bows pointing at the island and keep in this position," I call to Arcelio and Pedro.

"We'll have to hop into the water one by one, raise the outboard engines and then hold the pangas as we unload the gear," I tell Cabeza.

Cabeza has an idea of his own.

"Shiese. We can and must drive up onto the shore." He doesn't see the rocks just below the surface there.

"Get closer," he shouts at the drivers.

This pisses me off no-end but I keep my calm. "Stay here," I shout to Pedro and Arcelio, "We don't want to get too close to the rocks. We jump in here and unload." They both understand the situation but Cabeza obviously doesn't: he raises his voice several notches and babbles at me aggressively in German.

"Speak English." This infuriates him. He goes nuts and I don't understand anything he says. I stay calm.

"Listen Ca…. Herman" *I almost called him Cabeza.* "Calm down. The only way to get ashore is by getting into the water and getting wet. You'll have to accept it or find another landing site."

He glares at me and begins ranting again until the other group members calm him down. After a long discussion, we slip over the side and into the sea. The water is waist deep, so it is tricky unloading all the boxes whilst trying not to get our legs trapped in the large rocks beneath us.

Cecil stays in his panga filming Cabeza until everything is unloaded. Then, bugger me, if he doesn't insist on Pedro driving him right up to the beach so he can step out without getting wet. I can't believe it.

"Listen, you'll have to give the camera to someone else and let them carry it ashore. It won't get wet if you lift it above your head," I tell him reasonably.

Cabeza is upset by this. Standing on shore he shouts at me loudly. "The camera is too valuable to get wet. Get the panga closer."

"Look, I will help Cecil but he will still have to get into the water and walk ashore. If you are so worried about it, you should leave Cecil and the camera onboard the Searcher." This pushes a button that changes his whole persona. His piggy little eyes almost fall out of their sockets. His faced instantly turns crimson. "Aschlock shiese Englander! Get the boat in closer," he screams at me, along with a mouth full of what I presume to be expletives in German. This is absolutely the wrong thing for him to do. It's a long time since I've allowed anybody to scream at me and get away with it.

Bounding through the water, I scramble over the rocks towards him in a rage. There is nowhere for him to run as I approach, so he takes a swing at me. *Fuck me rigid.* He misses, then puts his right arm out to ward me off but I grab his outstretched hand in both mine and twist to the right, at the same time bending up sharply at the wrist, forcing his hand backwards towards the inside of his forearm. The swift movement causes him to scream and turn his body away from me. As he turns, I kick his legs from under him, letting go of his hand at the last minute. Landing flat on his chest he screams in pain. I wait for him to get up, but he lies there with the wind knocked out of him looking totally shocked. Kneeling on his back I grab him by the hair with my left hand. With my right thumb I apply pressure to the belly of his trapezius muscle, eliciting another scream. Fearful of snapping his head back too hard I whisper in his ear, "don't ever, ever, shout at me again. Do you understand?"

Before I am tempted to damage him, I let go of his hair and shove his face down, standing back to watch as he retches and gasps for breath. The police rush over to me, and grab my arms.

"Tranquillo Capitan."

"It's ok," l tell them calmly.

If they don't let go of my arms there is no telling what will happen next. This whole thing might be all over here and now.

Luckily, they both let go and everyone breathes a sigh of relief, except Cabeza who thinks I am going to twat him again. His face is as white as a nun's arse. Glaring at me he rubs his wrists and neck at the same time. Staring fiercely back at him I tell him slowly, "There are two ways to do this my friend. You can keep your comments about me to yourself and we can carry on as if nothing happened, or you can keep being a prick and I'll kick your arse and take you back to the boat right now. It's up to you."

With eyes of fire he mutters, "I will tell Jimmy about this. You can't treat me like this. You assaulted me. I have witnesses here. I will have you fired."

"Okay, get back in the fucking boat, this trip is cancelled."

What the hell am I doing?

"You cannot do that! I have paid for this trip," he spits.

"I don't give a shit whether you paid or not. If I make a judgment that something is unsafe, you'll just have to fucking well live with it, and if you want to shout abuse at someone, you can do it to some fucker back in Europe. You will not shout at me again, because if you do, I will seriously hurt you – do you understand?" I am standing on dodgy ground but I have to try and bluff my way out.

"Wait, stop it you two. This is crazy. Fighting? - for what? This is all Shiese. You must stop. Let's get on with this thing, without fighting." This comes from Günter. He speaks rapidly to Cabeza in German, and I understand him saying he can fight or he can report me after we get back to port, if that's what he wants, but this expedition is too important to sabotage.

Standing up slowly, Cabeza holds his wrist. Looking around sheepishly, he brushes himself off. I wonder what the hell has gotten into me. The group is suddenly deathly silent. I could chop the tension with an axe.

I have no idea what he is going to do next but I wonder again why I let my temper get the better of me, even though no fucker shouts at me and gets away with it.

Julia walks over to me, looking at me strangely but I ignore her and stare at Cabeza waiting for his next move.

"Okay, let's go," he says slowly, breaking the silence and the mood.

Walking past me he avoids eye contact and joins the rest of the group by the slope. One of the cops slaps me on the back, "Usted debe ser a Capitan cuidadosa. Estancia sereno. Ok?"

"Ok lamento, pero El Cabeza esta' tocado." They laugh at that, and it eases the tension between us.

We are at the bottom of an overgrown, steeply rising gully that I have been longing to carve through since first coming to the island. I think we are going up through the gully. From the position Cabeza showed me on the chart, I thought this was where the cave is, but he directs us to a take a path to the right, up a steeply sloping hill. I am astounded. I naturally assumed we would take the route up the ravine but he completely ignores it, as though it isn't here. The direction he leads us is way off to the right.

Looking at the island from the sea gives no indication of how difficult it is to negotiate the rugged terrain. Even though there has been very little rain lately it is still surprisingly slippery. There are very few flat surfaces anywhere on the island, and the path we take is steep. We climb up a narrow winding gulley, over jagged, earthen-covered-rocks, squeeze between trees and hack through patches of tall razor-grass, brambles and thick, sharp ferns – much to the disgust of the park officials. Some sections almost require basic mountaineering skills. Poor old Orlando and Joachim struggle to keep up and are way behind as we climb steadily higher. Orlando suffers the worst, having to sit and rest frequently on the trail. Progressing slowly, slapping away the bugs, I think about my stupid outburst on the shore. What was I thinking? Of course, once more I wasn't thinking at all. My reaction was bad. And to do it in front of the police was completely idiotic – I may have just lost my potential buddies. It wouldn't be so bad if they weren't there as witnesses. Orlando and

Joachim may even thank me for it later. I try to put it out of my mind. There is no point dwelling on it.

We have to climb at the pace of the park guys, which is very slow. They call for frequent halts. They are supervising and it is their call. As we climb, each of us covers the person below with showers of earth, small rocks, and dastardly ants that crawl everywhere. The ants bite every bit of exposed skin at every opportunity. It doesn't help that they bite in places that have already been sliced by the tall, sharp blades of grass. The bloody ants and other unseen creepy crawlies nibble away at us constantly – *I hate bugs*.

After negotiating the first part of the escarpment, we are forced to cut our way through thick vines with machetes, and then climb up another steep zigzagging slope, this time using saplings and roots to pull our way up. We pull clumps of grass and small roots out by the handful. Having so much equipment makes it doubly difficult for us, but the older guys are really struggling to keep up. Fallen trees of all sizes litter the slopes and have to be climbed over with care, in case they slide down and injure someone below – I make sure I am not below Cabeza. Orlando takes advantage of any rest stop he can – he is suffering badly. The higher we climb, the more bemused I become.

This is a load of old bollocks as far as I'm concerned.

"This is strange isn't it Mac? I would have taken the ravine route," Julia whispers to me. "We are heading way too high. It's no place to hide anything, let alone several boatloads of treasure."

"I was thinking exactly the same thing," I tell her.

We have often discussed possible burial sites between us, and she is on constant lookout for new possibilities. I liked the idea of exploring the ravine, but that is now way below us, over to our left.

I once explored a ravine over by Wafer Bay that had potential, but it took a great effort and too much time to hack through the undergrowth on my own - I was always strapped for time. I suggested a few places for Julia to explore but we haven't got around to exploring the ravine here on our left, because I thought we might be spotted by rangers if we tried. If they sneak up and catch us - which they are quite capable of doing because they all take their jobs so seriously - it might be difficult explaining what we are up to.

Making frequent stops, waiting for Orlando and his mate, the climb takes more than an hour. The air is getting hotter and hotter and more and more humid as we climb higher and deeper into the jungle. Cabeza constantly utters German expletives and complains about 'shiese' this, and 'shiese' that. Of course, it would be much easier without all the equipment we have to carry. The weight of all the food and drink alone would cause a team of Himalayan Sherpa's to give up and go home - there is enough to feed Napoleon's army in those boxes. I tried getting them to cut down on some of the supplies, but they know best. The bags the police are carrying don't look light either – they must be wondering what the hell they have gotten themselves into. Their nice little cruise is turning into the voyage from hell - what with the mad German nerd leading them into God knows what, and a violent, psychopathic skipper ready to kill at the first opportunity. They must be thinking that it's a bit premature bringing their bags on the first excursion. They <u>will</u> need weapons and camping gear if a treasure of inestimable value is found because it will need to be zealously guarded from pilfering persons such as myself. I am betting they wished they had waited another day before bringing their heavy bags on this climb.

Making my way up, thinking about the folly of the trail we are taking, I convince myself it is utterly crazy. Unless there is a cave up there that has at some time been open and visible from the sea, I can't imagine anyone wanting to put themselves to so much trouble. And with such a heavy cargo and so little time, the pirates would have had a problem carrying it all this way up the side of such a steep hill. It's hard enough for us - and our load is light in comparison to what the pirates would have been humping. There is a theory that the treasure might have been winched up with blocks and tackles, but I'm sure it wasn't from this distance – it's not feasible. Reaching the ravine to our left would be much less trouble because it is possible to anchor in the sand further out and still be close enough to run a line into the gully, from where there is a direct line of sight. I keep telling myself these guys know what they are doing. Cabeza must have invested a lot of money to be the one in charge right now. And the boat doesn't come cheap. Then there are all the flights, and the time spent in hotels and who knows what other expenses. Besides, Dietmar has been searching for seventeen years and surely, he knows what he is up to. I sincerely wish Dietmar was here instead of Dickhead Cabeza.

Suddenly out of nowhere we reach a small clearing and I am almost impressed. Although we are ridiculously high up and about thirty meters from the nearest summit, we are still only a short distance inland. A fast-flowing stream winds down the slope to the left of the summit above us, running away to our right and disappearing into the trees. In front of us, behind the stream, an almost sheer vertical grass and fern-covered slope

175

rises up 30feet towards the summit. At the top of this rock wall, just visible under the grass, I see blocks of rock that look man-made. "That could very well be a cave under there", I tell myself.

Over to the left we can almost see the sea through the trees. We lay all the equipment out and wash ourselves in the stream. Then we rest until Cabeza calls his group together. Standing by the stream they discuss the place to start digging. I listen intently. As far as I understand, this section has been tested with the void detecting apparatus by the two operators who apparently showed Cabeza exactly where it is on the map. Then I understand Günter saying he's been to this spot before, but his memory is playing tricks on him. Quiet at first, then becoming more heated by the minute, their deliberations turn into argumentations until I can't understand a bloody thing they are talking about - it makes no sense at all. Gesturing all around they keep saying it isn't the right spot but Cabeza flies into another rage and becomes more and more belligerent until Orlando jumps up and calms things down again.

Once they decide where to start digging there is another problem: Orlando and Joaquin don't want too much earth dug away from the wall. And because none of the crew are really sure of the exact spot they want to dig; it seems to them to be a harsh judgment. They have the idea they can dig away the entire side of the mountain but Orlando is having none of it.

"You must pick your place and dig - one place and nowhere else!" he warns.

There follows a further heated discussion between Orlando and the group, with Cabeza doing most of the talking. He cannot grasp the concept of not having carte blanche to dig willy-nilly wherever he wishes. He is getting more and more pissed off. I think we may see his enormous head erupt at any minute.

"But there are many millions of dollars under here! We must dig where we can." he shouts.

"Yah. It is not possible just to dig in one place. Look at it. It's crazy, we must dig it all away," joined Günter.

"We cannot destroy this island. Maybe there is nothing here. Then we make a catastrophe for nothing." Orlando is obviously not an optimist.

"Shiesse," shouts Cabeza.

I thought they knew exactly where they were going to dig but they really have no idea. They are only allowed to dig in one place. This whole thing is going to pot. I see it being a big bloody disaster. This will probably not take long at all. To me it is very simple: either they find the treasure here or they won't find it at all. They have no alternative. There is one hell of a wall of dirt in front of us though.

Pacing backwards and forwards in front of the wall and measuring lengths and breadths and heights, and uttering lots of profanities they decide on the place to start. *So much for German efficiency!* Orlando informs us that the earth has to be piled up neatly so we can replace it in the exact same spot it came from once we are done. From the time of my confrontation with Cabeza I've had the feeling things will go downhill rapidly. And they are.

We dig for two slow fruitless hours. The mood has gone from extreme excitement during our pre-landing to high tension during the actual landing, to sheer exasperation, to the beginnings of somber dejection. The knotted grass makes digging difficult, especially since Orlando forbids the use of pickaxes because of the possibility of damaging the rocks. He must be plagued by nightmares about expeditions that came before his time, when treasure hunters used copious amounts of explosives to achieve their goals, blasting away at anything that stood still long enough.

I could shift all that dirt and rock for them in no time; and blow a bloody big hole in the wall to boot, with a little touch of the magic stuff. I could even make some for them, if they ask me nicely. As it is, we take turns laboriously digging away in the heat and humidity, with an army of insects nibbling on exposed body parts that were previously covered in insect repellant that has since become washed off by our continuous outpourings of perspiration. Neither Orlando or Joachim, nor the cops join us in digging. They are quite content to sit on a blanket under a tree watching but not really enjoying, the sight of us mad bastards carving up the island. Orlando and Cabeza's faces are as red as beetroot and both look due for coronaries. As the heat and humidity continues to rise, we continue to melt.

I notice the hunters disappearing into the brush to our left during frequent breaks, which I think are potty breaks until three of them go off together. Since none of them speak to me anymore I can't be bothered asking what is so interesting over there.

I decide to see for myself.

On our next break, Julia and I walk over to the left and along a small gully through the trees. Emerging from the trees, we stand on the edge of a cliff with a sheer drop of about fifty feet. Below us, we see the top of the ravine with the overgrown foliage – the spot we both thought was such a good place to search. The ravine leads up to a small plateau with a lonely fig tree sprouting long roots pointing in every direction, including up. Above the plateau to the right, a wall of rock rises up to another ridge on our right side, where a huge boulder sits, bridging a small gully sloping gently backwards into a thick canopy of trees. "Wow, what a great view, if it wasn't for the bugs, I might consider having sex with you right here on the edge of the cliff," Julia says in my ear.

"At least that would make this crazy climb worthwhile," I reply.

"What madness this is. All the time and money they have spent to arrive at this spot. You would think they know what they are doing."

"That plateau down there looks like the perfect spot for a cave, why aren't we down there?"

"I'm buggered if I know girl."

We hold hands and silently take in the view a while longer before wandering back to the dig.

By the time the digging stops at four o'clock, we have barely scratched the surface of the wall. With only a fraction of the rock face exposed and not a single sign of a cave or its entrance evident, I look at the pile of earth and rock we have removed, not believing we'd made such a small dent in the wall – how is that possible?

"We need to return to the boat before sunset or we will be eaten alive by a million things that come out at night," I tell the group. "Also, the climb down will be dangerous in the dark."

As it is, the trip back is accomplished in a fraction of the time it took to climb up - partly because we leave most of the equipment behind us. We make it back onboard in time for a sundowner on the top deck.

Julia and I sit alone, discussing the events of the day. Cabeza is still not talking to me – he made a bee-line for the boss when we got back onboard. I didn't hear what he had to say then, but he is now whining about lack of progress and the amount of money this has cost him. The other members of the group sit around looking as if they have been sucking lemons all day.

If they can't take a joke they shouldn't have joined.

"We must make an earlier start tomorrow," Cabeza tells Orlando.

"You will have to wait until I am ready, "replies Orlando.

"Shiesse."

Cabeza comes straight over to me. "Tell Pedro to take me and Günter over to the island early; I won't start digging until Orlando arrives."

"Fuck off. You'll have to wait for Orlando, just like he says."

He glares at me, but fuck him, I am already off his Christmas card list and there are only two days left before we depart back to the mainland - although I don't really look forward to that either.

I wonder what is happening back there. I am still curious about the two mysterious callers in the early hours. Why didn't they come back in the morning? Were they cautious in case the police turned up at the dock again? Do the police still want to talk to me? I hope the bash I gave to the side of Macho's head didn't leave a bruise. And I hope they haven't found Flora - that really will suck. And while I'm hoping, I hope these guys don't find any treasure.

After dinner, Jimmy takes me aside. "What happened this morning Mac.?" I give him my version. Yeah Herman is an asshole but I'm surprised you lost your temper. You should hold it in; it isn't good for business."

Nor is it when your captain is a murderer, I think, looking straight through him.

Later that night Pedro and Arcelio approach me in the wheelhouse. "Cappy, Mr. Herman, he offer us money to take him to the island early in the morning," says Arcelio.

"He did what? I hope you said no."

"Si senor, we tell him it is not possible without we ask you first."

"Well thanks for telling me but we cannot do it. Go and tell him to fuck off if he asks again." Arcelio is completely shocked but I don't really give a fuck.

I already stepped over the line before the trip began; and now I have assaulted a guest. What the hell am I doing?

In bed I am too preoccupied to have sex with Julia, even though she makes it crystal clear she wants it. Even thinking of Queen and country I can't muster one good enough to get the job done.

Julia is far from impressed.

What is happening to me?

Chapter 17
The 'Cave'

"How much more grievous are the consequences of anger than the causes of it."
Marcus Aurelius

THE PILE OF DIRT IS ENORMOUS.
The rock face is now completely uncovered and a wide section of flat, solid rock in front of the wall appears like a giant cave door.

This is it!

Cecil, Thomas and Cabeza are on one side, and Günter, Julia and I are on the other, all pulling on the huge pry bars wedged into the gaps on each side of the rock door.

Nothing budges.

We try again – nothing. We make several more attempts to loosen the huge rock door without a result. Cabeza rallies the troops and reminds us what is at stake. Our next effort is almost superhuman. The huge rock teeters slightly then topples away from the wall, crashing down onto its face, uncovering a gaping hole in the side of the hill.

A dank smell escapes from inside the dark hole. Gathering together in a row we peer inside. Orlando and Juan look shell-shocked.

It is difficult judging the size of the interior until Cabeza appears behind us with a flashlight. Standing at the entrance, he shines the light inside. With my shovel I sweep away a curtain of cobwebs at the entrance.

"I will go first," says Cabeza, "I paid a lot of money for this."

"Okay," whispers Orlando. He is so completely stunned he wouldn't go in first if he were offered directorship of all the national parks in the world.

Cabeza slowly disappears into the void followed closely by Günter.

"Oh, mien Gott. Dis is super. Oh mien Gott." Cabeza's high-pitched voice echoes eerily from inside the cave.

"Kom! Look!" cries Günter.

We all rush to join him inside.

The first thing I notice is the skeleton with its armored breastplate and conquistador style helmet – just like in the dream I had in San Jose.

Then I see the statue.

It is the Virgin with child, and even after nearly two hundred years the glow of her golden patina is astonishing. Reflections from Cabeza's flashlight bath us all in the Virgin's golden sheen. In the darkness her golden rays reach every corner of the cave. I move closer to the life size statue – and discover that it really is encrusted with jewels. I touch it in awe, feeling the cool, smooth, precious-metal with my palm. Piles of golden trinkets are stacked everywhere. Kneeling down in the dirt to examine the contents of a rotten wooden box, I am suddenly shaken rigid by two simultaneous explosions echoing through the cave. The explosions hurt my ears and scare the crap out of me.

I think it is a booby trap.

Another explosion comes from behind me. I spin around just in time to see Cabeza's huge head disappear from his body. His headless trunk stands there for a split second, blood pumping from its neck, before it slumps into a crumpled heap on the earthen floor. I notice the once golden statue is now red with blood. My head reels. Turning swiftly to face the door, I see the cops, our former friendly protectors, silhouetted by the sun in the entrance. They are blasting away at us with shotguns. Trapped inside the cave under a hail of ferocious gunfire I watch our small group expire one by one. I see deadly patterns of lead shot ripping great chunks of flesh from bodies inside the cave. Kneeling in a trance, bathed in a bloody red haze, I am terrified and fascinated. Regaining my presence of mind, I fling myself down into the dirt.

Lying there completely frozen I am totally defenseless against the two cops with their shotguns. I wonder why I haven't yet been hit. Very soon one of those blasts will put an end to all my happy years of shagging. I want to stand up and confront them but I think that maybe I deserve to be terminated for my sins. But maybe they will leave me for dead if I can just stay still long enough. I am covered in warm sticky blood.

The shooting stops as suddenly as it began. I try closing my eyes but somehow, they won't close.

In the sudden silence I am aware that I have stopped breathing. I see Julia falling on top of me and everything starts going black. As her body presses down onto mine I feel wetness in my ear. Is it blood? What the hell is it? I open my eyes and look into Julia's face above me. This is madness.

She is smiling.

She puts her tongue in my ear and I suddenly realize I am in bed in my cabin and the back of her head is moving down to my lower regions. Amazingly, despite the sight of Cabeza's head being blown apart, I have a hard-on.

Bloody Hell! If I don't stop dreaming, I'm going to give myself a bloody heart attack.

Lying in a sweat, I revel in Julia's expert attention. All thoughts of gold, treasure, and mass slaughter recede from my mind. I feel waves of pleasure as Julia's head bobs slowly up and down, taking me to the edge and beyond - towards a different kind of madness.

God Save the Queen.

From that point on the day is real.

At breakfast, I think I will be banned from the day's excursion but Cabeza wants me to dig, so I go along for the ride. The day is pretty much a repeat performance of the previous day but without any confrontation with Cabeza. I dig and sweat and watch Orlando for signs of a heart attack, and try not to listen to Cabeza's constant whining. He carries on like an Aussie forced to give up cricket and beer. Bored with this whole business I wish I'd gone diving for a bit of real excitement instead. But Malesh - I only have to endure this bullshit for a short while longer.

The rock face is about half uncovered by the end of the day and there is still no sign of the fabled rock door. The rock has a curious formation, as if it is manmade, carved out of blocks - but there are two tiny basaltic islets south of the island that have exactly the same solid square block formation. This is a natural feature of volcanic origin and not something built by any human.

Cabeza's rubbery lips pout more and more as the day wears on.

When it is time to pack up and return to the boat, I feel happy about all our efforts being wasted. I am now pretty sure there is no treasure buried in the vicinity of that rock, and don't really give a rat's arse if there is. With only one more day to go, I feel sorry for Dietmar, but the fact that Cabeza has spent his money fruitlessly cheers me up no end.

Back onboard Cabeza speaks to me for only the second time since our altercation on the beach. "We need to stay one more day. Is this possible?" He asks sullenly.

He has already asked Jimmy, who told him to ask me, which must have pissed Cabeza off no end. Once we get back to port there is a lot of preparation to do for the next trip so I tell Cabeza I will let him know the answer the following day. I will have to call the office on the single sideband radio, or get the rangers to call their office to relay the message by phone to Mano in Punta La Pesca. Even though I have no inclination to help him personally, his request appeals to me. On our return we will be in and out of port in half a day.

The less time I spend in port the better.

Unless the police suspect my direct involvement in the bad bastard Macho's death - for example if Flora reappears or if Maria breaks down under interrogation, I assume they won't take me in for questioning. But the more time I spend in port the more vulnerable I am. Maybe I will do a runner later, but as it is right now, I will stand my ground and deny any accusations coming my way.

After careful consideration I decide to stay at Cocos for the extra day.

In the morning Jimmy decides to go to the island with the group while I stay onboard and contact the office on the radio, to let them know we will be in port a day late - it won't be the first time we've turned the boat around in one day to accommodate guests.

Taking advantage of the relaxed situation onboard, Julia and I swim, sunbathe, and shag, making the most of a gloriously relaxed, fun-filled day. How many more days like this do I have left?

My crewmembers are not so happy.

Carlos and Pedro confront me on the top deck. "Is it true we are staying aqui one more day?" Pedro asks.

"Si Pedro, pero why don't you and the rest of the guys have a beer tonight and relax; I'm buying." I very rarely allow the crew to drink alcohol on the boat but I feel like giving them a break.

When the team arrives back onboard at the end of the day, I know by the looks on their faces that it was another unsuccessful excursion. The extra day they have tomorrow only gives them time to cover up the mess they made of the hillside.

In the morning Orlando doesn't feel too good, and because I am the medic, I stay onboard to keep an eye on him in case he has a funny turn. I don't want to go traipsing back up to the 'cave' anyway. I am well over it.

I hope it will rain and cause them to abandon their efforts, but it doesn't; it remains dry - so dry that the waterfall in Chatham Bay almost disappears. During the five years I have been coming here, I have never seen it like this before – it always flows fast. El Nino has to end soon; if it doesn't, Cocos might become a desert island.

After lunch I go off for a dive with Jimmy and Julia, but to my disappointment there are still no big schools of hammerheads to be seen. We see a few Silky Sharks cruising about, and we swim into the path of a huge Tiger Shark, but he turns and swims off before I have a chance to stab Jimmy with my knife.

I feel so good being underwater again, surrounded by this amazing sea life that I actually look forward to the next trip. I notice that some of the corals are turning white, which is a really bad sign – it means they are dying – but that is the least of my problems.

I expect to see some sorely disappointed faces amongst the team when they arrive back onboard later that afternoon, but they all seem surprisingly up-beat.

Once the pangas are lifted on deck and all the equipment is packed up and stowed away, I say a sad farewell to Julia. I like her even more after the past couple of days, and really look forward to seeing her again in a couple more days, providing I'm not stuck in the calaboose.

I'm not surprised by the buoyant spirits of the two park chiefs and two cops as we leave the island, but I am surprised by the mood of the hunters. Orlando and Joachim are relieved that the whereabouts of the island's treasure remains a mystery, despite what it would do for the country's economy. The police are also relieved because they don't have the responsibility of guarding the country's new found wealth. Inexplicably, the hunters seem upbeat about the whole thing.

Orlando joins me in the wheelhouse during my watch. "I will never allow those treasure hunters back after the damage they have done to the island. They left a really big mess up there. Joachim fell asleep during the day and the team pulled a big part of the wall down and didn't put it back properly. You know the government is considering a blanket ban on all treasure hunting trips in the future, and after I report back, they will put it into law pretty swiftly." He treats the island as his own private property and takes it as a personal affront when anyone "desecrates the holy ground" - as he put it. Well good for him.

"Bravo Orlando."

Although I am happy no treasure has been found, I am unenthusiastic about returning to Punta La Pesca.

The police are friendly to me on the way back, realizing I am making certain they have everything they need and are treated as special guests. After spending all this time with Cabeza they are sick of him too.

Jimmy spends more time than I like in the wheelhouse with me, discussing the running of the boat, the behavior of the crew and the way El Nino might affect future bookings.

"So, what about a pay raise Jimmy?"

"Times are tough and we have to go to Panama for dry-docking again, and that will be expensive. You know you should try and calm down a bit with the guests."

"Calm down? What do you fucking mean, calm down, you little cunt?" I shout at him *in my head.*

What I actually say is: "Yeah, right."

He doesn't ask if I need any time off though - *the little wanker.* The last time we speak together he looks more uncomfortable than ever; as if he wants to say something but can't quite muster up the right words. Looking at his gold Rolex reminds me of what a little prick he is.

I manage to avoid Cabeza for most of the trip back - eating in the wheel-house, whenever I can, and not spending any time in the main salon. My only conversation with Cabeza, since our spat at the island, was the one where he asked to stay for the extra day, but his presence still drives me nuts. If I could just kill one more person, please let it be him.

The atmosphere amongst the hunters is now suitably depressing. Willy excels himself, consuming a record number of beers and passing out for a whole day in the salon.

Joachim tells me again about the mess the hunters made. Apparently, it is really bad at the dig site. They trashed the hillside and were unable to get everything back in place. I nod sympathetically, not really giving a shit. What does it have to do with me? And why should it affect my life?

Arriving back in port at eight in the morning, two days after leaving Cocos, I really don't give a shit about anything except what will happen in the next few hours.

Rather than anchor on the seaward side of the peninsula in the early hours of the morning waiting for high tide, as I normally do, I reduce speed and time our arrival at exactly high tide.

The weather is changing - it is cooler and the sky is thick with clouds. The brilliant red sunrise is a sign of bad weather to come.

I approach the dock tensely and anxiously, but to my huge relief, only Mano and the two maintenance guys are there waiting for us. The hunters are champing at the bit to get off the boat and back to San Jose and I am just as eager to see them all leave.

We have twelve hours to get the boat ready for the next trip. Luckily there are no bills to sort out this time, because all the drinks were complimentary and we haven't sold any T-shirts. There is also no tip, which doesn't really surprise me but pisses the crew off no end.

Malesh.

I think about doing a runner while I can. I don't really give a flying fuck about anything anymore - until Mano tells me my passport still hasn't come back from immigration.

Chapter 18
You Always Hurt the One You Love

"The enemy is anybody who's going to get you killed, no matter which side he's on."
Joseph Heller, Catch 22

MY STOMACH IS in knots again.

Once everything is secure and the engines are off, I walk over to Mano on the dock. I am seriously anxious to hear the latest developments in the 'bad bastard affair.'

Fortunately, Mano is keen to impart his inside knowledge.

"Holy shit Mac, by the looks on the faces of these guys it looks like you didn't find no treasure," he says with an extra wide, tobacco-stained grin.

"Yeah complete waste of fucking time Mano. Que pasa?"

"Well boss, everything is ready for you. I got you full oxygen tanks, and the gasoline tanks are ready for you. All the rest of the supplies should be here at nine o'clock pronto. You didn't order diesel. I guess you must have enough for this trip. What about laundry? Do you have enough clean sheets on the boat?"

"Yeah, we have lots to spare. We've got just enough diesel in the tanks for this trip, but we'll need a full load when we get back. I don't like getting this low on fuel but we'll manage. There are plenty of clean sheets on the boat. During this trip I'll get the guys onboard to launder the ones Juanita changes today. I still have plenty of gasoline. We didn't use the pangas much so I just need a few gallons to top up the onboard tanks. Did the office say what time the guests are arriving? I don't want them hanging around while we get the boat ready."

"They should be here around seven thirty tonight. What time do you want to leave?"

"I guess I'll leave at around eight thirty. There should be enough water under the boat by then. Have you seen Claus; is he up yet?"

"Si, I saw him earlier with another 'novia'."

"He's such a dog."

"He sure is boss, worse than you! Oh, by the way the police found that girl they were looking for, the one you had onboard last time."

My blood runs cold.

"Yeah, it's terrible. Esta muerta boss."

"Oh Jasus." I am truly stunned, and I have to say I am also truly relieved.

"Yeah, I'm sorry boss; they say that bastardo Macho killed her, and now they think her boyfriend killed Macho." This is really good news. The heat could be off me.

"And you know what? I just heard they picked up your friend, the big gringo."

"What?" *Holy shit!* My rapid relief turns instantly into deep anguish.

"Yeah... you know that Yankee that was here when you came back from the Caribbean - he's in jail. He was at Macho's place around the time he was killed."

"You mean Al?"

"Yeah, that's him."

"When did they pick him up?"

"I don't know for sure, maybe yesterday."

"What did he have to do with Macho?"

"Well boss, he is involved in the drug business."

"That's bullshit."

"Hey, I don't know nothing. But how come he has that big focking house and he never works? How can he afford to live without working?"

I don't feel like explaining to him that Al has family money and a successful business behind him in the States.

"How did you hear all this Mano?"

"I have my sources boss, you know that," he says proudly.

"What else have you heard?"

"I heard the police found a lot of guns at his place. You know he always carries a focking gun, right?"

Fucking hell.

"Anything else?"

"Not much, but the shit is flying here. A lot of people been picked up by the police lately."

"Has anybody been asking after me, Mano?"

"What, the police?"

"No, anyone else?"

"Like who?"

"Like Maria?"

"No. Nobody boss, looks like she don't love you no more." He smiles at that too.

This is both good and bad news; at least the cops haven't been around, nor the two 'night prowlers'. But I am deeply shocked about Al being picked up - that is bad news in the extreme. I hope he can talk his way out of it; I always said Al could talk his way out of a concrete block and that's just where he is right now. My, my; this is not good.

"Okay Mano, I'll be on the boat if you need me. Tell Claus to come over if you see him."

"Okay boss. By the way, the weather is changing. We're gonna get rain at last, maybe a storm headed our way, looks like the focking El Nino is on his way out."

"About time too. I can handle the shitty weather as long as the diving is good. Maybe the diving will be better this trip. Can you get me a proper forecast?"

"Sure can boss; leave it to me. Oh, the National Park guys came with their new generator yesterday. They said they spoke to you about taking it to the island for them. It's big."

"How big?"

"Focking huge boss."

"Where is it?"

"They will be back with it today. They couldn't get it off the truck without a crane yesterday."

"Okay. I don't think it will be a problem, as long as they can transport it in on their panga once we get to Cocos. I'll load it onboard for them as soon as they get here."

"Okay, you're the boss."

"See you later."

Just as the bus arrives to pick up the group, I'm surprised to see Claus in the *Searcher's* salon, in deep, animated conversation with Cabeza and a bleary-eyed Günter. They are speaking in German but the conversation stops abruptly as I get close. I greet Claus and tell everyone else the bus is on the dock ready to leave as soon as they are ready. They don't take long to get their gear together; they leave all their tools on the dock, for us to put in our bodega ashore. Mano will probably end up selling them because after my conversations with Orlando and Joachim I seriously doubt the hunters will ever use them again – at least not at Cocos.

When they are gone, I motion Claus up to the wheelhouse.

"Claus, what's happening?"

"Hey man what did you do to upset Herman?"

"He's a fucking weasel. What was all the talk in the salon? You looked like you didn't want me to hear what was going on."

"Of course not, you asshole. He sure is pissed at you, man."

"Well fuck him. What's happening?"

"You heard the news about the girl and the gringo?"

"Yeah, looks like the shit really hit the fan. Have you seen Maria lately?"

"No, I haven't seen her. She finished working in the Royale."

"I'm not surprised. What else has been happening around town, any more murders?"

"Not since you were gone buddy," he smiles.

"What's that supposed to fucking mean?" I smile back.

"Nothing Mac. It just seems kind of peaceful around here when you are away."

"Yeah right; so what's really happening?" I know Claus is dying to tell me the latest news.

"The police are looking for Flora's boyfriend. I heard a rumor that the gringo killed him after they both killed Macho. There is also a rumor that Maria had something to do with it."

"Rumors, rumors; the town thrives on this kind of shit." This thing is obviously out of control, and now Al and Maria are caught right in the middle. The problem now is: I am very close behind them. If Al talks, I am dead. If Maria talks, I am dead. I'm sorry about Flora but I'm kind of glad that now she can't tell her tale and get me involved.

Have I always been this big of a bastard?

Sometime later, mulling over my predicament and pondering how I might be connected to Al, I have an alarming thought - I hope they don't check his phone records.

I used Claus' mobile phone to call Al last week. Although there is nothing unusual about that, it does connect me to him the day of the murder. My only hope is Jake, my alibi, but he is an older friend of Al's than I am; and at the end of the day, his loyalty is probably with Al. I am teetering on the edge of a precipice about to fall into a very deep and dark hole.

I can't wait to get out of town.

Roberto the dive master arrives at around ten o'clock, wanting to chat about his nice vacation week and how many girls he's bedded, but I'm too busy, and not the slightest bit interested, because the truck has arrived with the rangers' generator. Mano didn't exaggerate – it is a big heavy bastard. I use the crane to load it onto the aft deck, along with the rest of the rangers' supplies. After making sure the generator is lashed down properly, I spend the rest of the day in a state of nervous apprehension, expecting a visit from a SWAT team at any moment.

In the late afternoon a Mackerel sky appears over town, the white puffy clouds mimicking the pattern on a mackerel's back. Never long wet, never long dry – we are in for a beautiful sunset and rain later.

At six o'clock, when Maria calls on the phone, I am wound tighter than a piano wire. Her voice is weak and shaky.

"Mac, le tengo que hablar inmediatamente a usted." She is using formal Spanish - she never speaks to me like that, at least not since my first Spanish lesson.

"What's up mi amor?"

"Yo gustaria usted viene inmediatamente mi apartamento." It doesn't sound right.

"Why? I'm waiting to meet my guests and I have to leave soon. Can't you come here?"

"Usted debe venga ahora capitanee! Si es tan amable." She is crying.

"Who's there with you, the police?" I ask rapidly in English.

"No, por favor venga ahora."

"Okay, but I can't stay for long. I'll be there shortly." The phone goes dead.

This is too strange. Although it is a major inconvenience, it is a major development and I have to see her. She is my lifeline in this affair. I wonder who is with her.

I will find out soon enough.

I have less than an hour to see her, chat, and get back before the guests arrive. I debate about taking the Glock with me but decide on the Berretta.

Approaching her apartment in the darkness, I wait a few minutes in the street to be sure no one sees me. The last time I was here, Maria said the other apartments in the block were empty. I sincerely hope they still are.

Drawing the Berretta, I creep up to the front door and knock hard, then run full speed around to the back. Thankfully the back door is unlocked. Slowly and silently I open it, easing the door just enough to see inside. I look into the tiny kitchen and through the room divider into the bedroom. Maria sits in a chair by the bed with her back to me, looking in the direction of the front door and the two goons standing beside it. The one with his head poking out the front doorway holds a weapon in his right hand, behind his back. There is no mistaking the extension on the barrel; he has a silencer. His buddy tries hiding beside the window on his right-hand side. I can't see whether he is armed but if they both have guns I should either run away or shoot them both in the back. I open the back door further and walk into the kitchen with my Berretta drawn, sighted on the goon with the gun

"Hey una pistole. ¡No rechazar cerca!" I say menacingly, moving toward them. Of course, they both do what most people would do in that situation: they turn to face me before I have even finished speaking. The gunman by the door isn't quick enough to aim and fire before my weapon spits out three small pieces of screaming hot metal. At least two hit him somewhere in the region of his solar plexus and he doubles over, clutching himself in pain. Luckily his partner isn't armed.

"¡Cagier la pistola!" I shout, moving swiftly into the bedroom.

Maria screams and turns in my direction as the second guy makes a dash for me. What the fuck is he thinking? Seconds later he isn't thinking anything. He is barely an arm's length away from me when I squeeze the trigger again, sending two hot rounds flying from my gun barrel into his face; one round disappears into his right eye, dropping him like a stone. Maria stands up transfixed, as the gunman by the door raises his gun again and fires. The shot hits Maria. I don't see where it goes in, but it comes out through her neck, hitting the wall beside me. Bullets from his weapon whizz beside my head. I duck to the side and fire twice more - this time straight into neck. He screams and drops his gun, before bending over and slumping to the floor. I'm out of ammo. I leap over, stand on his gun hand and kick the front door shut with my other foot. I grab his gun as he starts convulsing. Bending over him I fire two shots in succession straight into his brain. Stepping over him quickly, I do the same to his buddy. Looking at Maria's body I can tell immediately she is dead. Rolling her over gently, I look into her lifeless eyes. There is a large flower-like opening in her neck and a bloodstain where the bullet entered her chest. I am stunned. I fight the urge to shout out, *and* I *almost cry but don't have time.*

What a waste. Why didn't I bring the fucking Glock?

I consider putting the Berretta in Maria's hand, but after my coup de grace on the other two bodies it will be pretty pointless and unbelievable. I leave the scene just as it is. After cleaning my prints off the goon's weapon, I pick up my shell casings and account for them all before cleaning the doorknob and then flying from the rear of the building, slamming the door shut behind me. Reaching the street, I slow to a fast walk. It will be a miracle if nobody saw or heard anything during that little incident. Everything happened so fast I barely had control over the outcome. Now even more deeply embedded in a world of turmoil, I have just dug my grave a bit deeper. I am shocked and saddened by the idea that I am totally responsible for Maria's death - *me and my bright ideas.*

Hurrying down the street, I turn the corner of the block and bump straight into "Guaro Guapo" and "Marco the Pump". *Fuck me.* Firstly, I can't believe Guapo is walking around at this time of the day sober, and secondly, I can't believe I just bumped into two people who know me, not a hundred yards from the scene of a murder that will have the whole of Costa Rica talking.

"Hey Capitan, que pasa? Donde esta moi rapido? "You want to go for a drink?" *They know I'm always good for a free beer.*

"No es impossible. I have to get back to the boat, we leave very soon."

"OK Buenos noches Capitan. Hasta Luego." They both wave me off with a smile. This is all I need – fucking witnesses. Not just one, but two of the fuckers. Maybe they won't say anything, but then again, I don't know what they will do when they hear the news, which they surely will soon enough. I break into a sweat on my way back to the boat.

When I arrive at the dock, Pedro, Raul and Roberto are doing the last of the cleaning on deck, and although I am sweating like a racehorse, I try not to act suspicious, which in itself probably looks suspicious. I saunter up the gangway and make my way to the wheelhouse with my heart thumping in my mouth. I need a bowel movement. In my cabin I strip off my clothes and sit on the toilet for a few moments in a slight panic. *That poor sweet girl.* I can't believe she is dead. My pulse races and sweat pours off me. I calm myself down with some deep breathing exercises but this isn't a good exercise to perform after having a bowel movement. I turn and dry heave into the washbasin. Standing under the cold shower I take stock of the situation. Fuck! I just turned myself into a serial killer. My life has gone awry in a period of less than two weeks. I really am a dead duck now. Fucking Guapo and Marco showing up like that completely put the shits up me. Did anyone else see me, or hear the shots? It's a good job I didn't take the Glock; that would have alerted the whole town. How the fuck am I going to get out of this mess? There aren't too many gringos around town with my build and looks. Maybe the police will think it is another drug related killing. If I can get away on the boat tonight, I might still have another ten days to try and work things out in my head. Now it really is all about timing.

I hide the Berretta under my bed before dressing, then walk past the galley and make my way to the crew's quarters up forward, calling down for them to get up on deck ready for the guest's arrival.

Waiting on deck, I can't stop sweating. My heart is still in my mouth. I try to stay calm but can't keep my eyes off the dock gateway. I expect flashing lights and sirens and police cars zooming through that gate at any second. I wait for a SWAT team to start manning the surrounding buildings, with snipers placing me in their rifle sights. I don't know if they even have a SWAT team in Punta La Pesca but I am now completely and utterly paranoid.

I wait an eternity for the bus to arrive. When it does, it gives me a jolt. At first, I think it is full of cops. When the passengers start disembarking, I breathe an audible sigh of relief. Rushing everyone onboard, I direct the crew to get the luggage onboard as quickly as possible. I am ready to leave even before the cabins are assigned. Before anyone has a chance to ask a single question, which is a new record, I tell everyone I have to leave right away to make high tide, and will give a briefing as soon as we are out of the estuary. Instructing the crew to cast off the lines, I almost drive off before realizing I haven't seen Molly for a few hours.

There is no way I'm going to leave without her but I can't hang around much longer. We tie the boat back on the dock. I call her name. All the guests look at me as if I am demented. I check the boat again but she's not onboard. Fuck. I shout over to Claus to look in his bodega - a favorite resting place of hers. Two minutes later he walks out of the bodega doorway clutching her in his arms. As soon as she is onboard, I wave farewell to a bewildered Mano, Claus, and a couple of the crew's tearful wives on the dock and before anyone can say "hold that boat" I drive off down the channel.

Talk about timing; it couldn't be any better.

After rounding the point, I look back through binoculars towards the area of Maria's apartment building, trying not to make it obvious I am looking in exactly that direction. It is too dark to see anything, and anyway, I can't see behind the trees lining the promenade. The good news is: I don't see any flashing red and blue lights or hear any sirens, so maybe the bodies haven't yet been discovered. I might be lucky - at least for ten days. Anyway, now I have to put it out of my mind completely and get on with the charter.

As soon as we clear the shallowest part of the gulf, heading towards open sea I put Pedro on the wheel, gather the guests together and then smilingly give them the routine boat briefing. As I speak, I can't help but think about what happened less than an hour ago. These guests have no idea whatsoever that their captain has just slotted two men and is responsible for the death of at least two other people this week: nor do they realize the potential danger they are all now in.

Chapter 19.
The Dive Charter

"It is absurd to divide people into good and bad.
People are either charming or tedious."
Oscar Wilde

WHEN EVERYONE IS gathered in the salon I study the guest's faces; there are twelve in all; four Germans; four Brits; two Americans, and a French couple. I spoke briefly with them all when they came onboard but I can't remember any of their names except for those of two familiar faces.

I used to tell everyone when they first came onboard that I was pleased to meet them, but if they are repeat guests, this greeting upsets them. Nobody likes being forgotten. I've lived with hundreds of people doing this job so maybe it's not surprising that some faces blur into obscurity.

Prior to the guests arriving onboard I am usually armed with information about each; the office sends me completed questionnaires the guests filled out at the time of booking. On paper I know names, addresses, ages, occupations, diving experience, and even their weight. I know if there are repeat guests, but I don't always recall their faces.

The section in the questionnaire about diving experience is interesting, especially the part where they grade themselves as divers from novice to expert. I am always wary of the experts. During the past twenty years I've made thousands of dives, in various roles, in many different locations but still don't have the audacity to call myself an expert.

Some people think they know it all. The two faces I recognize are of that ilk. They have more money than sense, and no sense of humor. On their last trip with me there was another group onboard who wanted to have fun - of all things. The group joked around all day, played cards in the evenings, and drank a few beers, which for some reason pissed off these two twerps. On that trip I put the good group together in Roberto's panga so they could have fun, while I suffered with these two, and the four other miserable buggers they brought with them. One day, Jim, one of the fun groups, joined me in my panga because the other panga left without him. As a joke Jim asked me where we kept our beer because he said there was a bar in the other panga. Everyone in my panga looked horrified because they actually believed there was a bar serving alcohol in the other panga. After the trip they had the temerity to complain to the boss that I didn't stop the fun group from enjoying themselves and. the boss asked why I allowed beer drinking in the pangas before dives! The bastards! They also said the other group made too much noise. They even complained about Molly – *the fuckers*.

Now these two miserable bastards are back.

I look them up on the questionnaire: David and Mari. If these two arrogant toffee-nosed twats cause any problems on this trip, I will shoot them dead.

I don't think I should even be here right now.

At dinner I face the usual barrage of questions and give the usual standard replies. I could just plug in a tape recorder and play it back. I feel weird: detached, as if I'm seated on a big cloud watching everything below me. I wish I were somewhere else. After dinner, sitting alone smoking a cigarette on the top deck, I can't stop my heart racing. What am I doing? *Bollocks!* This is such a mess. When some of the group joins me, I don't listen to a word anyone says; the conversations are a load of mindless twaddle to me.

The wind is picking up. Plastic glasses and cans start rolling off the tables. Everyone disappears below decks but I stay for a while, willing the wind to blow my bad karma away. I think how nice it would be if we were headed towards Panama, where I could just hop off and disappear.

If the shootings had happened yesterday, I would be long gone by now - on my way to some other exotic destination. I should have fled the country alatool, right after slotting Fat Macho.

Why *am* I still here?

Apart from having no passport, maybe it is my arrogance and sheer stupidity. Do I think I am so damn smart I can get away with murder? That *really* makes me a stupid bastard but after the shooting at Maria's I didn't really have time to think.

Well, I am truly screwed now.

The sea is rougher than we've seen it for ages. I spend the midnight watch thinking about the trouble I am in. I can't believe poor Maria expired in front of me like that. She was so nice and so kind. Maybe she *was* misguided, but she was a lovely little woman. I am still stunned by the suddenness of her death. There is no doubt I caused it. I don't even know who the two gorillas were. I assume they were the midnight ramblers - the ones paying the early morning visit to the dock gates. They must have something to do with Macho but I don't know why they were after me, unless it was something to do with the book I took from his safe. Maybe they were just out for revenge. Who knows and who fucking cares? They both got what they deserved.

I'm doubly glad I killed them. I wish I could do it again. In my mind I kill them again but it isn't anywhere near as good as it was the first time - like the very first orgasm.

I've got Molly the cat to stroke but I wish Julia was onboard to take my mind off things.

My main concern now is Big Al. If he talks to the police I am sunk. And Guapo will surely know I just left Maria's apartment when I bumped into him, even with that Guaro fucking up his brain. I shouldn't have gone to her apartment but I did, and now she is dead and there is nothing I can do about it. I toy with the idea of dumping the Berretta overboard but decide to keep hold of it for a while – I might need it. I don't expect a visit from the police out at the island - it will take more than this incident to send the patrol boat out. The police certainly won't go to Cocos on a fishing boat. Anyway, all they have to do is wait until we get back there in ten days.

I am really in the shit.

During my watch I leave the wheelhouse every hour, on the hour, to check the engine room and the national park's bundle of goodies lashed down on the aft deck. I don't want the load thrashing about and causing damage to the boat. When Raul relieves me at four in the morning, I am bright eyed and far from sleep. Back in my cabin I lay in bed with Molly and think about Julia, trying to get my mind off my troubles. The time drags like never before. Night becomes day before I drop off to sleep.

I sleep for only two hours. Bleary eyed, knackered and starving, I wander down for breakfast. The sea is rough. We're rolling around so much only two guests have managed to make it to the dining table; the rest are staying in their cabins. This is very unusual but it's good that the rough sea is keeping everyone in their bunk. I don't feel like talking anyway. After breakfast I move out onto to the aft deck. Dodging the waves washing over the deck, I check the lashings on the generator and fuel drums once more. The generator is covered with a tarpaulin but I am sure it is getting wet underneath. After loading it at the dock I warned the two rangers about covering it properly. If it doesn't work when it eventually lands at Cocos it's their problem, but why am I even concerned about it?

Back inside I check on the galley crew.

"How are you feeling guys? Sea sick?"

"No Cappy. Gracias Dios no mal-de- mar ahora. No too bad." Says Arcelio despite looking pale.

"Did you hear about the girl who was found dead Cappy," he asks, concerned.

I feel uncomfortable. "Yeah that's terrible."

There is an embarrassing silence. "She is the girl you were with no?" asks Ronaldo." I assume he is talking about Flora and not Maria. How would he know about Maria?

"What about that loco gringo drug dealer? You know the girl's novia killed Macho," interrupts Arcelio before I can answer.

"Well he got what he deserved, I guess. I heard bad things about him. Very bad man." Says Ronaldo.

I feel we've already had this conversation but I wonder if they know about Macho's evil predilection for youngsters.

"Si Cappy we hear too much bad things. In Punta La Pesca everybody know everything."

Maybe they do.

Wondering what else they know; I suddenly have the urge to leave the galley.

Back in my cabin, lying in bed with Molly, the rest of the morning passes slowly. I know people in town are questioning my involvement. In the local bar, where I first spoke with Claus about Macho, Claus, bless him, can't keep his mouth shut about anything, so what is he saying there now, about me and Flora? And maybe Al, "the loco gringo," will spill all he knows to the police. Maybe Maria's death and the killing of the two goons will take the heat off him because they only just happened, and he is probably locked up miles away from Punta la Pesca - maybe. Maybe he can explain his extensive armory to the authorities; after all it isn't illegal to have weapons in Costa Rica. Maybe Al can buy an alibi or even buy the alliance of a crooked cop; maybe even the one who allegedly helped Macho stay out of trouble with the law; and maybe they will find out who really killed Flora. And what about her boyfriend, what happened to him? *Bollocks!* There are too many maybes in this tangled web. My brain hurts just thinking about them. I can't believe all that's happened in the last ten days.

At one o'clock I am scheduled to make the usual radio call to the office in San Jose. My daily calls are important: they are the only means of communicating with the mainland from the boat. I usually give the office a synopsis of the crossing, the diving, and the general mood of the punters. More importantly, if I have any problems concerning the safety of the divers, I can contact them for help - although help is at least thirty-two hours away. The radio reception depends on atmospherics and isn't always good, so if I am not able to contact the office, I can ask the rangers to send a message with their radio, on the island, to their own Headquarters in San Jose. The National Park HQ will then telephone someone in our office and relay the message back to me via the ranger's radio, which they keep on all day long. It may seem complicated but it is effective, and it's good to know that if there are any problems, I can contact someone during daylight hours. After dark – forget it, everyone will be in bed. We are totally isolated without the radio, and in my current situation, this is great.

I call in at one o'clock but the reception is so lousy I can't understand a word over the airwaves. After just a few minutes I give it up as a bad job.

Usually the guests use this day of the crossing to get their equipment ready for their first dive the next morning, but the weather isn't conducive to standing up inside the boat, let alone being out on the aft deck. In the late afternoon we hit several squalls that make us bounce around like baboons in a box. Molly sits up in the wheelhouse with her little body moving from side to side in opposition to the movement of the boat – fully gimbaled, she is amazing to watch.

I don't get any shuteye in the afternoon even though I am dead tired. I keep checking on the crew because I don't want them too sick to do their watches. I estimate our time of arrival at the island to be three thirty in the morning – not much sleep forecast for me during the coming night either.

At one point, with the boat tossing around all over the place, I find Pedro stretched out across the wheelhouse floor. He points to his mouth and I think he's been injured but he is just seasick. I kick his arse and send him to bed, finishing the watch myself.

Seasickness might be all in the mind. Although it's a physical sickness, I believe its severity can be controlled. If I ever feel seasick, I won't admit it to anyone. What kind of confidence would the crew and guests have during a trip if their captain is seasick? If the captain lies in his bed sick, who will save all the other poor seasick souls from the inevitability of the ship sinking?

I hate rough seas and anyone who says they like being tossed around on the ocean like a bouncy cork is a wanker. If I ever feel the slightest bit ill, I have to shrug it off. I've seen people wanting to throw themselves overboard once they succumb to the 'Mal de Mar'. Some people want to be off the boat at any cost, and if that means escaping from the lingering pains of a woeful death by drowning - so be it. I feel sorry for these poor people and thankful I'm not one of them.

From experience I know that the best remedy for those suffering from seasickness is sleep. If you can't do that, wear a scopolamine patch behind your ear. These patches release measured doses of medication over a period of three days, and from what I've seen, this is one of the few effective remedies out there. My American guests tell me the patches have become hard to get lately; they say the US Navy bought them all because they are expecting a war somewhere. Who knows? Claus probably started that rumor himself.

By six thirty the few guests who were up had abandoned the main salon. Ronaldo and I visit each cabin to see if anyone wants anything to eat or drink. Eventually I have to send Ronaldo to lie down because he starts turning green too.

Nobody makes it to dinner, which is just as well because Arcelio is completely fucked and Raul has taken over his duties in the galley, and even though he's done his best, the food is a disaster. He makes big lasagna but drops the pan taking it out of the oven. Despite him scraping the lasagna off the floor and trying to tidy it up with a couple of slices of tomato and a sprig of parsley, it looks very un-appetizing. One look at it and the guests will be heaving.

I give it a miss and make myself a cheese sandwich.

Chapter 20
Cocos Island Day 1
The Dive Briefing

"I've learned that people will forget what you said;
people will forget what you did;
but people will never forget how you made them feel."
Maya Angelou

URING THE LONG NIGHT I slow our speed to stop us slamming into the oncoming sea. By the time we arrive at the island it is five in the morning. Carlos returns from the engine room and is trying to hold the binoculars still as he gazes through the bridge windows.

"No Delphinus Cappy?" He asks.

"I haven't seen any." Maybe the absence of a dolphin escort is the first bad omen.

Foolishly, when it started to get rough, I told everyone that once we reached the island we would be in a calm protected bay and everything would be wonderful again. But I am wrong. The swells sweeping into Chatham Bay are huge, causing the boat to rock and roll like Little Richard.

"Oi-Oi-Oi," says Carlos, "Mucha problemas for the pangas and the generador."

If I don't find somewhere calm, unloading both our pangas and the big generator sitting on the aft deck will be a nightmare.

I drive the boat around to Wafer Bay to see if it is any calmer there. As I suspected, because the bay is shallower the swells there are even higher and more confused. The southern end of the island is being pounded by even bigger waves and I only need a quick peak at the eastern side to know it is even worse there. Wafer Bay is three quarters of a mile west of Chatham Bay as the crow flies. But if you don't happen to be a crow it takes at least an hour and a half to trek there, after a long steep hike through tall grass, then up a steep ridge through thick trees, bushes and vines before stumbling down a winding, slippery, uneven hill trail on the other side.

Close to the beach at Wafer Bay, in a small clearing on the very edge of the rainforest stands a wooden building containing a bunkroom, kitchen, and small office that is the headquarters of the half-dozen rangers protecting the island from raiders. To the left of the HQ, a small brick building houses a number of wild pigs captured by the angers during mad-cap hunts. We give all our waste food scraps to them to fatten the pigs for slaughter, providing fresh meat for the ranger's barbecues.

To the right of the ranger's station, the Genio River, one of the island's largest watercourses flows into the sea from a small creek. Behind the creek, across a small wooden bridge constructed by the rangers, a large wooden barn houses an extraordinarily huge collection of fishing paraphernalia worth thousands of dollars - confiscated by rangers from long liners imprudent enough to lay their fishing gear too close to the island. A fifteen-mile, no-fishing zone is implemented and strictly enforced around the island to protect its unbelievably rich sea life.

Sometimes I help the rangers rescue sharks and other large fish caught up on lines inside the prohibited zone. You can't imagine what it's like trying to unhook a big thrashing raspy skinned shark flashing a mouth full of surgical scalpels, whilst trying to convince it you are its friend. It isn't just a matter of cutting the nylon line - sometimes the sharks are so tangled up they have to be untangled manually or they will die. Why bother, you ask? Well, that's what the rangers are like; they want to do the right thing. Sometimes I have to laugh though, watching them carry out their perilous task staring serious injury in the face while I drive the panga for them - which is all the help they get from me on this one.

When I discover floating lines or nets during trips to dives sites in the pangas I have to be careful the fishermen don't find out I've informed on them. I will have a war on my hands pretty damn quick if they do find out; pretty much like the war I'm engaged in now probably.

The two rangers' pangas are moored on long ropes strung between trees overhanging the creek. During low tide the boats rest on the riverbed.

I call the ranger station on the VHF radio, the short-range radio, operated by line of sight, used by all marine craft. The rangers have a tall mast installed at the highest point of Chatham Bay to transmit signals that will otherwise be blocked by the mountains.

"Ola, Victor. Como esta?"

"Ola, Cappy. Todo bien e usted?"

"Todo merde Victor. The weather is crap. It's too rough here in Chatham to unload your generator. You can come and pick up your buddies and your food supplies whenever you want but I can't unload the generator or your fuel yet. Have you seen the size of the swell? It's moi grande. Have you had a weather report on the big radio?"

Mucho juevia aqui Cap. Dos dias mucho rain. Pero, maybe it's better soon."

"How soon?"

"OK... So... Maybe we can collect the generator at midday. Mucho tiempo con no power aqui Cap. We need the generator pronto. I don't want to trouble you, having it on your deck too long. At twelve o'clock we can drive straight into the creek."

"I don't know if it will be calm enough Victor, but we will see."

"Can you come over and help me put out an anchor? I will tie to the mooring but I need to keep the boat heading into the swell so I can unload my pangas safely."

"OK Cap, no problem, I will come over with Jorge."

"Muchas gracias. Hasta luego Victor."

High tide is at eleven thirty. That's why they can drive it straight into the creek. I know they are running a very small portable generator but the big TV satellite dish in Wafer Bay has been idle for months and they haven't seen any decent TV since the last generator broke down. If they miss high tide today, they will have to unload the next day and even though Victor says it will be calmer later today, the swells might be even worse. I can refuse, but it is inconvenient having all that stuff on deck.

Unloading at the regular mooring in Chatham Bay is my only good option.

Driving the boat towards the mooring, I notice something really strange – the waterfall has completely dried up and Victor just told me it rained a lot during the past two days so this does not make sense: the waterfall should be gushing down. In five years, it has never stopped, but I have more pressing problems to worry about than waterfalls.

With the help of the rangers in their small patrol boat I am able to lay a kedge anchor astern, which keeps the Searcher's bow heading into the swells while I unload our own pangas. The launch isn't easy. Before lifting the first panga into the air I shunt the guests out of harm's way. Judging the swells rolling in I hoist the first panga during a slight lull. The crane wire sings as the crew struggle with the ropes trying to stop the heavy boat swinging perilously from side to side. The panga bounces around so dangerously all the onlookers rush inside the main salon. To stop it from swinging wildly out of control I have to drop the second panga onto the deck with a loud booming sound that echoes around the boat, putting the fear of the almighty into the punters sitting in the salon beneath. Anyone still in bed will think a war has just broken out.

Luckily neither panga nor crew members sustain any damage. I decide not to lower the heavy platform on the transom because it is sure to be damaged in the swell. We don't really need it until tonight anyway, by which time the sea will hopefully be a lot calmer. The huge steel platform is slatted with 6" x 4" planks of heavy hardwood. The recreational swimming platform is vital for night dives because without it, it is virtually impossible for the average diver to get back onboard wearing diving gear.

The generator, together with all the other equipment for the ranger station takes up most of the free space on the aft deck, but I don't want to unload it in this weather in case I sink their little boat doing it. Besides, their panga could tip over on the way to shore. After seeing the swells ripping into Wafer Bay earlier, I think it's madness to even attempt taking a boatload of gear ashore there.

After breakfast I gather everyone together in the main salon for the major dive briefing. Surprisingly everyone seems to have recovered from the rough trip and although we are still rolling around, they are itching to get into the water. I have to give a dive briefing before we can do anything further. I switch to auto.

"Okay, I hope you're all back in tip-top shape after the bumpy crossing. I deliberately left the dive briefing until this morning so everything will be completely fresh in your minds." I look around to see if everyone is paying attention.

"I couldn't have done it sooner anyway, with that atrocious weather we had. How many of you thought you were going to die?" *No one put a hand up.* "This won't take long, but it may be the most important dive briefing you'll ever get so please digest everything I tell you – your lives depend on it." *This is absolutely true.*

"I want you to think about the passage we just made from Punta La Pesca. It takes about thirty-two hours to get here when the weather is calm. As you all now know, it's a hell of a long way from the mainland. Think about that. Think about it and remember that if you decide not to follow any of the dive plans or if you get yourself into difficulty and have a decompression problem - it will be a very, very, long time before we can get help from another source. The closest recompression facilities are in Panama - five hundred miles away. No helicopter has the range to fly out here and back, and no fixed wing aircraft can land on the island. Seaplanes can only land on the waters of Chatham Bay in extremely calm weather, so we are completely on our own - isolated from the civilized world except by radio contact. We have tons of oxygen onboard for the primary treatment of decompression problems, but that's not the situation we want to be in. Think of this and remember it well - if any one of you has a decompression problem we will have to head back to the mainland. This means the trip will be over for everyone." *I do not want to have to go back to Punta La Pesca prematurely before I have a plan formulated in my brain.* I've been running this boat for five years now and haven't had one single incident. We haven't lost anybody or had a decompression problem during that time and we won't have any problems if you follow the rules. We haven't made safety rules just for the sake of having rules. Rules are vital to your safety out here so I suggest you remember where you are at all times.

I strongly suggest that everyone use a dive computer; if you don't have one, the boat can rent you one for a nominal fee. When you use your computer, you must follow the profile and pay particular attention to your ascent rate. It's been known for some time that a slower ascent rate and a safety stop at ten to fifteen feet, that's three to five meters, for three minutes or more is highly beneficial to the diver. The computer's algorithms are based on a relatively slow ascent rate – slower than the rate of one foot per second, which you may have been taught when you did your course. An alarm will sound on your computer if you exceed that rate; so please pay attention to it and you will all be going home safely.

We will be making two dives in the mornings. The first dive is around eight o'clock after breakfast, and the second at around ten thirty. The first two dives will be the deepest of the day, and the afternoon dive will usually take place in a relatively shallow area. This ensures that you off-gas sufficiently to allow you to reach the deepest allowable depth the following morning, and are able to spend the maximum time allowable there. There will also be a night dive available each night, but for safety reasons these are all done at the mooring wherever we happen to be that night. The night-dives aren't compulsory, but the day dives are." I stop and smile to gauge their reaction and to see if they are all still paying attention.

"Each day I'll move the boat to a different location around the island, where I will moor or anchor in the sand - we're ecologically sound here. From there we will use the pangas to transport us to the dive site of choice, which is totally dependent on the weather. We will probably be returning to Chatham Bay for the night now that the weather seems to have changed for the worse. But don't despair over the weather because it could mean that Hammerhead sightings will go up drastically." This brings a lot of smiles.

"Early each morning I will take a panga out to check the conditions around the other side of the island. Believe me, sometimes it may look great here but as soon as we poke our noses out around the corner they might get blown off. If I say it's too rough to venture out and dive in any particular area, it is because it IS too rough. My primary concern is for the safety of all divers."

There are times when I've been out in the panga in the morning to check on conditions around the corner, and then arrived back at the Searcher dripping wet and covered in salt spray. I've reported to the guests that it is too rough to dive in the designated spot for the day and then been called a virtual liar by some arsehole who thinks I am trying to rip them off for that particular dive. If that happens more than once with a group, I have to waste time taking the Searcher out just to prove that I am telling the truth. *The fuckers!*

"You all have designated dive-gear lockers, and each of you has a dive cylinder marked with your name on a piece of tape. The lockers on the port side have tanks with yellow tape and the ones on the starboard side have blue tape. These are the designated teams, which will be in separate boats. Once you have all your equipment together the crew will pass down everything you need into the respective pangas.

Arcelio will be driving the yellow panga, which is on the port side with me as guide, and Pedro will be driving the blue panga, which is on the starboard side with Roberto as guide.

You will be responsible for putting your auxiliary equipment into the pangas: fins, weight belts, masks, snorkels, dive computers and cameras if you have them. The crew will pass these items down into the pangas for you if you want, but it's up to you to make sure you have them when we reach the dive site. Some of the sites are a long ride away, so you will be buying a round of drinks for everyone onboard your panga if you forget anything and we have to return to the boat to collect it. We have spare sets of masks and fins in the pangas but it's best to check that you have everything before we leave. When we get back onboard here after the dive, the tanks will be filled in the pangas, using the extra-long filling hoses extending from the deck on each side of the boat; so, you don't have to carry your tank at all, it stays in the panga. We might start to see some rain now so your gear will get a good rinse off from it. The only time you need to touch your tank is when you put it on or take it off after the dive."

There is a mass look of wondrous adoration at this last remark.

"I will give you all a full dive briefing before each dive and hopefully tell you everything you need to know about the dive site: the topography, the current strength and its direction. I will also tell you what kind of corals, fish and pelagics you can expect to see there and where best to see them, and I'll give you a dive profile - which I very strongly suggest you all follow. Roberto will be diving every dive and I will make all of the morning dives and some of the afternoon ones. Occasionally I will have to take care of routine jobs onboard (like having a siesta or a shag; but I don't say that). Every diving excursion will be prefaced by a thorough briefing. I can even suggest what lens to put on your camera and I can tell you right now that you should never put a macro lens on for the morning dives." This brings a big chuckle from the photographers because the macro lens is only good for small close up stuff.

"Nobody in their right mind will want to shoot a close up of a barnacle when there are serious numbers of sharks flying about all over the place just behind you. There may be a swell on the morning dive sites too, so you may be bobbing around a bit under the water.

Once at the dive site, the guides - either Roberto or me - will check again on the direction and strength of the current. Sometimes I can look at a dive site from a distance and tell you how the current is likely to be there; like at Manuelita Island over there where we are making our first dive today. Usually I can see from the lines the current is making off the end of the island what its direction and strength is, but at some sites this is not so easy. At these sites it is usually critical to jump in at the right spot or you will go zooming off into the blue and have to be picked up and re-deposited. Today the swells are pretty big so it is much more difficult to spot a diver on the surface from the panga, but always remember that whatever happens – if you follow the rules you will be okay.

After we check the current, the drivers will position the pangas for your entry into the water. At a lot of sites, the entry spot is crucial. If you take too long to get yourselves together and don't enter the water sharpish when a strong current is running, you will already have gone past the best point of entry. If that happens, wait for the driver to reposition the panga before you make another attempt at hopping in.

Entrance into the water from the panga is made by executing a simple backward roll holding your regulator and mask in place with one hand, whilst holding your mask strap behind your head with the other. NEVER, EVER, go in until the driver or dive master says it is safe to do so, and even then, make sure you look behind you before you roll in. It really makes your eyes water when someone does a back flip with a heavy dive tank and lands straight on top of your skull. I can stitch up that big hole in your head, and give you an aspirin, but you probably won't be able to dive for a day or two afterwards.

There are only two dive sites where we actually anchor the pangas, so remember that these small boats will be moving with the wind or current while the engines are in neutral, and for obvious reasons we don't want to be running the engines while you jump in.

Once everyone is at the dive site, it is really up to you whether you follow the dive guide or not. So many things happen underwater here that it is virtually impossible to keep the group together, and with the currents running like they do sometimes it's like dropping a handful of marbles on a concrete floor - everyone goes bouncing off in different directions.

Once you are in the water, swim away from the boat immediately and make your descent. If you need the driver to hand you your camera, he will do so - just tell him how you want it passed down to you, and once you have it, swim away from the boat.

When you make your descent, pick your nominal depth and start looking around. Remember to look out into the blue - this is where you are likely to see schools of hammerheads. If the current is very strong it may be necessary to hold on to the rocks, but be careful, the barnacles are very sharp. If you have gloves wear them.

If you are too slow in entering the water and you find that the current has taken you away from the dive site don't panic. Come up to the surface immediately and the panga will pick you up and drop you back in. Photographers, you can do your own thing here. If you lose your buddy and are happy with it stay where you are and carry on photographing whatever takes your fancy. If we carry out the lost buddy routine here at Cocos, we will probably spend more time on the surface of the sea than under it. Nobody will get a bollocking from me if they lose their buddies. I treat each and every one of you as the mature and experienced diver you obviously are, but having said that, this next part is very, very important.

The reason I can say "don't worry about your buddy if you get separated", is because you must all carry out this next procedure – because your life depends on it.

If any one of you sees a school of hammerheads, or a whale shark, or some other such creature, and you decide to swim off and play with it, and then find yourself so far away from the reef that you cannot see it, you must come to the surface. Don't go swimming off looking at your compass saying, "I know it's 240 degrees so I'll just follow the compass". You will swim for ten minutes and you still won't see the reef. You'll then say, "Oh maybe it was 140 degrees", and then after a further ten minutes swimming blindly you will go to the surface and take a compass bearing and you'll see that it really was 240 degrees, but by then the dive site is way off in the distance. It's funny how it's always 240 degrees - I'm doing a thesis on it." *It isn't really.* There are a few blank looks.

"Anyway, after you re-submerge yourself and start kicking away like mad to reach the dive site, following the compass bearing of 240 degrees, you will eventually surface and will be staring at the approaches to the Panama Canal, which is very strange because the compass bearing from Cocos to Panama is 076 degrees. I'm not kidding - the currents here ARE that strong. In fact, you would be very lucky to be staring at Panama - it's more likely that you would be staring at nothing more than the sea and sky.

Remember that even if the compass bearing is correct, the current can sweep you out to sea in no time, and with no point of land as reference, there is no telling how far or fast you are hurtling through the briny. If you lose sight of the reef, come up, give the okay signal with your arms held high, or one hand touching your crown, and wait for the panga drivers, who will be only too happy to drive you back to the dive site, no matter how near or far away you are. It doesn't matter if the panga picks you up a hundred times; it stops the drivers from becoming bored. They will be waiting and watching the moment you go into the water, and they have very good eyes. Another thing you have to consider here is the rain. Whilst you are underwater there may be a sudden squall, which can obliterate the surface visibility down to zero. Remember that if you lose site of the dive site - surface immediately. I can never emphasize this point enough.

You may have noticed that hanging on each tank there is a small mesh bag. Inside each bag is a whistle, a cyalume light stick, and an inflatable safety sausage. These are to be carried with you on every single dive. If you find yourself on the surface, and in the unlikely situation of not being able to catch the attention of the panga driver, blow your whistle and inflate your sausage. If you thrust your sausage into the water, it will stand up proud."

There are lots of titters as I unravel a six foot, elongated plastic red sleeve and give a demonstration.

"The panga may be picking someone else up, so be patient. If you give anything other than the okay signal, like waving your arms rapidly in the air or splashing the water, the driver will come to your aid immediately

The panga WILL always come and pick you up.

If you find yourself drifting off, don't worry. We know in which direction the currents are traveling and we know how long you have been in the water. With this knowledge and a simple mathematical formula i.e. time, times speed, plus direction, we can estimate the position you will likely be in. We haven't lost anyone yet and I don't intend breaking my good safety record on this trip.

Typically, the first dive of the day is to the maximum allowable depth here, which is the industry standard: 130 feet or forty meters. Make that dive the deepest of the day and make each subsequent dive at a shallower depth. Don't be tempted to break that law. If you do, you will find that your residual nitrogen is so high you will be severely restricted on subsequent dives and by the end of the week your computer will not even allow you to step under the shower. After we have been to our maximum depth we spend a lot of time in the intermediate depth range of sixty to eighty feet, because it's a good depth for seeing hammerheads; that's why nitrox is such a boon to us and anyone interested in doing the course can enroll any time today; but more about that later.

I'm hoping that this change in the weather signals the end of El Nino, and the re-appearance of the big hammerhead schools, but whatever happens on this trip – IT'S GOING TO BE GREAT.

If you want to see hammerheads you have to look out into the blue. They come into the reef area frequently for cleaning, but are very skittish when divers are around. If they come into the reef stay still and calm - any movement towards them will send them shooting back off into the blue. Although theses sharks congregate in great numbers and are huge and fearsome looking, they are very nervous of divers. The rest of the marine life here is not nervous at all, and one of the reasons for that is we do not touch anything under the water except barnacles, and you can play with those as much as you like. Please do not touch anything else. Don't try riding the mantas or the whale sharks, do not puff up the poor puffer fish, or poke the lobsters. If you want to do anything like that, I suggest you go elsewhere. If you try interfering with any of the marine life here, you spoil it for every subsequent visitor to this fantastic place. It is also illegal to touch any marine life here. Sometimes the Rangers will be diving to check up on you, so be warned. There might be a big fine involved." *This is a blatant lie.* "

Cocos, is a wild and natural habitat for a myriad of wonderful creatures and we want it kept that way. We don't feed fish here. We don't need to; they have more than they can eat and you will see them all feeding naturally. Sharks zoom around in hunting parties, right before your very eyes here. If you chase anything it will get scared and scarper quickly, just like you would if you were walking down a street in New York City and you were approached by a gang at a trot with maniacal looks in their eyes; you'd run away wouldn't you?

Don't forget to ascend slowly and make your safety stop at ten to fifteen feet, or three to five meters, for at least three minutes at the end of the dive. Try to do it close to shore so you are not getting swept away in the current. Having said that, sometimes at the end of a dive, if the group is still together with the dive master, we may all go off for a drift with the panga following. You may choose to follow the dive guide or you may do your own thing. This is not one of those tours where you see the dive guide swimming like the clappers being closely followed by a line of divers in brightly colored suits and color coordinated equipment, snapping pictures of everything that moves. Roberto and I will flit around making sure everyone is okay. We will always be there if you need us. We are usually the last ones to leave the water.

Once you are ready to be picked up, the drivers will place a ladder over the side for you to climb onboard. Just take your fins off and climb up. If you have a back problem you can take off your gear and hand it up to the driver, but try to climb up first because the driver can assist you and it is far easier than struggling with your equipment.

After the dive, and once back onboard the boat, you can leave anything you want in the pangas. We will pass your cameras back up to you and you can place them in the fresh water rinse tanks situated on the aft deck. You can hang your suits on the hangers between the dive gear lockers. Now a few words about wetsuits - it seems that every night someone comes onboard and pees on them."

This brings looks of horror on most faces.

"Because I know that none of you would ever pee in your suits, would you?"

Now there are looks of comprehension.

"If it does happen, rinse your suit in the sea, because fresh water doesn't work, it won't kill the smell. There is nothing worse than standing on the aft deck breathing in the fresh unpolluted Cocos breeze and being suddenly smacked in the face with a pissy dive suit."

There are smiles *and* cringes among the group.

"Okay. Any questions?"

"What's the water temperature?"

"It has been as high as 86 degrees in the last few weeks, but now it's about 84. The thermoclines, the cold underwater currents we find at some deeper dive sites, could be as low as 65 degrees.

Oh, and at Manuelita, there is sometimes a down current."

This elicits a few concerned looks.

"It's nothing to worry about if you realize what is happening to you. If you find that your bubbles are going down instead of up, or they are not going anywhere but staying level with you, you are in a down current. Sometimes it is very difficult to swim up in these down currents without help from your buoyancy jacket, so use your inflator if you have to. Inflate your buoyancy control jacket and swim up, but be very careful. Once you are out of the down current keep your hand on the purge valve of your jacket to vent off the excessive expanding air as you ascend. You do not want to shoot up rapidly to the surface. Does everyone understand?"

There are lots of nodding heads and a few relieved looks.

"Okay, I'll give the actual dive plan briefing, for the first dive, outside on the aft deck where I have the dry erase board."

The white board outside is mounted on top of a series of built-in box units fixed to the aft salon bulkhead, in the alcove underneath the steel boat deck. Each box houses a guest's camera or other piece of equipment needing to be kept dry.

When everybody is dressed, I draw a three-dimensional plan of the site on the board and explain every detail of the coming dive to them.

Now the fun commences.

Chapter 21
Un Problemo Pequeño

"Relax. Nothing is under control."
Adi Da Samraj.

THE DIVE GOES WELL. Some guests even see hammerheads and nearly everyone is excited about the number of white tipped reef sharks swimming around. In other parts of the world you might be lucky to see one White Tip during a whole weeks' diving. But after a couple of days at Cocos, divers start ignoring them and even stop categorizing them as sharks – even though the very first shark many divers see is a White Tip. After the very first encounter these divers probably boasted to their friends about seeing a "big shark in the wild" and were totally pumped about the machismo of being in the same bit of ocean with the dreaded killer and they probably regaled anyone who would listen with tales of it for months afterwards.

Anyway, the punters are now all happy, except for David and Mari who are disappointed at "not seeing anything at all" - *the fuckers.*

At 10am precisely, the rangers show up wanting me to unload the generator and fuel drums. Although the swell has died a little, I still think unloading is a bad idea. I could refuse, but it is inconvenient having all their stuff on deck. To see how they will fare transporting things ashore, I offload the fuel drums first.

Although sturdily built, the park's patrol boat is only slightly longer than one of our pangas. Their boat is painted blue with the park's emblem emblazoned on its bow. The small forward cabin covers a third of the boat's length. Beneath the flat deck, the inboard diesel engine occupies the other two thirds. After carefully loading the fuel drums onto their deck I watch them take off across the Bay.

Once they are out of sight, I expect a radio call from them saying it is too rough to have the generator sitting on their deck, but instead they are back in forty-five minutes just as I am getting dressed for the second dive. They want to take the generator ashore.

Thinking they know what they are doing I oblige. The crew attaches lines from various angles to stop the big generator swinging as I lift it off our deck with the crane and lower it as gently as I can on the small boat's deck. The generator occupies most of the deck space. Shaking my head in disbelief I watch them take off. That is one unstable looking load.

In the middle of the dive briefing Ronaldo appears on the aft deck with a worried look on his face. Waving his hands, he tries catching my eye. I hope there isn't a blocked toilet or something equally as nasty waiting for me inside.

After finishing the dive briefing, I take him aside.

"Que pasa?"

"Su barco los parques hay un problema grande, Cappy."

"¿Eh algo problema?"

"Ha zozobrado."

Fucking hell! It capsized – I knew it.

"¿Con el generador?"

"Si Senior."

Shit. "¿Adónde?"

"¡Sobre la playa Capitan!"

"Está a todo el mundo seguro. ¿Nadie fue herido?" I asked if everyone was okay and if anyone was hurt.

"¡Sí todo el mundo sea ok nadie fuiste herido - pero el barco esté muerto!" *Everyone is okay but the boat is dead.*

If it is on the beach and nobody is hurt, there is not a lot I can do. I am already late for the dive and need to go. I tell Ronaldo I will send the panga over to the rangers as soon as we get back.

What a disaster. The generator will be totally fucked now, and it sounds like their panga is totaled too. Ronaldo rushes in to call the rangers' station on the radio while Roberto and I round everyone up to go on the dive.

The rain starts before we even get in the water. If anything, it makes the dive better. We see a few Hammers and couple of Mobila Rays. Returning from the dive in the rain everyone is in a good mood except whiny David and Mari.

Back in the bay, the waterfall is slowly flowing again, along with several new ones.

After showering in the rain, I speak with the ranger station on the VHF radio.

"Victor, que pasa amigo?"

"Disaster Capitan, el barco is finished, it turned over."

"Yes, I heard. Where?"

"Close to the beach, a big wave came in and hit us on the side. We cannot pull it. The generator is underwater now and the boat is upside down. The waves are too strong. Hijaputa. Can you help please Cappy?"

I take Carlos, Roberto and Pedro with me in one of the pangas to go and appraise the damage. In Wafer Bay the swells are still rolling in and five rangers are in the sea, struggling to get the boat on the beach. There is no sign of the generator.

"Fooking hell!" says Roberto.

"You got that right Roberto."

"Ok Roberto, Carlos, Pedro can you jump in and help? Be very careful, watch your legs over there, and don't do anything dangerous."

"Si Cappy."

I maneuver as close as I can to the beach. The swells are short and high.

"OK guys, go."

They all jump over the side and swim to assist the struggling rangers. I swiftly maneuver away from the beach. Watching them battling the surf trying to pull the boat ashore I can see that it's pretty futile.

"OK guys forget it for now, it's too dangerous. Come back." I shout.

Realizing that they are fighting a losing battle they rejoin me.

"You know they tried using their little panga but that is upside down too." Roberto tells me.

"Si, all caput."

"Wow, that's very bad."

"We can't do anymore until these swells die down completely."

"Maybe I can help them fix the boats Cappy." Carlos says optimistically.

Well maybe their pigs will fly. I think uncharitably.

217

"Maybe you can help later Carlos, we'll have to see."

Back onboard, I pass on the afternoon dive, I really need to take a catnap - I feel quite knackered. Once the divers have gone, I lie down in my cabin and try to clear my mind. All this excitement has taken my mind off my troubles. I think of Julia again before dropping off to sleep, hoping she will call me later. She usually comes over with a pile of laundry as soon as I arrive at the island.

Emerging from my cabin later, I look outside and see it has stopped raining and the swell has calmed down some more. Thick clouds fill the sky, and out beyond the bay the wind is still whipping up the sea. The dirt brown waterfalls are all now flowing much faster, cascading into the bay, muddying the sea around the boat.

Now safely back onboard from the third dive of the day with Roberto, several punters want to do a night dive.

"Don't bother," mutters David, you won't see shit."

I could slap his smarmy face.

I address the guests. "The brown, muddy water around the boat is just the top layer, it's nice and clear a couple of feet below that and the current will soon take that top layer of sediment out to sea anyway. So, a night dive is on,"

Later, standing on the aft deck watching the night-divers kit up for their dive, I feel slightly peeved at not hearing from Julia.

I gave up doing night dives a long time ago – they bore me after the excitement of the day dives, and besides, a long surface interval between the last dive of the day and the first morning dive helps rid the body of its residual nitrogen build up, which makes longer bottom times possible at deeper depths.

I used to night dive regularly in the Red Sea; the underwater world at night on those reefs is phenomenal. But at Cocos I can never work up enough enthusiasm; even though there are usually a gang of whitetips hunting and the occasional couple of silky sharks swimming around the boat at night. Night dives just don't blow my kilt up anymore.

Most of the punters come out to watch David and Mari, who have decided to dive after all, and the other American couple Marty and Roberta, go on their dive. Marty and Roberta are a bit of a hoot together. In his late sixties, Marty is constantly being reminded by Roberta about where he leaves his equipment. He jumped in without his fins on the first dive and forgot his dive mask on the second. As dive master I usually check all the divers' equipment before sending them into the water, but this morning I was too preoccupied with troubled thoughts to check everyone properly - and that isn't good.

On the night dive the divers scare the shit out of the nightlife under the boat with their big bright flashlights. Standing on the aft deck, I really don't care. I am too distracted to chat with anyone, and don't follow anything anyone says. I think of Maria. I can't shake off the vision of her lifeless eyes and limp body lying on that bedroom floor. Before all this shit with Macho she was a warm, happy, and beautiful woman. Now she is miserably cold and dead, and it is my fault. If she hadn't colluded with Macho none of these bad things would have happened but she didn't deserve to die. The only thing I'm not sorry about is killing the bad bastard Macho and those two goons.

I look around at the guests; I still don't know all their names - not even the other English couple who are keeping a distance from the French couple who are constantly kissing and cuddling each other, behaving is if they are on their honeymoon. Apart from the language barrier, the French and English do not generally understand each other, but there are things to admire, such as their food, fashion, and wine. But why are they so bloody contrary? Apart from being tres-chic and mysterious, in a way, some are similar to the English in that they worry excessively about money and have a deep fear that everybody is trying to rip them off.

The English are usually fun as long as everything goes their way. They generally see injustice in many different and obscure ways, which to me makes no sense. They suffer in silence for a while, muttering amongst themselves until they can't stand it any longer. When they explode, they usually do it with a torrent of abuse and sometimes with an unspoken threat of physical violence.

The four middle aged German guys are all enjoying themselves; laughing loudly around a pile of empty beer cans on the camera table. I decline their offer to join them. I always enjoy having German groups onboard - even those who take themselves a trifle too seriously. Most are good at heart and I enjoy chatting to them, although my pretense at not understanding them is difficult at times, listening to some of the things they say.

I think briefly about Cabeza. I was too hard on him really. He didn't do me any harm, so why was I so rough on him? I soon put him out of my mind.

My crew members are fascinated by the hairiness of some of the Germen women we regularly have onboard, particularly under their arms and around the bikini area. My guys are shocked at the way some walk around naked before getting ready for their dives. During those trips crew members all rush to bring out hot towels and snacks after a dive, then stand around on the aft deck waiting for a flash of flesh. Embarrassingly, more men than women strip their kit off completely.

"What? Shit! So, they now have no boat at all?" We use a lot of air freshener on those trips.

The dive is followed by dinner, after which, I sit in the main salon nursing a glass of wine, detailing the dive plan for the next day and ignoring the guests boring dive stories until it is time to turn in. I still feel strange. I'm totally disconnected with this group. I really don't give a shit whether they enjoy themselves or not.

This is a first.

On the way to my cabin I peer out of the wheelhouse window; it's started to rain stair rods again. I can't get over the change in weather since last week. If the treasure hunters had chosen this week it would have been a complete washout - literally. Through the window I can just about make out the flashing lights of a couple of long-liners anchored close by. It must be miserable onboard those little boats. And where the heck is Julia?

Lying in my cabin I think again of the events of the last few days.

Although I am a bastard as far as women are concerned, I previously thought myself a good person. I always enjoyed making people happy. I made a right balls-up of that lately though. To prove it, there are five people right now because of me; and they are just the ones I know of. Poor Maria was a diamond and Flora seemed like a nice girl too, at heart. They might both still be alive if wasn't such an idiot. Who the hell were the two guys I slotted in Maria's apartment? I have no idea and quite frankly don't give a shit. *How strange, killing people you don't even know.* As for Macho, the bad useless bastard, I could slot him again in a heartbeat, only this time slowly, while he is conscious.

I am still worried about Al too. How the hell will he get himself out of jail? Will he even be able to? And if he can't, will I go down with him? I suspect I will. He wasn't too pleased with me after I did Macho in.

I am falling into a deep pit, but I don't intend holding my breath until I hit bottom - I will die first.

Chapter 22
Cocos Day 2: A Discovery

"They always say time changes things, but you actually have to change them yourself."
Andy Warhol

THE RAIN BEATING down on the steel roof of my cabin sounds like a dozen dope fueled drummers practicing for a heavy metal concert. They bash about on the roof above my head until dawn, when the jazz drummers take over.

I don't get much sleep. And it isn't just because of the noise. Evil thoughts are crowding my brain. I am in deep shit and need a shovel, or a plan. There are plenty of shovels onboard but only one plan – and that is to kill everyone onboard and take the boat to Panama.

This may sound absurd but it is doable.

I am a skipper with weapons. The only way anybody on the mainland knows where the boat is once we leave, is if I tell them over the radio where we are.

The problem is we don't have enough fuel to get to Panama. There is just enough diesel fuel in the tanks to get us back to base with a little in reserve in case somebody goes missing on a dive and we have to search for them.

I wrestle with the problem for hours.

This really is bonkers. I need to pull myself together. I am way off the charts.

221

Outside, Chatham Bay looks like a floating Japanese garden. Floating leaves, plants, and trees are strewn all over the bay, washed into the sea by the floodwaters. The waterfall is a torrent once again, with several subdivisions cascading furiously off the shoulders of the exposed rocks nearby.

Although the fishing boats are gone, the sea is still rough out beyond the island. Normally I would move the boat on day two, but today it will be more comfortable staying in Chatham Bay.

No big deal, we'll take the pangas over to Dirty Rock; one of the finest dive sites in the world.

Situated close to Wafer Bay, about three hundred yards offshore, Dirty Rock is a twenty-foot-high, pointed craggy rock, covered in bird-shit. Under the surface the rock rises up from two hundred and fifty feet and serves as a major cleaning station for droves of Hammerheads. As the schools of Hammers slowly passed by, they are greeted and groomed by groups of resident Angel and Barber fish.

Diving dirty rock is like standing beside a major highway during rush hour. I had one of the best dives of my life there once, when a school of dolphins cruised by with a shit load of silky sharks swimming amongst a massive school of yellow fin tuna. After a manta ray buzzed us all, closely followed by a flotilla of Mobila rays, an army of hammerheads appeared, as though in a Pink Floyd movie. The white tips were going nuts hunting and an enormous pile of male marble rays were trying to mate with a female ray in the sand. To top it off, two sailfish and a whale shark swam by.

I swear. I couldn't even make that dive up.

The only dive sites that come close to Dirty Rock for consistent excitement, are Manuelita Island, which is usually better in the winter months; and Alcyone, a sea mound that is a massive hammerhead cleaning station. Manuelita can be hit and miss in the summer. Because the punters make the first two dives of the trip at Manuelita, some are reluctant to do it more than once. For me it is a great dive site.

Alcyone in the southeast is even better, although impossible to dive in this weather.

The rain eases off as we leave for the first dive. If there is a major storm, and it absolutely pisses down with rain during the day, as it did during the night, I will postpone the dive because good surface visibility is essential for the pickup.

I am also a bit concerned about one of the panga drivers being deleted by a lightning bolt.

Staggering the departure times of the two groups, I instruct Roberto to take his panga forty-five minutes after I leave. This will give my group time to complete their dive before his group arrives at the dive site.

The dive isn't one of the best I ever made but I am happy to see some Hammers around. And so is everyone else, except David and Mari who had told everyone to expect hundreds of hammerheads.

By the time the second dive is due the rain has stopped and the sun shines between the clouds. A rainbow arches over the Bay; ending or maybe beginning on the beach, on one of the spots where treasure is reportedly buried. I've seen a rainbow there several times. Is that the reason so many expeditions dig there?

Returning from the dive I don't care that everyone complains about problems with the current and the shitty visibility, and that I dropped them on the wrong side of the rock. I don't care, because standing on the aft deck with a huge smile on her face, is Julia.

I hug her long and hard. "How long have you been onboard?"

"Long enough to have a nice hot shower."

"How did you get out here?"

"I swam. Let's go to your cabin, I have something to tell you." She almost drags me up there. I want to strip her naked in seconds flat, but she sits on my bed and holds her arm out fending me off.

"Mac, you won't believe what I found!"

"Don't tell me you've found the treasure," I laugh.

"I think I might have!"

"What?"

"Yes. I tried hiking to where we dug last week. I tried twice in two days to get there. It is very difficult to find. Climbing over the top of all those steep hills is treacherous — there are many big hidden holes up there. I got caught in that damn rain storm so I had to come back. But I did make it up there, Mac. You won't believe the mess up there. The rain washed away all the earth from the wall and now there are trees and rocks all piled up in front of it like a dam. The pigs have been digging around up there searching for grubs - they love new overturned dirt. The new dam has diverted the stream and it's now running over the top of the rise down to the ravine. Do you remember walking through the trees along that small gully and looking over the edge of that cliff? That's where the stream flows now. There's a huge waterfall pouring down onto the plateau, washing away the earth. I managed to make my way around to the opposite ridge where I could see properly and I swear it looks like there is a cave there. I couldn't get down because of the damned rain, but I swear to you Mac, it looks like a cave. I wish I could have gotten down there, but it was so treacherous with all the water rushing down. It's amazing, Mac. You have to go around there."

"Bloody hell! You haven't told anyone else have you girl?"

"Of course not."

"What about the ravine, can we go up there?"

"Well, from the top it looks like the waterfall has hollowed out the plateau - it looks like a big round bowl with water spilling over the top, pouring down the ravine."

"Wow. This could be something big. I had a funny feeling about that ravine."

"Yeah, isn't this exciting. Do you really think I could have found the place that hundreds of people have been looking for all these years?"

"You know babe, I was convinced the treasure was still here, and I thought you would be the one to find it."

This is too good to be true.

"We've got to check this out. I won't dive this afternoon; we'll take the kayak and paddle around there. I was planning the dive over at Lobster Rock next to Isla Conico, but now I'll send everyone off in the opposite direction: to Isla Pajara."

"Mac, I also have a funny feeling about this. I'm sure it's the cave."

"I hope you're right girl."

"Me too. Now I feel sexy. I missed you Mac."

"I missed you too babe."

She strips off her clothes and stands naked before me, head tilted to one side.

"What about lunch. Aren't you hungry?" I ask, stepping out of my shorts.

She grabs me by my stiff dick and kneels in front of me. "Yes, but what about hors d'oeuvres first – you want room service?"

And I do.

The galley crew saves us lunch but can't control their smirks when we arrive in the galley later. We eat by ourselves up in the wheelhouse.

"What if this is the treasure Mac, do we tell the National Park?"

"You must be bloody joking. Listen sweetheart, we don't tell a soul."

"How would we get it off the island without anyone knowing?"

"I haven't got a clue right now, but don't worry I'll come up with something."

"Where would we sell it?"

"I'll think of that too. But this may all be academic; let's find it first and *then* think of something."

Stashed in the forepeak there are a few tools from the German group that I intended giving to Julia anyway, to make it easier for her to rummage around on her pig-studying excursions.

From what she tells me, the earth and rock we dug away from the rock face has fallen into the riverbed, making a dam, causing the stream to flow into a gully and then through the trees over to the left, where we stood looking down onto the plateau that day. The dam and diversion created a waterfall that bombarded the plateau like a giant water cannon, washing the earth away. Julia saw what looked like a big hole in the side of the cliff face below the ridge.

So, this is why the waterfall in Chatham Bay stopped - it is only flowing now because rainwater is running down the hill and surrounding areas below the dam. Although it is some distance from Chatham Bay, I am willing to bet my soul that the stream up there feeds the waterfall here. I am eager to go and see.

Perhaps the Cabeza is cleverer than I think.

I should have known he is not as dumb as he looks — he must have a brain the size of a bucket. The hunters mentioned "eine umleitung"- a diversion - but I thought they were talking about creating a diversion from the park officials so they could do something else. That's why I was confused about some of the stuff they talked about.

Those crafty fuckers!

It rains again as we eat lunch. I wait until 14.30 before sending everyone off on the dive; switching the location to another site so Julia and I can explore the ravine. I send both groups to Bahia Weston, a small islet in the center of a small bay to the west of Chatham. Unfortunately, there is no room to anchor the Searcher in the narrow, channel between it and the island; it would be a great mooring site. The divers will need a shovel if they want to go deeper than 60 feet there. It isn't the most exciting dive in the world but it gets them out of our way, and they may even see the three resident frogfish there.

As soon as they are gone, Julia and I grab the tools and launch the kayak. The kayak is super handy. Made from molded plastic with space for two people to sit on top with legs extended, it moves across the water pretty fast. Unlike the collapsible, ocean going Klepper I used in the military, this one is only safe to use close to shore because when the wind catches it, the little kayak flies along and you need arms and shoulders like Arnold Schwarzenegger to paddle against the wind.

With both of us paddling, we disappear around the corner pretty sharpish. Passing Conical Rock and nearing the landing site I see straight away that it isn't going to be easy getting ashore. The swell crashes up onto the shoreline, meeting a brand-new river pouring in a torrent down the ravine. Small streams and mini waterfalls cascade down both sides of the gulley. The little river is so strong it makes a small tunnel through the vegetation before spilling into the sea across the narrow shoreline. Even if we manage to beach the kayak without injuring ourselves in the surf, it will be dangerous trying to climb the slope with the water gushing down like that.

We don't even try to get ashore. Disappointed, we arrive back onboard before the divers return from their dive.

Before dinner I instruct a Nitrox course with the Brit couple and the Germans. I do it because it will give me a bit of cash in my pocket after the trip is over. I have no idea what I am going to do once we get back to port, or even if I really want to go back there. If I get arrested, I am in big trouble. I try my best not to think about it. I give everyone free wine during dinner. Because of that, there are no takers for the night dive. Julia and I drink a couple more glasses of wine before retiring to bed early, leaving the punters to their own devices. I don't want to hear anymore crap or answer any more personal questions, and I don't really give a running fuck whether everyone is enjoying themselves or not. The next day is the fifth day of the trip, which means that there are only four days left at Cocos.

I have four days to decide what to do.

Up in the cabin, Julia and I discuss the prospects of finding the treasure and becoming extremely rich, before I fall asleep dribbling like a sloth.

Chapter 23
Cocos Day 3: What Next?

"Don't waste your time with explanations: people only hear what they want to hear."
Paulo Coelho

DESPITE MY FLIPPANT answers to Julia's questions the previous day, the irony of my situation is not lost on me. If we do find this treasure, how *will* I get it back to the mainland without anyone except Julia and myself knowing about it? And what is waiting for me back in Punta La Pesca anyway? I might be arrested for murder immediately the boat arrives back in port. If I'm not arrested, there may still be friends of the two goons I slotted at Maria's place, waiting for me up a dark alley. I might never know who they are. And even if I find out, it will probably be too late anyway. They obviously didn't realize who they were dealing with until it was too late. But if there are any more where they came from, they certainly know how dangerous I am by now. The fact that those two guys were waiting for me with weapons drawn obviously means they were intending to have more than a friendly chat with me over a cup of Earl Grey tea.

I find it difficult to stay focused on the guests. I have to put everything out of my mind and carry on as normal, but I'm not really bothered anymore. I shouldn't even be doing this charter, but I don't really have much choice. There was no time to think after the incident in Maria's apartment. Leaving immediately on the boat seemed like such a great exit.

If I had run off before the charter started, I would be proclaiming my guilt.

It is all about timing – but so far, mine is sucking.

The weather has turned out nice this morning; the rain has stopped and the sea has calmed down a bit, which means we can go to the south end of the island. Normally I would try and get to the dive sites in the south at the beginning of the week; especially during the rainy season because the weather is so unpredictable at that time of year, and it could be rough for days. Right now, I think more about trying to arrange the diving schedule around another outing for Julia and myself than I do about pleasing the punters. Although we need to explore that ravine, I still have to make a bit of an effort for them.

My criteria for diving in the south, is the sea state. If it is rough, with big swells rolling in it isn't much fun for any diver being tossed around inside a panga like a losing lotto ball in the state lottery. But the over-riding thing is this: if a diver is swept away from the dive site in a rough sea, he or she will be very difficult to spot from the panga between the high waves.

So, the bottom line is: I will never put divers in the water if I think it will be difficult to see them once they surface, and I don't care how much they protest about not diving every dive site during their trip. They cannot intimidate me – *the fuckers.*

My plan is to nip around to the south for the first two dives and then return to Chatham Bay, spending the rest of the day and evening there so Julia and I can try and make it to the cave.

Driving the *Searcher* past Isla Conico, I scan the ravine through binoculars but can't see anything through the foliage. I do notice a strange looking object lying at the bottom, close to the shoreline, to the right of the opening in the trees. After further scrutiny it turns out to be a dead pig with all four trotters sticking straight into the air. I am glad we didn't attempt to land there yesterday.

The anchorage I favor on this side of Cocos is close to Tea Cup Island a small rock outcrop in Iglesias Bay, just off a palm-fringed shoreline. One hundred feet above the line of palm trees a waterfall cascades into the interior, creating a stunningly picturesque scene. I anchor in the sand close to Tea Cup and not too far off the shoreline.

Two good dive sites are close by. The closest is Submerged Rock, which we pass on the way. Further south, a fifteen-minute panga ride from Iglesias Bay takes us past the southernmost point of the island to

Shark Fin Rock; so named because the rock's triangular pinnacle sticks out from the sea like a giant shark's fin.

With just a rolling long swell and no choppy waves, both dives go well. Most divers see dolphins and silky sharks. The three Germans saw a sailfish at submerged rock, and everyone spotted at least one hammerhead. The colossal school of resident horse eye jacks at Shark Fin Rock causes the biggest sensation – they are an impressive sight swirling around in an immense cloud measuring a hundred feet or more in width stretching from the surface to a hundred feet or more below. Everyone is happy. "OK everyone, we'll leave back to Chatham Bay after lunch." I am looking forward to leaving.

"What about going ashore to the waterfall, asks David, "it's a whole part of the Cocos experience. We went last time and it was fabulous. We should all go." They are right of course; but not on this day. I actually toyed with the idea of sending everyone off there with Roberto.

"I'm sorry but not today, the swell is too dangerous. It might not look it from here but there are big boulders on the beach area just waiting to break your legs if you get caught in them."

"Bullshit," muttered David.

"Did you say something David?" I glare at him. He doesn't answer.

"The conditions on the beach may look okay from the boat but wading ashore in a big swell is a very dangerous procedure. There is no way we can beach a panga because the whole shore line is a mass of different sized boulders, above and below the surface – each one waiting to trap anyone foolish enough to try and walk in the surf-line. Coming off shore, back into the sea is even more difficult. When the swells come in and you have an ankle trapped between the rocks there will be a loud snapping sound followed by an even louder scream – this will be a broken ankle you just heard. Unfortunately, unless you have already been in that surf with that kind of swell battering the bejasus out of you, you really can't visualize it." I explain.

If someone breaks their ankle, or worse, I will have to take them back to the mainland for treatment right away; we can't stay there for another four days while their bones fester and their limbs drop off. In no way do I intend going back to Punta La Pesca before it is time to do so. Bollocks to them; they will have to wait another day – even though I don't really plan on coming around this side again unless by popular demand. Some are grumpy at my decision but the majority, are okay with it.

I plan to move off after lunch - I am more than eager to get back to Chatham and check out the cave.

That plan changes during lunch.

Is anything going to work out as planned?

David and Mari want to dive these two sites again; they don't want to do Lobster Rock or Manuelita again. Right here they say, are two good dive sites and by golly they want to do them again this afternoon. They are the ones paying, they say, and unfortunately the rest of the punters agree. Of course, I have no objection to doing the closest of these sites again under normal circumstances; I often do, but now I have a possible half billion dollars waiting for me and all I have to do is grab it and run - if it is there of course.

I don't want to face a hostile group for the rest of the trip and have my karma reduced any further (how much lower can it go after murdering three people and being responsible for the death of at least two others?) Reluctantly I relent and plan the next dive at submerged rock at two-thirty, a nice safe dive not far from the boat. It will give me time to give Julia a quick one after lunch.

At two fifteen, after a nice session with Julia, I walk out onto the aft deck to prepare for the dive and notice one of the pangas is missing. I look over towards the shore and see six people on the beach. Raul is driving the panga and they all seem to be shouting at him at once.

They went over to the beach anyway, the silly bastards!

I rush up into the wheelhouse and grab the binoculars, training them on the beach. It looks like David, Mari and the other two couples. The three Germans are swimming back to the Searcher. I see one person lying down holding their knee.

Fuck a duck; the fucking idiots.

I call on the VHF radio to Raul in the panga. "What's going on Raul?"

"One of the guests twisting her knees trying to get off the beach," he replies in a high-pitched panicky voice.

"Serves the fuckers right," I think grimly.

The surf is so high they are all having a problem getting off the beach and out to the boat. This may get even worse.

"Raul," I say over the radio, "throw the line from the front locker. Try and get them to grab hold of the rope while you pull them out. I will be over in the other panga in a minute."

I am fucking fuming.

I put my wet suit on. "Pedro, can you drive me over to the beach? Where is Roberto?"

"He swam to the beach to help."

When I'm close to the beach in the second panga I see Raul has managed to get John and Helen into his boat. John is bleeding from a cut above his left eye and is holding his left shoulder. Remarkably, Helen seems Ok. How I stop myself from calling them all the idiots under the sun I don't know.

Marty and Roberta are at the water's edge, ready for an attempt at wading out past the surf line, but they keep getting knocked over by the waves. Roberta is crying. Marty is trying to console her.

"Okay, listen," I shout to them. "The only way to do this is by trying to duck into the waves as soon as you can. Take your fins off and try to lean forward. Don't let your feet become trapped in the rocks. Watch the swell. Every seventh wave will be smaller than the rest, so wait for that seventh wave and go for it. Don't hesitate once you make your move. I will try and direct you," *you fucking idiots*, I add silently.

Marty and Roberta manage to make it after being battered about a bit, but Mari is having problems standing up. She is so skinny I think she might snap in half if her legs get trapped. I am in such a bad mood right now I might laugh at that.

"Okay, I'll go back to the boat in the panga and bring the kayak. I'll have to try and bring you out on that."

Returning several minutes later with the kayak aboard the panga, I lower it into the water and lie on it, front first. Paddling with my arms, I arrive ashore surfing a wave right in front of the two wankers.

"Sorry Mac," says David, wanker number one.

I don't reply, giving him a steely look instead.

I manage to get Mari standing on one leg with her arm around my shoulder before hoisting her up, piggyback style.

"Right; as soon as the kayak is in the water lay on it, face down and grab the sides as tight as you can. Forget the pain. This is the only way out. David, you and I have to do this together. You need to get the kayak in the water close to us and I will put Mari on it. As soon as she is holding tight, we have to go for it. Don't let go of the board unless you are about to be turned over by a wave. We have to be fast and strong."

I wait for the lull and give the instruction to go. We manage to get through the first onslaught of waves, but David lets go of the kayak and I am knocked sideways, twisting my own ankle in the process. Somehow, I manage to grab it again before it turns over.

"Get on Mari. Quick." I have to hold on tightly to avoid having Mari thrown off into the surf again. Managing to keep stable, I propel the kayak in front of me with my legs going full throttle. Reaching the rope in the water I grab it with one hand and hold tightly to the bow of the kayak with the other as the panga pulls us out. We manage to get Mari into the panga without further mishap but my ankle is killing me.

I limp back onboard to a group of silent guests on the aft deck.

"Okay," I say, "whose idea was it to go ashore."

"David said it was easy," Roberta tells me. "Yeah," says Marty "he says he did it on his last trip and it was no problem."

I shake my head in exasperation but say nothing.

Mari is in tears nursing her knee.

"Ronaldo, per favor. Get me two ice packs from the fridge." One is for my ankle; it feels buggered.

I limp inside with David. I am so angry with him I feel like grabbing his t-shirt and yanking it up under his chin but I stare coldly at him. "You are a fucking wanker. I warned you about going ashore here. If anybody had been seriously injured, we would be on our way back to port right now; dive trip over for everyone. If you ever pull a stunt like that again I will pull all of your fucking teeth out with a pair of rusty pliers. In fact, if I ever see you again after this trip, I might just do that anyway. Just keep out of my fucking way from now on."

Marty nurses his shoulder while I patch up the small cut on his eyebrow. *He'll live.*

"You'll probably be okay to dive tomorrow."

"Thanks Mac. Thanks for helping us."

"I'm sorry David led you astray." I reply.

"Yeah that asshole," Marty surprisingly chimes back.

Luckily John and Helen are ok and the French couple didn't go ashore; they are in their cabin.

The Germans are the only takers for the afternoon dive, so I send Raul and Roberto off with them and stay onboard with Julia.

They are only gone an hour.

As soon as they return from the dive, I move the *Searcher* back to Chatham with the two pangas being driven ahead in the rain. By the time we arrive it is too late for Julia and I to go on our outing. My ankle throbs like hell anyway. Luckily it isn't too swollen and it isn't broken - what a disaster that would have been.

At dinner, David and Mari are totally subdued. I hold a grudge and am still pissed about the remarks they made to the boss after their last trip.

David is probably planning to bring a law suit against me for assaulting him and causing his wife to have a mental breakdown, but it's their own bloody fault.

John, Helen, Marty and Roberta actually apologize to me but I sense a new feeling amongst the whole group, and it isn't a good one. This is what happens when you ignore your guests. I've never done that before and I don't like it now, but screw them, I have more important stuff filling my brain. Later, sitting with Molly in the wheelhouse pondering what dives to do the following day, I hear a voice from the ranger station calling me on the radio.

"Ola Cap, Lena called us from your office."

I forgot to call again today.

"Thanks Victor, any messages for me?"

"They asking if everything is OK."

If that's all they want, that's good news. *No manhunt for me underway yet then?*

"OK gracias, I'll call them tomorrow. How are your guys doing?"

"Not good without our boat Cap."

"Yeah, that's too bad Victor. Anything I can do?"

"Give us one of your pangas…"

"Sorry buddy, that's not possible right now, but maybe I can leave you one when we leave, if you promise not to sink it. I'll ask the boss tomorrow."

"Ha, that will be moi bien Cap. Gracias. Please keep a look out for illegal fishing. Hey Cap, is Julia onboard with you? We need her to be on the island tomorrow to do her duties." whatever that means. I know the rangers are all jealous of the treatment I give her onboard. Unfortunately for them, they will never get the same treatment from me as long as they have a toggle and two between their legs. Sorry lads - wrong sex. I wonder how long it will take the fishermen on the mainland to find out that the island's potentially lush fishing grounds are unprotected. A while back, when the rangers were without a boat because of engine problems, it only took one boat to anchor overnight in Chatham Bay for the news to travel over the airwaves to all the other boats in the area. Most have SSB radios onboard. A fleet arrived shortly at the island not long after word got out.

I was planning to send Julia around to the cave in the morning, while we are out diving, wherever that might be, but now, because she is needed on the island, our little project will have to wait until the afternoon. I don't want her getting into trouble and being kicked off the project; she is too valuable to me. She and I have the ideal situation going - she has the comforts of the boat at her disposal and I have the comforts of her presence at mine. I did think if I ever met a girl I truly liked, I would ask her to live onboard with me. But that isn't a good idea because it won't be long before she tries taking over as captain; they inevitably do - endorsing the old naval expression that 'The hand that wanks the captain rules the ship'. I'm not sure why I am even thinking this way because I have decided that this is going to be my very last trip, one way or another.

Chapter 24
Cocos Day 4: Boat Gypsies

"Sailing: The fine art of slowly going nowhere at great expense while being cold, wet and miserable."   Irv Helle

---

I'M PREOCCUPIED WITH thoughts of escaping with a boatload of treasure. What will I do if we find a cave full of treasure? How the hell will I get that stuff off the island and onto the Searcher secretly? The crew takes turns in keeping watches at night even though they probably sleep through them. I could give them a break and tell them they don't need to be doing watches anymore during the night. I'm sure that will please them all. Then I'll have to teach Julia how to drive the panga so I can do all the heavy humping. And then there is the small problem of stashing the booty onboard. If I do manage to get the stuff onboard, I might not get the chance to dispose of it in Costa Rica before being arrested. The police may be waiting for me on the dock.

In a way, I hope there is no treasure. Maybe that's why I make lame excuses to myself, putting off visiting the ravine. For half a billion dollars I should be climbing that ridge right now. I did some gnarly things in the Navy, trudging through rotten mud in full diving gear dragging a hundred pounds of weight and jumping naked from a 60-foot tower into a frozen lake to swim in its icy waters at midnight. Compared to climbing up the side of a moving ship at night in the stormy Irish Sea, or scaling the leg of a North Sea oilrig during a dark winter storm, how bad is climbing up a little ravine? A twisted ankle is no excuse. Under normal circumstances I would be only too excited to have a pile of gold, sparkling diamonds, and a golden statue of the virgin standing before me, but I am now stuck between an abyss and a deep crevice; with no idea whether the treasure will be of any benefit.

I ought to be optimistic about my situation but I'm too much of a realist. Maybe I should just hang myself from the nearest yardarm.

Moving the Searcher out of Chatham Bay through the channel between Manuelita and the mainland, I notice a small sail on the horizon far off to the North. Sailing boats sometimes stop off here on their way across the South Pacific to the Marquesas Islands. But it's far too late in the season for that: most boats cross during the summer months, when the sea is calm. Normally, they stay at Cocos for only a couple of days, unless they have a big budget. The park rangers charge a daily anchorage fee, per boat, per crew member, and collect it judiciously - we pay the fee for every guest we have onboard, every trip.

Because we were in the Caribbean during the best part of the crossing season it is a while since I saw a sailing boat here, which is not a bad thing. Some yachts are a pain in the arse. My crew always gets excited when they see a yacht but I don't always share their enthusiasm. Some the smaller yacht owners expect us to fill their dive tanks for free and take them on dives for free, and give them fresh water, even though there is a million tons of it on the island. Some ask for fuel and food and sometimes ask if our engineer can fix problem machinery. I don't mind helping anyone out if they are in real trouble but I have a charter to run with paying guests to take care of and some yachties take liberties. Obviously, they are not all like that, but there have been enough to make me cynical of any approach by them.

There was once a guy and his wife in Chatham Bay aboard a yacht so small and scruffy I wondered how they made it there. One of the park rangers came over to *me* to see if I could help the old couple onboard with an engine problem. Being a good egg, I went over with Carlos to see what I could do.

Arriving at the boat, Carlos and I looked at each other in amazement. We couldn't believe the conditions they were living in. The yacht was a floating pigsty. The captain and his wife were both in their sixties, on their way to Australia. The tiny interior space was taken up by a filthy, garbage strewn bed covered with a mangy throbbing sleeping bag. They were both encrusted with oil, dirt, and salt and their dank dirty hair stood on end, making them appear like frightened scarecrows. Our engine room rags were cleaner than the clothes they wore. Obviously, there were no mirrors on the boat but surely, they looked at each other, and surely, they noticed that they both looked and smelled like shit. The boat stank like an Aussie sheep shearing station in summer.

The captain had a gaping, weeping wound on his leg, but had nothing onboard to treat it with. His wife told me he suffered from epilepsy but had run out of medication. When he smiled it was like a crocodile's arse exploding. Sitting scrunched up in the tiny cockpit with his fetid breath hitting me squarely in the face I don't know how I stopped from gagging. To be honest I wanted to dive overboard to clean myself up. The couple kindly offered me a cup of tea, which I refused when I saw the dirty jam jar she was drinking from. Although I tried not studying the jar too closely – I could see it was covered with alien cultures and held what looked like bilge water after the sanitation tanks had overflowed. Carlos, who was lucky enough to be sitting on deck during all of this, did ask me afterwards if she had bilge water in the jar.

Lots of skippers taste bilge water, unless they have an engineer to do it for them. If you ever find your bilges suddenly full of water, you need to find out where the water came from pretty damn quick. Did it come from outside or inside the boat? Is it salt water or fresh? The best way to find out is to taste it. I've tasted bilge water a number of times but there was no way I was going to drink that fucking tea; it certainly wasn't Lapsang Souchong, that's for sure.

That little boat was a total mess. The mainsail was ripped and they had nothing onboard to repair it with; the engine was fucked and would not start, and even if they had managed to start it, there was no fuel left in the fuel tank anyway - only fumes. They had somehow lost their life raft and their little inflatable tender, and had no means of survival if the yacht sank - and the chances of that happening were pretty high. To top it off, they had run out of food. But the truly amazing thing is this: they had only traveled 450 miles from their last port of call, Panama, and still had more than 3000 miles to go!

We helped them all we could. I did some first aid on his leg and when everyone went diving, let them both clean up onboard the Searcher; they said it was the first freshwater shower they'd had for two years. Carlos fixed their engine problem and gave them fuel; Raul gave them food supplies and I even got our office to phone the guy's brother to wire some money over because they were broke. When I offered to take them back to port onboard the Searcher they accepted. But after delaying my departure from the island for a couple of hours they changed their minds.

We took their main sail back to port with us and had it repaired and Mano persuaded a doctor to give him a prescription for the epilepsy medication. The park rangers were great and uncharacteristically let the couple stay at Cocos for free for a couple of weeks, while we sorted all this stuff out for them.

But eventually, after everyone's patience was pushed to the limit, the couple was told to pay the park fees every day or leave. The following morning the boat had vanished and to this day I have no idea what happened to them.

Although that is an extreme case, these kinds of circumstances make me reluctant to have any contact with boat gypsies. Whoever is headed toward the island right now won't be getting a friendly welcoming radio call from me - unless there appears to be at least one nubile lady in a bikini onboard – just for my crew to look at, you understand.

I am heading towards the lamentably named Punta Maria, two miles west of Wafer Bay. I named the dive site there 'El Sphinx Sin Cabeza', because beneath the weather-beaten cliff face, a small bay has two separate rock ledges stretching into the sea on either side like enormous long lion's forefeet in repose. To me it looks like the front end of the Egyptian sphinx, minus its head.

Passing Wafer Bay on the way to the dive site, Pedro takes Julia over in a panga and drops her off at beach in front of the ranger station. I plan to pick her up on the way back to Chatham Bay this afternoon. My anchorage for this morning is at the very western edge of Wafer Bay, opposite a spectacular waterfall - a smaller version of the one at Iglesias Bay on the other side of the island, where the gusts got in trouble on the beach yesterday. Because this waterfall doesn't require a long hike, I intend sending everyone there once the swells die down.

The dive site itself is made up of a series of sea mounds a mile from our anchorage. Both pangas anchor there while the divers descend the anchor rope to the top of the tallest pinnacle, at a depth of sixty feet. After swimming around the sea mounds for forty minutes the group level off at twenty feet and drift together, parallel to the shore in the current. Roberto and I each release a brightly colored float on the end of a thin line for the panga drivers to follow. When each diver gets low on air, they surface and are picked up by the nearest panga. Although this is a nice dive site, it's really a dress rehearsal for the site planned for the following day: 'Alcyone' is a much larger, more challenging undersea mound named by Jacques Cousteau himself.

The sky is overcast and gray when we surface and I hope it isn't going to pour down with rain again - I am now very anxious to visit the 'cave'.

Roberto takes everyone except the injured David, Mari and Marty over to the waterfall. When he returns, he tells me the pathway we normally take through the undergrowth up to the foot of the falls is once again covered by rocks and trees. The pathway changes drastically every month. When it rains heavily after a dry period, debris washes over the cliffs, landing in a mass of tangled branches and tree trunks that gathers more earth and debris that constantly changes the landscape.

When it comes time for the second dive my ankle bothers me so much, I give it a miss. As soon as everyone is back onboard after the dive, we take off for Chatham Bay. Driving slowly, I eat lunch in the wheelhouse while Molly the cat sleeps. I think about Julia. I'm looking forward to seeing her again tonight. I might not see her again after this trip; I might be in jail swatting horny hoodlums away from my arse.

At one o'clock I make the scheduled radio call to the office in San Jose; and promptly wish I had not.

"What time exactly will you be arriving back in port Mac?" asks Lena. This gives me another attack of paranoia. Usually no one asks that question until the day before we are due in. They know what time high tide is because they have a tide table in the office. They know what day the charter ends so why is she asking me now?

"We have to schedule a time for the bus to pick up the guests," she says as if to answer my unasked question.

"I should be right on schedule. Did you hear about the rangers losing their boat and new generator?" I ask, changing the subject.

"Yeah we heard all about it from Victor. He asked for you to leave one of the pangas for them when you leave. Jimmy said that was ok, but it better not be damaged because they will have to pay for a new one if it is."

"Well, don't forget that we will be in trouble if they do damage it. We have divers to transport to dive sites. Without one of the pangas it will be a nightmare." *Why am I even making this comment?*

"But you will get it back when you return to the island, next week."

There won't be a fucking next week.

"OK Lena, no problemo."

Why haven't you called before? Why can Victor get through on the radio and you can't."

"Better radio, I guess. Anyway, I can't sit by the radio all day I've got a charter to run."

"Ok, Mac. We'll see you when you get back. Is everything going OK?"

"Yeah it's all great Lena, no problems," I lie.

"OK bye for now."

Arriving back in Chatham Bay I am surprised there is no sign of the sailboat I saw on the horizon earlier. Wafer and Chatham are now the only two safe bays to anchor; anywhere else will be potentially too dangerous and uncomfortable. But 'blow-boaters' are a different breed from us 'stink-potters'. 'Blow boaters' are used to discomfort: they seem to spend most of their time at sea slanted sideways anyway, but they seem to thrive on it. I will be very surprised if they don't stop here. Maybe they are sailing around the island sightseeing before mooring up at Chatham for the night.

Once at the mooring Raul and Pedro secure their pangas along each respective side and start charging the dive tanks in the pangas. Standing there on the aft deck, the sound of Julia's voice startles me for a second – I hear her in stereo, her voice coming from the radio in each panga. Jumping down into the port-side panga I answer her call. She has to spend the night in Wafer Bay; there is work to do there. She hopes to see me tomorrow. That's it. I am miffed. Raul and Pedro smile to themselves.

Deciding to take a panga ride anyway, I carry Molly from the wheelhouse and sit her in the front of the panga; she likes riding on the bow like a dog. After starting both engines and releasing the lines, I slowly drive off. I feel good getting away from the boat. I've really had it with the charter with the punters and with everything else.

If I get the chance in port, I will disappear as soon as possible. Maybe I will jump overboard just before we get in. Mind you, it would have to be dark and there are some gnarly sharks swimming around in those waters - it's okay diving with full gear on, but swimming around on the surface at night in a strong current?

I don't know about that!

Chapter 25
Fancy Meeting You Here

"True friends stab you in the front." Oscar Wilde

FROM THE PANGA, I see the sailboat as soon as I turn the corner: possibly an 80-footer; anchored close to shore about three hundred yards south of Isla Conico. They must know this area well to be anchored there but why? Are they trying to avoid paying park fees? It isn't a spot I would choose to spend the night; it's far too close to the shoreline. If the wind picks up, they'll be in big trouble. Drawing close I see the name *Toucan* in gold lettering on the stern.

My curiosity turns to agitation when an extremely large head appears above the cockpit.

Fuck me rigid. It's Cabeza. The bastard!

When I see the blonde-haired guy standing next to him, I almost go into shock.

Claus smiles at me. I should have suspected something was afoot when I saw him talking to Cabeza onboard the Searcher when we arrived back after the last trip. They won't be here long though, once I inform the rangers of their presence. They'll sail out a lot faster than they sailed in, if they don't want to end up in jail

"Hey Claus, hey Herman, what's up?" I shout.

"Mac; how's it going?" Claus has a huge shit-eating grin on his face, but Cabeza lasers me with his piggly eyes.

"Do you have permission to be here?" I ask, tongue in cheek.

"Sure do buddy - from the president himself."

"Yeah. Right. You lying bastard. Where are the rest of the officials?"

"WE are it. We are the official delegation. Come onboard and have a beer. I have news for you," offers Claus with a smile that broadens by the second.

"I can't stay long, I've got to get my divers in the water; and by the way; we're going to be diving over there at Lobster Rock this afternoon so you'd better make yourselves scarce - particularly since I'll be speaking to the rangers on the radio when I get back to the boat."

"You asshole; take your divers somewhere else," says Cabeza.

"Oh, asshole is it, you fucking freak? Watch your mouth or I'll tear your fucking tongue out and feed it to the fish, you ugly twat." *I can't help myself.*

"Hey, calm down you two," says another voice inside the cockpit. *Fuck me gently; it is Dietmar.*

"Well, well. Happy families is it? How many more of you are here?"

"Just us," replies Claus.

The lying bastard. He must have more crew with him.

"I thought you had a heart attack," I say to Dietmar.

"Well, not quite," he smiles.

The crafty old bastard.

"Here, take my line," I say to Claus as I secure the panga alongside.

Once secure, I climb onboard and stick out my hand to Dietmar. "Hey, good to see you mate. What are you doing hooking up with this arsehole?" I ask, nodding towards Cabeza.

Dietmar takes my hand but doesn't answer. Cabeza tries again to drill a hole in me with his beady little eyes. I want to smack his fat face but Claus takes me by the shoulder and steers me up to the foredeck.

He looks at me sternly and speaks in a soft voice. "You, my friend, are in all kinds of fucking trouble."

"Why so?" I ask.

"Maria is dead." He waits for that to take effect. "There's a taskforce waiting to arrest you when you get back to port."

"What?" I am genuinely shocked by the mention of a taskforce. "Maria is dead? How?"

"Don't tell me you don't have anything to do with it, Mac."

"Why do you think I had something to do with it?"

"Mike told me that the police visited him. He said they want to question you about Maria's murder, and the murder of that girl Flora. And do I need to mention Macho's death? And a there were a couple of other murders too. Sounds like you were busy, Mac. The police came to see me too. They still have your gringo buddy in jail. They found out from his phone records that I called him on my mobile phone the day Macho was killed, and they also want to know why my phone records show a call to Maria at six thirty in the morning the day after Macho was killed."

"What did you tell them?"

"Well, of course I couldn't tell a lie, I told them it was you." He smiles again.

"What? Did you really say that you prick?"

"Of course not, but I know it was you, you fucker."

"Look, I had nothing to do with any of it, but it does look like I'm more than a little bit in the shit, mate."

"You could say that."

Claus smiles but doesn't answer. He doesn't need to; he knows. It is as simple as that."

"Do they want to arrest me, or just question me?"

"As far as I know it's just for questions, but they aren't stupid Mac. I would be worrying big time if I were you. I saw one of the patrol boats on my way out here yesterday. I spoke with them on the radio. They wanted to know if I was coming out here, but I don't have permission for this trip so obviously I couldn't' tell them I was. They were on their way here but had engine problems and had to turn back. Maybe they were coming after you. Why else would they come?"

"Maybe they were coming out on one of their family cruises. How the fuck would I know?" I am really rattled.

"What do you expect? Did you think you would get away with something like that, in that small town?"

I don't even bother denying it further.

"Okay, it looks like I'm fucked, but let's forget about all this shit for a minute. What are you doing here? You could get in deep shit yourself if you're caught here with these guys onboard without permission. And what the fuck is Dietmar doing here?"

"I'm not gonna be in anywhere near as much shit as you Mac, but who is going to catch me, now the rangers no longer have a boat?"

"How the fuck did you know that?"

"Mano told me. He had a call from the park's head office. They told him about their boats being destroyed. They were really pissed about it, and boy, are they pissed with you for unloading the generator in the big

243

swell. They blame it all on you Buddy. They are saying that you made them take the stuff off because it was in your way on the boat." He laughs at me again.

Those fuckers! But what can I say? Being blamed for causing the loss of a couple of boats and a generator is nothing compared to being chief suspect in the Punta La Pesca serial killings. I want Claus to stop grinning; it is starting to piss me off.

"Whose boat is this?" I ask.

"Bruce Foster, a gringo. You've probably seen him in the 'Cabana Bar'. I got a good deal for renting it. He might let me do more charters with it."

"Great." I say unenthusiastically. "How long are you going to be here?"

"Depends on what these men here want. I could stay for a week or more if they want. I've rented the boat for two weeks. They are pretty determined to find the treasure. They say they may have been digging in the wrong place last week."

"No shit, Poirot'."

"What? You think they were in the wrong place?"

"Well, considering they didn't find anything on the last trip, it doesn't take a fucking genius to figure that out. It seems to me like a pretty unlikely spot they chose anyway: it's right up in the fucking clouds almost. You don't need to be Albert Einstein to figure out that nobody would bother hiking all the way up a fucking big hill with eleven tons of treasure on their backs. It seemed pretty stupid to me. Hey, what happens if these fuckers find the treasure? Where are you going to take it?"

"They have a contingency plan; and a buyer who will take care of everything."

"Where?"

"In Panama."

"You won't be able to fit eleven tons of treasure into this little boat - it will sink."

"They have a plan for that too."

"What? Another boat?"

"I can't say any more."

"This could involve a hell of a lot of money Claus. Do you trust them?"

"What do you mean?"

"Well, if they do find treasure, you're a witness. How do they know they can trust you? They may decide they don't need you."

He looks uncomfortable. "They wouldn't do that."

"Why? Because you're German?"

"You are such an asshole Mac. Of course I trust them. You know; these guys found out from their lawyer just before the trip with you, that there is an old law still in existence in Costa Rica that would stop them from claiming any of the treasure. If it is found on an official expedition, the government gets everything and these guys get nothing."

"Are you serious?"

"Of course I'm serious man. They wouldn't have been able to keep one colone if they found anything last week. So, if they find something now, it's all theirs."

"Maybe not." I say in a low voice.

"What do you mean?"

"It might be millions Claus; think about the possibilities."

Claus looks at me suspiciously. I lower my voice. "Who knows they are here? If it's not official, then there is no record of them. I could do the dirty business in an instant. I'd love to bust that huge head open."

"But there is another boat standing by to come here to take the treasure to Panama. They are waiting for a radio call from Herman."

"And if they don't hear from Herman? Or he calls them and cancels? And when I say *he* calls them I mean someone who sounds like him on the radio calls them.

"You are such a bastardo, Mac"

"Maybe I am, but this might be your one and only chance of becoming rich my friend. You might end up dead instead. German or not, I wouldn't trust them. Dietmar may be okay, but look at that other twat. Look into those shifty little eyes of his and ask yourself if he is trustworthy."

Claus eyes me suspiciously for a second or two.

"I could handle everything. You wouldn't have to do a thing, except transport the treasure." He stares at me and I can almost see the cogs turning inside his head.

"Where are you staying tonight?" I ask

"My only choice is Iglesias Bay. Where are you diving tomorrow?"

"It depends on the weather. I'll probably dive Dos Amigos and stay around the other side all day, but after tomorrow I have to come around here and dive Alcyone. You'll have to go for a sail at around 8.30 in the morning and hide yourselves. I'll stay in Chatham Bay all day after that. There's no point in trying to talk on the radio; I won't be able to reach you on this side anyway. I'll try to nip around and see you later tomorrow. I have to go now and so do you because I'll be back here to dive with my group soon, and you don't want anyone to know you're here, right? You'd better tell Herman that I can bring the rangers around any time I like. He ought to be nice to me - the fucker. I'd better go. I'll see you later Buddy - have fun!"

"Okay, Mac I'll catch you tomorrow, you asshole."

I watch Dietmar and the Head appear on deck again as I leave. What an unlikely pair they are together.

Chapter 26
The Real Cave

"Plan for the future because that's where you are going to spend the rest of your life." Mark Twain.

The punters are already getting dressed for the dive when I get back to the *Searcher* with the panga. I let Roberto know I won't be diving and ask him to give the briefing while I prepare for my own excursion.

I figure Claus will now have taken the *Toucan* around to Iglesias Bay, to anchor there for the night and will probably go back to the ravine in the morning to drop off Cabeza and Dietmar so they can spend the day in the cave area.

I aim to get there before them, hopefully after the next dive.

The shovel and machete are still in the forepeak wrapped in a bin liner from the time Julia and I tried to go to the cave. As soon as both pangas leave, I walk out through the side door of the wheelhouse and cross the top deck with my gear. Leaving everything on the rear edge of the boat deck I walk down to the aft deck hoping I won't bump into Arcelio or Ronaldo because they will be curious about what I am up to. Making sure no one is around, I take the gear from the top deck, launch the kayak, and place everything onboard before paddling off. At Punta Pacheco I keep myself hidden from the pangas on the other side of Conical Rock. With the rock between us, I pull myself up to the shoreline and stash my goodies under a row of thick ferns, before quickly paddling back to the

Searcher and securing the kayak to the swim platform. The whole operation took twenty minutes.

Thirty minutes later, when the first panga rounds the point on its way back from the dive, I sit back on the Kayak; I don't want anyone asking to use it because I will have to refuse, and even now I still worry about my karma. Setting off slowly, I wave with the paddle as each panga passes. I don't receive a single wave back – but fuck them.

I recover the bag of tools from the ferns on the shoreline and then paddle furiously through the small gap between it and Conical Rock, heading towards a landing spot close to the ravine. Pulling the kayak onto a small rocky strip of shoreline to the right of the newly formed stream, I secure the bowline to the base of a palm, and stand staring at the water pouring through the mass of tangled foliage. I walk quickly towards the overgrown gully.

The stream has cleared a tunnel through the undergrowth. The entrance is big enough to crawl into. I crouch down, and wade in between a mass of brambles, trees, and vines. Once inside, the passage becomes higher and wider, as if it has been hacked away by someone. Further up the ravine it narrows until it is no longer possible to stand upright. I take out the machete and start hacking. Chopping my way through, I let the stream carry the fallen branches down to the sea. Crouching on the slippery bed of the fast-flowing stream, I struggle to get enough purchase to cut away the brambles around me, gradually hacking my way higher and deeper, creating a larger tunnel through the vegetation. Here and there, beams of light filter eerily through the trees. The ground beneath the stream becomes spongy and I get the nasty feeling I might be swallowed by a massive hole if I'm not careful.

Climbing gingerly, chopping and gaining rhythm, I'm grateful the stream carries away most of the smaller branches and vines. I'm also grateful for the neoprene wetsuit that is saving me from being eaten alive by constantly attacking ants. I beat the bastards off, glad for the protection of neoprene gloves and the ingenious cap with built in mosquito netting covering my face.

Why is my meat so sweet?

Sweating like a sinner at the gates of hell, I hack away for almost an hour. The ravine gets narrower, steeper, darker and then lighter again until I see light pouring through a large hole in a wall of rock ahead. It looks like a cave. Suddenly I don't have to cut anymore. I stand there with my heart pounding in my ears. The stream spills through the opening, and runs down into the gulley towards me. Peering through the opening in the wall of rock I'm not sure what I am looking at. It is not a cave, but a big clearing and there is a giant spider in the middle of it. *Fuck me!* I almost want to run back down the gulley screaming. Standing as still as a post I stare through the opening, trying to identify the strange looking object I see there: lots of spindly legs and a thick body. I dare not move. I almost crap in my pants. My heart races so fast I think I am going to pass out with fright. Do I go up or run down?

The object doesn't move, so I decide to go up.

Moving closer, I suddenly realize what it is; and feel sick with relief. Behind the rock wall is a huge hollow and in the center of the hollow, stretching almost to the far wall, a giant fig tree lays over on its side, its massive long roots, completely confused by the upheaval, reaching out in twenty different directions in search of nourishment, just like a giant spider. I can't believe I scared myself that much over a bloody tree. Wading over the rocks through the gap, I turn right, and enter into what looks like an amphitheater. The scene takes my breath away. Hidden from the seaward view behind the rock wall, a waterfall plunges from above. Walking into the clearing, I stand close to the waterfall and watch the roaring water bouncing off the jagged rock face above me, sending a refreshing breeze my way. To the right of the waterfall, a fifteen-foot mound of earth leads up into a giant cavern.

Hallelujah! What is this?

Inside the clearing, the sights, sounds, and smells engulfing me are overwhelming. I walk to the pile of earth at the threshold of the massive cavern and gazing up at the towering portal I feel a sudden and unexpected sense of foreboding; but that doesn't stop me trudging up the mound of dirt blocking the entrance. At the top of the mound I stare into an opening just big enough to crawl into; it looks like a long horizontal mineshaft. I feel a sudden chill and have the uneasy feeling that I am now standing at the gates of hell.

Shivering involuntary, I feel someone walking over my grave. Climbing back down, backing away from the entrance, I look up once more. I see the ridge at the top of the bluff, where Julia and I stood looking down that day. I'm surprised there are still trees perched on the ledge up there; the water runs right between them, cascading over the edge.

The left side of the hollow is lower than the waterfall side on my right. Half way along the wall, opposite the opening, I see a small gulley about thirty feet up, with a huge boulder sitting precariously close to its edge.

Maybe that is where Julia was when she spotted the cavern. She wouldn't be able to see it from up on the ledge. I make a mental note not to stand too close to that rock wall.

I decide to climb back up to the cavern's earth filled archway. My legs sink into the soft mud up to my shins, as I climb. Overcoming my feelings of dread, I crawl into the space beneath the earth and the rock ledge above it. Peering into the narrow hole, I can just make out a small tunnel but it's too dark to see the end of. I get the willies again. I am not crawling into that hole without a flashlight - no way Jose. I take off my backpack.

With the hair on the back of my neck standing upright, I shine the light inside, and just about make out a wall at the end. Slowly, on my hands and knees, like a tiny beetle, I crawl inside, slithering on my stomach when it gets smaller. I suddenly stop myself. What am I thinking? Am I crazy? If this lot collapses, I will be crushed. I really get the willies then; big time. Even the hair on my arse stands on end. With my heart thumping yet again, I scramble backwards as fast as I can. My mouth is as dry as a nun's nasty.

The attack of heebie-jeebies is followed by an attack of common sense. I crawl out of the tiny blind alley; run back through the archway in the wall and down into the foliage tunnel, heading back to the boat before you can say "incy, wincy, spider". Before scrambling all the way down to the shoreline, I bury my bag of tools in the tunnel brush.

I will return early in the morning.

Jumping into the sea in the fading light, I wash off the dirt and sweat before recovering the kayak.

On the way back, my brain starts working furiously again. Incongruous thoughts bounce around the inside walls of my skull. Is that really Aladdin's cave? I curse myself a hundred times for not getting there sooner. I am rapidly running out of time. This is the Royal Flush with accumulator; the Mega ball and Power Ball jackpots, the Star of India and everything I ever dreamt of winning; and it is just sitting there waiting for me to pluck with my grubby little hands. Well, maybe it is.

There are just a couple of small problems to overcome. Not least of which is the possibility that this is my last charter ever - and there are only two days left to beat Cabeza and Dietmar to the punch.

I am so preoccupied I forget it is barbecue night on the top deck. What an appropriate night for a party! After a couple of beers and a few glasses of wine I don't care that Julia hasn't shown up. I thought she might sneak over or give me a call. She likes the barbecue nights.

Feeling slightly drunk, I brief the punters about the planned dive site for the following morning and then sit in the salon and drink more wine, staring distractedly at the boring underwater video that threatens to send me to sleep dribbling all over the sofa. Usually I paint the toenails of anyone falling asleep in the salon, but those days are over. I don't care about the punters.

Removing myself from the salon, I stroll up to my cabin in a trancelike state. I wonder briefly why Julia didn't come back onboard. I'm ready to sleep like a dead dog, but bugger me; as soon as I get into bed, I am wide awake; my mind racing like a greyhound. I fantasize about murdering everyone onboard and feeding them to the sharks; or making them walk the plank in the middle of nowhere - it won't take long for them to be gobbled up out here. Well, maybe I could do it to the guests but not to my crew.

But despite this, my drunken thoughts continue: Could I coerce the crew into becoming part of it? The crew situation and the lack of enough diesel to get me anywhere other than Punta la Pesca are my biggest problems. The rangers have the supply of diesel I brought for their boat and generator, but it won't be enough to help me out – the Searcher's engines gobble up more fuel than the Apollo moon missions. Anyway, Carlos knows exactly how much fuel we have onboard and he knows we have enough to get back to Punta La Pesca so I can't ask the rangers for fuel without making Carlos suspicious. If I steal the fuel, I will have to slot all the rangers and that means Julia might have to go as well. I think about dumping all my crew and punters on the island and disabling the rangers' radio, but fishing boats are always stopping by.

I must be going crazy. I could not possibly do anything like that - Even if I did have enough fuel to reach Panama. Is this the real me thinking all this stuff? What happened to the nice bloke who can't do enough for his guests?

I'm not really sure of anything until a cunning plan hits me like a giant cricket bat.

Chapter 27
Cocos Day 5:
A Bright New Morning

" We cannot solve or problems with the same thinking we used when we created them."
Albert Einstein

DAWN IS JUST BREAKING as I ease myself out of bed.
I have a great plan.
The time has come for extreme action and today is all about timing. My plan is simple and drastic.
Someone is going to die today.
But first, before anyone else wakes up there is work to be done.
The success of my plan depends partly on the weather: if this heavy rain continues it could scupper my plans. By the time my first chores are finished I am delighted to see the sun peeking through the clouds and there is just a slight drizzle of rain. The morning's first dive is scheduled for Alcyone: the big undersea mound a mile off the eastern side of the island within sight of Iglesias Bay. I take the panga out to make sure that the sea state is calm enough for us to dive there. I don't have to go far to see that it is perfect. I haven't the time to go all the way to Iglesias where Claus is, but I hope he took me seriously and has moved off out of sight.

I know it is going to be a beautiful day – no matter what the weather.
After a good breakfast and a dive briefing, we are ready to go.

Rounding the southern tip of Chatham Bay in the panga, heading towards the dive site with the group, I'm relieved that the sea state is no worse than it was earlier this morning when I drove around alone. With all engines purring loudly our two little boats fly together across the slight sea swell on the two-mile drive towards Alcyone.

From the area of the sea mound, I'm relieved to see no sign of the *Toucan* in Bahia Iglesias.

The only navigational aids we have in each panga are a compass and depth sounder, but people sail around the world with less. If you know what to look for, finding an unmarked sea mound is a piece of cake. The features I take a bearing on are a small rock pinnacle, a small cave, and the contour of a ridge that lines up with another small pinnacle. It isn't possible to pinpoint trees or anything like that on the island because the landscape is being continually transformed by landslides and whatnot. Once I line up on the bearings, it is just a matter of driving out on a set compass course for a set time. Then, when we are close enough, the depth sounder locates the top of the large sea mound for us.

The numbers on the depth sounder's digital display decrease with the depth as we approach the area above the center of the sea mound. I keep the panga in position by heading into the wind and running the engines with just the right amount of throttle. Raul has the anchor ready to drop from the bow. As soon as I give him the nod, he drops it into the blue, watching until it disappears on its winding path below. Landing on top of the rocky mound, the little anchor drags slightly until it catches behind a rock or in a crevice. The line at the bow suddenly snaps taught and the panga stops dead, swinging around in the current and coming to a standstill facing south. The current sweeps past us on its way north, and judging by the wake streaming off the transom, its estimated speed is about one and a half to two knots. This is perfect.

I wait, making sure we are secure before beckoning for the yellow panga to come closer so Roberto can go down and check the anchor. We need to make absolutely sure it is wedged tight and isn't about to come loose. Roberto is already dressed in his equipment. At my signal he rolls over backwards and makes his way down the anchor line with masses of silver bubbles streaming behind him until he is out of sight. The visibility looks to be about fifty feet vertically. Looking down from the surface the visibility is different than it is looking horizontally underwater. Light carries further vertically. Today, all I am really interested in is the vertical visibility.

Alcyone can be a very tricky dive when the current is strong; that's why we usually keep it until the end of the week. Some divers have to be worked up to it because the best part of the dive doesn't start until reaching the top of the sea mound 100 feet below the surface. When the pangas approach, the noise of their engines frightens off the hammerheads, scattering them like shotgun pellets. Then the noise and spectacle of two boatloads of divers splashing into the water with masses of bubbles streaming behind them, creating a massive Jacuzzi effect over the seamount, freaks the Hammers even more, making them wary about coming back. Fortunately for us, their desperate need to be cleaned of parasites overcomes their suspicions. As soon as everyone is settled on top of the mound the Hammers line up once again for the big march past. Alcyone is a site where, if everyone stays still and calm, hundreds of hammerheads hover around at any given moment. Of course, no group ever sits still and calm, because we all know that the grass is always greener on the other side, right? Well, in case you don't know it, and for future reference, it's not.

Raul ties a long-knotted rope to the anchor line at the bow, throwing part of it overboard before attaching the other end to the transom. The divers can now pull themselves along it if they need to. Holding tightly to the rope when descending into the current is a necessary precaution, because anyone foolish enough to let go and try swimming will be swept away in the current. If that happens, they will need a taxi back to the dive site. Most divers that come on our trips are proficient underwater. I hope this group makes it to the mound in one go. Sometimes the current is stronger on top of the mound than it is on the surface. Divers can easily be lulled into a false sense of security about the strength of the current. If they let go of the line half way down, thinking they can swim the rest of the way, they find out too late that the force of the current coming up from the depths and sweeping over the top of the mound is much stronger than they imagined, despite my warnings about it during the dive briefing. The current down there is often too strong to swim against.

When we reach the top of the mound, we have to hold onto the rocks tightly and pull ourselves hand over hand while finning like mad to get into the lee of a rock or crevice and evade the current. It is often like a Charlie Chaplin movie down there, with divers holding on with straight arms, and their bodies flapping around in the current like sheets on a washing line on a windy day.

If anyone lets go of the rope on the way down and is whisked away by the current, the rear panga will detach and pick them up. Then, if there is enough air left in their tank, they will be deposited back on site.

Because this is a relatively deep dive, the divers have to pay particular attention to their pressure gauges and decompression computers. Moving around isn't really necessary because once we reach the top of the sea mound everything happens in front of our very eyes — it's an underwater amphitheater.

Some divers expend more energy here than on a regular dive. With the combined effort of holding tightly to the rope while descending, and then using a combination of leg kicks and hand over hand pulls, divers suck in a whole lot more valuable gas than normal.

On leaving the bottom, divers also need a good reserve of gas in their tanks to be able to complete a safety stop at fifteen feet. At Alcyone this is crucial.

Everyone has to avoid going into decompression at all costs. There's nothing much worse than having no gas in your tank at the end of a dive to do the necessary decompression stops — it's like having a heart attack on a canoe in the middle of nowhere. There might be a chance that somebody in the group has enough gas in their tank to share with you while waiting for an extra tank to be lowered from the panga, but it isn't something to be relied upon. And if a whale shark appears, there won't be a soul around to help you anyway. Whale sharks show up frequently on this dive, and that causes total bedlam. Everyone goes nuts, swimming furiously, trying to get close to the big beasts, leaving more people low on gas than there are spare tanks.

Yes, this can be a tricky dive alright.

Our panga rides up and down on the anchor line in the swell as we wait for Roberto to check the anchor is secured properly on top of the seamount. It doesn't take long but everyone is impatient to get into the water. Pedro drives the second panga ahead of us, and on my signal puts the engines into neutral, indicating for his divers to roll over into the water one by one. Because they are ahead of us, they don't need to swim against the current to get to our anchor rope — all they have to do is drift back onto it. Once the divers from both pangas have submerged, Pedro will tie his panga on to our stern and hang behind us.

The divers from my panga struggle to pull themselves along the rope to the bow, but to my relief, they all make it down the line okay. I watch them slowly disappear into the depths. Making sure they've all made it to the bottom safely, I call for the yellow panga to come and tie to our stern. When it is secure, I put all my equipment on, open the valves on my rebreather and roll over backwards into the sea.

In about sixty minutes the shit will hit the fan.

Chapter 28
Goodbye Cruel World

"The best way to escape from a problem is to solve it."
Alan Saporta

VENTING MY BUOYANCY jacket in the swift current, I hold the line tightly and descend ten feet beneath the panga. Checking my equipment, making sure everything is working properly I wait two minutes before starting my descent, - I can't afford any problems on this dive. I maintain my equipment religiously and today I am relying on it totally to get me out of trouble.

Absolutely sure everything is functioning correctly I sink down fifty feet on the rope, gazing at the silent scene beneath me. Strung out on the undersea mountain top below, the divers are all looking away from me, facing west. Every time they breathe out, masses of gas bubbles explode from their regulators. Sparkling streams of reflective bubbles burst behind them in the fierce current; the bubbles expanding and ascending continuously towards the surface. Looking through the long stream of bubbles I see hammerheads moving in. I'm not interested in them today though, except as a distraction. I don't intend staying to watch a flight of fluted hammerheads right now – oh no; I'm going flying myself.

Diving really is like flying; but without an aircraft. Wearing a rebreather underwater makes me a stealth diver. I am a fish; a part of the ocean.

After diving with scuba gear and having the constant roar of gas bubbles streaming past your ears, rebreathers are stunningly silent. Depending on whether you use 'closed' or 'semi-closed circuit' equipment, few if any bubbles escape. I'm wearing a 'closed circuit system'. My small integrated gas bottle contains enough oxygen for a six to eight-hour dive. All my unused breathing gas is re-circulated – giving off no bubbles and making no noise.

The panga drivers are busy keeping a lookout for anyone popping up to the surface. They won't see a single sign of me on the anchor rope below them when I let myself go and stretch myself out, allowing the current to take me backwards.

The sea mound looks smaller and the divers all disappear from view as I turn and start finning like the clappers to the west. I swim away from the sea mound and away from the divers; away from my old life heading for another level.

If I get this wrong it will be disastrous.

After swimming in a northwesterly direction for ten minutes, I turn slightly. My destination is to the west, but once closer to land the current might take me east, making me miss the island altogether.

I hope I'm not being swept too far east, but there is no way of knowing where I am without a point of reference other than my compass. I can't go to the surface for a sneaky spy hop just yet, I have to keep swimming, hoping I am moving in the right direction.

I've spent many hours following compass courses underwater, although they were not always 240 degrees despite what I say in my dive briefings.

I swam miles in the Navy; silently and secretly submerged under raging seas in the dead of night, enveloped in the heart of darkness; wrapped in a blanket of obscurity, with nothing to see except the tiny luminous dials of a compass and depth gauge mounted on a small, hand-held swim-board. We were constantly preparing for the day we would be facing the dreaded Ruskie Commies from The Soviet Union.

In retrospect our "attack" role was a big exercise in futility.

When we were lucky, we swam in the warm, tropical, shark-infested waters of the Far East, but mostly it was under the cold storm-tossed seas of Northern Europe - sometimes on clandestine 'sneaky beaky' raids; swimming for miles in fiercely hostile weather conditions. We carried practice explosive limpet mines intended for the destruction of 'enemy' warships. At other times we may have an underwater camera and underwater drawing implements for the reconnaissance of 'enemy' beachheads.

Breathing from black antisocial rebreathers, we always maintained a steady rate - taking maximum advantage of the number of breaths in our two small oxygen cylinders. We wore heavy rubber jet fins, not the long lightweight fins I now use. These long fins developed for free-divers, work magically underwater; propelling me quickly through the sea. The current is taking me with it, and with powerfully swift, long-leg kicks I am positively speeding away from Alcyone.

This is my most important underwater mission yet and I better get it right or I will end up a dead duck.

Cranking up the kicking action I feel I'm whistling through the water at a great rate of knots. A number of curious silky sharks almost turn in their tracks to follow me. Normally I would turn towards them menacingly because they don't expect their prey to be chasing them, but right now I can't be distracted or turn my body away from the course I am following. The thought of a group of silky sharks silently following me makes me nervous, until I see a school of hammerheads below; their presence strangely reassures me.

If I have calculated correctly, I will soon be in shallow water, and will be able to see the bottom. I don't want to pop up to the surface just yet; but if I have to, I can probably spy hop without being seen – I've had enough practice.

During countless exercise compass swims all kinds of boats zoomed around trying to catch us. Sometimes after planting dummy limpet mines on a warship's hull we were told to give ourselves up. I'll never forget the explosive sound of automatic rifles going off beside my head when I surfaced one night with my buddy and one of these boats spotted us. The Royal Marines firing those weapons really wanted to kill us.

Now, suddenly I see shadows below me. I see large shapes on the sea floor. I can tell by my movement over the bottom that I am moving at a fair old pace. I have been swimming for forty minutes and if I have calculated correctly, I will soon be in the vicinity of Cabo Descubierta. Once there I can follow the underwater ridge back to Iglesias Bay. If I am wrong - who knows where I might be? I am very glad to see the bottom. I stop finning to see which way the current is taking me. The current is going east.

Trying to swim against it gets me nowhere fast.

I am still hoping to be able to swim straight to Iglesias Bay and climb out there, where it will be easy to disappear into the jungle alatool. However, there is an element of risk attached to that plan because of the possibility of being swept past the south end of the island and out to sea. I really will be in big trouble if that happens. Nevertheless, I am lucky; I am now in shallow water and will hit the island very soon. I will soon be able to get out and hide. If the current gets weaker, closer to shore, I can swim to Iglesias Bay and still be okay - it doesn't really matter as long as I stay out of sight.

If I weren't used to diving and swimming in swift currents three times a day, I would never be able to make it this far in such a short space of time without becoming completely exhausted. Even so, I will suffer from a furious headache later because despite the effort of swimming hard and fast, I still breathe navy style to preserve gas; controlling each breath - one every eight seconds.

I estimate that the first divers at Alcyone will be making their way to the surface very soon and expect Roberto to be completely confused as to why I have not dislodged the anchor and sent it to the surface with the lifting bag, as I usually do. Roberto might not have enough gas in his cylinder, or enough bottom time left to go down and lift the anchor. He is probably looking around for me right now. But none of the other divers will even notice I'm missing. No one will be worrying about me just yet.

I decide to keep heading due west, and once close enough to shore to try a sneaky peek. With land close behind it will be difficult for anyone to spot the top of my head if I make a quick spy hop. Hopefully I won't be spotted from the panga.

I swim until the water is so shallow that the swells swing me backwards and forwards involuntarily. Raising my body into the upright position I squeeze all the air from my buoyancy control jacket and very slowly stick my head up. My eyes just break the surface. After taking my bearings, I am back underwater in a flash; without even making a ripple. The spy hop was perfect but my navigation sucks. I am a long way north of where I am supposed to be - *so much for all that naval training.*

I've only gone about a mile but the current swept me further north than expected – I am over two miles from Iglesias, which is two miles further away than I planned. I am so close to Isla Montegne that there are two different choices to make. The first is to try and climb onto shore behind the small islet and wait until the current dies down and then swim to Iglesias. The second option is to try and make my way to Iglesias Bay against the current.

If I try climbing ashore behind Isla Montegne there is the small possibility of being seen. Although I will be only partly shielded it is still a good prospect - if climbing out here is physically possible. If I try swimming against the current to Iglesias and have a problem with my equipment, I will have to surface, and in that area, there is insufficient cover for me along the shoreline. Even if I make it, I might be too knackered to do anything by the time I get there. I have to make up my mind fast, before they start looking for me.

There is one other possibility. I could try to make it as far north around the shoreline as possible, and maybe reach the cave site, about a mile away. But then again, if I do that, I don't know whether the current will be against me when I round the curved shoreline ahead. Just because the current heads north here it doesn't mean it will be going in the same direction around the corner. The current swirl around the island causing eddies at each cardinal point.

I decide to go for Isla Montegne.

Checking my computer again, I see I have been in the water for forty-seven minutes – it is definitely time to get out. With plenty of gas left, I have no doubt I can make it to Iglesias in one go but not right now. I'll go ashore here and wait a while.

Swimming into the narrow channel behind Montegne, I make another spy hop, but this time making a 180-degree sweep, looking for the pangas. I can't see them from behind the islet, which means they can't see me either. I decide to risk landing on a narrow strip of shingle. There is enough undergrowth to hide.

Now it's time to really test my luck.

If any divers are still in the water, they will probably have drifted quite a way north already, and the pangas will be following them. They may already have picked everyone up and started to head back to Alcyone to search the surface area there. They might even be waiting for the anchor to appear with its lifting bag. I have no idea what is happening right now, but once everyone is picked up, a very nervous dive master in the yellow panga will ask if anyone has seen me. When the reply is in the negative there will be a lot of nervous divers not knowing what to think.

Because I usually spend an hour in the water on each dive, rarely surfacing earlier, there is at least another twenty minutes left before they start thinking anything is wrong.

When the pangas have waited in the immediate area long enough to realize I'm not there, they will start heading in the direction of the current. They probably won't look close to shore until later. Roberto and the drivers will assume I am floating around in the vicinity. They know me well enough to know I normally stay close to the dive site until the very last moment. When I don't appear, they will start thinking that maybe I drifted off. They have a float onboard each panga with a weighted pole and flag. When the pole is thrown overboard it floats with the current, simulating a diver. They will probably use it. Only when they can't find me around Alcyone will they think I have drifted further out to sea, or made it ashore. It won't be until much later, after a fruitless search, that there will be the unpalatable feeling that maybe I am sleeping with the crabs. After the search is abandoned in favor of the Dances with Crabs theory, my decision to wear the rebreather will stimulate all sorts of theories about the possible reason for my demise.

Maybe it was oxygen poisoning, because I had the wrong gas mixture in my cylinders. Maybe I dived too deep on an oxygen rich mixture, and, racked with convulsions, drowned. Or maybe there was not enough oxygen in the mix and I suffered from hypoxia and drowned. Or the CO_2 absorbent became too damp, causing carbon dioxide poisoning. Or maybe the absorbent was out of date or I used it too many times, and, breathing too rapidly, fighting for each breath, I panicked and drowned. Or maybe seawater leaked into my CO_2 absorbent canister from a loose connection giving me a soda lime cocktail, causing me to choke on the caustic solution and drown.

They will have a field day with this one. There are plenty of potentially juicy topics for discussion here - all with the common denominators of drowning, death, and me.

Popping up to the surface, I am ready to duck back down in an instant at the first sign of a panga. Luckily, they are nowhere in sight as I approach my point of exit – so far so good.

Chapter 29
Freedom

"Man is free at the moment he wishes to be."
Voltaire (Francois-Marie Arouet)

THE LANDING IS a bit tricky.

Bouncing up and down in the swell, I fin like mad to catch a breaking wave that gathers me up and throws me onto the rocks like a soggy sponge, knocking the wind from my lungs. Although it is a hard, ungracious landing, I'm not looking for extra points for style. Clinging on to anything I can grasp, I scrabble up the shoreline as fast as I can. I don't normally wear gloves on a dive but I made sure to bring them today. Lying completely flat, with very little room to maneuver, I shrug off the rebreather and remove my fins and weight belt. My fashionably black wetsuit was chosen specifically this morning - no bright neon colors to attract attention.

Dragging the rebreather up the incline as quickly as possible, I rest under the first row of palms. Lying on my back out of sight I regain my wind. The trickiest part of this whole operation is now over; if I had missed the island altogether, I would have ended up at sea hoping to be picked up by one of the pangas. And if I were seen climbing ashore here, this particular plan would be over and it would be embarrassing trying to explain what I am doing here. As it is, I am in pretty good shape.

Only a few places around the island make a landing like this possible. The precipitous nature of the islands' shoreline limits the possibility of beach landings anywhere except in the bays. This is a good spot; completely hidden from view. The pangas won't be able to get close enough to shore to see me because of the rows of small rock pinnacles along this section of coastline. I don't have to climb a rock wall to get to the interior of the island from here either. Completely out of sight, I crawl up slowly through the tall grass and ferns, dragging my rebreather.

Uncontrollable bramble branches snag my wetsuit, making small slits in the nylon covering. The neoprene rubber protects my skin from sharp thorns and attacking ants as I slowly move on up. I have bags of time. I just need to get to a point high enough to see what is happening with the pangas.

How long will they search before dropping the punters back off at the boat? How long before they call the rangers and the office in San Jose? This is going to create all kinds of ripples across the pond of everyday life aboard a dive charter boat. It will also slow down Claus and company onboard the *Toucan*. They won't have a clue what is going on with the panga activity around this side of the island. They will be unable to go back to Conical Rock until the pangas have stopped searching and that won't be until nightfall. If the *Toucan* shows itself, I am pretty sure the crew of the Searcher will ask for assistance in searching, which will put Claus in the difficult position of trying to help in the search whilst trying to hide his illegal guests.

From the pocket of my rebreather buoyancy jacket I take out a pair of neoprene booties and my jungle green baseball cap, with its sewn in mosquito net. The booties protect my feet from the sharp thorns and rocks but don't provide much traction on the slippery earth. The mosquito net is vital, as I said before – I'm a magnet for biting bugs.

I hide the rebreather amongst the ferns.

Free of the cumbersome piece of equipment, I crawl more rapidly through the trees and up the slope, looking for a good lookout spot. I stop when the whole search area is in sight. The pangas are specks in the distance. They will estimate that I might have traveled at least a mile with the current during the last hour. I imagine their anguish, searching an ocean that suddenly seems a far greater expanse than they imagined an hour or so ago. From the low vantage point of a panga, the whitecaps out there make it difficult to see far into the distance.

One of the pangas turns and starts heading back toward the island. Through the tall grass, I see it clearly as it passes close to the shoreline. Most of the divers onboard are standing, studying the island. The other panga is still way out in the distance. The drivers are smart; covering both options at once. They will not yet have the feeling I am lost forever.

It will take time for the realization to dawn on them that Mac might never come back. There will be a major panic amongst the crew as they try to figure out what to do next. One of them will have to drive the Searcher back to port. They could probably all do that, but Raul will be in charge and will shit a brick at the thought.

There is one more day of diving to complete and I bet a whole bunch of money that my disappearance will not stop them doing three dives tomorrow - the fuckers.

I am thankful the ranger's panga fleet is out of action; it keeps them confined to land; either at Chatham or Wafer Bay, making it impossible for them to do a search of their own. All I need to do is wait awhile before going overland to the vicinity of the cave; although it will be a nightmare trying to get there through the thick matted jungle in my path.

Having never stepped foot in this particular area before, I have no knowledge of the terrain on top of the rise, but there is sure to be a tangled mass of vegetation up there. The cave is not that far to walk in a straight line, but a swath will have to be hacked out with my little dive knife and that could take until my 90th birthday. I promptly rule out that idea. The only real option is to wait until dark when the search ends, then swim around the island close to the shoreline.

The inside of my mouth is as dry as week old armadillo shit. I need a drink badly. Since climbing ashore, I haven't stopped sweating. Crawling on my belly I head for a small palm. Pulling on a flowering stalk, I cut off the tip, allowing the sweet sticky nectar to drip steadily into my parched mouth.

Sweating like an old pork sausage I lay there for an hour amongst the ferns on the bank. Have done the right thing? Well, the plan is in action and there is no going back. My mouth and throat have the consistency of balsa wood. I desperately need a long cool drink. Moving to an area further up, I pick through the vines, looking for one with nice thick shoots. With plenty to choose from, I select one with a rough bark, and taking a chance, stand up quickly and cut a notch as high as I can before kneeling to cut the vine off at the base. I watch in anticipation as the clear fluid oozes out - if it were milky, I wouldn't be able to drink its poisonous sap. As it is, I manage to quench my immediate thirst.

Occasionally poking my head up, I see the pangas driving around frantically searching. After an hour and a half, to my delight, they both disappear back in the direction of Chatham Bay, probably to drop off the punters and get more fuel for the pangas.

Once they have gone, I crawl up to the top of the ridge and stare at the massive tree covered expanse ahead. It is just as I expected: thick with closely woven trees, more vines, and still more brambles. There is no way to get through it quickly without a machete. Earlier I thought of trying to hide a machete inside my diving equipment but couldn't take the chance of it being accidentally discovered before the dive. I imagined dropping it from inside the rebreather jacket and it landing on the deck of the panga in front of everyone. How would I explain that to the punters? "I just thought I'd bring this machete along in case we meet something really gnarly on the dive"?

The weather is changing: rain is coming in. I will soon have more fresh water than I need. With my little knife, I cut my way far enough into a growth of trees to make a small hide, and when I am done, I curl up for some shuteye.

The rain comes shortly after one o'clock in the afternoon - and it pisses down. The good news is: I can now quench my thirst. Even though I have fairly good shelter under the palm leaves and vines, and despite wearing a makeshift poncho made from a large plastic bin liner, I am soaking wet and cold.

I start shivering.

Huge, heavy raindrops hammer down. Gales seem to be blowing from all directions. The visibility is down to a few feet and the wind blows fiercely straight into my little hide; it looks as though the rain is in for a good while.

Unable to bear it any longer, I decide to get back in the water to get warm. I could swim further around the shore towards the cave; no one will see me in this weather. The pangas won't be out searching in this anyway; they will be unable to see anything in this rain storm. I crawl back down to where I left the rebreather, put the anti-mosquito hat, plastic bag, and booties in the jacket pocket, strap the heavy piece of equipment on my back again, and slide down into the sea.

The sea is warm against my skin under my wet suit.

Swimming swiftly underwater in the shallows, pumping my legs, I follow the shoreline. Rounding Cabo Atrevida, I can tell by looking up at the surface that the rain is still beating down. A group of white tips follow me, probably thinking a hunting party is about to begin, but I ignore them and continue swimming as fast as I can until reaching a long finger of rock. I know exactly where I am now. The rock stretches away from the shoreline at right angles, continuing underwater toward a deep sand bed. Swimming across the rock, I reach an area where thick brown mud is being washed down from a river ashore. Suddenly it is dark underwater; I seem to be swimming in a bowl of lentil soup. I swim a while longer before slowly raising my eyes above sea level. Tree branches and leaves are floating around everywhere on the surface. The visibility is crap, above and below the surface. I could get out right here and crawl up the bank without being spotted by anyone further than five feet away. The only problem is: there is now a small river pouring down the ravine through the trees, and it is even wider than it was this morning. Can I propel myself through it? Summoning another burst of energy, I fin ashore to the side of the river. *If the pangas appear now I'm fucked.*

Sharp stones dig agonizingly into my knees and elbows as I try crawling across the narrow, rocky shoreline. I claw my way up for a few yards but the river washes me backwards and I have to lie flat, trying to take my fins off with the river rushing over me. I curse a dozen times into my mouthpiece every time I get washed back. I try moving away from the river to get onto the shore but it is treacherously slimy and I can't get a grip. The rebreather cuts into my back, twenty times heavier than it was in the water. Desperately frustrated, I scramble to get out of the sea, trying to reach as far up the bank as possible before slipping back down in the mud. The diving booties don't help - they just make my feet slide out from under me.

I am extremely vulnerable right now. I have to get up into the brush as quickly as possible or I will have to swim all the way back to where I just came from, or even further - to Iglesias Bay.

Even though the torrential downpour makes it difficult as hell to climb, I am thankful for the cover, because without it, I wouldn't even be here. I am starting to tire. My breathing is labored as I try pulling himself up. The rain is starting to ease off and I suddenly feel panicky.

If the rain stops altogether there is a danger I will be seen from miles away. This is not good; if I get caught my plan is ruined. The rebreather weighs a ton on my back. The straps dig tighter into my shoulders, restricting the circulation but I have to keep it on until I am completely hidden in the brush. The fins don't help either. I stuck them inside the waist straps of the jacket and they are so long, they get in my way. I can't dump them – I will need them later.

The more frantic I become the longer each second ticks by. Sheer desperation forces me to scramble wildly up the incline like a hermit crab on fire. Gritting my teeth, silently, screaming as loud as I can, I eventually make it up the bank to the opening in the brush where the river bursts through. Pulling myself inside through the mud and leaves, I grab any plant I can for leverage. I rip roots and rocks away by the handful. As fast as I pull them up, I grab more. I scrabble on my elbows and knees. I would use my teeth if they weren't clamped tightly onto the mouthpiece of the rebreather still strapped to my back. The muscles in my arms and legs scream for me to stop and rest - but I can't, not until I am completely safe and hidden.

My persistence pays off.

Inside the tunnel of foliage, completely out of sight, I sit firmly, and as fast as I can, unbuckle the straps of the rebreather and shrug it off. My sigh of relief can probably be heard in Chatham Bay. Pushing the rebreather between the trees and vines, I move it out of the river's path before retrieving the cap and bin liner from the pocket. After turning off the cylinder valves, I jam the equipment in as far as it will go before covering it with branches and leaves. Sitting to the side of the small ravine, with my feet wedged in amongst the roots, I allow the river of muddy water to wash down over my body.

Free of the rebreather, I no longer exist. I have simply disappeared and hopefully will never be found. I am Monty Python's Parrot: dead, deceased and for the moment, resting in peace.

I have taken a radical step towards regeneration. Although it is a huge gamble, I see no alternative; it is the only way I can squirm my way out of the quagmire. If I have to, I can live on the island for months - not that I intend doing that - the bugs will drive me nuts. There is plenty to eat and drink, and if I can avoid injury, I can go anywhere on the island I choose. The only thing I am sorry about now is leaving Molly behind on the boat. I will miss her. We are alike - constantly surrounded by people but always alone; not giving a shit about anything or anyone except ourselves. Old Molly is the only one who is always there. Thinking about her brings home the seriousness and finality of the situation I just brought about.

The world is standing still for me right now. I am in limbo. I have not yet reached the point of no return. Everything could change in an instant. I could put my gear back on, jump back into the sea and float around to the boat, giving everyone the surprise of their lives. I could tell them I was swept over to the island from the dive site and have been waiting for them to rescue me. I could take a nice warm shower, eat a nice big steak dinner, drink a few glasses of wine and then crawl into bed with Julia. I could finish the trip and go back to port. If I were lucky, I could be arrested and thrown into prison for who knows how long with a bunch of other desperate criminals. If my luck runs out, I could be slotted by someone I don't even know.

Despite what I've done, I still don't consider myself a real criminal. Well okay, I don't suppose everyone would make the same decisions I did. Am I just a victim of circumstances? What do I have to lose now, that I wouldn't lose if I stayed on the boat — my job?

On reflection I probably made the best decision.

The rising noise level surrounding me makes me think again. The island is coming alive; I'm in the middle of a choir practice for millions of insects and hundreds of birds. Every living thing around me is suddenly screaming like a demented idiot.

Until you study the island closely, the only signs of life you see are a few large frigate birds and boobies, and the occasional deer or pig, but when you look closer: stone the bloody crows; there are millions of creepy crawlies everywhere; the little bastards.

Shivering, I think of all the unwelcome companions I'll be sharing the jungle nights with. I hate bugs; always have done. No-see'ems, ants, ticks, lice, millipedes, centipedes, scorpions, spiders and mosquitoes all love me — the fuckers.

I only begin to relax when the rain starts pouring down again, beating on the jungle canopy, drowning out all other sounds. Although not everything has worked out exactly as planned, I have reached this stage without being detected and it is now just a matter of time before the next stage begins.

All in all, everything has gone remarkably well - so far.

Chapter 30
Preparation

"No matter how rich you become, how famous or powerful, when you die the size of your funeral will still pretty much depend on the weather."
Michael Pritchard

L YING IN THE BRUSH I think back to when I woke earlier this morning, before dawn. My first conscious thought was of the rain rattling the roof, making me unsure of whether it was a good or bad start to stage one. Wrapping a few clothes in a jungle-green poncho, I squeezed them together into my backpack along with a few cans of food I liberated from the galley. Next, I dug out my special waterproof bag; the one I intended keeping my valuables in should the boat sink one day. The fact that I have no valuables is neither here nor there. I put both my handguns, a few boxes of ammo, and a few other items in the bag before rolling the top down tightly and securing it closed. Wrapping the shotgun and more ammo inside a double layer of bin liners, I secured it with duct tape.

When everything was ready, I took the bags down to the aft platform. Everyone was still sleeping in their cabins. Quickly and silently I launched the kayak, loaded the bags, and took off into the pink twilight, paddling away from the boat like an Olympic canoeist on a diet of ginseng and Costa Rican coffee. Sitting on the loaded kayak, disappearing around the corner of the bay I thanked the pouring rain for hiding me from anyone who might be up and about. Passing Isla Conico, heading for the landing spot, I saw that the stream was fuller and faster flowing than the day before; it would be very difficult climbing ashore there. I paddled back to the shallow area behind conical rock where there was hardly any swell. Standing groin deep in the narrow channel behind the rock, I unloaded my bundles onto shore; hiding them beneath the thick brush line some distance from the new stream. If all goes well with my plan, I won't need any of these items until tomorrow anyway.

I was back onboard before anyone even noticed I'd gone. On the aft deck, I prepared my rebreather, charged the CO_2 absorbent canister and checked the pressure of the O_2 and air diluent bottles. I then put my booties, mosquito cap and bin bag into the rebreather pocket. Satisfied everything was prepared correctly I climbed the steps to the boat deck and sat in a chair beneath the awning. Lighting a cigarette, I studied the island through the now drizzling rain, going over my plan once more.

The cigarette made me so lightheaded I resolved never to smoke again.

I had made up my mind what to do and nothing could stop me except the rain. If it rained hard all day, we wouldn't be able to dive at Alcyone because the surface visibility would be bad. There was always the next day, which is the last day of the charter but I had to execute my plan today. After spending all day searching for me, everybody would assume I was dead. They might continue the search tomorrow, but I very much doubt it; the punters will want to dive.

Even if they do decide to have another look for me, they will still have to leave the island on time, to arrive in port on time, or everyone will miss their flights. This means they have to leave Cocos around 5 pm, by which time everyone will have given up all hope of ever finding me.

There will be no point in sending out the patrol boat from Punta La Pesca because if I really were floating around somewhere, I would be plankton twice removed by the time they arrived here. An aircraft might be sent out but they probably won't spend too much time looking; everyone would be thinking the worst after a day and a night had gone by. It is unlikely anyone could survive floating around in the waters off Cocos Island for that length of time without being gobbled up by at least one wicked beasty. And even if someone survives being eaten — the currents would sweep them into the middle of nowhere in twenty-four hours.

Passing by the galley I stopped to chat with Raul and Ronaldo, gratefully accepting their offer of a fresh plate of Gallo Pinto.

At 6:45 back up in the wheelhouse, deep in thought, ready to listen to the BBC news on the radio, Ronaldo brought me breakfast. The sports report is usually on until 7am, but I'm not interested in that. I sat at my desk savoring the black beans, rice, and scrambled eggs. At 6:55 I switched on the radio, and as soon as I tuned in to the BBC, I knew something major had happened. The somber announcer wasn't talking about sport.

Something had happened in Paris.

Gradually it became clear that there was a car crash in a tunnel. I almost choked on a chipotle when the reporter announced that Princess Diana, the Princess of Wales, had been killed in a car crash. I was flabbergasted. One of the most famous and most protected women in the world had just died in a car crash – unbelievable. I sat there completely stunned. Was this some kind of omen for me? This is a day people all over the world will remember for the rest of their lives. I will certainly remember it, and so will the punters - even if my plan doesn't work out.

I sat at my desk in the wheelhouse for a full hour devouring the news filtering in. At 8am I wandered down to the aft deck in a kind of daze and gave the punters the bad news. Everyone was deeply shocked, and amazingly some were sympathetic towards me, as if I had personally lost a family member. Speaking with me for the first time in days, the Brits were dumbfounded and devastated.

The mood on the boat hadn't been good since the David and Mari incident. Those two twats couldn't have cared less if the total population of the British Isles was annihilated – in fact they would probably have welcomed it as long as it didn't affect their diving for the day. Since David told the others he was assaulted by me, nobody wanted to talk to me anymore; not even the Brits. But I stopped caring about anyone once I formed my plan. I even thought about slotting the two of them underwater in one last act of nastiness; and if the opportunity arose, I promised I would think about it more seriously- as a special treat to myself.

Back in my cabin for the last time ever, I changed into my swim shorts and looked around at my home for the past five years. There is nothing on display. The cabin has no personality. There are no pictures or photos and it is just as it was when I moved in. I haven't added a thing. There is no need to remove any private letters because I never received any. There are no secret things I don't want anyone to find – my arsenal is in the bag hidden on the island and now there is nothing of value, and nothing personal left in the cabin. The only things I left behind are an expired British passport, a stack of useless credit cards, a couple of hundred colones, and a few clothes. The crew won't have to fight over anything I leave behind except the expensive cologne. Everything else I own will soon be made into cleaning rags for the engine room.

There was only one last task before I left. I had to say goodbye to Molly. She was sitting in her favorite position in front of the wheelhouse windows, gazing outside at nothing in particular. I tickled her under the chin. She brushed her mouth over my fingers, giving them a last quick, rough lick. I whispered into her ear quietly, "Sorry old girl. I know you'll be okay." But she didn't look at me; she just turned away and continued gazing out the window.

I left her there without looking back. I didn't even look back from the panga as we all drove off to Alcyone. This chapter of my life was already closed.

Or so I thought.

Chapter 31
Whoops!

"Use your enemy's hand to catch a snake."
Persian proverb

I THINK OF MOLLY.

What a great companion she was. During the past four years she spent more time with me than any woman; and now we are both alone. I'm sorry I left her on the boat but what could I do? What will happen to her? But s*he's a bloody cat, does she even care?*

What about the death of Princess Di? I didn't know her personally; never met her or even saw her in person; I read about her, and saw her on TV occasionally, just like millions of others, but her death is as much a shock to me as Maria's was - and I was almost in love with Maria. Thinking of how closely protected the Princess was makes me realize again that no one is really safe in this world.

Her tragic death is a damn shame, but it means the death of a lowly dive boat skipper in shark infested waters off a remote island in the Pacific won't even make the back page of the Shropshire Sheep Shaggers Sentinel. Everybody will be preoccupied with news of Princess Di for months, and even if someone who knows me hears about me croaking, they will probably forget about me in a millisecond.

In the big scheme of things, I am totally insignificant; just like I was in the navy, regardless of my own opinion of myself. But unlike then, I now prefer it that way.

There is nothing odd about my thought processes or my priorities. I am close to being officially announced dead. I am thinking of my own mortality. I am dead and alive, and living on Cocos Island. I am also close to what I hope will be a legendary cave full of fabulous riches. I didn't plan on being in this exact location now though. I originally planned to be in Iglesias Bay, where things would have been a whole lot easier. With no swell it would have been a piece of cake climbing ashore there. I could have built a little hide in any of a hundred places in the area around the palm trees along the shore; and Julia has a little camp in the interior, only a couple of klicks away. Julia sometimes stays in a tent there, and who knows, she may even be there now. What will she make of my tragic disappearance; a major inconvenience? Now she will have to seduce the next skipper to get her laundry done.

Since I am not now at Iglesias Bay, I plan to spend the night in the shelter of the cave opening. There is also the unexpected bonus of being able to retrieve the bags I planted earlier this morning; I'm starving, but I don't fancy eating palm hearts, grubs, worms or cockroaches just yet.

I can't afford to bump into anyone but Julia from now on. Somewhere along her regular trail, undetectable to the other rangers, Julia told me she made a new path to the ridge above the hollow. The only other ranger that ventures far from Wafer Bay is Jorge on his pig shoots; but he won't be out in this rain.

I'm eager to see what progress the hunters have made.

With the wind still blowing through the trees, the jungle canopy over the ravine protects me as I start up the steep slippery slope to the cave. Wading up the incline through the muddy running water is not easy. The stream comes up to my knees, its force straining the fibers of my tired leg muscles. Piles of branches washing down from above form small dams in several areas causing water to cascade over the tops in a series of mini falls. In other areas where the earth has been washed away completely, the bare rocks underfoot make it easier to get a foothold but the sharp edges dig right through my diving booties into the soles of my wet feet, making me curse my choice of footwear.

At the top of the ravine, breathing hard, I reach the opening to the clearing and am about to wade through when something stops me in my tracks. I saw movement and above the roar of the waterfall I hear shouting. Ducking down to my knees I try making myself invisible.

I totally discounted Cabeza and his pals landing here this morning. I had looked out for them at the crack of dawn after sneaking away on the kayak trip to unload my stuff. Later, taking the panga to check on the sea conditions at Alcyone, I missed them again. I assumed they would steer clear until after our group dive at Alcyone. But why would they? They have a lot of work to do up at the cave.

Well, maybe this is good; they will be shifting the mound of dirt for me sooner than I expected. All I have to do now is wait until they finish digging and then reap the rewards. Brilliant!

Scuttling back down the trail as fast as possible, I stop where I hid the rebreather. I need a knife. As puny as it is, my knife still has a job to do. I need a place to hide quickly. Climbing about a third of the way back up the gulley, I hack out a hole just big enough to crawl into and then carve my way in until invisible inside the foliage. Half asleep, I lay on my stomach in my small nest until I hear voices coming down the gully. I hear them long before I see them slipping their way past. The group stumbles and curses their way down, oblivious to my presence. Claus is probably waiting at the bottom with the *Toucan* or the small inflatable boat. Has Claus run into the search parties in the pangas? Are they still out searching? If they are still searching, Claus may have to leave his group here until dark.

No longer hearing voices – except the ones in my head - I listen intently for sounds other than jungle noises, just in case there is anyone else coming down the trail. I wait a while longer before emerging from the den. The rest period did me the world of good; I feel it in my legs as I climb back up to the cave. I will definitely stay there for the night; it is the best area to make camp and if I can hide somewhere close by, I can keep an eye on the group's progress tomorrow.

I'm eager to see what progress they've made. They probably improved on their work rate of the previous week when they did such a convincing job of looking like a bunch of disorganized wankers at the other dig site.

Inside the clearing, the waterfall has washed a little more earth away at the bottom of the mound - but not enough to make a significant difference. The cavern's roof overhangs the mound, protecting it from rain. Looking up at the entrance I see there are now a series of steps making it easier to climb. At the top of the mound they have dug out a substantial amount of earth from the cave opening.

I climb the steps to the opening at the top, and standing upright, walk inside a little way. Unlike my previous visit when I had to crawl inside on my belly, there is now enough space to walk in a crouch all the way to the rock face at the rear of the cave. A series of small steps lead down the dirt pile at the rear rock wall. Several buckets on long ropes lay where work has been abandoned for the day. The steps appear to stop about half way to the bottom. Since the group's water trick hasn't removed all the dirt from the entrance, they are uncovering the entrance at the rear of the mound instead of tunneling through it or moving all the earth away, which would take weeks. If, as legend has it, a huge stone door rolls aside at the entrance, they will have to shift all the dirt from the sides too. I am impatient to see what their actions will be tomorrow.

The cave is cool and sheltered; the perfect place to spend the night. Although I could just lie down right now and sleep, I need to find a hideaway for tomorrow. I need to be up early in the morning. Pacing around the perimeter of the small clearing, I look for a place to turn into a hide. Apart from hollowing out the fallen fig tree over by the far wall and worming my way inside, there is really nowhere suitable. I try scaling the mounds of earth piled up against the rock face opposite the cave, but they are all too soft and muddy. Attempting to reach the rock face above the mound, every plant I grasp comes away in my hands. It's impossible without climbing equipment.

Standing on the trunk of the fallen fig tree I study my surroundings. There is no way to climb up high inside this huge rock bowl.

In the morning I will have to go back to the hide I made inside the brush and wait there for the rest of the day. I don't relish the thought but I have to stay hidden until the Searcher leaves the island.

Or do I?

Chapter 32
This Changes Everything

"It is useless to attempt to reason a man out of a thing he was never reasoned into."
Jonathan Swift

MY BACKSIDE ITCHES like mad. I've worn my wetsuit all day but now I need to take it off to have a good scratch.

In the evening twilight, the waterfall looks inviting.

Descending the earthen stairway, I look for a spot to stand under the cascade. I need somewhere to stand that won't put me in danger of being walloped by a falling pig or tree trunk. The weakest part of the cascade is at the side, I walk through a gap between it and the rock face. Now standing behind the falling torrent of water, I strip off my wetsuit and trunks and scratch my arse, before walking into the cold refreshing stream, letting it massage my head and body. Standing there naked, I feel rejuvenated and as horny as hell. I fantasize about Julia. What is she doing now? I made love to her under a waterfall once. Why didn't I do it more often? I suppose running the boat got in the way.

Refreshed and hungry, with my arse no longer itching, I step out of the waterfall and put my wetsuit back on.

It is time to retrieve my bags from behind Conical Rock. I hope I thought of everything this morning when packing.

The stream has slowed a little, which makes the trek down the ravine slightly easier. And to my relief, the sea has also settled down; the swells are much smaller than in the afternoon. Sliding into the sea I swim along the shoreline towards Conical Rock where I stashed my bags this morning.

I don't stop for the bags; instead I decide to continue along the shoreline, to the edge of Chatham Bay.

I wonder if the Searcher is out looking for me. Will they be out searching with so little fuel onboard? On reaching Punta Pacheco I see the answer. Fully lit up under her ultra-bright spotlights the *Searcher* still sits on the mooring. I didn't really know what to expect, but it is strange watching her there now. I see a lot of people on the aft deck but no-one sees me. I hear laughter. They are actually doing a night dive - *the fuckers*.

They should be grieving over the loss of their illustrious captain; or at least out searching for me. They aren't supposed to be enjoying themselves. *The bastards!*

I am pissed. I am so pissed I am going to cause chaos to reign upon them all. *You may as well have a drink and a little fun now my friends, because it will make you nice and tired after your long day, and you won't notice me paying you a little clandestine visit later.*

The moon will be rising at eight o'clock and by the time I pay them a visit it will be high in the sky with roughly ninety six percent of its surface illuminated. The clouds will obscure some of that light, but even in bright moonlight they won't see me coming – they will be sleeping like Russian spies in the C.I.A. They have no clue that I plan swimming silently through the night to sneak up on them.

Later tonight I will right a couple of wrongs that are bothering me.

Swimming back to Conical Rock I retrieve the backpack and two lifejackets but leave the wrapped shotgun under the ferns. Back at the landing site, climbing into the complete blackness of the brush it isn't easy making my way up to the cave in the dark. Although I don't really want to, I have to use the flashlight from the backpack. And as soon as I switch it on, I am converged upon by a cloud of flying bugs and it really puts the willies up me. I thank my lucky stars for the mosquito-net cap. I don't believe I can survive without it.

Back inside the opening of the cave I have a few hours to wait until my planned visit to the boat. Now is the time to eat. But first I have to cover my hands, face, and neck with bug spray - I have never seen so many mosquitoes. The thick cloud buzzes around my head, attacking me through the bug spray haze. Eating a combination of tinned corned beef, mixed with flying bugs and beans, causes a bout of indigestion. I hope it doesn't last all night.

After checking that the Glock and spare clips are completely dry in their baggies, I put them inside a clear waterproof camera bag. In theory the bag is meant to hold a video camera down to ten feet underwater, but in practice, it can only be trusted not to leak in the rain. Deciding I might have to use non-deadly force, I put a zapper in the bag for good measure. Sitting up in the cave entrance in a trancelike state, burping and occasionally farting, I am looking forward to the new stage of my plan.

A few days ago, I was concerned about letting the punters have the use of the kayak, worrying about my karma, but now I plan to do something that will ruin my spiritual glow forever. Malesh. I am buoyant and eager to get it over with.

Midnight rolls around not a moment too soon.

My plan is very risky but worth it. Nobody will be standing a watch onboard tonight. They will probably be up at first light to go off and search for me again. With no one to stop them drinking tonight, the crew won't be able to abstain. The whole crew, with the exception of Raul, may even be drunk. He doesn't have a strong enough character to take charge of any of them. The guys always joke about him sleeping like a horse and farting like a donkey. They will walk all over him.

Well, now, in the midnight hour, my ghost is about to walk all over them.

Chapter 33
As Nutty as a Fruitcake

"Roses are red, violets are blue, I'm schizophrenic, and so am I."
Oscar Levant

I WAIT UNTIL well past midnight, before setting off for Chatham Bay.

With the rebreather once more on my back, I swim on the surface to Punta Pacheco. The *Searcher* is still on the mooring; the current keeping her parallel to the shoreline. The current will be useful later. With her spotlights off, she lays silently dormant in the dim glow of the deck lights. I'm pretty sure everyone is fast asleep by now, including the crew.

Clouds obscure the moon.

Things couldn't be better.

On the far side of the bay, in the shallower, more sheltered area, two fishing boats sit at anchor close to the beach. They prefer it over there, and tonight I am glad they do. Swimming, underwater against the current, towards the sleeping giant, I hope not to wake her once I board - stealth is now my strongest weapon. The closer I approach, the louder the hum of the generator. A large shadow swims by me, but without a light to see what it is I ignore it, hoping it will go away without biting me.

Surfacing slowly under the swim platform at the stern, I pop my head above the surface, listening intently for the sound of voices. The only sounds are a hum from the engine room and the sea lapping against the hull. The surface of the bay is almost flat calm, with just a very slight swell. The aft platform is stable; not bouncing up and down as it does in bigger swells. The conditions are perfect for hanging here with my head above water, listening.

I need to be absolutely sure no fishermen are onboard visiting. They sometimes come over at night to chat with the crew members on the aft deck, happy to be off their little long-liners for a couple of hours.

Maybe someone is on watch.

Ducking below the surface, I make my way underwater past the bow, swimming far enough in front of the mooring to see into the wheelhouse once I bob to the surface. The wheelhouse lights are out, confirming my suspicion that nobody is on watch. If they aren't on the aft deck talking to the fishermen, whoever is on watch usually sits in the wheelhouse reading; supposedly doing rounds of the boat every hour.

Swimming back past the *Searcher*, I stay far enough away from the port side to scan the salon windows, looking for the telltale flickering from the television screen. The only lights I see come from the dim night-lights glowing in the main salon. Every cabin light is out, the darkened portholes indicating that the guests are asleep. Swimming to the starboard side, I find the same conditions there. Now, quite sure everyone is turned in their bunk I swim to the panga secured by a bowline to the boom on the starboard side.

Closing the mouth-cock of the rebreather so water won't enter the system, I slip out of the straps and turn off the tank valves before suspending it underwater by a bungee cord that I attach to the pangas bowline. Taking the camera bag from a jacket pocket I swim slowly to the back platform, alert for every alien sound.

From this moment on everything has to be exactly right.

Very slowly, I place the bag on the platform and slip off both my fins, placing them carefully beside the bag, before inching my body up and lying flat across the wooden board. I am almost breathless. My heartbeat sounds to me like a freight train.

Lying motionless on the platform as the boat gently rocks gently from side to side, I breathe deeply, willing myself to relax. I pull my mask down so it is hanging around my neck; I don't want to lose that. Taking the Glock from its package I stick it inside my wet suit and slowly raise myself until I can just see onto the aft deck.

There is no one around.

Creeping onboard slowly, I rise up on my feet, tiptoeing across the wooden boards, aware of every creak. From the deck I see that all the punters dive equipment is still in the pangas.

This is great.

Suddenly there is movement from the area of the camera locker alcove.

I freeze and tense for action, but it's Molly; up from her sleeping position on top of the camera lockers. She jumps onto the deck and runs over to me, meowing at what seems like a deafening volume before brushing herself against my legs. I stop and bend down, trying to make myself as small as possible. Taking Molly in my arms, I stroke her until she is purring like a lion. Creeping slowly over to the port side, I drop her gently into the panga, where she lands on her feet and looks up at me inquisitively.

Standing by the camera lockers, inching my head up, I peek into the salon through the rear windows, making doubly sure no one is asleep on the sofa: it's all clear. Ducking beneath the port side windows I silently make my way to the engine room hatchway.

At the bottom of the ladder I stand as still as a statue in the machinery room, listening for any sounds above the hum of the air-conditioning unit next to the ladder, and the murmur of the generator behind the engine room door.

Walking over to the work bench against the forward bulkhead, I stare at the 24-volt fuse panel above it, before opening the door and gently pulling one end of the bilge alarm fuse from its bracket; just enough to disable it but not enough for to be obvious at first glance. I do the same with the VHF radio fuse. Back at the bottom of the ladder, kneeling beside the air conditioning unit I silently lift a small deck plate. Below the plate, beneath the air conditioning unit are several hoses running seawater to and from the unit. The inlet and outlet hoses are connected to open valves on the hull. Adjacent to them is a closed valve with no hose: a spare inlet. Carefully, I open this valve slightly, allowing a trickle of water to enter the boat, before replacing the deck plate.

Back on deck, I swiftly and silently make my way over to the starboard side and untie the stern rope of the panga before silently stepping down onto the bench seat. At the stern, ducking down and kneeling next to the two big outboard engines fixed to the transom, I reach into the bilge and remove a small square hatch cover and pull out the rubberized bung beneath the engine supports. This is the drain plug that empties the panga bilge. It only drains water out when the panga is running at speed; at a standstill the bilge fills with sea water. This is what's happening right now. Moving forward to the bow, I unclip the bow rope and rapidly climb back onboard the *Searcher,* pushing the panga away and watching it drift backwards with the current. Once clear of the boat, it will drift out to sea and sink with all the dive gear onboard.

No more diving for you lot, once I release the port panga. Ha-ha-ha.

Even if the panga doesn't sink entirely, but floats just under the surface, it won't be seen; someone in Hawaii might get a nice little Christmas present though. With my heart in my mouth I glide back to the aft swim platform, wrapping the Glock back up in the waterproof bag, before putting it inside my wetsuit.

I feel lucky right now. Thank heaven I didn't need to use the weapon on anyone.

With my mask and fins back on, I ease myself into the water and swim on the surface to the bowline of the port-side panga, where I left my rebreather hanging. Ducking beneath the panga, I put the rebreather back on, open the mouth cock and almost feel like singing as I swim happily beneath the hull, heading for the main mooring rope up forward.

Regular scuba gear is unbelievably noisy under a boat. The racket the bubbles make traveling along the hull can easily be heard in the cabins. They could easily wake somebody. Luckily my rebreather is noiseless. Moving silently beneath the hull in the darkness, all I have to do now is swim along to the mooring rope; cut it enough that it will break later, and then swim back to the other panga, secured to the port side - a piece of cake; except that the current is a lot stronger now than when I swam over earlier.

I start cutting the big rope with my ultra-sharp dive knife. It's not too difficult because there is a lot of tension on it. I cut through to the final strands and stop; watching in horror as the rope-strands start spinning furiously until they all break completely.

Now free from the big anchor holding the mooring in place, the mooring rope, which is still attached to the *Searchers* bow, takes off backwards in the current. Taken by surprise, I have to grab it or I will be in serious trouble. Desperately reaching out for the rope, rasping for breath I just manage to grab it as it starts floating up to the surface. Swimming along the line, pulling myself hand over hand, I let go just before it hits the surface. I will be much too vulnerable on the surface in front of the bow. I have to swim like a bastard underwater, trying to catch up with the now moving *Searcher.* If anyone onboard happens to notice the boat is moving, they will immediately go to the bow and take a look at the mooring line.

I have to reach the port panga; the one Molly is now being dragged along in. I have to set it free – I need that panga.

I've lost it.

I can't seem to make any headway; it takes a tremendous effort just to stay level with the Searcher's bow, but because earlier I released the stern rope holding the panga, the panga has now turned completely around on its bow rope and its stern faces me as the *Searcher* moves away backwards. Suddenly I see another slight problem - the *Searcher* is now heading towards the shoreline.

For a horrible moment I think she is going aground on the rocks at Punta Pacheco. But at the last minute she changes course slightly and heads away from the corner, out to sea. I don't have time to sigh with relief; I have to get between the *Searcher* and the panga to stop it banging against the *Searcher's* hull.

I am rapidly running out of time and strength but I need that panga badly — regardless of Molly being stuck in it or not. I stop myself from growling loudly like a mad bear. Sucking on the mouthpiece of the rebreather I swim towards the pangas stern. My head is throbbing. This is not good. This is the perfect scenario for hypoxia — struggling on a surface swim and sucking all the oxygen from my mixture will be deadly. I would swim a lot faster without the rebreather on but I can't drop it just yet — not until I've cut the panga free. I spit out my mouthpiece. Right now, I need to make a decision, I am tiring fast. Gritting my teeth, I power my legs and do what I never do with diving gear on — I swim like shit on the surface using my arms, making just enough headway to reach the panga.

There is nothing whatsoever to grab onto beneath the panga; the fenders are all tied to the *Searcher.* Holding on to the panga outboard engine for dear life, I gag for breath as it pulls me backwards. I try getting between the panga and the *Searcher* to stop them banging together, but I have nothing to hold onto. I manage to swim to the bow to cut the rope free, but when I get there, I can't reach the rope. It's too high up out of the water. The island is getting further away and I'm stuck here with it, until I cut the panga free. Someone onboard is going to wake up any minute and it will all be over...

I take out my knife and cut my rebreather off; dumping it for good; letting it sink into the dark depths below me.

I have to cut the panga free quickly now because the sea chop is starting to bounce the small boat against the *Searcher's* hull. Without the rebreather on, I gain enough momentum to kick myself up out of the water, grab the panga bow rope and cut it. *Oh, the sweet wisdom of always carrying a dive knife.*

Swimming like the blazes, I drag the panga behind me, heading like a maniac towards the island. Although the panga feels like a big heavy bastard in the water I am able to distance myself from the *Searcher* which is now drifting away pretty fast sideways,

I curse my stupidity. I should have used a long rope to tie the panga to the mooring anchor, but I tried doing everything as quickly as possible. Ironically, I didn't want to swim to the mooring rope with the panga because I thought that with the rope tied to the anchor, the panga would bang against the *Searcher's* hull as it moved past. I almost screwed that up completely. I hope it didn't waken anyone.

It took a lot longer than expected to accomplish everything I set out to do.

With that seawater valve open in the *Searcher's bilge*, I'm not exactly sure how long it will be before the machinery room bilge fills with water. The air conditioning unit is below water level so that will stop and blow the electrical breaker. The *Searcher* won't sink because the machinery room is a watertight compartment, so I'm not going to get anyone onboard killed. But however long it takes, it just adds to the excitement.

Oh well, the crew can handle it, I trained them well enough.

I feel like the Prince of Darkness.

I start singing:

"I'm a bastard, I'm a bastard,

I'm the dive boat skipper from hell,

I've fucked my way around the world, now I've fucked you all as well."

I can't help laughing, imagining the panic that is going to break out when they discover they have no pangas, no dive gear, and they think the boat is sinking. All the guests will be panicking like fuck.

I'm pretty confidant no one will die because the boat has two good life-rafts and lots of lifejackets; and on the top deck there are two EPIRBS (Emergency Position Indicating Radio Beacon) that will send out emergency signals to a satellite, pinpointing their exact location to someone sitting in a rescue center.

I could have been really nasty and disabled the EPIRB's too, but I don't really want anyone to die except David and Mari - *the fuckers*.

Swimming along, hanging on to the frayed piece of the panga bowline, I am extremely happy. I managed to move some distance towards the island.

As soon as the *Searcher* leaves the protection of the island and moves into open sea it will start bobbing about a bit, and that will be the first sign of a problem to anybody awakened by it. When Carlos goes down into the machinery room he won't immediately see where the water is coming from beneath the air conditioning unit. There will be a lot of damage, but nothing life threatening. This should distract everybody and now, hopefully, they won't be interfering with my plans for tomorrow. After I fiddled with the fuse box, they won't be able to use the VHF radio to call on any fishing boats in the vicinity for help, until they fix it.

I was worried that before the *Searcher* left to go back to port, the crew would leave a panga for the rangers to use, as I had promised, but now there are no pangas and no dive gear and I don't have to worry about anybody roaming around this side of the island to dive and upset my plans for later. No sir.

I'm sure the crew will handle everything ok; we practiced enough drills since the government-training course, that they are ready for any eventuality. The punters and crew will all have their fifteen minutes of fame and I will have the satisfaction of knowing that at least two nasty punters have been paid back for the grief they caused me. The rest of the group will be happy to have a story to tell that beats most other dive boat stories hands down. Maybe Jimmy will have to pawn his nice gold Rolex.

What does a ruined dive boat business matter to me? It doesn't. Not having a dive boat at the island for a while might even be good for the sea life. And the crew might get a nice break with their families for a few weeks.

I realized a few days ago that once you cross the line into evil, anything is possible. Now there is no going back. *I am flying high.*

Chapter 34
Too Clever by Half

"Never give a sword to a man who can't dance."
Confucius

DRAGGING THE PANGA behind me, I swim on; trying to get back to the island as fast I can. But the island doesn't appear to be getting any closer. I'm not too worried about that just yet though, because I just need to be far enough away from the Searcher that nobody sees me.

Luckily the cloud cover is thick.

Swimming around to the back of the panga I try finning and pushing the transom but I can't see where I am heading. My legs are cramping up. I keep straightening my legs and stretching my fins but I can't shake it off. I can't swim anymore; I'm fucked. I am definitely too old for this shit.

I need to get into the panga and *drive* it to the island.

Reaching over the transom, I pull each engine release lever in turn, lowering both outboard engines into the water. Slipping off my fins, I throw them into the panga and step onto the small protruding skeg plate next to the propeller of the starboard engine, grabbing the engine cowling and pulling myself up into the boat. Keeping low, I pump the small, rubber bowl in the fuel hose, priming the engines with gasoline before pressing the starter switch. The two outboard engines spring to life.

I am now going to pay Claus and company a visit onboard the *Toucan*.

I have plans for them too. I am such a clever man. My plans have worked out great so far; more or less. And now it is all just a piece of cake.

Yes!

Molly girl: you and I will soon be cozy, fed and possibly very, very wealthy.

Oh yes!

I am so smart.

And suddenly both engines die.

What the f…!

If I am such a clever bastard why didn't I notice that the portable fuel tanks are missing?

I can't believe my eyes, or my stupidity. I hadn't even thought about checking for fuel tanks – there are always fuel tanks in the pangas. *But there aren't any in this one.*

There was just enough fuel in the engine and fuel hoses to start her up, but that was it. *Holy Shit.*

I always insist the drivers fill the gasoline tanks at the end of each day so the pangas are ready to use at any time; but tonight, the fuckers took out the tanks for refilling and probably left them sitting on the boat deck - or somewhere else equally useless.

One of my crewmembers has unknowingly dropped me right in the shite.

Their revenge has come prematurely.

Bobbing about in the darkness I can just about make out a light from the *Searcher*. I look down at Molly at my feet. *Bollix*. The panga is still moving out to sea and if I don't get in and start swimming, I am in danger of catching up with the *Searcher*. And I have to take Molly with me.

I dig out four lifejackets from the forward locker and secure them together; then tie Molly on top; but she doesn't like it one bit. Before I leap overboard with her secured to the lifejackets, I open the small inspection plate on the deck and pull out the main drain plug. The panga will soon sink but it is as useless to me now as a chocolate frying pan.

Diving at night with flashlight in hand, on a nice coral reef is one thing, but swimming on the surface of shark-infested waters without a light of any description, is another.

The only time I was really nervous diving amongst sharks at Cocos was during my first dive on a bait ball. Diving alone, surrounded by hundreds of frenzied sharks of all shapes and sizes, some of which were too curious about my presence for comfort, I thought that if just one shark decides to find out what this strange looking animal swimming around in front of him tastes like, I will be history, with the pack tearing me to shreds and processing me into shark shit in no time flat. I soon put that thought out of my mind.

Apart from that one experience, I've always felt comfortable diving with any number of sharks. I've swam amongst more sharks than most people can possibly imagine, but years ago, as part of an underwater attack team in the Far East, I regularly swam at night in pitch darkness through shark infested waters to plant dummy limpet mines on the bottom of darkened warships at anchor – and that really put the willies up me.

At that time, we had no real understanding of shark behavior – most divers imagined sharks to be vicious man-eaters gobbling up people at the first opportunity. We Navy divers were protected by little bags of shark repellant, which we activated on entering the water. Whenever I could, I wore two; but the only guarantee we were given as to the repellant's effectiveness was: "Don't worry if you are gobbled up by a monstrous shark; it will probably puke you up afterwards."

Whenever the repellant was changed for a new variety, which, we were told, "might work better", our confidence plummeted. The only reason we carried our big ugly knives was: in the event of a shark approaching us we could stab our buddy and swim off like the clappers. The only reassurance we had about not being attacked was the legend written in the Royal Naval Diving Manual stating quite categorically that 'no Royal Navy diver has ever been attacked by a shark.' *Until one was - then that really put the shits up everyone.* We weren't all quite as roughy-toughy as we liked people to believe we were – at least, I wasn't.

So here I am, in the water, swimming on the surface in the dead of night, pushing a fucking cat who hates water, on a pair of lifejackets with dozens of sharks all around.

At this point I'm not sure who is more afraid: Molly, or me.

I swim on my back in the upright position, just as I did hundreds of times in the past. Only this time I'm dragging a terrified cat on top of a pile of lifejackets; who at any second, is going to leap on to my face and claw my eyes out before jumping into oblivion. I try not to splash, which isn't really difficult considering how tired my legs are. Stretching my legs and pulling on my fin tips eases the cramp in my calf muscles but the thought of ending up in the middle of the ocean at night with no hope of rescue spurs me on. There is nothing like panic to get the adrenaline pumping, and it pumps right down to my tired legs as if my life depends on them – which it does.

If anything touches my legs, I will shit myself.

When I finally make it to the shoreline there isn't a happier man or cat alive. Totally knackered, Molly and I have survived.

Out to sea there is no sign of the Searcher, which actually worries me a bit.

I've landed well south of Isla Conico, but it's too dark to get proper bearings; I estimate I am about three quarters of a mile from the ravine, but I need moonlight, and that doesn't look as if it is coming any time soon.

The rest of the night is a blur.

I am so tired after making it back to the landing sight and crawling up to the cave with Molly that I go straight to sleep – which is another dumb move.

Chapter 35
Big Trouble

"While you do not know life, how can you know about death?"
Confucius

IWAKE UP AND know immediately I am in big trouble.

Molly's pitiful cry followed by the boot I take in the face gives me my first clue.

The voice I hear next gives me the second.

"Nein Herman, Nein. Die ist übel."

It is Dietmar's calm voice, but it is El Cabeza's boot that breaks my nose.

Opening the two swollen slits that are now my eyes I stare at the leg in front of me, trying to focus. What the hell just happened?

My gaze follows the leg up to the distasteful sight of Cabeza pointing a gun at me.

I lost my trusty mosquito cap - maybe it is in the jacket pocket of the rebreather lying somewhere in the deep – but anyway, all night long I've been under attack from creepy crawlies, despite using the bug spray. During the night I had lain half asleep on top of the mound in the cavernous entrance, swatting bugs until I fell into a semi-coma.

Now at dawn, my face is a mass of lumps and bumps and Cabeza has just broken my fucking nose and has a gun pointed at me. This is about as bad as it gets before you die.

I don't understand why Cabeza doesn't just shoot me there and then. If it were the other way around, I would slot him in an instant. Cabeza kicks me in the mouth again, shouting insults that refer to the size of my brain and the length of my dick.

"What are you doing here aschlock?" he shouts with his annoyingly tinny voice, through those rubbery lips.

"Just looking for some peace and quiet," I mumble through lips that are now strangely huge and rubbery themselves.

He obviously doesn't see anything amusing in my reply because he makes the mistake of kicking me again. This time I am ready. I grab his foot and twist, sending him sprawling in the dirt. Leaping on top of him I push his face in the dirt and scramble for his gun hand.

I didn't think he was so strong.

He twists over, pulls me down by the hair and whacks me on the side of the face. *Fuck me.* My strength is almost gone, but single mindedly I grab his gun hand with both of mine and hang on. I don't know how he does it but somehow, he clocks me again; a good one, right in the eye; and it hurts. I hold onto his wrist and twist until he drops the gun. I reach for it but Dietmar's raised voice stops me in my tracks. "Drop it Mac, or I will shoot you - several times." I hesitate, thinking that he won't do it because he might hit Cabeza. Cabeza's Walther feels good in my hand but I don't have time to turn and fire accurately. I don't even know exactly where Dietmar is. And even if I did, it would do no good; I can hardly see through my swollen eye slits. "If you shoot me, he goes too," I bluff.

"But you will be dead Mac. What is the point? Drop it now - last chance." There is not a trace of emotion in his voice. I know he is serious. I drop the weapon and lay there next to Cabeza, whose face is now a mask of fury. I am close enough to see white spittle sticking to his lips, and for the second time since being woken up only a couple of minutes ago, I wait for the sound of a shot to ring out. It doesn't look as if this is my lucky day. I watch Cabeza slowly raise himself. "Umbringen ihm, Dietmar!" He shouts. He wants me dead.

"Just get the gun, and don't do anything foolish," Dietmar tells him, to my relief.

Cabeza picks the gun up and starts fiddling with it until Dietmar tells him to calm down. I turn to face Dietmar and see he holds a very nice weapon in his hand; I recognize it instantly: it is my Glock. I took it out of my wetsuit last night because it was so uncomfortable. I don't know how long they have all been standing here but Dietmar even had time to remove the weapon from the waterproof bag. I am such a bloody idiot.

Günter and Thomas stand by him. Thomas is armed with a shotgun, but it isn't mine. I am very lucky; if I had turned around with the gun I would have ended up as offal. I wonder why they brought weapons with them. Did they intend killing any rangers who happened to come this way? And how long have they been here?

Günter sorts through my rucksack.

"Jasus guys, were you expecting me, or did you think the Costa Rican army would be here?" Nobody smiles as I try to stand up, holding my nose.

"Sit down Mac," says Dietmar coolly, "What are you doing here?"

"What do you think? I know this is the cave you've been searching for. Let me help you; at least let me help you dig."

I know, and he knows, that he is going to have to kill me sooner or later, but only if there is actually any treasure here. If there is no treasure, there is no secret to be kept, and unless he, like me, has killed in anger before, there is no need to even go down that road. Cabeza would love the chance to bury me and dance on my grave but I don't think Dietmar or the two guys standing beside him will really kill me unless they have to, and I really don't plan on doing anything foolish.

"So, Mac, you want to help us, huh?" asks Dietmar reasonably. "Why do you think we need your help?"

"You have a lot of digging to do and I can help. I presume you want to find the treasure and get out of here as quickly as possible. I'm strong enough to do the work of two men." *That is not strictly true right now, I feel shattered.* "After you have done here, I could also be a valuable guard for you. I don't want much in return, just enough money to buy myself a one-way ticket to oblivion. Obviously, I can't go anywhere to tell anyone about any of this. Hey, you can even send me in first to see if the cave is booby trapped." *Sometimes I am such an idiot I can't stand it. But right now, I am desperate to survive.*

I watch him mulling it over in his mind. It makes me think he doesn't intend killing me right now after all. Even though he can't trust me, he knows I might be a valuable worker ant. I know he won't allow me to go with him once he has the treasure. He also knows that if he gives me enough hope of surviving, I won't do anything foolish. What he obviously doesn't know, and what I am really thankful for, is the proposition I put to Claus onboard the *Toucan* about stealing the treasure from him. I hope Claus hasn't told the group about the Macho story; but he probably has.

"Okay, Mac, you can help us dig but if you try anything suspicious I will shoot you dead, and if you don't do exactly what I tell you, I will shoot you dead, and nobody will ever know; because you are already dead, no?" He actually laughs at that, and so do the others, but I am only too glad I am alive. If I were holding the gun and I had to make his decision - there would be bullets flying everywhere and a big heap of dead bodies lying in the clearing.

I ask him if Claus was caught up in the search for me the day before, and he tells me all the fishing boats in the area are converging on the island to help look for me. I want to ask if he heard anything from the *Searcher* but I refrain – I don't want to explain why I am asking. I also figure that Claus won't be able to hear anything over the VHF radio because of his position, tucked in at Iglesias Bay. The high terrain will block any radio signals from all but the South East.

"Looks like they want to find you badly Mac, but I can't think why," he laughs again. "They even sent an aircraft to look for you; that was amazing. Claus thinks you killed someone in Punta La Pesca, is this true?"

So, Claus did tell him. "Who me; what do you think?"

"It doesn't matter what I think, Mac. Just remember that you are already a dead man and if you want to be resurrected: you must be a very good boy, no? You can help us and I will let you live, but any sign from you that you are not cooperating with us in any way will mean your death - instantly. That is a promise."

"Just tell me what to do and I'll be as good as gold; I promise."

"Can you see through those eyes? What happened to you?" he laughs.

"I forgot my bug spray."

He laughs again – *at least I am good entertainment for him.*

"Okay let's go to work."

After such a bad start to the day I feel rather lucky to have survived it.

Dietmar allows me to change out of my wetsuit into a pair of shorts, a tee shirt and a pair of hiking boots from my bag. I've had the wetsuit on for almost twenty-four hours and it feels orgasmic putting on loose fitting clothes. Cabeza stares a little too long at my cock as I get changed. I hoped he isn't planning on shagging me before he kills me. If he is, I hope he wears a condom.

I take old Molly to the fig tree in the shade. She is wondering what the hell has happened to her life in the last twenty-four hours.

I am starving.

"Do you have anything to eat Dietmar, I'm starving."

Everyone laughs as Cabeza points at Molly, before throwing me a shovel.

Watch your heads, you bastards.

We dig dirt all day. Everyone takes it in turns to dig, with me doing more than my fair share, despite having difficulties seeing and breathing. Dietmar acts as technical advisor and my guard. I don't believe anyone except Cabeza will shoot me in cold blood unless I make a dangerous move, so I make sure not to provoke anyone into doing anything foolish. Dietmar instructs everyone to keep their distance from me as we alternate between digging and hauling up dirt from inside the cavern.

I wait all day for a chance to grab someone and break their neck but the right circumstances don't present themselves. My nose throbs and my face and hands itch like mad, despite Dietmar taking pity on me and giving me cortisone cream to rub into the bites. My eyes bother me the most; they swelled even more after the kick from Cabeza; but at least I can see slightly in front of me.

I vow to kill Cabeza at the first opportunity.

I gather a lot of dirt and a lot of information from Dietmar during breaks. Although I am ravenously hungry, they still refuse me food; feeding me information instead.

Dietmar loves to talk. It may be another reason he's keeping me alive.

He suspected for years the cave was in this area. He tried exploring here many times but the thick growth in the ravine prevented exploration - the rangers never allowed any of his teams to cut through it. He tells me that on his last illegal trip with Claus the rangers caught him, which is the main reason he had so much trouble getting permission for the last trip with Cabeza.

Claus never mentioned that.

Dietmar says that during his three-month expedition on the tugboat, his group managed to distract the rangers long enough for the two big Russians to climb down on ropes from above and survey the area of the plateau with the void detector.

Well, that explains their presence on that expedition.

Apparently one of the documents Dietmar came across in his research mentioned 'one cave leading to another,' so he thought the area he needed to search for was in a hollow. It may have been filled with earth during the earthquake of 1821; the one that killed all but one of the visiting ship *Nora's* crew just after the treasure was buried. But when I ask how he knows exactly where it is, Dietmar tells me he found it from the other side. I think he means from the other side of the rock, but he really does mean from the other side - one of his clairvoyant pals saw it in a vision.

Do clairvoyants specialize in winning lotto numbers? Have any won? If I survive, I vow to look one up.

Dietmar has aerial photographs taken from a DEA aircraft; he also has a geological survey map of the island from the University of Costa Rica. He has photos taken from the microlite aircraft. He thinks he has images showing more detail of the terrain than has been seen by anyone else alive. His coup de grace is a series of images he commissioned from NASA, which he just can't resist talking about.

With Cabeza providing the funds, Dietmar booked a satellite to take a series of infrared images accurately pinpointing any voids beneath the island's surface. The same technology deployed by the military to detect underground bunkers was used to help him find the richest buried treasure on earth.

Precious metals radiate heat when buried for long periods. And at night, when the surroundings cool down, any heat radiated to the surface by precious metal is easily measured. The air in caves or tunnels acts as insulation, cooling down at a slower rate than the surrounding rock or earth, making caves easily detectable.

But so great are the demands for images from the satellite, Dietmar had to book well in advance on a specific day at a specific time. The best time to detect any heat differences is at night, but the images he needed couldn't be transmitted through cloud, and Cocos has cloud cover ninety-five percent of the time. Dietmar fortuitously picked a time when the sky was crystal clear above the island. Dietmar also had luck in calculating and forecasting correctly the period of the current El Nino. No other treasure hunters ever had this kind of technology at their disposal. Dietmar already knew the island like the back of his hand, even before he had these images.

With his luck he is wasting his time looking for treasure; he should go straight to Las Vegas for his vacations - he'd win millions.

Diverting the stream on the last trip was a stroke of pure genius on his part too. Apparently, the theatricals of the group pretending to argue about where to dig were partly real. When they got to the site, his little band of worker bees couldn't agree on where best to make the diversion, even though Cabeza figured it out using computer graphics, with Thomas the engineer utilizing mathematical equations.

I ask Cabeza why he bothered with all the filming on the last trip if they weren't really looking for the treasure. Wasn't the film worthless? It seemed such a strange and unnecessary subterfuge. Cabeza proudly explains that the film has already been sold to a television network, and no matter what the outcome, he will make money from it, and more importantly will become famous in Germany.

What a wanker.

Dietmar won't tell me how he plans to dispose of the treasure so I take that to be a good sign, thinking that maybe he really doesn't plan to kill me after all.

Maybe that is just wishful thinking on my part because I am in such a bind.

The harder I work, the more relaxed they become with me; that is, everyone except Cabeza, who still wants to kill me slowly and horribly provided he doesn't have to touch me with his bare hands.

I think a blowtorch would be his weapon of choice.

We dig down deep, all the way inside the cavern until late afternoon when I hit rock bottom. Despite my slitty eyes and aching body I burrow like a termite to prove I am a keeper. And now, illuminated by an oil lamp, I stand alone in an area at the bottom about eight feet square.

"Looks like it's a dead end", I shout up to Dietmar.

"Come up," he shouts back.

I feel buggered as I slowly trudge back up the steps. Outside, at the bottom of the mound, Dietmar joins the rest of the group and beckons me to join them. He has managed my position with such Germanic efficiency throughout the day that I despair of ever having a chance to escape.

Cabeza disappears back up into the cavern with a large stiff brush in his hands. *Typical; keep everything squeaky clean and organized.*

Ten minutes later Cabeza reappears with a huge shit eating grin on his ugly mug.

I thought the rock face was just a solid mass, but apparently, after brushing away all the earth clinging to it, there is little doubt in his mind the large rock blocks some sort of entrance at the bottom.

Cabeza, Thomas, and Gunther go back down with flashlights and huge pry-bars to try and move the rock. Dietmar, with gun in hand, tells me to sit over by the fig tree where Molly is still sleeping. With one puffy eye on Willy the shotgun keeper, I take a seat on the fig tree over by the far wall of earth and rock. Someone has carved all the branches and roots off the tree; a big pile lay off to my left.

Dietmar joins me by the tree, keeping a safe distance.

"This is it Mac. I told you it was here. I dreamed of this moment over and over for twenty years - even before I came here, I knew I would find it."

"I'm really glad for you old mate. You deserve it. But what do you intend doing with me now?"

"It really depends on how much treasure we can take with us. If we can take it all, I will leave you here; you'll be no harm to us."

"If it's the Lima treasure, you won't be able to take it all on the *Toucan*."

"Mac, do you think I haven't thought about this moment?"

"No, but it's such a small boat."

"There will be a bigger one here very soon. Everything has been arranged."

"What if you can't take it all...?"

"Oh, I think we will, but if we can't... I'm still not sure Mac. You know that Herman will kill you now if I let him?"

"Yeah, I know that."

"So, let us wait and see."

"Do me a big favor, Dietmar."

"What is that?"

"Take my old cat with you, would you?"

"I can't take him back to Germany with me."

"I know that, but maybe Claus will look after her."

As he mulled it over, I hear screams above the noise of the waterfall.

I dearly hope they are screams of pain.

Moments later Cabeza appears at the top of the mound and I know something big has happened.

"Ya. Mien godt." Screams Cabeza. "Dietmar, com, schnell."

It sounds uncomfortably like the dream I had on the boat – if Cabeza's head explodes next, it will be perfect.

Dietmar looks at me with tired eyes and a wistful smile as Cabeza comes rushing over to tell him excitedly in Germen that they managed to make an opening and Thomas and Gunther are now inside the cave, and there are lots of wooden chests, but Cabeza can't squeeze himself through the hole.

Dietmar tells Willy to give the shotgun to Cabeza, and for him to guard me carefully. I feel a bitter taste in my mouth – the odds on my survival aren't too good right now.

"At least let me see the treasure before I die," I plead with Dietmar.

He doesn't answer. He just leaves Cabeza and me alone. I watch pensively as he climbs the dirt steps and disappears inside the cavern. I sit in silent panic, staring at the ground with my head in my hands. My face feels horrendous. Neither of us speaks. I suddenly feel dog-tired and doomed. Slowly raising my head, I survey my surroundings.

The big hollow is a solid bowl of rock with only one escape route: the opening to the ravine twenty feet in front of me. The waterfall and cavern are off to my left. If I try making a run for it or try rushing him, Cabeza will blast me to smithereens with the shotgun - he can't possibly miss. The only thing I can do is to try and get him closer to me somehow. The light will be fading very soon and if I can just hang on until dark, I might be in with a chance — but they might kill me before then. Cabeza keeps turning towards the cave, waiting for the treasure to appear. If he would just stare that way a while longer…

While I debate my options, Thomas emerges from the cavern carrying a small metal chest. He makes his way down the steps whooping with delight, stopping to place it in the middle of the hollow. "Kommen Herman. Blicken sie."

Cabeza looks at me evilly. "Stay there. If you move, I will kill you." And I know he will. I've heard that phrase too many times for one day.

He walks over to Thomas and helps him sort through the contents of the chest. There are pieces of jewelry everywhere; millions of dollars right there. Thomas rummages through a very large bag and produces a stack of smaller, thick canvas bags. He takes an arm-full back inside with him.

Cabeza faces me, watching with one beady eye as he sorts through some of the larger pieces of jewelry. I judge whether to make a run for him when Gunther comes out of the cavern smiling broadly, dragging one of the canvas bags behind him. Placing it beside the small chest, he punches the air and slaps Cabeza on the back before rushing back up the mound.

Cabeza finishes sorting through a pile of jewels from the chest and places them inside the canvas bag Gunther just brought out.

I feel sick to my stomach and look at Molly curled in a ball by my side. "Well old girl, what are we going to do?" I ask quietly. She doesn't acknowledge me; she is pissed she hasn't eaten all day.

"Hey, Herman, how about some food for me and my cat?" I shout.

He smiles; but it isn't a nice smile. "You don't need any food, - not for where you are going."

"Come on Cabeza, you're not going to kill me, are you? Think of your Karma; it would be ruined forever if you did that."

He stops rummaging and looks at me full on. "What did you call me?"
Bloody Hell. I didn't know he understood Spanish.
Walking towards me, he stops several feet away.
Just a little bit closer, I plead silently.
The plea goes unheeded.
He looks down at the shotgun briefly and then back at me.
He is going to shoot me - the fucker.
If I don't do something quick, I am going to meet my maker right here
and now

He raises the shotgun and aims. "I am going to kill you," he says
superfluously. I don't say a thing, instead I involuntarily move back
against the wall of rock as he steps closer. My plan is to lunge at him as
soon as he is close enough but I suddenly feel very nervous and afraid of
the shotgun – I know what it will do to me at close range. I am literally
backed up against a wall and I am bollixed. Earth starts falling on my
head as I look at him defiantly, even though my bum feels very squeaky.
He starts fiddling with the safety catch as if he doesn't know whether it is
on or not and I feel the sudden resolve not to die like this. I can't allow
myself to be slotted by a slimy gutless bastard like Cabeza no matter how
big his fucking brain is.

I am about to charge towards him when a whole pile of dirt and small
rocks rain down on me. Strangely I feel pain in my head, and then blood
runs down my face but I don't hear the blast from the shotgun. I duck
down, holding my arm up in a pointless attempt at shielding my face. I
drop to my knees thinking he fired and missed, but he stands transfixed,
staring at something above him.

I relive the next millisecond a thousand times – in slow motion, in 3D,
in brilliant Technicolor and with quadraphonic surround sound.

One minute Cabeza stands in front of me with a shotgun ready to kill
me, and in the next instant he disappears altogether. I see his glasses
flying into the air and I hear the sound of crackling bones and a gurgling
sound, together with a loud thud like a giant hammer smashing an
enormous egg. And he is gone. In the space where his body was, there is
now a huge boulder.

He disappears before my very eyes and ears and I think God has done
it - until I run out into the center of the hollow and look up at the top of
the ridge thirty feet above me.

It isn't God, but as seen through my slitty eyes, it is the closest thing to it I've ever seen. Julia is there on top of the ridge with Jorge - and I never saw such a wonderful sight in my life.

"Run, Mac. We'll cover you," she shouts down.

I don't need telling twice. Scooping up Molly in one hand, I run. As I pass the canvas bag in the center of the hollow, I grab it with my other hand and leg it like a rabbit at a dog track. I shoot through the opening in the rock and scoot down into the ravine as fast as I possibly can. On the way down I hear shots but I don't stop to see if anyone is shooting at me. Slipping and stumbling, dragging the bag, I run down the ravine as fast as I possibly can. Molly hangs on to me for dear life, digging her claws deep into my chest as I run. I don't even care if there is anyone within sight when I come out of the hole in the brush at the bottom of the ravine; I just keep on running around the shoreline until reaching the place I hid the shotgun. I take the weapon out of the brush and shove the canvas bag full of booty, inside. Hoping she'll stay put, I gently place the very grateful Molly on top of the bag inside the brush. Unwrapping the gun as I go, I run back into the tunnel of green. I am going to kill the lot of them. *The bastards.*

Going back up the ravine, I hear a gunshot and I realize it is unlikely anyone will be chasing me. They will either be under attack from Jorge with his trusty rifle, or will be looking at the two mangled legs sticking out from beneath the boulder. I have to laugh. *What a glorious sight that was.*

I creep back up the ravine to my little hidey-hole and crawl in. I can only imagine what is going on up there now. How long were Jorge and Julia watching us? What an astonishing turn of events. That was the last thing I expected to happen. I wondered what happened to Julia, but I should have known she wouldn't just ignore the cavern. After all, she actually found it. I also should have known someone else was shagging her. It explains why she went back to the island "to work". Well, I'm glad Jorge is the one – good luck to them. They saved my life.

That was too close.

I noticed that huge rock on top of the ridge but never imagined it would be used as a weapon. It was a fucking brilliant idea. They could have killed everyone with it if they had waited a while. Anyway, I'm safe now. I'll just wait for those treasure hunting bastards to come down and then ambush them. The light is fading fast. They will try to leave under cover of darkness. When they do leave, I will be waiting for them.

But I'm worried.

Will Dietmar and his gang stay where they are? Will Julia and Jorge make their way back to the rangers' camp and tell the rest of the rangers? Are they the only two up there on the ridge, or do they have other rangers with them? My mind is flooded with questions but dry of answers.

The hunters will be foolish if they come out into the open with someone shooting at them from above. They are in a no-win situation in that hollow. Al told me Jorge was a hell of a sharpshooter. He loves that M1 Garand. And there is a treasure trove right there, that can be all his and Julia's.

I can't stay where I am; the mosquitoes and ants are causing me problems again - they are eating me alive. There are bites all over me and blood is still running into my eyes from several cuts on my head from the fallen rocks. My head feels enormous.

I hear a horn sounding from the bottom of the ravine. It must be Claus calling for his buddies. I wait thirty minutes, but no one comes down the ravine. They probably dug themselves in for the night up there. I can't stand it any longer. I have to do something. I have to get away from the bugs at least.

I crawl out of the dark ravine into the dark night. If the guys up there want to get out now, they can. So why don't they? I'm not about to go up there and find out; I need to get as far away from them as possible.

Emerging from the hole in the trees on the shoreline I think I might find Claus still waiting in the *Toucan* or their small boat tender, but there is nobody in sight. It will be nice if I can make it to Iglesias where the *Toucan* is anchored, but there is no way I can get there in my present state; I am totally knackered.

I decide to go around the shoreline as far as I can towards Chatham Bay. Maybe I will stay at the ranger's hut there. There is a first aid kit there and I can wait for Julia and Jorge to come back. There is no other choice. It has to be Chatham Bay; I am so close I can smell it.

I take the fins, mask, snorkel and lifejackets from where I left them the night before, and walk around the shoreline. Molly is sleeping on top of the bag where I left her. I put her on the lifejackets once again and wonder what she thinks of all this. She looks a bit moth eaten right now. When I made the plan, I knew it wasn't going to be easy, but I had no idea it would turn out like this.

I leave the bag I liberated from the hunters, plus the shotgun, in the brush under a pile of rocks. I have no idea when I will be able to collect them, but there is no way I can take anything except Molly with me right now. Carrying Molly and the lifejackets, I stumble along the shoreline as far as I can before taking off my boots and putting the snorkeling gear on. I put Molly and my boots on top of the bundle of lifejackets and slip into the sea once more. The saltwater stings my head like hell. Chatham Bay is close, but without a wetsuit, and wearing only shorts and a tee shirt the swim takes a lot more effort. And here I am again swimming on the surface of shark infested waters at night, only this time I am bleeding. *Way to fucking go, you dumb shit.*

Reaching the bay, I half expect to see the *Searcher* there but the mass of flashing lights all around the bay takes me completely by surprise. My heart is in my throat until I realize the bay is full of long-liners. I hope nobody is in the rangers hut because I desperately need to lie down and die for a while.

Looking around the bay I notice one small white light shining way up in the sky, with another, dimmer light below it. The light is on top of a mast. There is a sailing yacht anchored right in the middle of the bay. There can only be one sailing yacht here at this time of year; it will be too much of a coincidence if there is another. This one is supposed to be in Iglesias Bay; *Thank God, it is Claus, my savior.*

I am so excited to see the *Toucan* anchored here that I start swimming over; completely disregarding my aches and pains and the caked blood and associated danger of sharks. Sharks are the least of my worries; it will be much too ironic being munched by a big fuck-off shark at this stage of the game. I am frightened out of my tiny mind. I decide that irony is a huge part of my current state of affairs, and it is distinctly possible I will be eaten alive by a renegade shark. I vow never, ever to snorkel in shark infested water at night again.

By the time I reach the boat I am completely exhausted. Lifting Molly into the tiny inflatable boat tied to the stern is easy enough, but my arms just about give out as I struggle to drag myself out of the sea and climb into it myself.

The aroma of food coming from inside the boat is mouth-watering – a five-star restaurant smell. My digestive juices suddenly become over excited, making me realize just how ravenously hungry I am. I haven't eaten anything since the tin of corned-dog and tin of cold beans the night before. With the hunters deciding not to waste any of their precious food on me it is a wonder I have the energy to keep my slitty eyes open. I am truly knackered.

I wait in the tender a while, to be sure there is no one else onboard before pulling on the bow line to get close enough to inch my way onto the deck. The only visitors Claus might have onboard would be rangers. If he has fishermen onboard, one of their little boats would be tied to the stern. Claus probably came into the bay under the cover of darkness. None of the rangers would be idiotic enough to swim out to check him out and he wouldn't have gone ashore to pick the rangers up in his tender; besides there should not be anyone at the Chatham Bay station – Julia is out, and the other rangers will be in Wafer Bay tonight.

I creep across the deck to the cockpit, standing there in the darkness listening intently for the sound of voices inside; I am sure Claus is alone. In what I believe to be a silent manner, I creep across the deck to peer through the hatch but Claus obviously hears me and sticks his head out of the main hatch, and I swear his blond hair stands on end.

His eyes go wild and wide and his mouth hangs open.

"Looks like you just saw a ghost." I laugh, enjoying the spectacle of his white face.

He is speechless for a moment.

"Hope you're not going to shit yourself, my old fruit," I say in a low voice.

"You fucker, I didn't recognize you with that fat face," he explodes; his mouth turning from a big 'O' shape to a big smile. "You fucker, I knew it you fucker..." *I have no idea what I look like.*

"I'll have to teach you better English my old mate; you're getting boring."

"You bastard."

"That's better; a bit more variety there."

"What the fuck happened to you; you look like caca?"

"It's a long story mate, but I think your men are all in the shit."

"I was supposed to pick them up before sunset. I waited and they didn't arrive."

"No, they're pinned down by the Apaches, and they might not be back until morning."

I tell him the story, surmising that Jorge and Julia would be long gone from their spot up there by now. "Maybe they are all dead Claus. Jorge is a fucking ace with that rifle of his."

"So, what do we do now?"

"You could just leave them there and take me to Panama."

"Yeah right, you asshole."

"I was just joking. We'll wait to see if they are okay. If they're still alive, I'll kill the fucking lot of them and we'll split the booty. If they're dead: we finish taking out the treasure and split it between us and I'll even let you have the lion's share.

"What about Julia and Jorge?"

"I'll take Julia and you can have Jorge, how about that?"

"Fuck off Mac. Seriously, what do we do about them?'

"Well, assuming they aren't going to share the information they now possess with the other rangers, or the higher authorities, we'll have to cut them a deal. No sweat; there must be pot loads of treasure in that cave and we'll have enough to live comfortably for the rest of our lives. If there isn't; why are we even having this conversation? Don't worry buddy, it will all work out. Now get me a big whiskey, some hydro-cortisone crème, a box of band aids, and then give me a big plate of whatever it is you're cooking, I'm fucking famished."

Chapter 36
Jacque's Back & the Head's Dead

"A real friend is one who walks in when the rest of the world walks out."
Anon

BEFORE DINNER, I convince Claus to move the *Toucan* over to the *Searcher's* second mooring close to Manuelita Island. I want to discourage any members of Cabeza's group from swimming over to us if they manage to escape from the cave; although I can't imagine any of them having the courage to do so.

Our new mooring spot is nice and peaceful.

It's time for me to clean myself up.

Seeing my face in the mirror of one of the tiny bathrooms comes as a shock. In the cupboard beneath the sink I find an array of grooming products, amongst them a hair trimmer. Carefully and painfully I shave all the hair from my head, so I can dress my wounds properly. After shaving off my beard, I don't recognize myself. With two black eyes, a face covered in lumps, bumps, small cuts and abrasions, and with no hair or beard I look hideously ugly. To my utter dismay I actually look a lot like Cabeza; even though my head is still not the size of his. But the good news is: I won't be recognized because I am almost unrecognizable as a human being right now. I take a welcome shower, watching the blood-soaked water run down the drain.

After the initial shock of seeing me emerge from the bathroom in all my ugliness, Claus has a really good laugh. He is still laughing as we sit in the cockpit enjoying a fantastic meal of lobster, garlic sautéed prawns, pilau rice, and fresh vegetables. I am so grateful to Claus I could marry him. After sucking down several glasses of chilled white wine I look at Claus and consider giving him a blow job. *No, of course I don't.* I just threw that in to show how grateful I am for him being there.

Sitting in the cockpit with a full belly, enjoying the nice balmy evening, we talk of this and that, and discus what we will do with our share of the treasure. Molly is sprawled out with a belly full of leftovers. I can't believe my luck. I wonder what will happen next.

Claus tells me he heard chatter on the radio about the *Searcher* being in some kind of trouble. He wasn't able to hear the transmissions clearly because the signal kept breaking up, but he thinks they are making their way back to port with some kind of engine trouble. I don't mention anything to him about my little act of sabotage - I prefer keeping that to myself.

"You know an aircraft came to look for you Mac, and a whole fleet of long-liners abandoned their fishing grounds to come here and join the search."

I am touched.

"Your crew were devastated by your loss, I don't know why, you asshole." That is too touching for words, and actually makes me feel a bit guilty for doing what I did to them. But malesh, they seemed to be having too much fun last night when I saw them on deck before my visit to the *Searcher.*

"There is another boat on its way to the island. I heard Dietmar on the radio with one of his partners in Panama last night. He apparently arranged for a boat to leave there as soon as possible. He spoke with his guys about a big boat called the *Anastasia,* and men with "tatwaffen" - weapons. They were leaving from a small port in the north of Panama, about 450 miles away. Depending on the boat's speed, it will take between forty to forty-five hours to arrive at the island."

That means we have to leave as soon as possible tomorrow - after we find out what had happened in the hollow, and hopefully, after we grab bag loads of swag.

Claus spoke to the rangers on the radio this morning, convincing them he was out sailing alone to escape from a girlfriend, when he heard the news about my disappearance. They gave him permission to stay in Chatham Bay for as long as he wants, which is a welcome break for him, because the time spent anchored at Iglesias was rough, with swells rocking the boat all day and night. Anchored so uncomfortably close to Tea Cup Island trying to duck out of the swells, Claus was awake most of the time, so is a bit knackered his self.

Despite us both being in an exhaustive state we arrange to keep watches between us during the night, with Claus taking the first watch. I trust Claus; he is a good guy. Luckily, I manage to make him see the precariousness of his own situation. If the amount of treasure is as great as rumored, there is no telling what it will do to someone who has it in their possession, or to others with designs on making it their own. Fueled by greed, we humans traditionally act with barbaric ruthlessness. *Look at me for example.*

Claus is a witness to the treasure hunter's illegal search and discovery, and as such is extremely vulnerable to being slotted by them. I am Claus' vital ally, which makes me feel safe sleeping while he is on watch.

Lying on the bunk in the small cabin up forward, without a noisy generator running, and with just the sound of the waves lapping against the hull, I fall asleep in an instant - but I am already awake when Claus comes down to wake me for my watch; I have been for a while. The yacht is now rolling around quite a bit. The increasingly rocky movement is accompanied by the sound of birds screaming and screeching outside. I was just about to go up on deck anyway because I know what these signs mean.

"I think there is a storm coming", says Claus concernedly, as I follow him up on deck.

He is dead right.

The sky is completely black. Clouds roll rapidly past the moon and the wind is starting to howl. Red Footed Booby birds screech all over the sky. The fierce wind has the frightened fuckers flying about everywhere. Dozens land on the boat; some on the deck; others balancing precariously on the guardrails swaying erratically in the wind. Still more fight for a position inside the small inflatable dingy tied astern. Regurgitated fish and bird shit are scattered everywhere on deck.

Manuelita Island has come alive.

Boobies always panic before a storm. They have good reason to: sometimes their homes get blown away. In such conditions I always move the Searcher away from Manuelita, closer to the beach to get out of the wind and swell. The wind howls from the west and if it continues from that direction, the closer to the beach we anchor, the calmer and safer it will be.

Claus starts the small engine while I tip-toe on the slimy deck to hoist the bow of the inflatable up onto the transom, rendering several booby families homeless. Slipping and sliding my way up to the foredeck, kicking and shoving boobies out of my way to release the mooring rope, I slip on a pile of slimy, half-digested fish remains and have to boot two boobies overboard after the bastards bite me with their big sharp beaks.

I'm starting to feel like a traffic accident victim.

The wind velocity increases just as we start to move off. In the gap between Manuelita and Colnett Point, the strength of the wind causes the yacht to list sharply to port, almost knocking us off our feet. Suddenly the heavens open and we lose sight of everything but the rain. From the cockpit I jump down into the salon, sliding the overhead hatch closed. Grabbing my diving mask and a foul weather jacket for Claus I crawl through the cockpit hatch and hand them to him at the helm, before going back below. The depth sounder is already running and I watch it carefully after switching on the radar. Claus steers by compass whilst waiting for the radar to warm up. He is only five feet from me but I can hardly see him through the torrent of rain. He must be almost completely blind outside, with no shelter. But luckily, we don't have far to go. When the radar screen comes to life, I direct him to a safe anchorage position a short distance from the long-liners, close to the western shore where the island's heights shelter us from the worst of the wind.

This is a major storm. This is a Jacque Cousteau storm combined with a special one for Princess Di. This is like being in the middle of a bombing raid. Through the deck hatches above us in the small salon, we watch bright white flashes light up the sky. Jagged forks of lightening split the dark night apart with simultaneous cracks, sizzles, and bolts of booming thunder. The small yacht rocks and the wind howls through the shrouds as it brings more rain – more rain than whole continents receive in a year. Ear-rendering explosions shake us and leave us partially deaf as we sit rocking inside the small yacht. The noise is horrendous. Judging by the way the boat reverberates under the explosive crashes of thunder I'm sure the lightning conductor at the top of the mast is hit more than once. The rain beating down upon us has a fury I never before witnessed – and I have been through some terrible weather during my years at sea. I am very happy to be anchored here and not out sailing in the middle of the inhospitable ocean.

We both feel vulnerable, but luckily, we are moored in the only bay at the island where there can possibly be shelter from the wind. Thankfully it is from the west otherwise we would have no shelter here at all. We don't have to worry about dragging anchor or being hit by a fishing boat dragging theirs. I think about the guys on the *Searcher* and hope they aren't struggling through it somewhere.

If I was religious, I would pray for them.

The rain no longer falls in stair rods - it has become a continuous deluge. I feel I'm inside a barrel, rolling over Niagara Falls. Poor old Molly is wedged into a corner, paralyzed by fear. I wonder if her heart will hold out after what she has been through in these last couple of days.

With me up on watch in the salon, Claus goes down to his cabin and tries to sleep. I don't expect any visitors to the boat tonight. I hope Julia and Jorge are safe somewhere. If not, they could be toast - maybe literally.

Bored with just sitting around, I rummage through the cabins that Cabeza and company used. Going through their belongings I find a nice pile of cash. I also find their passports. Browsing through them makes me suddenly feel exceptionally high. One fits my needs perfectly.

Irony of ironies - I am about to become El Cabeza himself. It is said that if your passport photo matches your face, you are in urgent need of medical attention. Well, Cabeza's photo matches my face and I do need medical attention, and provided I wear a baseball cap and nobody notices the difference in head sizes, his photo will pass as mine in a cursory inspection. My German language skills are good enough anywhere except Germany, but I don't intend going there. I hit pay dirt once more when I find a bundle of credit cards. Cabeza has a stack that he won't need any more.

The storm's fury lasts all night, only easing off just before dawn. In the early morning light, I survey the bay through the rain; fishing boats are anchored all over the place. The bay is calm but it's a mess; whole trees and hundreds of leaves float around on the thick, muddy brown water. The sea's mud content in the bay is now greater than its salt content. With so much plant debris floating around it looks as if all the long-liners are stuck on a mud bank. There must be millions of gallons of fresh water cascading down every slope in sight, running straight into the sea. Everywhere I look, the once green, grassy hills are replaced by muddy brown slopes.

What is it like up at the cave?

Those guys are probably thanking their lucky stars they had a cave to shelter in for the night; but what of Julia and Jorge? Surely, they won't still be there. Did they manage to make it back to the ranger hut okay? The island is a mass of rivers and waterfalls. I hope they are both okay.

I am eager to get around to the cave and clear up.

I cook eggs and bacon for Claus and myself and give Molly a bowl of milk and some of the fish left over from the night before. We all tuck into breakfast as if it is our first meal ever. After breakfast Claus turns on the VHF radio and listens to the continuous stream of chatter from the fishing boats; they are checking whether everyone made it to the shelter of the island, but it sounds as though there are a couple of boats missing. I hope the *Searcher* made it home okay. I now feel really bad about what I did to them. If I made it out of this okay, I will do something good for them. I will change my life, which is easy to do when you have milliards of dolleros.

Not wanting to go around to the ravine in the small inflatable we lift the anchor and slowly make our way past the long-liners towards Punta Pacheco. I stay below. Fishermen with sullen looks wave to Claus as we pass. It must have been hell for them last night.

After passing Isla Conico I go on deck. The sea is very confused. Big swells crash onto the shore further to the west but at the landing site by the ravine it is relatively calm. Upon reaching the landing site I am totally shocked. There are no trees in the ravine; I mean there are absolutely no trees at all. There is just a huge, fast flowing river, belting down a steep rocky slope.

This isn't what shocks me most. The waterfall above is now pouring into a giant pool up there. Holy Guacamole, I can't believe it. The hollow is no longer a hollow — it is a lake. Water cascades fiercely over the front of the rock bowl and is pouring down the slope. The opening in the hollow isn't visible because of the amount of water cascading over the top of a wall of rock surrounding it. At the top of the ridge, where Julia and I stood looking down that day, there are now no trees at all. They have all been washed into the hollow.

The other ridge beneath it, from where Julia and Jorge lobbed the giant boulder, is also completely bald. There are no signs of trees or other vegetation up there whatsoever. There isn't even any earth; just huge jagged rocks. Everything has been washed down into that hollow, blocking the opening and causing the whole place to fill with water from above. Surely those guys couldn't survive that.

If they got stuck in the entrance to that cavern, they may even have ended up inside the cave; underwater - with the treasure. *Wouldn't that be poetic?*

I suddenly have a horrible thought.

"Fucking hell Claus, can you drop me over by Conical Rock? I have to look for something."

"Okay but you'll have to jump in."

"No problemo."

I gather up my snorkeling gear and jump in as soon as he is close enough. I swim through the sea of dirt and leaves to the shoreline behind Conical Rock, where I left the bag and see immediately that it is gone. There is a big hole in the brush, with water running through it.

The sea all around is filthy but I duck under the swell and try looking around. I know it can't be very far away: if it is still here. The visibility is zero underwater. I spend about thirty minutes searching the area before I find it. I can't lift it from the bottom. I don't remember it being this heavy, but I was fueled on pure adrenaline dragging it down the ravine, running for my life. Claus throws me a rope, but it takes another ten minutes to find the bag again. I secure one end of the rope around the canvas bag and swim back to the boat, handing Claus the other end. Claus keeps the boat as close as he safely can while I haul the big heavy bag onboard. The frown on Claus' face turns into the biggest grin I ever saw when I untie the bag and pull out a huge, gold and jewel encrusted broach; and then show him a fistful of diamonds.

"Okay, Buddy let's vamanos, as fast as you like."

We hoist the sails, and with the big bag of priceless artifacts at our feet, we watch a wet Cocos Island slowly disappear behind us in the rain and mist as we sail away under a mackerel sky.

Central American Times

EL NINO ENDS IN NIGHTMARE
WIDESPREAD DESTRUCTION IN THE NORTH
Death and Heroism on the High Seas

As water temperatures slowly returned to normal along the Pacific coast, The National Oceanic and Atmospheric Administration (NOAA) officially announced the end of El Nino, but not before it took a further toll in lives and caused millions of dollars more in damages. In the early hours of Friday morning a tropical storm swept in from the Pacific and blasted the coasts of Costa Rica and Nicaragua. High winds and flooding caused widespread damage to property. At sea, two boats are reported missing, their crews feared dead.

SEARCH FOR MISSING DIVE BOAT CAPTAIN CREDITED
WITH SAVING THE LIVES OF FISHERMEN.

The search for a missing diver may have saved the lives of dozens of fishermen who were operating in the Pacific during the storm. Several long-liners, fishing in an area approximately one hundred miles West of Cocos Island, cut short their fishing missions last Wednesday to join in the search for the captain of the Punta La Pesca based diving vessel Sea Searcher.

The captain, Davies Macan, a British national, went missing on Wednesday, whilst leading a group of tourists on a dive at Isla Del Coco. The fishing vessels were searching for the captain in the area, and when the massive storm struck, were close enough to the island, to seek shelter there. Many fishermen believe that had their boats been in their original positions they would have been at the mercy of the storm in the open ocean, and that would have been a disaster.

SHARK ATTACK
It is thought that Captain Macan may have been the victim of a shark attack. Despite the island being a notorious haven for man-eating sharks, the Sea Searcher took tourists there on diving excursions.

Heroic Crew Saves Dive Boat Passengers
In a further twist, the Sea Searcher was forced to abandon the search for Captain Macan on Wednesday evening, and return to port early because of extensive flooding inside the vessel, after a passenger accidentally left a valve open on a toilet. The seven crewmembers are being hailed as heroes by the passengers after their valiant actions saved the boat from sinking. The crew battled to keep the Sea Searcher afloat as it was hit by the tail end of the storm. Fortunately, the Sea Searcher missed the brunt of the storm and was not in its direct path, as it would have been, had it left the island the previous day as scheduled.

Two Vessels Still Missing After Storm.
The tugboat Anastasia, a Panamanian vessel still hasn't been heard from since she left port on Thursday, heading for Costa Rica. Authorities report that the vessel left without applying for proper sailing permission so it is not known how many crew are onboard.

The long liner *Macho,* which sent out a mayday call, is also still missing. The *Macho* was the only boat not to join the search at Cocos Island and was caught in open seas. Several vessels reported hearing a Mayday call on their radios but the fiercely hostile seas prevented them from leaving the safety of the Island until late Friday morning.

National Parks Mourn Losses.
Two Park Rangers Missing

Two National Park Rangers working at Isla Del Coco were also reportedly still missing this morning. Julia Adair and Jorge Campos failed to return from a routine research expedition. The Island was battered by hurricane force winds and torrential rain on Thursday evening. Parts of the island have been completely devastated.

Sailing Yacht Reported Safe in South

The sailing yacht Toucan was reported to be in the safety of Golfito after being reported missing by its owner American Entrepreneur Bruce Foster. It was feared the yacht had sank after leaving Cocos Island on Friday morning, but lone yachtsman Claus von Doll, who chartered the yacht, had decided to seek shelter in the safety of the South until the weather improved.

De Tega 400 N. 200 E.
Condiminio Al Dente
San Rafael de Escazu,
Costa Rica.

You Asshole,

You have no idea the trouble you put me through. I thought if I ever got out of jail I would come looking for you, to kill you.

While I was in jail my wife sold our house, took the money and went back stateside. She wants a divorce and for once I'm happy giving her what she wants.

After I saw the charges the cops were planning to bring against me I thought I would rot in prison for the rest of my life. They took the number of my car when it was parked out at Fortuna that night. The cops thought I was a member of a big burglary ring and drug cartel.

I have to tell you Mac that the shit sure started flying here while I was in jail. The drug guys were killing each other left right and center, (as you would say with your British accent). It seems the police got some kind of inside information and started rounding people up all over the country. The lawyer said the police received some kind of notebook in the mail, and I'm guessing that had something to do with you.

I see now why Macho had to die. You should have told me about the young kids Mac, I would have gladly done it myself if I had known. The police were glad to be rid of him.

I have to tell you Mac I was very relieved when the big, hotshot lawyer arrived to represent me. I guess he did the right thing because they dropped all the charges.

I bought a place out here in Escazu with the money you sent. I have a nice little Tica maid looking after me now, and I'm a happy man.

I hear Claus is doing pretty well too, with his new hotel (or brothel is what it really is.)

I heard through the grapevine that the crew of the Sea Searcher all received big fat Western Union checks in the mail. Where would those come from I wonder?

I hope you are doing okay Mac. If I knew where you were, I would pay you a visit, but I guess that's privileged information. I sure hope you get this letter OK. The lawyer said he could get it to you. He said you have a PO Box somewhere in the Far East.

Take care, old pal.

I'm glad you didn't forget me.

Al.

PS

Macho Gordo was officially pronounced dead from a heart attack. They say he had lots of alcohol and all sorts of narcotics in his system.

PJ Probert joined the Royal Navy at the age of 15 and served worldwide for 12 years, leaving as a Leading Diver. Subsequently he worked as a deep diver on the North Sea oil rigs in the 1970's, and as a diving instructor and dive boat captain worldwide.

He is now retired and lives in Wales.

This is his first novel.

Made in the USA
Las Vegas, NV
30 November 2021

35614213R20187